For Kelley,
the star in my life
who fell from the sky
to perfectly complete me.

BURLOI
Necroth and the Citadel of Ar'lenon
The Northern Desert
The Western Wood
The Waterfall
Fort North
Gunning's Place
Ilfena's House
Henri's Home
Donher's Abode
The City of Quentin
Borderline
The Hemmed Land
Coastal Town
Crysalia
The Sea of Serpents
N W E S
RESGERIA
The Endless Wall

Dragon Offspring

The Sword of the Dragon

Book 2

Scott Appleton

Other books by Scott Appleton:

The Sword of the Dragon series
Swords of the Six
Dragon Offspring
Key of Living Fire
The Phantom's Blade

The Neverqueen Saga
Neverqueen
Neverqueen 2: The Suffering Chalice

Anthology
By Sword By Right

For more info visit: www.AuthorAppleton.com

DRAGON OFFSPRING

The Extended Edition

Original concept sketches by artist *Amber "Vantid" Hill*

Oganna and Vectra cross the Hemmed Land

THE RAGGED PROPHET'S PROMISE

The black dragon Valorian had laid waste to the forces that opposed him on the Plains of Galaban. Mortally wounded, Xavion had hidden in a deep cave. His loyal apprentice, the prince of Prunesia had tried to protect him. But the famed warriors of the Six had betrayed Xavion and slain the prince. In the midst of that treachery the dragon Albino arrived on the battlefield, his rage falling like a storm upon the men that had betrayed him.

The white dragon's teeth ground into Clavius's body as it raised him high off the ground, breaking him in half. The traitor's sword clattered to the ground as the dragon's claws raked the earth, breaking stones as he faced the next traitor: Letrias.

Auron froze as he gaped at the sight of the mighty white dragon with its lips parted, dripping the bloody entrails of Clavius onto the stones as its pink eyes locked on Letrias. The remains of Clavius lay about on the ground. Auron knew that he should move. Knew that he needed to escape while the beast was focused on the other traitors. But his legs felt as if they had turned to stone, and all he could do was watch with increasing terror.

Flames roiled in the dragon's half-open mouth and Letrias's eyes widened. Letrias had never shown fear in front of Auron. Not that the man could remember. But the look of fear now was undeniable in his eyes. Letrias had been instrumental in this betrayal and he had promised Auron a path to greatness, and freedom from the rules of the prophets and their Creator. He had been so certain, so filled with confidence in the supremacy of the wizards in this war.

Had he been wrong? Had Auron chosen the losing side? Now, as he watched the white dragon engage Letrias, his heart fell into despair. Nothing could oppose Albino. Nothing! He had betrayed Xavion in the hopes of a lofty destiny, one where he would exercise power over others. Now the wizards would have all they could do just to survive Albino's wrath.

Auron swallowed his soul in one breath. May the wizards help him, he had chosen the losing side! His mind screamed for him to run but his body refused to budge.

The great white dragon loomed tremendously in front of Letrias, every muscle in its body sharpening as liquid iron beneath its scales. The flames in its mouth burned white-hot in preparation to roast the traitor alive.

Letrias dropped his sword to the ground and

spread his hands toward the dragon. As the sword clattered beside Letrias's feet, electricity sizzled along his palms. His lips trembled as he spoke. "You are not all-powerful. Hermenuedis is more than a match for you, and he has taught me" –bluish light amassed between Letrias's fists— "how to wield extraordinary power!"

The energy shot from Letrias's hands in the form of bolts that sped toward the dragon's chest. Hope surged in Auron's chest, hope that he had underestimated Letrias's abilities. But the energy sizzled through the dragon's scaled body as though he were a ghost, as if the creature had no physical presence, and then it splashed uselessly onto the distant ground. Auron's heart fell again and Letrias stumbled back from the creature. Letrias glanced at each of his hands then back at the dragon, then he spat in the dust.

Dark clouds rolled overhead, gathering together until the sunlight faded from the Plains of Galaban. Auron thought that the air turned cold, but that could have been his imagination.

Albino the dragon drew back his head, flames roiling between his teeth. "I will waste no more breath on you," the dragon said, and fire streamed from his mouth.

But before the flames reached Letrias a cloud spiraled to the ground and a dark humanoid entity passed from the heavens to the earth. Hermenuedis landed between Albino and Letrias, crouching for a moment, then straightened like a bird preparing to take flight. The wind played along the Art'en wizard's back, ruffling the feathers of his voluminous, furled wings.

Auron swallowed hard at the sight. Most of the winged humanoids were the size of a man, but Hermenuedis was a giant among them. The fierceness of his high cheekbones and the gray palor of his skin appeared as a visitation of death to the fight.

As the dragon's flames reached the wizard, he held out a black sphere that absorbed Albino's flames. The Art'en did not flinch beneath the dragon's attack. Calmly he held the sphere as the flames swelled it to the size of a boulder.

The white dragon's hard gaze riveted on the wizard. Hermenuedis flapped his wings as the flaming barrage slid him backwards. The dragon took a step toward the Art'en. All power. All righteous indignation and strength. Albino would not be denied.

Auron remembered then that the dragon would come for him next and at last his foot moved. He cursed his legs for refusing to move any faster. The Art'en wizard would lose this battle and the white dragon would come after him next. Auron turned and ran. His sword grew heavy in his hand and he dropped it like a lead weight.

The dragon roared and the ground quaked. As Auron fell, he glanced back.

Albino rose in terrible majesty and flung a black dragon down the slope, its dark body digging a rift in the hard earth. So, Valorian had joined the battle. The black versus the white. Two wizards against the dragon prophet and still it had the advantage against them.

Auron stumbled to his feet and raced eastward. The dreadful sounds of the battle on the Plains of Galaban diminished behind him and he did not look back. He did not care who lived and who died. He cared for one thing and one thing only. Living. He had to stay alive and he had to be far away from the fury of the titan monsters that he had witnessed. It was their world. He was insignificant in comparison and he knew it.

For five days he fled. The sky remained cloudy, and rain pummeled him night and day. Eventually he found shelter on the forested slopes of a mountain. That night he fell into an exhausted sleep, but he awoke not long after with something cold pressed against his throat. He opened his eyes and the tip of a stone dagger played at his throat.

A familiar handsome face grinned at him over the blade. The clouds must have thinned, for moonlight fell through the trees.

"Letrias? You're alive!" Auron exclaimed. "How did you survive?"

Letrias clamped a hand over Auron's mouth and withdrew his crude weapon from Auron's throat. "Silence, fool," Letrias said. His gaze darted about the trees on the mountain slope. "Someone has been following me."

At that moment a fair-skinned man with blond hair stepped from behind a tree. He was dressed in a ragged cloak.

Letrias bounded to his feet, prepared to run. The man raised a hand and said, "Stay in your place. I know who you are, Letrias. And I know thy companion Auron."

"I don't know how you found me, but I'm warning you to keep your distance from me," Letrias said. His eyes widened, and Auron felt his own body freeze in place. There was nowhere he could look except at the stranger.

The man's body glowed as if with holy light. It hurt to look at him. His eyes blazed like small suns from his face. Spotless white robes grew over his rags, covering him from head to toe, and his hair radiated light as golden as Yimshi's rays.

"I was sent to tell you that the Creator sees all," the man said. "There is only one Ruler of the universe and he has seen your wickedness and the innocent blood that you shed on the Plains of Galaban. There will be a reckoning for you both. Your deeds will be returned upon your own heads. This night God delivers a message and a curse, for in turning from his holy law you have brought His wrath upon yourselves."

"Get out of here before I kill you," Letrias said. "Serving your Creator has brought you to rags! Just look at yourself and consider it." Letrias chuckled and shook his head. He seemed to have regained his boldness. "What are you? A homeless tramp looking for money no doubt! You find wanderers and convince them with magic tricks that you are some prophet? Ha!"

The strange man raised his hands, his gaze penetrating. "You have made your choices, and I pity you for them. God lingers for the redemption of the wicked and he pleads for their souls. Now, to you is given this promise of a curse: You will not find rest, for the wrath of the Heavenly abides on you. Age shall not change your bodies. For the centuries will pass and you will remember your sins until you repent or fall upon the swords of the righteous. God is forever."

The light died in the stranger's eyes and the white robes vanished. He stood there catching his breath as if physically drained by the experience.

Auron stared at him, stunned. What a strange sort of prophet, and dressed in rags from head to toe.

Letrias lunged at the man, the dagger in his hand thrusting at the man's throat. But the man vanished and Letrias's momentum flattened him against a tree. Loudly cursing, Letrias picked himself up. He glanced around for the strange man but, not finding him, he cursed again and ran off into the forest.

Auron trembled as he walked to a tree. He leaned his forehead against the rough bark and wept. Not tears of remorse for the wrongs he had committed, but tears of fear for himself. He should have stayed with Albino and tried the way of righteousness. Now he had fallen beyond redemption. Betraying Xavion and killing the prince should have secured a place for him at the side of the all-powerful Hermenuedis. But if what he had seen of that wizard's last battle with Albino was any indicator, the wizard would be fortunate to escape with his life.

He scraped his skin along the bark. Somehow the feel of his warm blood dripping down his face seemed a penance. He should have remained loyal to the prophets.

So began the wandering of his lost soul. A soul and a body disconnected from the reality of his sad existence. Neither of them at peace, and his spirit often sinking into madness.

A hundred years passed. In Auron's heart it felt even longer. Believing himself to be beyond redemption, he let the power of his guilt solidify his rebellion and harden his conscience. He needed no God, he needed no allies. So he told himself.

At the end of the hundred years, his loneliness and his powerlessness were more than he could bear. He set out eastward, keeping his head down and his ears open as he journeyed across strange lands. Rumors of a powerful sorcerer guided him on to find Letrias, the last living pupil of Hermenuedis. But the years were not friendly to him and for a long, long time he searched in vain. The passage of time blurred for him and his meaningless, miserable existence.

* * *

"Letrias, a stranger has come to the valley." The stump of a man cowered before his master and bit his thumbnail.

Letrias regarded the man in silence. His own slender figure would have deceived any stranger into believing him weak, but in his hand he held a metal staff. At its head the dark metal separated into several bands that wrapped about a small orb. He clanked the staff on the floor and calmly eyed the penitent figure. "Do not let your lips quiver, Mazmodel. Tell me what you know."

"Forgive me, mighty one," the little man said as he bit his other thumbnail. "I—I mean the stranger reported that he knew you. He said he knew you a long time ago."

Letrias looked over Mazmodel to the massive chamber doors, then stepped down to the man's level. "Place your hands on the stone," he commanded.

Trembling, the little man positioned himself on all four limbs with fingers splayed.

Letrias walked forward and landed his booted foot on Mazmodel's hand. The man cried out, but Letrias stepped past him, not even glancing down. "Ah, Mazmodel." Letrias laughed. "You must always be ready to give me a quick answer. Otherwise if your usefulness is at an end I will have no choice but to remove you from my protection, and your daughter as well. Now, tell me, who has come to my valley."

"He said his name is Auron," the little man said, and his lips trembled. He spat on the floor as if to ease the tension.

Letrias lifted his staff. It thrummed a deep tone that filled the room, and harsh, unintelligible whispers joined in. It was an otherworldly, evil sound that bespoke condemnation. Letrias laughed and faced Mazmodel. The evil he had fostered in his soul these thousand plus years had given him what he'd always desired. Power over others.

Mazmodel's body rose off the floor until his limbs hung loose in mid-air. His toes dangled in the air above the stone. Tears sprang from the man's eyes.

"So, Auron has returned to me." Letrias smiled while the power of his staff continued to hold his servant a prisoner. Swift-flowing lava spilled from a nearby hole in the rock wall, flowing through a channel carved beside him at the wall's base. The molten rock curved against the back wall and streamed past him on the other side, forming a perfect U of hot liquid that glowed orange-yellow.

Forcing all his fingers into his mouth, the little man stuttered, "I . . . I, he . . . he is . . . Auron wants—"

Letrias angled his ear toward the chamber's twin doors. A familiar presence entered his perception, and a smile creased his face. His leather clothes creaked as he lowered his staff to the floor. "And I had thought he, too, was dead," Letrias said.

Letrias let the staff's power drop the little man to the stone floor. Perspiration rose on the man's forehead and dripped down his cheeks. He took his fingers out of his mouth and licked his lips. "Please, Master, I . . . I . . . I . . . you . . . promised"—he choked on his words—"promised me home."

A chorus of muffled hissing and unintelligible words arose in the shadows behind Letrias. "Home? You were warned against mentioning this in my presence." Letrias sighed. "Your fate is in my hand, Mazmodel. As is your daughter's. You are my trophy, though a disappointing one you have proven to be. You are my trophy of war, a constant reminder that piece by piece Subterran is falling into my palm. But your pleas are wearying me."

At that moment the chamber doors lumbered open. Two wizards wielding scythes entered, their bodies garbed in heavy black leather. They stood aside as four broad-shouldered men shuffled inside bearing a man on a litter. Each of the litterbearers held a wizard's staff and wore black cloaks.

Letrias addressed Mazmodel without looking back at him. "If the whole land of Nostravium is filled with idiots such as you, my followers will feast on their corpses. They who have no strength have no use to me."

The staff's head glowed harsh gray light, and

energy blasted from it into the little man's chest. Letrias ambled over to the litter as Mazmodel's body crumpled to the floor.

Letrias glanced at the litter and the man that lay on it. Auron's sand-encrusted face returned his gaze. "At last you have come. Welcome to the Valley of Death," Letrias said with a frown. "What has it been, Auron? Only a thousand years since we survived the battle of Galaban? Age has not touched our bodies, nor has time dulled my memory. Xavion is long dead and forgotten, and his master has not appeared nor have I heard rumor of him in all this time." He leaned on his wizard's staff, letting his dark eyes return Auron's weary gaze. "If you have come to serve me, then I will save your life."

Auron coughed and then growled, "Didn't I come all this way?"

Letrias did not utter a word. He played his fingers along the staff's smooth surface.

"For these thousand years I have searched for you," Auron said. "I have not forgotten your promise to teach me. To teach me sorcery as Hermenuedis taught you."

Letrias stood back. How dare Auron treat with him so boldly! He swung his staff through the air towards the litter. The wizards who were holding it stood as still as stones. Auron's eyes opened, and he started to cry out. The staff knocked him full in the chest, causing him to spit bile, and the litter shattered into tiny fragments. Auron crashed to the stone floor.

"Do you want power, Auron? Or do you seek to evade the fate that that prophet decreed for you and I?" Letrias asked. He knelt in front of the man.

"You could easily say that the one will lead to the other. If you have power then you can evade your fate. A war is beginning. No! It has started already. A war against all who embrace the Creator and his prophets. And we know whose side must win if we are going to survive."

Auron struggled to his feet and Letrias rose before him, looking down upon him. Auron seemed so weak. No, Letrias decided, he was pliable. He was ripe and ready to receive instruction. This former member of the Six had potential in the ranks of wizardry.

Grabbing Letrias's shirt-front, Auron sought to steady himself. But Letrias captured him in the powers of wickedness and suspended him in the air as he had done to Mazmodel.

Letrias kept his gaze on Auron as he issued a command to the staff-wielding wizards that had carried the litter. "Leave us, and seal the doors as you go." The black-robed men turned to the door, and one of them stooped to grab the dead little man, Mazmodel.

"Did I ask you to do that?" Letrias asked as he raised his eyebrows and eyed the man out of the corner of his vision.

The wizard swallowed hard, withdrew his hands from Mazmodel and bowed, his eyes as wide as apples. "Please, Master, forgive my presumption."

Letrias pointed his staff at the man and lowered his brow. "Forgive?" he asked. Electric current snaked from the staff's base toward its head. "Forgiveness begets weakness." He thrust the staff at the man's head. "And God knows I never believed in helping or preserving the weak." Energy bolted from the staff. Before Auron could blink, another body lay beside Mazmodel, the other wizards had exited the room, and the doors thudded shut.

Letrias knew he had placed Auron in a fragile position. He had treated him as little more than a servant. They had once been friends, but today he must become one of many. He must see that he was not special, that he was a tool through which Letrias's power could be exercised. Letrias chuckled as Auron sat in front of him. The comradery of the Six no longer applied. People must live and die at Letrias's pleasure.

There was fear in Auron's eyes as he stared at the bodies. Letrias grinned. He would drive that fear out of him. Auron must fear no one except for Letrias. His fear of him must rise above that of any man or any god if he was to become a capable vessel.

Auron would need an instructor who feared neither man nor beast, neither angels nor God himself. Unfortunately the battles to the east of the valley kept his prize pupil, the Death Knight, occupied. Among the wizards who currently resided in the Valley of Death, only one possessed a similar fearless devotion to sorcery and to Letrias himself.

Wiping his dirty face with his shredded sleeve, Auron glanced at the ceiling. How far he had fallen from a millennia ago. What would happen to him now?

Letrias stooped next to him and nodded that he understood. "Yes, Auron, I do believe it is possible to escape the wrath of the prophets. I have escaped their wrath for a thousand years. The curse which that ragged man pronounced upon me has turned into my greatest ally. And one day soon I will be stronger than any man or creature that roams Subterran. I will be beyond the reach of even Albino himself. The Grim Reaper will envy me and Valorian will arise again. That black dragon will call me his brother, while the world falls under the sorcery I now teach."

He pulled Auron to his feet and said in hushed tones, "Stay in my shadow and all will be well."

* * *

Auron felt the bars of his heaven-bestowed prison rise around him. "I will stay in your shadow, as ageless as you, but I will serve in exchange for your protection from the prophets," he said as he looked up at Letrias, noting for the first time that the wizard wore a turban-like headdress.

"Very well then," Letrias said. "You will serve me. But I have no need of another pupil. Already some of my students have far surpassed you and my choice ones do not struggle with fear, as you do. You will learn from another. He is one of my strongest. Fearless and receptive to the power that sorcery gives. And he has few rivals in physical combat." Letrias marched to the exit doors and tapped them with the head of his staff. They immediately opened.

They walked down a long, high corridor until they stopped at an arched opening. Before them lay a large underground chamber. Auron followed Letrias inside past a fountain that spewed lava. The heat drove Auron against the wall, but Letrias dipped his fingers into the molten rock and pulled them out unharmed.

Letrias laughed. "Yes, not even an angel

would dare tread me beneath his feet now. Even a spirit would hesitate to harm me."

The chamber opened into a cavern, and the floor slanted steeply for a few hundred paces. Rivulets of lava spilled down the stone walls. The heat was nearly unbearable. But Letrias pointed his staff into the cavern to an arena far below. Armed men battled one another inside the arena. Sparks and bolts of energy abounded, passing from staffs that the wizards wielded. Auron coughed as he inhaled sulfur, but he growled, fighting it. He stepped forward, planting his feet next to Letrias, and crossed his arms. He still felt miserable, but Letrias was unveiling a purpose for him. For Auron, a purpose was enough.

Two wizards rushed at another who stood in the center of the arena. They approached him from either side, both of them wielding short swords in both hands. The movements of their bodies were smooth and precise, and they wielded their swords with admirable speed. But their opponent rose in the midst of the arena and Auron could not help but admire the man's physique. Even from a distance the man's arms and legs were impressively ripped, as a miniature monster. He was holding a metal rod in his fists and as the other two assaulted him he swung it past their defenses, thwacking each of them across their chests.

Both wizards dropped their short swords and collapsed to the black stone of the arena floor. The man lifted his rod like a spear, poising himself to impale one of them, but Letrias raised his staff. Even from that distance the victor noticed him and immediately stayed his hand. Letrias held his staff up for a moment longer, then chuckled as the wizard walked out of the arena.

"Ah, see the power that I now wield!" Letrias spread his arms as if embracing the combatants. "I have built an army, an army that communes with the spirits and receives power from them. This is no mere force of men, these are wizards. Their power is less than my own, but combined they are formidable."

The thought of all these men communing with evil spirits and learning magic from Letrias chilled Auron. Not that he, with his God-bestowed curse, was better off than they. In fact, this is why he'd come. He would learn and learn well. He would sell what remained of his soul if it bought him power to save himself from the prophets' wrath.

Suddenly the arena calmed. The wizards formed a circle as a giant of a man emerged from the shadows to stand at their center. When he raised his sword in one hand and a staff in the other, the wizards attacked. But he batted them back like so many urchins, his armored body glinting in the lava's golden light. Taking a closer look, Auron recognized the truth. This wizard had attached small blades of every shape to his massive frame, and they protruded from him at every angle.

Beside him Letrias spoke. "Meet Razes, a master among my followers. Your new master. Do not cross him, Auron, for he would end your life. Learn from him what you came here to learn from me." Letrias swung his staff, holding its end as he slammed its head into the ground.

Auron felt, rather than saw, the burst of lightning that seemed to erupt from the point of impact.

It threw him against the chamber wall. When he looked up, Letrias had engaged in a duel with another wizard who'd emerged from behind. The contest lasted only moments. Letrias stabbed the wizard through the heart and then stood over the body. "A waste," the wizard said, and he sighed and walked out of the cavern.

Left to himself, Auron felt dread building in his chest. Letrias had effectively surrounded himself with death and he reveled in it. Auron would have to claw his way through the wizard ranks if he wanted to survive this place. He stood, steeling himself against the challenges to come. He descended toward the arena, conscious of the molten rock that ran like fire down the chamber walls and the eyes of a hundred other men warily watching him. Razes was still standing in the arena, the blood of his adversaries still fresh on his blades. As the giant became aware of Auron's approach, it turned toward him. Auron felt the sweat running down his face and he considered turning to flee the impending introduction. But in his heart he knew there was no turning his back now.

Guardian of the Dragon's Offspring

Specter was leaning back against the cave's wall with his arms crossed over his chest. The early morning darkness barely touched him in here and the dampness drove a chill through his robe. He had left a fire burning low to keep himself warm, but that lay deeper in the cave and he knew he must wait out here.

He held his scythe's handle against his breast, momentarily reflecting on a time over a thousand years ago when he had been called by a different name. The name of Xavion, warrior captain of the ill-fated Six. He had fought in the War of the Trantureen. He had watched countless men and women die in that war, and then he had nearly died himself.

He glanced out of the narrow opening to the cave just as the great white dragon settled into view. The mighty beast landed with gentle grace in the woodland hollow. The albino's brilliant white scales covered its body better than any man's armor.

Specter stepped out of the cave onto the shelf of stone that bordered the the woodland hollow. The great white dragon angled its bony face down to him. Specter had been here in the forests of the Hemmed Land ever since the dragon's daughter, Dantress, had been married. She had died in childbirth but Specter had remained as a faithful guardian to watch over her child. The cave and a nearby abandoned cabin had been Specter's home in this strange land, and he had found it to be a respite from his previous journeys.

Here he stayed to serve at the dragon prophet's request.

"Master," he said as he bowed to the majestic creature. He left his cavernous gray hood over his head. Early morning darkness flooded the depressed clearing. Not a single owl made a sound and no bats hunted insects. It was as if they were afraid of disrespecting the mighty beast standing in the hollow, so they held their voices and listened instead.

The dragon's arm muscles rippled as he crouched closer to the man. "Give me your hand, Specter."

"I would prefer not to, my master," Specter said.

"No?" The dragon growled. "Of what use will you be without the full function of both of your hands?"

"It is not a crippling injury," Specter said. He extended his scarred hand, clenching and then opening his fist. "And it is a scar that I will be honored to keep, for it is the price of a life saved, a life that one day might save humanity from the evil of the warriors who turned on us. Warriors that I trained."

Specter studied his hand, half-smiling to himself. It only seemed right to let it remain burned. He had interceded when the dragon's own daughters had tried to terminate Dantress's pregnancy. They had shot a beam of energy from their swords, energy that originated with the power of their dragon blood, and he had placed his hand in its path. The cost had been painful but the child in Dantress's womb had been saved, and now thanks to his actions baby Oganna would grow into a woman.

Smoke wafted from Albino's nostrils. It settled around Specter like a fog. The dragon gazed intently into the man's hood as if he could see his blue eyes. "Do not think that I have forgotten that day, my friend," he rumbled. "Time has not wiped away the blood spilled by Letrias's treachery, nor has justice been thwarted."

"One, my master," Specter said. He could not suppress a growl of his own. "Only one of those traitors met with the fate he deserved." He clenched his fist. "And he did not even have the honor to seek that death in combat. Instead . . . instead he committed suicide."

"Do you condemn him for that?" the dragon asked thoughtfully.

Specter was silent for a while. The sky lightened in the east. The stars winked out one by one. The brightest ones remained visible a tad longer, twinkling even as the velvet sky turned blue around them. At last he whispered, "I loved them like brothers, trained them like sons. Kesla! Why him? He had a family. A beautiful wife and happy children. I would never have questioned his loyalty. If one of my students was above reproach . . . it should have been him."

The dragon flexed his wings and then folded them to his sides. His long tail twitched, and the scales on his neck rippled forebodingly. "Listen to me my friend," the dragon said, then he hesitated. The man's cloaked head had tilted toward the ground.

"Xavion?" the dragon asked, and Specter looked up into the prophet's pink eyes.

Albino spoke in a low rumble. "I think it is time for you to know the truth. The whole truth of who lived and who died a thousand years ago, and why it happened. It is time for you to understand. I do now, though I did not know at that time. I understand now why Kesla turned and I have forgiven him."

* * *

Kesla fitted his scabbard to his side and hugged his wife. His three boys and two little girls hovered behind their mother. His eldest son was almost twelve, the youngest no more than five. The girls were seven and eight years of age. The children waited until he released his wife, then they clamored for their turns, hugging him until he laughed. They laughed with him, filling the log cabin with the joyful noise. He smiled as he tore the last of his little girls' arms from around his neck. He stood her on the floor, tousled his boys' hair, and pecked his wife on the cheek.

"Go now!" She laughed with him. "I love you, too. Now be off with you. You have a goodly long distance to travel . . . It was your choice after all to build so far from the dragon's lands, and you must join Xavion."

Kesla sobered upon her reminder of that. It was true. Xavion would be waiting for him on the Plains of Galaban. He smiled again as he gazed around at all of the loving faces in his cabin. This! This is why he fought alongside of Xavion. This is why he served the will of the prophets, to protect his family and the families of countless others. He had wanted to check on their safety before facing the wizard's armies in battle again.

"Be safe," his wife said. "You know that you'll be in our prayers . . . as always." She pecked him on the cheek and shoved a glowing iron lantern into his hand. The light warmed her face as if she were an angel. In a way, she was. She was his angel. The brightest light of hope in a dark world and the one in whose arms he lost all thought for his troubles.

Leaving the house with its smoking chimney and long, rough-hewn walls behind him, he set off down the dark, narrow path. His white cape flowed behind him. He jerked his head toward the sky, opening his senses to the fresh, cool air. Innumerable stars shone in the sky above him. On both sides of the trail the trees rose protectively, while a border of soft thick grass carpeted the trail's edge. It was the night of new moon. Darkest night of the month.

The trail wended through the forest, a lonesome path but his by choice. He could have had a mansion in Emperia, under the direct protection of the great white dragon. But he'd fallen in love with this forest on one of his travels, and here he had determined to build his family's future. The trees were straight, tall, and sturdy, with little forest undergrowth. Deer abounded, though he did not care much to hunt them, choosing instead to lie in his back yard and watch the woodland creatures graze without fear. Thankfully, his wife sympathized with his sentiments.

But on this night he sighed, realizing that it might be a long time before he could return home. The War of the Trantureen seemed to continue without end. Though the addition of the valiant prince of Prunesia to the dragon warriors' ranks had given him a small measure of hope. There were still kingdoms of men that were willing to join the fight against the wizards.

Kesla strode swiftly down the trail, unconcerned for the dark clouds that rolled without warning from the south to cover the stars. An exposed tree root caught his foot, and he fell forward. The night turned darker than it should have, and the air around him bit with a sharp cold uncharacteristic of this time of year.

Turning to look at the sky, Kesla's heart beat with twice its vigor. His blood ran cold and sweat built on his palms as he reached down to check for his crystalline sword. Fear stabbed him with the force of a thousand blades as he heard a screech, as of an eagle on the hunt, but with far more volume. The screech echoed in the forest, rebounding from tree to tree, surrounding him with its dark cruelty.

Kesla spun on his heels and raced toward his house, sliding his pure blade from its sheath and holding it wide. The lantern in his hand became a burden, and he dropped it, shattering its chimney.

The clouds gathered above his house as he ran. They swirled, tornado-like, descending from the sky as if gravity forced them to fall. Something shaped like an oversized falcon dove from the midst of the swirling dark mass, dropping with incredible speed as if to catch its prey.

A sizzle of energy built inside of the clouds and they glowed green. Kesla gasped and picked up speed. A single bolt of green lightning followed the falling form from the sky to the ground, and the strike exploded into the cabin roof.

Such was the force of the blast that the paned windows shattered outward and the stone foundations trembled. The shockwave forced Kesla's arm over his eyes, but he ran to the front door, catching a glimpse of the falcon-like form again as it dropped through the hole in the roof.

Kesla burst into his house. The walls were charred, the fireplace was cracked and smoking, the floorboards which he had so carefully laid out were broken and twisted.

In the darkness and amidst the ruins, Kesla's eyes confirmed his greatest fears. A breeze swept through the broken walls, whipping his white cape around his legs. It blew smoke over the crumpled, soot-covered bodies of his wife and children, their sides heaving with shallow breaths.

Clouds of smoke billowed around a creature that crouched behind the bodies. Its black-feathered wings spread over and around them. Its eyes, glinting like gray-green metal, glared at him from the leathery face of a man. Black leather covered its entire body.

A flame grew in the ruined fireplace and its light flickered on the face of a smooth black sphere in the winged man's hand.

Kesla longed to rush forward. To gut the creature with his sword and feed it to the ravens, but he knew the foolishness of the thought. He knew his limits and fighting this wizard would be as useless as beating his sword on a boulder.

"Good, you have restrained yourssself, Warrior Kesssla," the creature hissed. It pointed its fingers toward each of the prone bodies, yet didn't touch them, merely wiggling its fingers as if they were a spider crawling through the air.

"Leave my family be." Kesla's mouth went dry, his sword hand began to shake. He knew that his helplessness showed in his voice, too. "Whatever you are here for they are of no use to you."

"No?" The wizard Art'en lowered his black sphere until it almost touched Kesla's son.

Kesla's knuckles whitened as he wrung his sword's handle. Its blade glowed with pure white light.

The wizard laughed, high and birdlike. "But you are wrong, my dear warrior. They are very useful to me. So long as I hold them in my power, you will do as I sssay, and you are integral to my plans."

"No . . . no I would never." But even as Kesla said it, the wizard touch his wife's cheek with an icy finger, and Kesla knew his declaration wasn't true. He would do anything to keep her from harm, even if he had to sell his own soul.

"Oh, but it won't be so hard as you think, my dear, dear warrior. Only a sssmall favor I ask. Just one! And then you can have your family back safe and sssound. Not a scratch on any of their precious heads." The wizard cackled, spreading his arms. "I promisss!"

Kesla swallowed hard. His eyes burned with tears that begged to be shed. But he felt as if he was no longer himself. He had been pulled out of his body and was watching helplessly the course of a horrid history.

The Art'en wizard stared hard at him and said, "You do know who I am."

Kesla knew, but he could not bring himself to name the wizard out loud. This being was the dread Hermenuedis. Only recently Kesla had traveled to the lands of the Eiderveis with the rest of the Six to try and assassinate Hermenuedis. But though they had infiltrated the temple they had not found the wizard himself.

"What do you want of me?" Kesla said in a voice too weak to be his own.

"Not too hard a thing, my dear warrior. I offer one life in exchange for many." It pointed at his wife and children. "For some time now Letrias has been my servant. With my help he has enlisted the aid of your fellow warriors, the members of the dragon's trusted Six! Now only you and your captain remain loyal to the white dragon. Your captain might not need to die, unless he interferes with your mission. But the prince of Prunesssia. Ah! I want his young blood sprayed across the path by your own sssword so that his people will withdraw their support from the prophets. Do this thing and then come to me at the Temple of Al'un Dai. If you succeed in thisss deed then I will keep my end of this arrangement. I will return your family to you unharmed and then I will leave you in peace from that time forward.

"Double-cross me, or fail to kill the prince, and your wife's carcass and those of your children will hang on the temple ramparts until the fowls pick their bones clean and until time turns them to dussst."

The smoke whirled around the Art'en's giant figure, hiding him and the bodies of Kesla's family from view. When it cleared, the wizard and his victims had vanished.

Kesla fell to his knees and beat his fists on the floorboards. "No! I will not do it! I will not betray them." But his wife and children filled his mind. He would do anything, become anything if it meant saving their lives. The prince must die. One simple act, one horrible deed and life could return to normal.

Normal? Not normal but a different beginning from which they had a chance to survive this hell. If Letrias, Hestor, Auron, and Clavius had already joined against the prophets then the famed Six were indeed beyond hope. Their support of Xavion during the mission to Al'un Dai had been nothing more than a farce!

He threw aside the pure white garments that set him apart as a warrior in the prophet's service, and donned a black cloak, deeply frowning all the while. His sword's blade glowed with only a faint light as if reflecting the condition of his soul.

He left his demolished home and journeyed into a foreign land south of Emperia. On the stone plains of Galaban he waited beneath a cloudy sky until Letrias, Hestor, Clavius, and Auron joined him.

Letrias took the lead, the edge of his mouth twitching in a sneer. "You see now, my fellow traitors, not even the mighty Kesla is above corruption."

"Silence!" Kesla shoved Letrias to the ground and stomped on his stomach. "As always," he said as he glanced at the others, "you will follow my lead. Let us be done with this . . . and quickly."

"It was I that made contact with the wizard Hermenuedis," Letrias spat. He thrashed out from under Kesla's foot and stood, dusting himself. "He holds me in high favor. Don't forget that and your family will be safe."

Kesla fisted the thin man in his jaw. "Why you! You lowest scum of Subterran! You told the wizard where to find them."

"Nothing else would have turned you," Letrias said.

Kesla drew his sword and grasped the warrior's shoulder, prepared to thrust him through. But electricity sizzled out of Letrias's hand, blasting Kesla to the ground. The other warriors grimly watched, though Auron almost smiled.

"I can kill you now and leave your family to die," Letrias said as he pulled Kesla to his feet. "Or you can lead us to Xavion and the prince of Prunesia, and your family will live. My new master has left the choice entirely in your hands."

Kesla chose to continue on his path, vowing that, when all was set right, he would hide his family and find and murder Letrias. He would beat the man's smug face to a bloody pulp, lash him to a tree, and watch him bake in the sunlight for days on end. Oh yes, Letrias would pay for this and he would pay dearly at Kesla's hand.

His hatred for Letrias grew in proportion to his self-loathing as he and the other traitors journeyed north along the Plains of Galaban. They at last found evidence of recent battle. Corpses peppered the landscape for as far as the eye could see. They walked among the dead and it chilled Kesla to his soul. He was to be a part of this bloodshed, part of the curse that the Trantureen had brought to their world.

At last he spotted the stone mountain where the young prince of Prunesia had found refuge from the wizards' carnage. Prince Brian greeted them warmly, his face showing great relief as he led them into a mountainside cave. There, Brian brought them face to face with the mighty but wounded captain Xavion. The armies of Emperia and their allies had engaged the dragon Valorian in battle on the stone plains of Galaban, and they had lost.

When Kesla and the other traitors had carried Xavion out of the mountain cave, they fell upon the young man and the old. Kesla's heart seemed to die within him as he committed the deed. Everything he believed in was epitomized in Xavion, yet everyone he most loved would die if the prince did not.

He thrust the prince through and wept over the still body. A roar filled the heavens. Looking up, he saw his former master, the great white dragon, coming in all his fury. In the dragon's wake the clouds divided like water.

For the first time ever, Kesla felt afraid of the powerful creature. It landed with such force on the stony battlefield that the ground split.

Albino raked his razor claws down Hestor's front, spilling his organs onto the ground. As Clavius started to flee, the dragon roared, then caught the man with his jaws and snapped him in two. Next he wheeled to strike Letrias.

The wizard pupil vainly cast bolts of lightning from his hands that passed through the dragon's body. Albino reared back his head, spraying such vehement flames that the dirt turned to glass.

Without warning, the Art'en wizard Hermenuedis fell from the sky with a screech and landed between his pupil and Albino, sparing Letrias incineration. The orb in the wizard's hand grew in size and absorbed Albino's flames until it became as large as a boulder.

"Be gone, cursed artifact!" Albino roared. He stretched out his claws toward the orb and flexed them but did not touch it. The orb burst into tiny fragments.

Kesla stumbled back. He dropped his crystalline sword and stared at its blade, now stained with innocent blood. The deed was done. His tears burned on his cheeks.

He glimpsed Letrias standing behind the Art'en wizard. Letrias's face paled ghastly white as the dragon swung its tail around, cracking it into the Art'en. "Hermenuedis," the dragon rumbled, "you have carried your wickedness to its final day."

"No, Albino, thisss day isss mine," the wizard screeched. "You have lost your champions!"

Suddenly, a large black dragon shot from the heavens toward Albino. With teeth bared he attacked, but he passed through the white dragon as if through air. Albino grasped him with his claws and flung him down the slope. The black dragon's body furrowed a canyon in the ground as it skidded to a stop. Kesla recognized the beast as the wizard dragon Valorian. He had seen the monster before on other battlefields. The black dragon was a foe of superior physical strength and a deadly practitioner of sorcery.

Kesla did not wait to watch more of the conflict. He raced south as fast as he could toward the temple of Al'un Dai and toward his family. The distance to the temple was vast. When he at last arrived, he found that he had not been fast enough. The Art'en wizard, wounded from his encounter with Albino, had taken refuge in the temple fortress, but the white dragon had followed. Fire gushed from the albino's mouth, and it called lightning from the sky. It broke the temple walls and at last cornered the Art'en in one of the great halls.

Rushing past the raging beast, Kesla stumbled through the rubble, becoming increasingly desperate as he searched in vain for his wife and children. As he leapt over a pile of rubble he spotted an opening in one of the tower walls. Above his head the dragon's tail crushed a stone column and the fragments fell toward Kesla. The man ducked, glancing across the courtyard to see the dragon strike again. The tail crushed Hermenuedis into another tower.

The wizard stood again, the battle renewing as he fought for his survival. Kesla barely saw or heard all that happened around him. In the gaping hole left by Albino's attack on the tower wall, he saw the bloodied bodies of his wife and children trapped beneath fallen debris.

"No!" he screamed as he raced toward them. Frantically he pulled away the stones that lay on top of them, but the great white dragon continued to pour out its wrath on the wizard.

Kesla pulled his beloved family from the ruins and laid their bodies on the floor of an untouched tower, hoping to keep them safe. At that moment the dragon crashed through the wall, his claws ripping Hermenuedis's wings out of his back while his teeth cut the Art'en's skull. The wizard's screams reached a pitch far more disturbing than anything Kesla had heard yet.

Finding a hatch with a stairs beneath it in the tower floor, he took the bodies of his family into the dark sublevels of the temple and, with a broken heart, buried them in the alcoves of a large, stone chamber.

In the midst of his despair a beautiful woman revealed herself to him. She consoled him, soothed him. In his loneliness he turned to her and lost himself to her. Even when he learned that she was the mistress of the dreaded Art'en wizard, he did not leave her. She taught him some of her master's dark arts, in particular she crafted a potion for him to drink, which kept him from aging. But an eternity cooped up with a mistress of darkness was still an empty existence. The world continued without him, unaware and uncaring of his lost soul.

* * *

Albino the dragon sighed as he finished telling Kesla's story. Then he spoke again to Specter. "When my daughters brought word that Kesla had slain himself on the sword of his captain . . . That is, when they told me that he had fallen on your old

42

sword, I wept in secret. For I was to blame for the death of his family. Was it not I that was so bent on slaying my enemy that I neglected the innocent? To my shame, I am to blame for his fall as much as he was. And if I could do it all over again, I would have driven Hermenuedis to humiliation and not have scattered his followers to the four winds. Now his evil spreads across Subterran more surely than it did before. For Letrias and Auron evaded capture that day and hid from me, so that for many years I knew nothing of their whereabouts. Only Dantress's child and the sword that I have given to Ilfedo can cleanse the stain of that day from my conscience."

Specter shook his head. "Forgive me, Master. My words were spoken out of ignorance and nothing more."

The dragon blew gentle clouds of smoke from his nostrils, filling the hollow, then its white-scaled sides shimmered and it became invisible. "A child approaches this hollow," the dragon explained, "You would do well to follow my example, Specter."

Specter chuckled softly. He waited until the head of a young boy appeared at the hollow's rim. He let the youth spot him for only an instant, then caused his cloak to shimmer with light, rendering him as invisible as the dragon. "It seems there are more people in this region than there were before Dantress married Ilfedo," he said as he watched the boy staring with mouth agape at the spot where Specter had been.

"Yes." Albino blew a greater cloud of smoke into the air, veiling his face. "The Hemmed Land is about to change. Its people were mostly leaderless, but now they are taking respectful notice of the young woodsman that saved the coastal people from the sea serpents and married a mysterious beauty. They have heard that he cleansed this wilderness of the man-hungry bears. More settlers will come, it is inevitable."

The dragon's pink eyes stared blankly as if seeing something beyond Specter's range of vision. "The sea serpents have again invaded the Hemmed Land, this time in greater numbers."

"Master, let me deal with them," Specter said.

"No, I did not give that task to you and, though you are strong, my friend, I cannot risk losing you in that battle. It is up to Ilfedo and my daughters who remain, to deal with those creatures," the dragon said.

"But if you would not send me for fear of losing me, why send them?" Specter asked. "They do not have my experience with such things."

"Because, my friend," the dragon rumbled gently, "though you are strong, Ilfedo is stronger now. And though you have the gift of invisibility, Ilfedo has the gift of the sword of living fire to which you cannot compare. No, you must remain in these forests and watch over my offspring."

Lifting his head to gaze at the trees surrounding the hollow, Albino said, "The boy is gone. Here, take these and keep them safe until they can be given into the hands of my newest offspring." The dragon opened the palm of his other clawed hand. Therein lay the rusted sword of Xavion and the blade boomerang that Dantress had retrieved from the fields around the temple fortress of Al'un Dai.

Specter took the weapons into his arms with near reverence. "I will do as you ask," he said. Both he and the dragon dropped the shrouds of invisibility and regarded each other with sober resolution.

"Ilfedo will soon leave his home to seek out the sea serpents," the dragon said. He snapped out his leathery wings, sending a wave of air across the woodland clearing. "He will soon know the extent of the power of the sword I gave him. At least, that is, the extent of its power when wielded by him. Farewell, my friend. I wish you the full blessings of God." With that the dragon crouched, digging his claws into the ground, and launched himself into the distant western sky.

When the dragon had gone Specter carried the sword and the blade boomerang into the cave. He hid them there and looked upon them, musing on their history. The sword he knew from long ago. Yes, it had been his own when the rest of the Six had betrayed him. It was the chief of the swords of the Six. Many years later the white dragon had given it to his youngest daughter and she had afterwards died in childbirth. Specter shook his head at the tragic memory. Dantress had been a beautiful soul. To die so young seemed unjust, yet the memory of her lived on in those whose lives she had touched.

Now, Specter would keep these weapons ready for the day that Dantress's daughter was old enough to wield them. Perhaps in her hands these weapons could at last forge a more complete and beautiful history.

He walked out of the cave, slinging the black-handled scythe over his shoulder, then proceeded across the hollow and into the forest. He rendered himself invisible again, choosing caution as he proceeded toward Ilfedo's house. On his way there he stopped at the abandoned cabin in the forest where he had made his temporary home. The door lay broken on its hinges and the furniture lay about. But the roof was still solid and the log walls were thick. He had hidden his food and clothing inside of the cabinets, cleaned up the place just a touch, and had even dared to start a low fire on a few nights. The cabin was on Ilfedo's property but the man seemed to avoid it as if it were haunted. Specter had speculated that it had something to do with the prolific claw marks on the cabin's walls and floor. Some beast, likely a bear, had torn the cabin's interior to pieces and there were blood stains still evident on the floor. Someone had died here.

Specter fetched an apple from the cabinet and then set off for Ilfedo's house again.

Some time later he stepped noiselessly between the trees that surrounded Ilfedo's clearing. Specter stood invisible on the hillside clearing. The clearing was filling with early morning sunlight. In front of Ilfedo's house a group of around forty people had gathered. They were lying down asleep on the grass. Their clothes were soiled, their hair was disheveled, and the assorted bags and other items lying about them served as pillows and blankets. Children curled under blankets with women and men. Many of the little ones' breathing seemed ragged and uneasy.

Specter marveled at the sight. These people had fled from something, and they had made a hurried trip through the wilderness to reach Ilfedo's house.

The house stood behind them on the hill, silent and lifeless except for two white birds. Specter saw the sunlight glint off of the birds' silver beaks, and he sullenly directed his attention to the northwest corner of the clearing where six figures now emerged from the forest. It was Ilfedo and the daughters of the white dragon.

Specter had seen them leave to bury Ilfedo's wife. They had taken the baby with them. Perhaps Specter should have followed, but he had decided to leave the mourners alone. Now that they had returned, Specter's vigil of protection over Dantress's baby could begin.

Ilfedo halted at the edge of the clearing, looking out at the mass of strangers sleeping in front of his home. When he had left with his wife's body he had been wearing a sword, but now two of them hung at his side. Specter tilted his head curiously. Something about that new sword reminded him of what the white dragon had said, "Though you are strong, Ilfedo is stronger."

Cradling his child in his arms, Ilfedo took a step toward his sleeping visitors. As he did so, several other people appeared on the opposite side of the clearing and Specter recognized a few of them as Ilfedo's close friends and fellow woodsmen.

Ganning walked with a decided limp as he skirted the sleeping individuals. Fast on his heels strode Honer. He was a taller fellow with sandy-blond hair and very broad shoulders. Behind him marched Ombre, a gray fur coat on his back. The head of the dead wolf hung limp over his back like a hood. All three of these men had been close to Ilfedo since childhood.

Two women accompanied them, one following Honer. Specter knew her as well, she was Eva, Honer's wife. The other lingered at the eastern boundary of the clearing, her eyes darting from one prone individual to the next. At last she also skirted the group and followed Eva. Specter knew from his time in this land that she was Ganning's wife.

Specter closed the distance between himself and Ilfedo so that he could better hear what transpired. As he approached, he got his first peek at the dragon's offspring asleep in her father's arms. Peaceful and beautiful she looked. Wrapped in a soft white sheet, Oganna slept with her mouth open.

The air that morning was warm and gentle.

"Ombre, Honer, Ganning." Ilfedo accepted a hug from each of his friends and then smiled through his tears as Honer's wife stood on tiptoe to kiss his cheek. "Eva," he murmured.

"Is this . . . ?" Honer's wife looked at the infant with tender blue eyes. Her blond hair fell over her eyes and she brushed it back over her ears with her fingers. "Is she yours, Ilfedo?"

Choking on tears, Ilfedo nodded, kissed the infant's forehead, and then held her out to the woman. Eva accepted the bundle as if it were gold. "She's as beautiful as her mother," she said with a sob.

For a little while Ilfedo's friends and their wives fawned over the child, then Ombre stood aside and raised his eyebrows. "Ahem . . . Ilfedo?" He swept his arm toward the five sisters standing like living statues half-a-dozen yards away. "Maybe you should introduce us?" he asked.

"Of course." Ilfedo wiped his face with his sleeve, smearing dirt through his tears. "Please," he said to Caritha, "do come closer."

One by one he introduced the sisters of his deceased bride, giving each a warm smile. At once their faces relaxed. His friends and their wives introduced themselves in kind and welcomed the sisters into their inner circle.

"You will have to join us for tea sometime," Eva said, rocking the baby in her arms. "I have a fine elderberry and herb tea."

"She makes it herself. Every year," Ganning's wife said quietly.

"Your invitation is very kind," Caritha said, inclining her head for a moment toward Eva. "But we are here for the child, to raise her and protect her."

"Protect her?" Eva replied. "What are you going to protect her from? We are all friends here. And between these men," she waved her hand to indicate Ilfedo, Ombre, Honer, and Ganning, "no place could be safer for Dantress's child."

Specter caught Ombre watching Caritha throughout the conversation. It amused him for a moment. Ombre, who always spoke of bachelorhood as the cardinal virtue. Ombre's eyes were taking her in and his uncharacteristic silence spoke volumes.

Aroused by the chatter, the people encamped in Ilfedo's clearing stood and ran toward him. The five sisters moved into position between Ilfedo, Eva, and the people, their purple skirts swishing over the grass as if they floated. Reaching down into their skirts they parted a hidden fold in each of their garments and drew out their rusted short swords.

The people stumbled over each other as they came to a sudden stop in front of the sisters. Ilfedo raised his hand and shouted, "Lower your weapons and let these people speak."

Laura stabbed her sword into its sheath and folded her skirt to hide it. Evela and Levena relaxed, sheathing their weapons as well. While Rozel frowned, then shrugged her shoulders and followed suit. Caritha started to do likewise. She pulled the fold of her skirt aside, revealing the sheath, but a rugged woodsman leaned close to see and she angled her blade toward him.

Ilfedo shifted his gaze to only her. "I command you to do this if you wish to remain with me. Otherwise take your weapon and leave us in peace."

She retreated a few steps, hiding her rusted blade in the folds of her skirt. Specter could see the struggle in her eyes. She had carried the responsibility of watching over her sisters for too long on her young shoulders. She needed to let Ilfedo lead. She needed to let him protect them all while she lent her support.

As Ilfedo nodded to the large group, a blacksmith stepped forward.

"You are Ilfedo Matthaliah?" he asked. When Ilfedo nodded the blacksmith put his big hand to his chest. "I worked a forge in the town of Endel. Have you heard of it?"

"No," Ilfedo said simply.

The blacksmith grimaced. "You won't hear of Endel now. It is gone. Wiped off of the map entirely."

Several women and children started to sob.

"Ours is not the only town," the blacksmith said. "On our way here we saw similar destruction in several of the larger coastal towns."

"Sea serpents," Ilfedo whispered and the words sounded as a curse from his lips. "You should move inland away from those monsters."

"Yes, but that is my point," the blacksmith said as he bit his lower lip, "Our town. The town of Endel was deep in the forest and the serpents still came. We were half-a-day's walk from the coast."

Ilfedo's face betrayed his growing frustration, and Specter could only imagine the tumult building within him. His wife had just died and now his homeland was in jeopardy from some oversized sea-dwelling snakes. Not exactly the welcome home that a man needs after a birth and a funeral.

"We are refugees now," the blacksmith continued. "Nowhere in the Hemmed Land is safe now. Nowhere! Those cursed serpents are killing everyone they find, seemingly just for the sport of it, and we can do nothing to stop them." He fiddled with his soiled brown beard and the eyes of everyone else turned toward Ilfedo. "We came across a young woodsman who pointed us in your direction. He said that you would remember him. His name was Ramul."

"Ramul. He is a woodsman now?" Ilfedo half-smiled at that revelation. "Yes, I don't know him well but we are acquainted."

The blacksmith glanced over his shoulder at those assembled and grinned. Hope shone in his eyes as he turned back to Ilfedo. "Then it is true! You are the slayer of bears and the savior of Coral Haven!"

"Coral Haven?" Ilfedo asked, puzzled.

The blacksmith furrowed his brow as he thought on the matter. "Ramul said that he used to work there at an inn called . . ." He glanced at the sky. "I think he called it the Wooden Mug."

"Ah, yes I do know the place," Ilfedo said.

The blacksmith pointed at Ilfedo with his thick hand. "Everyone has heard the stories of you. Whether it is the time you hunted the man-eating bears to extinction, or your battle with the sea serpents. You are the greatest hunter that the Hemmed Land has ever seen and we need you now. Please! Come to our aid. Kill these creatures and we will reward you with anything that you ask." Suddenly the blacksmith fell to his knees and behind him the others followed his example.

Ilfedo's face reddened and he wiped his forehead with the back of his arm. Then he pulled the blacksmith to a standing position. Resting his hands on the bearded man's shoulders, he turned to Honer's wife and glanced at his infant child. "Eva, will you watch over her until I return?" he asked.

"Of course," Eva replied. "It would be an absolute pleasure, and my children will get a thrill out of seeing her."

Caritha spun toward Ilfedo. "What? No, Ilfedo! We will watch over her—"

He shook his head. "I need you to come with me. If your recent vows mean anything then you must come with me. I can't do this alone."

She looked stunned at his admission. Nevertheless, with a slight bow, she promised her help.

"Rozel, Evela, Levena, and Laura," he said to the other sisters. "You are with me as well."

Evela smiled a bright little smile that warmed Specter from the inside out. Rozel harrumphed and crossed her arms. Laura said, "If that is what you need from us, Ilfedo." And Levena curtsied.

"Good." Ilfedo took off his extra sword, the one that had been a gift from his parents, and ran his fingers over its pommel. "Then we will head to the coast and face those cursed creatures. . . Don't worry," he said to Evela as she glanced at the ground, "I won't let any of you come to harm. You are my family now." He opened the door to his home and leaned his extra sword against the inside wall. Closing the door, he glanced over the expectant faces of the refugees and at his faithful friends who stood by.

"What about us?" Ombre asked with a frown. He nodded at Honer and Ganning. "You are going to just leave us behind on this one? I thought we were your closest friends."

"And so you are." Ilfedo looked at the eastern sky, breathing in deeply. "The serpents are intelligent beasts. If they have already invaded the coast, and penetrated the forests as well, then they will soon spread across the whole of the Hemmed Land. It will take some doing to scout the entire region, but if you three work together then it can be done. Organize whomever you find into hunting parties. We need a concerted effort to ensure none of those belly crawlers are left behind." He studied each of his friends' faces. "What do you think, Honer, Ganning?"

The men nodded. "If you think that needs doing, we'll see to it," Honer said.

Within an hour everyone had prepped for departure. Ilfedo set out first, leading the five sisters east. Later, Ombre headed northeast, while Honer and Ganning banded together and went southeast. The refugees remained, per Ilfedo's instruction, encamped in his yard for the time being.

Specter followed Honer's wife, Eva, south through the woods. She cradled the baby with motherly ease as she led him to her large cabin. Three young children greeted her at the door, oohing and awing over Oganna. Eva instructed them not to disturb the baby, then she entered the house, closing the door behind her.

Contenting himself with standing by a rectangular window next to the door, Specter watched through the glass as the woman sat in front of the fireplace in a rocking chair.

One of the children, a little boy, ran outside. He cut across the lawn in energetic bounds with a pail swinging from his hand. A wooden shelter with three sides had been built a short distance from the cabin, and a sort of stable had been attached to it. Specter smiled at the sound of goats crying, especially when the young lad exclaimed, "Hold still, Bella! Do you want the baby to starve? There . . . I didn't think so." He raced out of the stable with a bucket partly filled with milk and returned into the cabin.

As the cabin door closed behind the boy, Specter leaned on his scythe's handle and listened to Oganna's soft cries. Eva started to hum, and the child quieted.

He smiled again. The child was in good hands.

3

RISE OF THE LORD WARRIOR

Ombre watched the leaf of an oak tree bow toward the forest floor, gravity tugging at the pearlescent bead of cold moisture forming on its green tip. Miniscule droplets on the leaf's surface merged with one another, gathering into a single rivulet that fed the already precarious bead until its weight surrendered to gravity.

Rays of Yimshi's sunlight split through it as it descended through the calm air, dappling colors over its translucent surface. The sunlight winked through the tree branches, appearing, fading, following the droplet as it fell, until it struck his sword's blade, honed sharp. The droplet's molecules ripped apart, a few flying into the air.

Ombre looked at the long, straight blade of his sword. His gaze lingered for a few moments on the point where the dewdrop had landed. But his real focus was elsewhere. His ears were attuned to the silence in the forest. He'd encountered a trapper and together they had already found, fought, and slain one sea serpent. To his knowledge sea serpents had never ventured inland like they were now.

He and the trapper were scouring the deeper forest for any more that might have ventured this far inland. No chipmunks, no squirrels, no rabbits, no birds. He scanned the closely spaced trees for anything amiss.

"Garfunk thinks this's silly," a voice suddenly said from behind. "We should'n head to the coast."

Turning to face the trapper, but keeping both hands on his sword's leather-wrapped handle, Ombre shook his head at the man.

"What, so you think thar may be another big-gun snake out here?" The trapper turned his black eyes from Ombre's frustrated gaze and faced the broad base of an oak tree. He made a sucking sound with his mouth and shot a dark wad of spittle at it. "Yups . . . this's silly. I've been trappin' this part of the wilderness nigh five years. Garfunk thinks this's a waste of his time." He crossed his thick arms over his broad chest and stood with his legs set wide apart, bringing his height, which was still rather insignificant, below Ombre's chest. "Thar's no more serpents here," he said through his grizzly, black beard.

"If there aren't, then you've no need to worry, Garfunk." Ombre raised his eyebrows. "And if there are then you are going to put us on the short end of the fighting stick by alerting every critter from here to the sea of our presence."

"Bah! Garfunk thinks not!" The trapper

shook his head and seemed amused. "Go on, young one . . . Garfunk's takin' a nap." With that, Garfunk sat on the ground, where he'd spit, pulled his coonskin cap over his eyes, and rested his hand on his belt, just above the row of hunting knives he had sheathed there.

With a sharp, long whistle the trapper pierced the silence. As Ombre twisted his finger in his ear, trying to get rid of the highpitched ringing now playing havoc with his sense of direction, an old basset hound trotted toward them through the trees, then howled and lay next to its master.

"Thars Garfunk's boy." The trapper patted the dog's head. "Just a smidgen nap, I promise," he said to Ombre.

"Garfunk!" The ringing in Ombre's ear had finally stopped. He lowered his sword, backed up to the tree, and kicked the trapper in his leg.

"Yow!" The trapper leapt to his feet. His foot landed on the dog's tail, and it yelped, rolling to its feet as well. Both dog and master looked up at Ombre, neither hurt, but both with wide eyes.

Ombre sighed and shook his head at the man. "Come on," he said as he pointed his blade into the forest. "We've got a lot of ground to cover."

Behind him he heard the trapper muttering as he followed, though with a new note of respect in his tone. "Now thars a feller that'll get us both killed. You all right, boy?" His dog whined and the trapper seemed to take that as a yes. "We'll be takin' a nap . . . just not yet. Ombre's got the idea to hunt some serpents. C'mon," he said with vigor. "Mustn't disappoint the man."

Hours later, when the trapper started to complain again, Ombre left him and his dog to nap while he proceeded alone. The sunlight fell through the trees in perpendicular rays. It had to be about midday.

He'd left the trapper a good half mile behind. Now he stopped, sat against the rough bark of yet another broad oak. This region of the forests was not as hilly as where he and Ilfedo lived, and the trees were almost exclusively oaks with the occasional exception of a white birch or maple.

The forest was silent. He pulled the head of his wolf's skin over his forehead. It cushioned his skull against the unrelentingly hard bark as he leaned his head against the tree.

He thought back to the other day when Ilfedo had returned to his home without his wife, cradling his child in his arms. Ombre had never seen his friend so broken up. Not even the death of Ilfedo's parents had left a wound as deep as Dantress's loss.

With a twinge of guilt, Ombre remembered struggling with jealousy when Ilfedo returned to the Hemmed Land with his beautiful young bride. Not that he'd wished to deny his friend happiness, but Ilfedo and Dantress's bond prevented him from maintaining the close brotherly relationship he'd had with Ilfedo before.

All had changed for Ilfedo's betterment in the span of less than a year. Then his joy had been stripped away when Dantress had died in childbirth. Now Ombre wished that he could go back. Go back and willingly sacrifice of his time so that Ilfedo could enjoy a little more joy with Dantress. How could he not have been thrilled for his friend? Dantress was the most exquisite, delightful creature ever to step foot in their tiny corner of the world. Subterran had been brighter for her presence.

Now she was gone, and he could only imagine the depth of sorrow Ilfedo bore. To have loved so deeply, yet for such a brief time . . .

Ombre rested the hilt of his sword against his chest. The tip of its blade stuck in the grass at his feet.

He couldn't help wondering what Ilfedo was up to at this moment. He chuckled to himself, thinking that once again his friend had the beautiful woman with him. Or, rather, women.

Why couldn't Ilfedo have sent a couple of those devastatingly beautiful women with Ombre? Actually, it seemed odd that Ilfedo had taken them along at all. They were surely going into battle. Then again, all five of the sisters had been armed and seemed to wield their swords with practiced ease. There was more to them than at first Ombre had seen.

He'd caught Ilfedo sparring with his wife once, not long after the wedding. Dantress had surprised him with both her agility and her reflexes. In fact, he doubted that he could have bested her in a duel. Ilfedo had done it without too much difficulty. But Ombre? No. She'd possessed a mastery of the sword that was inexplicable for one so young and so feminine. Maybe her sisters did as well.

He let the silence of the forest envelop him as he closed his eyes. Sometimes when he closed his eyes, his other senses became more alert. Now his ears picked up the faint clopping of hooves on dry leaves, the sound of running water, and a child's playful laugh.

A child? Curious, he opened his eyes and looked around. Seeing no one, he stood and crept in the direction from which he thought the laughter had come.

Again the child giggled. This time he spotted her, dipping her small feet into a clear stream running through the forest. He couldn't see her face, but she had long red hair and she was young. If he had to venture a guess, he'd say she was so no older than eight.

Nothing seemed remarkable about his discovery until a stallion appeared behind the child and nuzzled her from behind. With a broad grin spreading across her rosy cheeks, the child turned. The stallion lowered its head, letting her run her fingers through its silvery mane.

Ombre walked closer, fascinated by what he saw. An Evenshadow stallion! The animal was magnificent. Never had he seen its equal. Its body rippled with muscle and looked at the child with eyes that glinted with silver and a touch of ocean blue.

The stallion raised its head in Ombre's general direction. The muscles beneath its pale-gray body rippled as it pawed the ground with a silver hoof.

At first Ombre thought he'd been discovered, but then a long black, scaled body slid through the forest growth ahead of him. A sea serpent! It had come even this far inland! Before he could react, the stallion charged through the trees. Rising with a scream, it bent its forelegs and struck the serpent's body with its sharp hooves.

The forest around Ombre erupted into chaos as the injured serpent's black head rose from behind several bushes. Its white eyes targeted the stallion, its fangs framing its gaping mouth.

The Evenshadow stallion reared, the serpent's blue blood now dripping from the tips of its silvery hooves. It whinnied, wheeling to face its opponent again.

The little girl screamed.

Ombre spotted another pair of white eyes rise from the opposite side of the stream. Another sea serpent had come to join the hunt. It pulled back its head, its open mouth twisted into a snarl.

With his sword gripped in both hands, Ombre leaped over the first serpent. Racing to the stream, he splashed into it just as the second serpent struck. As it brought down its head to strike, he slipped his blade between its fangs, ripping into the roof of its mouth. The sword passed through the serpent's mouth and rose like a horn out its snout.

The serpent's blood ran in blue rivulets down his blade, and Ombre yanked the weapon free. The little girl dashed to him and wrapped her arms around his midriff, screaming in terror. He tried to calm her, but that was difficult to do with the serpent's monstrous head only a foot away.

Behind him the stallion screamed. Ombre cringed. He feared that the serpent had sunk its fangs into the noble animal, but he dared not look because a third serpent now rose from the forest floor beside him.

Its tail whipped through the air, crushing his shoulder and sending him crashing into the water.

He rolled to his side to protect the child from the fall, and the pebbles in the shallow stream bruised his arm and side.

As he fell into the stream he pulled the sword with him. It left a hole in the second serpent's snout. The serpents hissed as they loosened their jaws and struck at him . . . and the little girl.

Sitting up in the cold stream, he pulled the child out of the way and lifted her to the opposite bank. Rolling onto his shoulder, he evaded the second serpent's attack. The third serpent almost nailed him with its venom-dripping fangs. Ombre climbed to the stream's bank, raised his sword over his head, and brought it down with such force on the serpent's skull that it erupted, spilling its brains all over his hands and arms.

Fighting his revolting stomach, he slashed at the remaining serpent. His blade sliced its jawbone, and he followed through with another cut that left half the creature's mouth hanging useless.

As the creature twisted on the ground, Omber stood to his feet. Pointing his blade at its head, he waited until it twisted into a convenient position and then he thrust it through the brain. It stopped writhing.

The little girl splashed through the stream and clung to his waist. He rested one hand on her shoulder, his sword in the other as he turned around to find out what had become of the first serpent.

On the ground nearby the stallion's hooves had left innumerable marks on the vile creature's body so that its blue blood now painted much of the forest floor. But the creature wasn't dead. Gray shadowed its usually white eyes as it stared up at the rearing stallion. Its head, held low to the ground, jerked from side to side.

Suddenly a dog howled from the trees, and Garfunk the trapper ran out from behind the wounded serpent, a long hunting knife in each hand. The serpent, already weakened, slowly twisted toward the new threat.

Garfunk's basset hound bayed from a safe distance while its master stabbed his armament of hunting knives into the serpent's head. When Garfunk backed off and stood with legs set wide apart, he crossed his arms over his burly chest. At least half-a-dozen knife handles crowned the sea serpent's head, and it collapsed to the ground moments later.

Ombre lowered his sword and breathed deeply of the cool, moist air. The little girl sobbed quietly. Nothing of her face was visible, only her red hair as she smothered herself in his soaked shirt.

He looked down at her, wondering how best to calm her. "You're going to be all right," he said, patting her head.

A soft snort made him look up. A pair of large, round eyes returned his gaze. The little girl's stallion protector. A breeze toyed with the Evenshadow's silvery mane. Its eyes swam with the beauty of an ocean, deep and blue. Yet thick strands of silver swam in that ocean, demanding something of him.

But what did the horse want?

The child released her hold on Ombre's waist and the stallion bent its legs until it knelt on the ground. The little girl grabbed a fistful of its long, silver mane and jumped onto its back. It stood, snorted at Ombre again, and galloped away, gracefully avoiding the trees and vanishing like a phantom. The only evidence of its passage were the prints of its silver hooves on the dead sea serpent's body.

"You know," Garfunk pursed his lips, letting out a shrill whistle of amazement. "I thinks I've seen everythin'. But I's never seen a horse like that. Heards of them? Yes! Seen? Nah." His hound trotted up to him, and he sat on the enormous serpent carcass. He punched the carcass with his fist and nodded at Ombre. "That thar was some good swordfightin' you did. You just 'bout killed these things yerself!"

"I'll take that as a compliment," Ombre said as he rubbed his bruised side and looked to the east through the trees. "I think we've covered all the territory around here. That is, between us and the other hunting parties. We should now proceed to the coast. It is a quick journey, isn't it?"

"I've been trappin' these forests a long time," Garfunk said, rubbing his hand along the serpent's skin as he sat on it. "Garfunk never thought to see one of these things inland." He stretched out on his back, atop the serpent, and closed his eyes. He jabbed his index finger eastward. "You'll find the coast thataway."

Ombre sheathed his sword. "I'll see you around, then." He jumped the stream and waved his hand without bothering to look back. "Thanks for your help."

* * *

Ilfedo let the tree branches slide across his face as he stepped out of the forest. The air was still,

64

the morning quiet. Dew from the branches moistened his forehead, and he didn't bother to dry it. The moisture felt refreshing.

Not a single cloud graced the blue sky. Beginning where the forest ended, the field where he walked rolled east to a distant line of white sand that was washed by the gentle waves of the Sea of Serpents. That vast body of water, in turn, stretched all the way to the eastern horizon. He imagined that the water beyond the horizon touched undiscovered lands full of green, rolling hills. Places he'd often wondered about and dreamed about after his first visit to the coast when he was only a youth. His father had taken him out here for supplies and his mother had accompanied them.

Off to the side stood a walled town by the sea. The wall had been made with stone, and smoke rose straight to the heavens from several of the buildings behind it. Ilfedo glanced over his shoulder. The five sisters emerged from the forest and stood in a line, their dark eyes staring back at him intently. Their presence soothed the ache in his heart where Dantress had been, and their quiet presence gave him confidence to move about. With all of them keeping their eyes and ears open it was less likely that some vile serpent would manage to catch him unaware.

Ilfedo beckoned for the women to follow as he set a brisk pace and made his way toward the town's gate. The tall wooden gates had fallen outside of the town as if they had been impacted from the inside, and the beams that had formed its frame were broken. Ilfedo ducked under a fallen beam and sidestepped one of the fallen doors. Caritha was right behind him with Rozel close as well, but Laura trailed a bit with Levena and Evela. They moved with such grace that their progress was as smooth as if they were dancing.

Inside of the town cobblestones paved the central street leading to the seaward gate. Those doors lay in pieces as well, having fallen inward from the wall and onto the street. Through the gaping hole Ilfedo glimpsed the white sand beach and the ocean water beyond that reached to the horizon.

The homes and businesses on either side of the street still stood, and the town was as silent as a tomb and seemed almost as cold as one, too.

"I want all of these buildings checked for survivors, but be cautious. Keep an eye out for sea serpents," Ilfedo said. "Caritha, Rozel, and Laura," Ilfedo pointed to a street leading north, "take a look in that direction. Be careful! These are not your ordinary snakes. They can swallow a person whole, if they wish, and sometimes they do exactly that. Keep your eyes open for any movement or variation of texture in the houses or in the streets. If a serpent wants to remain hidden it will be impossible to spot, except for those indicators."

"We understand," Caritha said as she reached into her skirt, through a fold in the outer garment, and drew out her rusted sword. She returned his gaze. "If a fallen beam seems out of place or not wooden, but rather like dust-covered scales, then look for a sea serpent." Her blade glowed with a faint light. She held the weapon in one hand, acknowledged Ilfedo's order with a slow nod, and then walked up the street.

Laura followed her closely, drawing her own

sword as well.

Rozel shook her head, muttering something like, "Here we go again." She followed the other two. As she drew her sword, its rust screeched against the sheath.

Levena and Evela watched them go, then Levena looked to Ilfedo. "What about us?" Levena asked.

Beside her, Evela stood with her hands clasped over her bosom. "Give him time to think. He has dealt with these creatures before. Surely he knows best what to do now."

"That is true, I have dealt with these creatures before," Ilfedo said. He reached to his side, slipping his hand over the cool pommel of the sword of the dragon. For a moment he considered leaving the remaining two sisters to watch the main street. But he could hear the crackling of fire in several nearby buildings, their wooden walls feeding the blaze. He'd feel better if he kept his wife's kin safely in sight.

"Come with me." He forced a smile as he spoke, but it was a weak smile, one born of necessity and not from his heart. That part of him still ached, trying to cope with the loss of his dearest love. Dantress had been his everything.

Casting aside his inner grief, he set off toward the southern end of town. At each building he expected to see a pair of white snake eyes peering back at him around the stone foundations. If he found one of those foul creatures, he would channel his grief into his sword arm, and heaven help the serpent that dared stand in his way.

The buildings burned around him as he made his cautious way through the streets. Most of the buildings were single-storied structures, some rose a couple floors higher than that. In places, the cobblestones had been stained red with blood that had not yet dried. But nowhere did he see any bodies.

Turning into a side street leading to the corner of town, he climbed a pile of rubble. Stones mixed with wood. He stood on the rubble and gazed around. Behind him Levena murmured, "Take care, brother." Evela stayed silent.

Few of the buildings remained intact. Gaping holes had been punched through most of them. Holes large enough for a horse to walk through. Telltale bits of black leathern snake skin ringed each gap and mixed with the rubble. He crouched and extracted a black scale from under a stone.

As he turned it over in his hand, rage built within him. The rough snake skin scraped over his palm. Curling his fingers into a fist, he crushed the scale, paying no heed to the pain it caused as it bit into his palm. The creatures had been here, that much was obvious. But where were they now? Hiding in the buildings, or already passed beyond the town and into the forest? They could be killing people in rural towns that were miles away! But, no, some of the blood on these streets was still fresh. This had happened recently and that meant his quarry was close by.

He didn't bother warning the two women. He dropped the serpent's scale and dashed through a gaping hole in a nearby building. Smoke roiled around him and stung his eyes. Rubble crunched under his feet. Flames spread up a stairway and over the wooden floors, threatening to burn him, too. But he pressed on through the building, past a table that had been broken in half and chairs that had burned to cinders. A shattered lamp lay beside the table, likely the start of the fire. There was nothing living in this place. That much was evident.

A large picture window on the back side of the house had been shattered and the curtains that framed it were on fire. He trampled the curtains on his way out through the window and dropped into the alley behind the building.

Here the cobblestones had been upended by the passage of something heavy, and Ilfedo gave a grim smile. He followed the serpent's trail down the narrow alleyway. The serpent's fat body had slipped between the walls with incredible ease but fragments of its skin had stuck to them. "I've got you," he whispered.

Up ahead the serpent had busted through the wall of another house. The timbers had bent and snapped like twigs.

Ilfedo climbed through the hole and found himself in a demolished living room. Fragments of furniture lay about and the serpent had punched another hole through the wall to one side. He followed the path, slipping through the hole so that he found himself in the building next door. He stumbled on something and glanced down. It was an anvil, cast off of its table during the serpent's passage.

Picking himself up, he gritted his teeth and skirted a blacksmith's forge in the middle of the room. This building was smaller albeit with a long roof. The creature had smashed the rafters and human blood had splattered across them. Ilfedo spat on the ground. The creature had taken another victim! The forge itself appeared undamaged, but the broken rafters had fallen into the blazing fire. A wall of flames spread from the forge, churned along the wooden walls, and splashed against what remained of the splintered ceiling.

With a burst of speed, he ran through the flames, reaching the other end of the blacksmith's shop unscathed. Here the serpent had again smashed through the wall of thick wood, though it had left three-foot-long strands of black scaled skin hanging across the opening. The strands flapped back and forth as the fire within the building sent waves of heat against them.

Parting the strands of snake skin with his hands, he darted through the wall. The rotten odor of the snakeskin lingered with him but he ignored it. He stepped out of the shop into the bed of a wooden wagon. But one of the wheels was missing and the other was ringed with flames, leaving its bed angled sharply toward the street.

He slid down and landed on the street. With cobblestones once again under his feet, he stood in front of a large, four-story building. No fire burned along its walls, no smoke rose from the shakes covering its roof. Unlike the surrounding homes and businesses it appeared relatively untouched except that where a set of double doors had marked the entrance before, now there was a hole higher than his head and broader than a rowboat. The double doors lay splintered into large pieces on the stone steps leading up to the building.

"Ilfedo, what's wrong?" Evela asked from behind him. She was breathing a bit heavily from keeping pace with him, and her voice sounded timid.

Without looking at her, Ilfedo took off his bearskin coat and dropped it onto the ground. "Stay here, my sister," he said as he firmed his mouth in grim determination.

"But . . . you are not going in alone?" Evela's voice rose to a high pitch, and he heard her take an uncertain step forward.

"No!" He turned and set his hand on her shoulder. Behind her Levena rushed to catch up with them.

Evela bit her lower lip, her eyes widening with fear.

The sea serpent's path of ruin led here, to this building. The giant serpent was hiding inside of it. Ilfedo felt certain of that, and he would face it alone. He would risk no life except his own on this venture into the jaws of death.

"That came out harsh, but I did not mean it to," he said to her. "Stay here for now. I must do this alone but I need you here watching my back." He let go of her shoulder and resolutely faced the hole in the building. The morning sunlight streamed from behind him through the billowing clouds of smoke from the surrounding buildings, but it did not illuminate the building's interior. The fires heated the air so that it felt as warm as a clammy summer day.

He ascended the steps with care. Sweat beaded on his forehead. Not only was the air extra warm, but knowing what he was hunting brought to mind his close encounter with death that first time he'd faced the sea serpents.

His fingers inadvertently reached under his loose shirt to his shoulder. He ran his fingertips over the parallel scars there on his skin. A reminder of just how close the sea serpent had come to killing him the last time he'd faced its kind.

He stood still in the building's main room, waiting for his eyes to adjust to the dimness of the building's interior. A grim silence permeated the space. Dust lay thickly in the air, forcing him to cover his nose lest he sneeze.

At last his eyes adjusted to the dimness. A carved wood pillar ahead of him twisted from the floor to the ceiling a dozen feet above his head, supporting an impressive arch that upheld the floor above.

Three portraits hung on the dark, stained walls. Judging by the fine apparel and aristocratic poise of the subjects, he guessed they were the town's mayor and other political leaders.

He peered into the gloom toward the middle of the room. Uncoiling beside an enormous stone fireplace against the back wall, were six enormous serpents. Their eyes were closed, else he would have seen their whites. Their bloated bellies undulated in an unnatural way devoid of rhythm. Bumps appeared as if from inside of their bellies. Ilfedo knew, beyond a doubt, that some of the townspeople were suffering a frightening death, suffocating and drowning in the snakes' bellies.

He reached down to the sword at his side. This day, he would spill their blue blood over the place of their feast. "Rise, you devils, and let us have at it!" he called out.

The serpents roused, their wedge-shaped heads lazily rising from their tangled mass. Their white eyes startled open, fixing him with haunted gazes. Their tails twitched as they attempted to move their burdened bodies.

Ilfedo reached to his side and grasped the two-handed grip of the sword of the dragon. He drew it from its scabbard as easily as if it had been freshly oiled. With both hands he held the blade, pointing it toward the ceiling. The flames within the shiny metal spread out, twisting to entwine around it.

The flames spread from the sword, up his arms and over his body. His muscles grew tauter and his shoulders squared with extra strength as the sword's energy raced through him. As quickly as the flames covered him, they receded, returning into the blade but leaving him adorned with an armor of white light. Indeed, flames danced inside of the armor that had replaced his former clothing. He appeared now as a being from another realm. He stepped into the heart of the room, his armor flexing with his movements with such ease that he could have forgotten it was there.

His awareness of the room around him, around the armor, deepened as if it were an extension of his senses. The sword and his armor lit every dark corner.

The serpents locked their eyes on him. Their forked tongues twisted out between their fangs.

Before they could advance or retreat, Ilfedo fell upon them. He thrust his flaming blade into three of the serpents' brains and slit the next one across its throat. He felt stronger than he ever had in his life!

The sword in his hand cut through the snakes as if they had been made of cheese.

As Ilfedo raised his sword to strike the remaining sea serpents, they regurgitated their prey. Coughing and choking on their own bile and that of the serpents, a dozen men, women, and children sprawled across the floor. Some got up on their hands and knees to escape the filthiness around them.

A few victims remained prostrate in the puddles of brightly colored liquids that reeked like rotting animal corpses. Ilfedo clenched his jaws, breathing rapidly. His fists wrung the handle of his sword even as his eyes looked away from the survivors. He burned his gaze into the serpents.

Rid of their burdens, the remaining serpents snapped their jaws at one another, untangling from one another and sliding across the floor to face him with their ghost-white eyes.

"Come, you vermin!" Ilfedo yelled as he started forward, swinging his sword wide. "Face me. Fight! I would have this no other way than to spill your guts in bloody combat."

The serpents drew their heads out of his reach. Their mouths hissed open, their fangs shining white, drops of venom forming on the tips.

In that moment, as the creatures rose in all their hideous strength, a thought passed through Ilfedo's mind. If only the flames inside of the sword of the dragon could extend beyond it. If they could burn through the space between and roast the creatures.

The serpents prepared to strike. Ilfedo retreated a couple of steps but pointed the blade's tip directly at the creature's white eyes.

Burn! Burn these beasts.

The thought took root and he felt the sword warping to his will. The fire in the blade raged out of it in a torrent of yellow and red tongues that gathered strength and threw themselves through the air.

Ilfedo felt his will merge with the sword as if he were in its blade. He gathered the sword's power as if from an unfathomably deep well and threw it. He threw himself. In his wrath he cast his strength against his opponents. His mind felt connected not only with his body but with the sword as well. One of the serpents avoided the sword's shooting flames and snapped its mouth at him, but he sidestepped the creature's attack.

The other serpent did not avoid the flames in time, and the vortex of fire burned the flesh from its head. Smoke curled out of the hole that the living fire had melted into its skull as it collapsed in a heap.

When the last serpent attacked him again, its fangs scraped but did not pierce his armor. The scraping of the fangs sounded like music in his ears. He held onto the sword with one hand and dug his armored fist into the serpent's eye with his other.

A scream tore from the serpent's throat, a sound halfway between an elephant's roar and a nuvitor's cry. It pulled away from him, shaking its head, trying to reacquire its target with its uninjured eye.

Ilfedo again gripped his sword with both hands. He approached the serpent and slashed the blade along its neck. The blade ripped through the creature's scales and burst open its veins. Blue blood pulsed from the wound, splattering the walls and spraying the human survivors. Some of the blood struck his armor but it steamed off of him, leaving the armor as clean as when the dragon had first given it to him.

Around him the survivors stood to their feet. They gazed upon him with eyes wide and mouths agape. "Who are you, warrior?" one thickly bearded man asked. The others gathered around Ilfedo while a few lingered to look at the corpses of those who had been less fortunate.

"I am no one of consequence," Ilfedo said, and he sheathed his sword. The living fire retreated off his body, returning to the blade. He tried to walk toward the door, wishing to get away from the reverent gazes directed his way.

"Wait!" one man said. He stood in Ilfedo's way and swallowed hard. "It's you, again. Isn't it?"

"It's who?" the bearded man asked. "For the sake of all that is just, man, who is this?"

"Ilfedo! Ilfedo Matthaliah, the sea serpent slayer! I saw you." The man pointed at Ilfedo. "I saw you at The Wooden Mug. It was you."

Suddenly five figures filed into the room behind Ilfedo. They brandished their glowing orange-red blades. Caritha stood front and center, nodding her head slightly as Ilfedo glanced her way. The sudden appearance of the sisters imposed confusion on the survivors, enough confusion to let Ilfedo walk toward the doors unhindered. But before leaving, with the sisters flanking him on both sides, he turned to the survivors.

"Our land cannot continue in this way without falling prey to the world around it," he said.

"Something must be done. And if no one else will strengthen us, then I will."

Uncomfortable nods followed his words as the bedraggled townspeople looked from the sisters to him and back at the sisters. But the man who had first addressed Ilfedo stepped forward, his face solemn. "Your reputation precedes you, Ilfedo. By killing the sea serpents you proved yourself brave and cunning. And in not asking much of the people whose lives you saved, you proved yourself wise." He dropped to the floor on one knee, head bowed. "Ages ago, as you know, our people followed a Lord, a warrior superior to all and envied by none. It is time for us to do the same and follow you as our Lord Warrior."

Each of the survivors knelt before him, pledging themselves to him. The floor seemed to spin and Ilfedo stepped back. Him, a new Lord Warrior? He remembered the tales of the Lord Warriors. Tales of men whose bravery held the ancestors of the Hemmed Land together. Perhaps that was the solution. A new Lord Warrior must rise in the Hemmed Land.

The five sisters did not bow, yet they watched him as he nodded to the people. It made sense. A Lord Warrior was needed and no one else could fill that role. Only a short time ago he'd have thought this impossible and undesirable. Now these people knelt before him, and he reached out, embracing the idea.

He did wish it. For the sake of his daughter, and now for all of the children in the Hemmed Land. They should not grow up in fear that the sea serpents or any other creatures might, at any time, encroach on their heritage and possibly take their lives. That fear was the reality that he had lived out when the man-eating bear had killed his parents.

He glanced at the sword now sheathed at his side. It offered him a chance to become a greater warrior than ever the Hemmed Land had seen. This weapon was the key to his future.

Except he no longer had a future, not without Dantress. His heart rent within him as he recalled the face of his beloved wife. So young, so beautiful. When she had been torn from him his future had died with her.

No! He chided himself. He had loved Dantress completely, without reservation and it had cost him his joy. Maybe he didn't have a future, but he did have the responsibility to build one for his child. Oganna was all that mattered. He would build a hedge of protection around her that nothing could penetrate, and he would use this sword to do it.

He addressed the townspeople. "If you will follow my leadership, then remain here and wait for my return. The serpents must be forced back into the sea from which they came, and I intend to make certain that this time they never return. Your town is in a shambles. Go! Put out the fires, clean your streets, tend to your wounded, and bury your dead. I will return." Without looking back he exited the building. On the ground near the steps lay his bearskin coat. He left it there. Left it in the dust. Behind him the sisters kept pace, their swords still drawn.

Ilfedo headed south, out of town. The fresh sea breezes cleaned the smoke from his lungs. The clear blue sky tempted his eyes upward, but he ignored it. His gaze searched the fields along the coast looking for signs of other serpents.

Once, he ventured to look back at the town, now receding into the distance. Only scant wisps of smoke wavered above the buildings, a good sign that the townspeople were following his instructions.

He sighed. By adopting the title of Lord Warrior he had allowed himself to become an icon, a hero to the majority of his people. This would change his life forever. To most he would be a welcome source of unity, while to others he would doubtless become a rival in their petty rule over the towns of the Hemmed Land. No longer would he be able to hide out in the wilderness. His name would be known, the tales of his deeds would be told.

Ahead lay a life far different from that which he'd come to love. But sometimes change, even this sort of change, destructive as it seemed to him, was necessary.

Leading the five sisters along the coast, he pressed southward in search of other sea serpents. The task of freeing his homeland had just begun.

* * *

As a gust of wind struck Seivar, he angled his white feathered wings to take advantage of the updraft. The warm air carried him a little higher, just enough to skim the top of an oak tree that poked above the forest.

Beside him and a little behind, Hasselpatch followed suit, gliding effortlessly in his wake.

Both of them searched the forest, their silver eyes darting about, sharp vision piercing the forest ceiling to scan for signs of sea serpents. Not many hours before they had found Honer and Ganning leading a party of hunters.

Hasselpatch had spotted a sea serpent slipping through the trees toward the hunters. She angled her wings for a swift descent, reversing her direction and returning in time to warn Honer and Ganning.

Forewarned, the men had spread out and surprised the serpent, falling upon it from all sides and efficiently dispatching it. Since that incident neither of the birds had seen anything of consequence.

Seivar glanced back at his mate. "Master must have reached the coast by now," he cawed. He noted with pride how the sunlight glinted off Hasselpatch's hooked beak. No nuvitor rivaled his mate's graceful form and, though they had not spent much time in the company of his kind, he had noticed envy in the eyes of other nuvitor males they'd encountered in the Hemmed Land's forests.

Hasselpatch twisted in the air and snapped her beak at him, unabashedly flirting with him. For that he admired her all the more.

But as he twisted in the air to return her play, a wedge-shaped, black-scaled head penetrated the forest's ceiling. A sea serpent closed its white eyes and opened its jaws to intercept Seivar's mate.

With a screech of terror and anger, Seivar pulled himself with natural fluidity through the air. He dove for the serpent's closed eyelids, ripping into them with his talons and pulling them apart. The big round, white eye of the serpent lay exposed for that moment and he opened his silvery beak as wide as possible, stabbing deep into the rubbery ball.

The sea serpent recoiled from Seivar's attack,

dropping through the tree. The creature's slimy body uncoiled from the tree branches as itmi fell.

Tightening his bite, Seivar yanked out the apple-sized eyeball and flapped his wings, using them to carry himself back above the forest. After flying a victorious circle around his mate, making certain she saw the prize he'd obtained in her honor, he dropped the eyeball into the forest and dove back in.

It was his intention to take the serpent's remaining eye, but the serpent was thrashing about, knocking into tree trunks. The commotion had brought several men armed with spears and axes.

Seivar left them to attend to the creature. He shot above the forest canopy to join Hasselpatch. Her silvery eyes regarded him with soft affection, and he indulged in flying another circle around her before leading her eastward.

The forest passed easily beneath them. Not much farther on and the birds reached the end of the forest. Here the trees were replaced by harvested fields of corn that stretched to the white shores of the Sea of Serpents. A town lay in the midst of the fields, smoke rising from several of its crumbling buildings. Much of the town was burning.

Black, shiny serpents slipped through the streets, crashing into the buildings with their tails. Other serpents slid from the forest, first a few, then more. They cornered a group of perhaps fifty people, who huddled together in the fields.

The serpents in the town left their destructiveness in order to join the newcomers.

Seivar angled his wings and turned along the coast, Hasselpatch flying above him. He watched the line of trees as the mighty sea creatures slithered out in great numbers. He stopped counting at sixty.

He had to find Ilfedo and warn him.

Sensing his urgency, Hasselpatch extended her wings with greater speed and followed him high above the gathering, coiling mass of serpents. They cut through the air, their talons curled to their bodies, their white feathers smoothed back.

In the distance, northward along the shore, six human figures approached. A tight cluster of smoking buildings lay behind them. Seivar knew before he reached them that he had found his master.

* * *

Ilfedo and the sisters followed the white sands along the seashore until it brought them within sight of another walled town. The waves of the Sea of Serpents crashed against the shore, then calmed, as if the Creator had touched them himself.

The sisters stayed behind him, except for Evela. She stepped up beside him as he surveyed the weathered, wooden buildings and the fields surrounding them. "Is something wrong?" she asked.

He looked down into her dark eyes. She gazed back with humble honesty, as if seeing through his flesh and into his soul.

"The serpents are here, my sisters," he said. And he had to admit to himself that he had avoided speaking directly to her on purpose. Evela was so close. Uncomfortably so. There was something about her that most reminded him of Dantress. He could easily reach out and touch her, finding comfort in her.

"Good, it's about time," Rozel retorted, just

in time to break his thoughts. "But this time, let's be clear, you're not taking them on alone. You have the five of us to help you. Put us to work hacking some of these creatures!"

"Agreed." Caritha set a hand on Rozel's shoulder, but rebuked her with a glance. She directed her attention to Ilfedo. "But we will follow your lead, Ilfedo."

Laura and Levena nodded. Evela stepped back and stood ready with her sword pointed at the ground.

Surveying the town up ahead, Ilfedo recognized the wall surrounding it. No high buildings poked above the barrier. This was the place where he first faced the Sea Serpents. Coral Haven, as the refugee had called it. Here, where it had begun, he would end it. Smoke curled up from near the wall and a dark, seething mass appeared. The sea serpents had come in force.

"If you are coming with me, my sisters," Ilfedo said as he drew the sword of the dragon out of its sheath and let the living fire cover his body, "then stay close." The sword clothed him in the armor of fire that glowed with white light, and he fastened his gaze on each of them in turn, raising his sword aloft. "As long as you stay with me you will be safe." He glanced at Evela. "I promise."

An eagle-like screech caught his ear. He looked up and smiled as his faithful nuvitors dove from the sky, flapping their white wings to slow their descent as they landed on his shoulders.

"Master," Seivar snapped his beak, "the serpents are gathering prisoners."

Hasselpatch fluffed her feathers. Her silvery eye regarded the sisters with mild curiosity.

"How many of the serpents are there?" Ilfedo asked.

Seivar cocked his head, his eye rolling as he considered. "Almost a hundred, Master. At least."

"You've done well, my friends." Ilfedo stroked Seivar's chest and then Hasselpatch's. "Now I want both of you to go to the forest and wait until the fight is over."

"Master!" Seivar protested.

But Hasselpatch responded by flying off of Ilfedo's shoulder and circling his head. "We will not leave you, Master," she cawed. Then, in evident rebellion, she landed on a startled Rozel's shoulder. The tallest sister cautiously stroked the bird's chest.

Ilfedo knew the nuvitor too well to try and change its mind. With a resigned sigh, he faced the town and walked toward it. The five sisters flanked him on both sides, their expressions hardening, their hands tightening around the leathern grips of their rusted swords.

Rozel's mouth froze in a frown. She glanced at Hasselpatch, but the nuvitor remained perched on her shoulder.

Pushing the sisters and the birds out of his mind and focusing on the fight ahead, Ilfedo put on a burst of speed to reach the serpents first. He could see their sinewy lengths gathered a thousand paces from his position. The first of the serpents' prisoners was plucked from their midst as Ilfedo approached. One of the vile creatures tossed the prisoner into the air as if the man were an item on the menu. Ilfedo's heart flamed within his chest as the helpless individual was ripped in two by a pair of serpents that raised their heads, one grabbing the legs and the other taking the torso.

Like a living firebrand, Ilfedo rushed upon the sea serpents. Seivar launched from his shoulder, pecking out the eyes of the first serpent that turned to face him.

"Come on!" Ilfedo screamed, laying about him with the sword of the dragon. "Face a real challenge. Face me and die, you cowards!" His blade opened the serpents' blubbery forms with ease, drowning the ground in blue blood.

Standing back as the serpents turned to face him, he pointed his sword's blade at them and willed destruction upon them. A torrent of fire rushed from the sword's blade, immediately felling five of the creatures.

Uniting with his blade in a mental bond, he half-closed his eyes, sensing rather than seeing his opponents around him. The serpents lashed out with their fangs and swung with their tails, stabbing at him. But he evaded them, ducking under their blows.

Three of the creatures slithered around him, working together against him. Their numbers were overwhelming. A few of them would have been difficult enough, now he felt a hundred pairs of white eyes focusing on him.

The townspeople in the serpents' midst ran for freedom, though some of them were killed by the massive bodies thrashing around and over them.

Ilfedo's blade sank into the serpents' bodies again and again, ending their vile existences as fast as his sword arm could move.

A tail slapped into his back, throwing him to the ground. He rolled, landed kneeling, and pointed his weapon at the attacker. His fingers clamped harder around his sword handle as fire shot from its blade and raged through the air, felling the serpent into a crumpled, smoldering heap.

Some of the serpents slithered after the fleeing people. Their fangs stabbed downward, impaling over half of the group's number. Men, women, and children screamed. They fell to the ground, twitching horribly as the serpents' venom spread through their bodies.

The five sisters screamed as they arrived on the battlefield. One by one they knelt on the ground. Tears poured down Evela's face and shone in Laura's and Levena's eyes. A dozen sea serpents rose around them with fangs exposed, drawing their heads back to strike.

Even Rozel dropped her sword to hold a little girl who'd been poisoned. Her eyes brimmed with tears. Caritha's face riveted on the bodies before her. Never had they seen carnage on this scale and it had stolen their will to fight.

"My sisters, what are you doing?" Ilfedo shouted as he stabbed another serpent between its white eyes. He swung the sword in a long arc, slitting open three more serpents' throats.

As the serpents' bodies slumped around him, he leaped over them and ran to the ring of serpents that had gathered and were preparing to strike Dantress's sisters. He landed in the sisters' midst, loped off a nearby serpent's head and sent flames from the blade into several others.

"Seivar, Hasselpatch," he yelled at the top of his lungs as his faithful companions flew at the serpents. "Go for help! There's nothing you can do here."

Tearing out a serpent's eye, Seivar screamed into the air and shot away. His mate set off in the opposite direction. Ilfedo knew that the birds were splitting up to cover as much territory as possible and bring whatever aid they could. In the meantime? In the meantime he was alone with five weeping women whose help he had been counting on.

"My sisters, rise!" He glanced at Evela, her shoulders quaking.

In that instant one of the serpents lashed out with its tail. The blow took him by surprise, sprawling him on the ground. The sword fell from his grasp and the armor vanished, leaving him unprotected.

Hissing with new confidence, the sea serpents lashed out at him. One of their fangs reopened his old shoulder wound, and he felt the venom swell his limbs.

Looking around for his sword, he spotted it not a dozen paces from his position.

One serpent's eyes followed his gaze. It rested its tail over the sword and opened its mouth in what resembled a sneer. Its fangs glinted with venom as sunlight struck them.

"No you don't," Ilfedo said. He rushed sluggishly forward, clasped his hands together and used them like a club, striking the serpent's nostrils.

The serpent snapped at him, but he dropped to the ground and rolled. He forced his arm under the serpent's tail, cutting his skin on its rough scales in the process. His fingers touched metal and closed around the vine-wrapped handle of his sword.

The metal blade rang as he drew it from under the serpent's scales. The flames leapt up, engulfed him, and clothed him in the armor of living fire. Immediately his wounds staunched. The poison seemed to surrender to the renewing energy that the sword sent through his body.

He poised his blade point up, and drove it through the serpent's lower jaw, aiming for the creature's brain. It dropped lifeless to the ground and the blade of his sword slid from the serpent's head, drenched in blue blood.

Flames roiled around the blade as he gripped it with both hands. The smell of death filled his nostrils. The serpents pulled back, stunned by his sudden victory.

"My sisters," he said again, this time shaking Caritha's shoulder, "now is not the time for this. I need your help. Now rise and fight!"

DEMISE OF THE SERPENT KING

Caritha heard Ilfedo pleading with her and her sisters to rise and aid him against the sea serpents. Deep in her soul she wanted to, but never had she been thus surrounded by death and suffering. Not to this extent. If only Dantress were here, she would have known how to draw the venom out of the victims' bodies. But Dantress was gone. Dead.

The strongest among the sisters had fallen prey to an early death. What was worse was the fact that Dantress had allowed it to happen.

No. Caritha stopped herself. Her younger sister had done the right thing. Just looking at the innocent child she'd brought into the world proved that. If Dantress were here, she would rise with the sword of Xavion in her hand, and fight alongside Ilfedo. If she were here, she would tell Caritha and the other sisters to do the same.

There was a time to mourn, and this was not it.

Summoning all of her strength, she rose from among the dead and the dying. Caritha raised her rusted sword in her hand. She deafened her ears to the pleas of those around her, turned her eyes away from the suffering, stepped over the bodies of the dead women, children, and men. She drew upon the power in her dragon blood until she felt it turning her sorrow into anger that fueled her for the battle.

Around her rose her sisters. They stood with her and she felt their anger, their lust for justice, their cold determination as they turned their dark eyes to the serpents' white ones.

Ilfedo was having difficulty fending off all of the beasts on his own, despite his skillful maneuvering and use of the sword's flame-casting ability. He met two serpents head-on, grappling with them in a strange wrestling match. His blade stabbed through one side of a serpent's head and emerged out of the opposite eye. Fire shot from the exposed sword tip, turning the other serpent's neck into a pillar of flames.

Wordlessly, the sisters advanced toward the serpents, slowly, patiently biding their time. Caritha wiped fear from her mind, feeling the strength of her dragon blood combine with that of her sisters.

Five of the massive Sea Serpents moved against the sisters. Their jaws hissed open, their long fangs glistened in the sunlight as they raised their heads above the sisters.

The sisters formed a close-knit line as a gust

of wind flung their long, dark hair across their faces. Caritha ignored the distraction and lowered her sword to point at the serpents. Her sisters copied her movement and touched their blades together with hers. Drops of blood fell from the weapons as blue energy sizzled along the rusted metal. A beam formed between the blades and shot toward the approaching serpents.

Severing the heads of the two nearest serpents, the beam continued on, leaving deep gashes in the necks of the other three.

Wide-eyed, a dozen of the creatures' companions slithered backward. But others attacked viciously. The sheer number of them overwhelmed the sisters. Caritha saw Rozel, Laura, and Levena disappear down serpents' throats. She would have intervened, yet the other serpents crowded around her and Evela.

Without the other three sisters, Caritha and Evela had to fight an impossible battle. Ilfedo frowned as he caught sight of them but he was too engaged in his own battle with a dozen more of the creatures. At least the creatures' carcasses were piling up around the man faster than they could replenish their numbers.

Not even half of the hundred or so serpents that had first met Ilfedo's attack were still alive. His feet stood in a river of blue blood, lit by the brilliance of his sword and armor.

Caritha stabbed the body of a nearby serpent, but the creature hardly twitched. The blade probably felt like nothing more than a nasty prick. Its head swung around as if to move away. She lowered her sword, looking about for her next target. The options were vast, the serpents were many.

But she had underestimated the wounded serpent. Its body had encircled her, separating her from Evela. She tried to jump as it tightened its coils around her. She was too late. Its body clutched her in a deadly embrace, squeezing until her breath was forced from her lungs in a burning gasp.

Her feet lifted off the ground as the serpent raised her into the air with its coiled tail, and the other serpents raised their heads to witness her demise with their ghostly white eyes. Her captor slipped his long, forked tongue out of its mouth. The twin tips of its tongue cooled her neck as they touched her. She looked down the long, red tongue and found herself gazing with helpless fascination down the serpent's gaping throat.

Beside her, another serpent captured Evela and hung her upside down with its tail. The youngest sister struck at the creature with her sword until it managed to pin her arms to her sides. "No! No, no, no. Release me," Evela yelled in terror. But the serpent tightened its grip.

Caritha struggled for air. If she didn't breathe she would black out.

One of the sea serpents rose beside her and opened its mouth as if to receive her. Suddenly the scales on the back of its neck rose as if they had been pushed from inside of its body, and the rusted point of a sword stabbed through.

The serpent's eyes seemed to pop out of its sockets. Its jaw opened as if in pain. But the rusted blade divided the back of its neck with an incision several feet long that laid bare the white vertebrate of its spine.

Rozel stood out of the serpent's body as it fell. Her shoulders were slumped with disgust as she lingered inside of the incision and spat on the ground. "All right! All right," she growled. "Fine. Humph! Take that, Ugly!" She glared at another serpent, and lunged for it. "You want a chunk of me, too?"

Rozel's blade cut into another serpent, and nearby two more of the creatures fell dead. Caritha gasped for air. Her captor seemed frozen by Rozel's actions. Its hold on her relaxed, though just barely, and its mouth opened and closed several times. But it was enough for her to catch the air she needed and to see why the other serpents had died. It had been Laura and Levena, for they had also killed their would-be-slayers.

The group of serpents surrounding the sisters slithered away from them. Caritha counted twenty of them racing toward the sea. A mere twenty more now remained to contend with, and these watched the sisters warily and tried to avoid Ilfedo's attacks.

Ilfedo dispensed with two more of them, sent three more scrambling to the water, and launched himself onto Caritha's captor. The sword of the dragon in his hands made mincemeat of the creature, dividing it into several sections before it had time to react.

Caritha breathed deeply of the fresh, salty air. She held her sword with both hands and joined her sisters, cutting the serpents with her blade at every opportunity.

* * *

The waves that crashed onto the shore seemed

to explode as a wedge-shaped head punched out of the Sea of Serpents. Ilfedo paused in the midst of his battle, catching his breath.

The seawater rolled off of a shiny black body sliding onto the shore, stretching to a length at least twice that of any sea serpent he'd encountered. Great bumps covered its face and its nostrils spouted water from its forehead as its white eyes bulged from the sides of its head. In its wake the creature left a depression in the ground which was so deep that a man could have stood in it. Yimshi's rays played off the gigantic serpent's white, scaled chest as it forged ahead.

As if responding to their master's domineering entrance, the surviving sea serpents stopped their retreat and struck with new energy, trying to bring the sisters down.

Ilfedo was torn between facing the approaching menace and helping the sisters. But if the monster joined its companions, he could only imagine how short the battle would be.

Ilfedo raced across the field. Standing halfway between the sisters' battle and the monster, he quelled his trembling body.

With a head the size of a small house, the sea serpent rose before him, its head looking down upon him from the equivalent height of a four-story building. Its lips curled up, and its jaws dropped open. Half-a-dozen fangs dripped thick black venom, spotting the ground with puddles of the sticky substance. Each of the monster's fangs was the length of a spear and the thickness of a small tree. Lesser teeth of shark-like quality filled the rest of its mouth.

Ilfedo felt light-headed just looking at the

thing. God have mercy, how was he supposed to survive this? But, no, he wasn't afraid. Why should he be? What was the worst that this creature could do? It could kill him.

Ilfedo smiled at the thought. After death he would be reunited with his Dantress, she who had been all things beautiful, sweet, and good in his life. Death did not hold the same dread to him anymore. "Thank you," he whispered to her across the divide of death. Thanks to her he could fight fearlessly and live to protect their daughter.

His fingers tightened around the sword of the dragon, and courage swelled his being. His armor flashed with light as if he were a miniature sun. Flames twisted around his sword's blade, rising to the tip and feeding into the air.

"Back," he shouted to the monster. "Go back into the sea where you belong, and take your minions with you!"

The gargantuan serpent lashed out a purplish, forked tongue. It did not touch him or his sword. Its eyes turned lazily in the sisters' direction, and it spat a wad of venom from its mouth. The venom struck Evela's face and upper torso. Her hands clawed at the venom, trying to wipe it off in order to breathe.

With a snap of its massive jaws that sounded like a small clap of thunder, the monstrous serpent looked back at Ilfedo as if waiting to see how he would react to the unexpected assault.

Racing to Evela's side, Ilfedo touched his sword's blade to her face. Its flames baked the venom into a crust. He dug his fingers into it, breaking it away from her mouth. She held onto his arm, coughing. Prying off what remained of the venom, he gently pulled her hands from his arm, noting that her beautiful lips bled where he'd torn away the dried venom.

Turning, he strode back to the enormous serpent. "You will return to the sea," he said, and he let flames shoot higher from his blade. "There you will remain. Or I will hunt your species to extinction."

"Hard words, thou brave warrior," the serpent ended with a hiss.

Ilfedo gazed into the malevolent white eyes. He could not believe his ears. The thing could talk. He lowered his blade a few inches and took a step backward.

"Before thy kind roamed this land, warrior, I dwelt in this sea. Before thy ancestors laid claim to this soil, I ruled it." The serpent's tail lifted into the air and then smashed the ground. Ilfedo set his feet wide to maintain his balance. "Now I have returned and all that is here, I claim to be mine. Even as all in the sea is mine, so is this land. Do you not know that I am king of the sea serpents?" Its fangs touched the ground as it lowered its head to gaze into his eyes. "I have battled the ancient dreads of Subterran, yes, even the Glorigathans and the Dudans . . . the Water Skeels, also.

"You presume to stand before me, little warrior, to do battle with me. But I can crush thee as an insect. Go your way, leave now, and I will let you go. I admire thy initiative, little warrior, but to stand against me thou hast neither the strength nor the means."

"But I am standing in your way," Ilfedo said

as he poised his sword to aim its point at the monster's head. "And for the crimes your minions have committed against my people, you will pay with your blood and they with their lives."

"Thou art brave, little warrior, to speak thus against me and mine." The creature hissed, pulling back its head and opening wide its jaws. A blade-like fin unfolded from its head, rising from the tip of its snout and arching back to the base of its skull. It lowered its voice. "I do not leave brave enemies standing. I prefer your death so that I may never confront thee again."

Ilfedo remained steady as the creature postured for attack. His life was on the line here and the odds seemed . . . towering. But when he considered the possibility of his own death, all he could see was the familiar face of she whom he loved. Death could only bring him back to her. It could only end his heart's ache and bring him to meet the Creator. To see his parents again.

No, he had nothing to fear from death. He had nothing to fear from anything, and to die defending those who could not defend themselves was a far better way to leave this mortal existence than to die of old age.

He faced the king of the sea serpents and held forth the weapon given to him by the albino dragon. His eye blinked involuntarily as a sunbeam reflected off of the silver band on his finger. The Eternal Band, its flame extinguished. He'd kept it nevertheless. It displayed to the entire world that his heart belonged to someone special. In his eyes it also stated that he would never give his heart to another.

A swath of flames ignited from the blade as the enormous serpent's head rushed upon him. The serpent's white underbelly blackened as the flames struck, but the creature remained unfazed.

Its head burrowed into the ground under his feet, ripping it out from under him, throwing him yards away as the head came up through the soil. The forked, purplish tongue lashed at him, roping his legs together as he fell.

Before he could react, the serpent tossed him away like a toy. It whipped him around, smashing him into the ground. He tensed his arms and swung the sword at the monster's tongue. But the purplish thing unwrapped itself from his legs, and he sprawled onto the ground.

The serpent's tongue returned into its mouth. Sucking in its cheeks, the serpent parted its lips just enough to spit a dark wad at his face. Ilfedo held his sword in the venom's path, and the black liquid fizzled harmlessly against the blade.

The serpent king's enormous tail snaked toward him from behind. Ilfedo dropped flat on the ground, and the hard tip of the serpent's tail stabbed the air where he had been.

Thrusting his blade upward, he stabbed into the serpent's tail. Blue blood spurted from the wound. Ilfedo immediately sent flames shooting from the sword, burning into the flesh exposed beneath the scales. A scream escaped the serpent king. The creature recoiled from Ilfedo, its white eyes wide open. Its blade-fin alternating colors between black and deep red.

"Thy skill surprises me, little warrior," the

serpent hissed. "Your manner is reminiscent of the ancient human kings, and the weapon you bear is no ordinary sword." The serpent's tongue slipped from its mouth, wetting its lips. "Perhaps you will prove a worthy challenge for me." Its eyes glinted with anticipation. "Perhaps I will bury thee in a bed of coral beneath the sea instead of feasting upon you along with the rest of your people."

"That is . . . not . . . going . . . to happen." Ilfedo dodged the serpent's swinging tail, jumped onto its back and drove his blade up to its hilt in the monster's body. As blood flowed from the new wound, he grinned. Life was in the blood. His mind merged with the sword's powers, latching on to the life force of the serpent king, drawing it into the sword. The weapon radiated white energy, burning deeper into the creature's body.

The serpent king screamed first in rage and then with fear. It slithered toward the sea as fast as it could move. Holding on to the sword with all his strength, Ilfedo concentrated on stealing the creature's life blood. He didn't understand his connection to his new weapon, but it had become an effective extension of his will.

He glanced behind him as the serpent king pulled him away to the sea. Several men were running to the sisters' aid, raising swords. Among them were Ombre, Honer, and Ganning.

Ilfedo only wished that someone could have come to his aid as well. But he was alone in this fight. A battle with a titan of the deep. Quickly the others receded into the distance. The gargantuan sea serpent splashed into the sea, pulling him with it under the cold waves.

* * *

Ombre paused his charge and watched aghast as the gargantuan snake dragged Ilfedo into the Sea of Serpents. The creature's seemingly unending length cut into the waves, immersing Ilfedo along with them. Ombre had always thought Ilfedo was a bit on the reckless side . . . but this seemed to carry his issues to a new extreme.

"What is he doing?" Honer's question came out as an angry yell, and his brow furrowed. "He must be mad!" The sword in Honer's hand dripped blue blood from its blade.

Beside him, Ganning limped toward the sisters who were battling the remaining Sea Serpents. He didn't say a word, only ran toward the fray.

Ombre shook his head as he took a final look at the sea into which Ilfedo had disappeared, then started running toward the nearby battle. Ilfedo was beyond his help but these women were not. He overtook Ganning and passed him, making for one of the remaining serpents as it sneaked around to attack Caritha from behind.

The serpents swung their tails at the sisters. They opened their mouths wide to expose their fangs and attempted to stab each of the young women. The sisters evaded the attacks, and the creatures' fangs sank into the ground instead.

Ombre vaulted the bodies of several lifeless serpents before reaching his intended target. The sea serpent must have heard his approach. It snapped its head around to face him, forked tongue tasting the air between its fangs. Taking it head-on, he whaled on it with his blade. The metal first bruised the serpent's snout and then broke through its scales, splitting its head apart. As it fell, he leapt another fallen serpent's body, taking position next to Caritha.

The sister looked at him, acknowledging him with a sober nod. Compared with her sisters, she had thinner eyebrows and longer lashes. Blue blood ran in rivulets down her purple dress. But her dark eyes shifted back to her blood-soaked blade as she brought it around, stepping forward to thrust it into a serpent's wedge-shaped head. She was magnificent.

With a gesture, she summoned her sisters to her other side. Rozel growled as she slit another serpent's throat and came to stand with the others. In unison they lowered their blades and closed their eyes. Energy shot from the handles, up the blades, joining at the tips. A bolt of blue light streamed from the blades. Ripping through the air with a crack. The light struck three more serpents, and burned through their bodies, leaving smoking holes in their flesh. The serpents closed their white eyes and slumped to the earth.

Ombre looked at them, raising his eyebrows at the sight. First Ilfedo had ridden a monster into the sea, and now the sisters had thrown deadly energy from their blades. This was an act that he and anyone else in the Hemmed Land would have to explain as magic. There was more to these beautiful women than met the eye.

As Ganning and Honer rushed another serpent, the woods seemed to blossom with lines of men. First the rest of their hunting party joined in the fight, then swarms of townsmen armed with whatever tools or weapons. The few sea serpents that had survived, now turned tail, too late.

The people cut them apart with knives and swords, stabbed them with spears and shovels, and pierced them with pitchforks. One large man, a farmer judging by his straw-brimmed hat, swung a pickax deep into a serpent's body. The battle was soon over. Everyone gathered around the five sisters. The young women's dark hair flamed red in the afternoon light and their swords glowed rusty-orange despite the blue blood.

The weary farmers and townsfolk cheered, screaming out, begging to know who the sisters were. But the sisters ignored their questions and ran toward the sea. The townspeople hushed into stillness, standing and watching.

"Wait!" Ombre ran after them alone. He caught up with them as they reached the white sand, their feet leaving clear imprints in the soft ground. Grabbing Caritha by the arm, he jerked her to a halt.

"Sir, let go of me." Her eyes burned back at his.

The other sisters stopped, staring back at her.

"Okay, first of all," he stated matter of factly. "Don't call me 'sir.' My name is Ombre. Second of all, what in Subterran has gotten into your head? If you're thinking of doing what I think you are—"

"I am," she said. She tugged at his arm, pulling from his grasp. "Now let me go."

He held her tighter. "Yeah right!" He forced a laugh. "And what do you think Ilfedo would say if he found I let you go? There's nothing you can do underwater, and if Ilfedo regains his senses, he will come back before he drowns. But I am not going to let you throw your lives away by swimming out there and trying to find him. You'd drown." He nodded his head at the other sisters, still looking into Caritha's eyes. Wow, even her dark eyes were beautiful. "They follow you. That is admirable. But this thing that you plan to do . . . is foolishness."

She looked at his arm. "Please, my Lord Ombre, let go of me." Tightening his grip on her arm, he waited for her to return his gaze. When finally her dark eyes met his, she bit her lip.

"I will gladly do so, my lady," he said, "if and only if you give me your solemn word that you will stay on dry ground."

She hesitated, glanced at the rolling sea. "We cannot let anything happen to him. We promised to protect him."

"And I am here to protect you." He sighed. "If there was anything that could be done, then I would be the first to go. Believe me." He glanced at the Sea of Serpents, the water that had swallowed his friend. "Ilfedo is on his own for now. All we can do is pray for his safe return."

Her dark eyes scanned his face. "Then I give you my word. We will stay."

"Thank you," he said in a voice too low for anyone else to hear.

She averted her eyes from his gaze and shifted her feet. "Please, let go of my arm."

* * *

Still holding on to the sword of the dragon, Ilfedo felt the slippery body under him losing energy as his blade leeched off its blood. The instant the monster pulled him under the waves, his head slapped against them as if striking a hammer. The cold Ilfedo could endure, but his head smacking the waves, he could not.

So hard was the blow that the world around him blurred and his conscious mind sank into blackness. He could feel the cold water filling his lungs, the saltiness of it covering his tongue. Was he going to drown here in the sea with only his adversary privy to his death? Was this the end?

Some time later Ilfedo awoke with a green light glaring at him from high above. His chest felt heavy as he rolled onto his side to ease his aching back muscles from the rigidity of the flat stones on which he lay. He might as well have had a sandbag weighing on his chest.

His body no longer glowed with the power of the sword of the dragon, so he deduced that his armor was not on him. He could also feel that the sword was no longer in his hand. His fingers touched a moist and blubbery substance covering the right side of his chest.

Blinking to clear his vision, he focused on a tubule connected to his chest. Long and narrow, it compressed and expanded with the regularity of a heart beat.

His vision sharpened. He stood to his feet or rather was pulled up by the tubule. Its end released its hold, popping off, sloshing liquids all over his chest. It retracted several feet over his head. He followed the movement and spotted a curious being towering above him.

It balanced on long, round legs that bent backward like a chicken's rather than bending forward like a human's. It slapped its frogish feet on the circular stones and leaned over him. Its bulbous body was transparent and resembled a jellyfish's hood. But the upper half of its body melded with the chest, arms, and head of a man.

Its angled ears tapered to sharp points. The muscles along its jawbone twitched, strengthening its handsome face. A green light shining from high overhead made its eyes glimmer like smooth pearls. Not a single hair graced its bald head.

Crossing its arms over its chest, the being bowed its bald head. Its eyes seemed to roll back into its head and the large, white shells that padded its shoulders swayed forward as the tubule retracted into the being's side.

"*Sevat,*" it said through the gill slits covering its mouth. "*Sevat eb Crysallis!*" Spreading its arms wide, it clumsily spun, raising its pearlish eyes to peer at the shell of an energy dome that held back the open sea which surrounded the plateau.

For the first time, Ilfedo took notice of the tableland on which he stood and the metal arch that rose over it, like a giant drafting compass with its arms set at opposite sides of the circular floor of stones. The arms of the compass dropped over the edge of the round tableland, but from their junction a couple hundred feet above him, a green star burned with blinding brightness.

Shielding his eyes with his hand, he traced four arcs of green energy from the star to sheer cliffs that rose beyond the dome into the darkness far above. A sliver of light glowed in the darkness.

It bent and stretched like a river into the distance. Turning he watched the river of light vanish into the dark distance. It was as if a slice had been carved out of the sky. But it was a sky unfamiliar to him.

Ilfedo's eyes alighted on the ruins of a city that stood in the bed of the sea. The buildings looked like grain silos, some larger than others, some low and others exceedingly high. The green light touched the ruins with faint fingertips, illuminating the seaweed that filled its deserted streets.

He blinked again to be sure he was seeing things the way they actually were. This place was under the sea. At the bottom of it. That river of light must be the light of day, far above him. Somehow he must have fallen through a rift in the ocean floor. Yes, that had to be it! He had killed the king of the sea serpents and had sunk deep beneath the waves. His body had not landed on the sea bottom but had fallen into a rift, a sort of canyon beneath the sea.

How impossible it seemed. The energy from the star formed an enormous bubble around the tableland. The ocean currents washed against it, and it shimmered, holding them back.

"*Trispal sevat?*" the being spoke again. It let its arms swing at its sides.

Ilfedo gazed into the creature's pearl eyes. When it shuffled its flat feet and waggled its head at him, he breathed in deeply of the salty air. "I'm sorry, my mysterious friend. I don't think we speak the same language."

Shuffling its feet, the being spread its arms wide.

Ilfedo stepped back, and his foot landed on

metal. Looking down, he saw his sword. Flooded with relief, he picked it up. The living fire sprang from the blade, braided up his arms and covered his body, in a moment transforming him into a warrior garbed in armor of white light.

The being standing before him did not so much as twitch a muscle in response. It regarded him with its pearl eyes, arms still spread.

With his mind focused on finding a way back to the surface of the sea, Ilfedo hardly noticed that the edges of the tableland were filling with members of the tall being's race. They were swimming through the depths, penetrating the green energy barrier, climbing onto the flat circle of stone rising from the midst of the city ruins. The green star seemed to sustain this bubble of air beneath the sea.

The creatures had him closed in on all sides.

"Stay back," he cautioned them.

"*Poonie,*" the first being said through its gills, gently gesturing at its companions and then crossing its arms over its chest.

Ilfedo lowered his sword and pointed cautiously at the being. "Poonie . . . is that what you call yourselves?"

The being shuffled forward, holding out its hand. "*Alartis!*"

Bowing, Ilfedo shook hands with the Poonie. Its pearl eyes dropped gold tears.

"I do hope those are tears of relief," Ilfedo said as he released the Poonie's hand and gazed around at the other beings. They were standing around him in silence.

Spreading their arms wide and moving forward on their ungainly legs, their frog-like feet slapping against the stones, their bulbous bodies dripping sea water from their recent swim, the Poonie said in unison, "*Sebat eb Crysallis!*"

Sebat? Was that their word for hello? He watched the congregation fix their pearl eyes on the green star hovering above the junction of the compass.

An icy hand touched his shoulder lightly. He jumped, spun around. But it was only the first Poonie, leaning over him. It pointed at the city around the tableland, and spread its arms wide. "Crysallis!"

"This city?" Ilfedo longed to break the language barrier and understand, but he thought he understood at least one thing. "Crysallis . . . it's the name of this place . . . this city. Your city?"

But the pearl eyes revealed nothing. Gold tears fell from the Poonie's eyes, filling the cracks between the stones on the tableland. Gazing around at the rest of the circular floor, Ilfedo caught his breath, seeing but hardly believing his eyes.

Gold tears flooded the cracks between the stones, falling from the pearl eyes of every Poonie present. The gold ran toward the center of the tableland, collecting around Ilfedo's feet. He felt the tears raise him off of the floor. First his head leveled with the Poonie's eyes, then he rose above them and faster and faster, higher and higher, gold tears surrounding him until he passed into the blinding brilliance of the green star.

The ocean fell upon him, roaring through a gap forming in the shield of energy that had kept it at bay. The sound of weeping filled his ears and he looked down to find the sea water crashing over the Poonie, whose gold tears continued to flow.

He pointed the blade given to him by the dragon, aiming for the ocean floor. Surely the powers in his sword could save these poor beings. But the star rose through the sea, carrying him with it, and he felt the surface of the Sea of Serpents break around him as he shot into the air, water pouring from his glowing armor.

Around him the green star vanished. Such was the force with which the star threw him that he shot through the air, over the water and toward the distant shore.

Before he splashed back into the water, he spotted the monstrous form of the sea serpent king slicing through the waves. Damn that beast! It had survived and was now returning to land. Ilfedo's trajectory landed him with perfect balance on the creature's massive head. With all his might he drove the sword of the dragon into the serpent's brain, spewing fire from the blade, cooking the creature from the inside out.

The serpent screamed a horrible sound that sent shockwaves through the water for a dozen paces around its head. It breached the water's surface within a hundred feet of the shore. Ilfedo saw lines of people building rank upon rank on the dry ground.

Ombre was standing closest to the water, his sword drawn, his face taut. Beside him the five sisters drew their swords and charged into the waves, soaking their purple dresses. A sea breeze wrapped their hair around their heads, wild and free.

Struggling to its last breath, the enormous

serpent shook Ilfedo off of its head. Its blue blood dyed the sea around it.

Ilfedo stood in the shallow water, aimed his blade for the sea serpent's neck, and threw it like a spear. He shouldn't have. The sword was not weighted properly for throwing, but in his eagerness Ilfedo forgot. The armor of light vanished from Ilfedo's body as soon as the sword left his hand. Somehow the blade lodged in the targeted spot, and the monster screamed again. It spat thick venom at the sisters. They ducked the flying poison, came within arm's reach of the creature's body, and sank their blades between its scales.

Ilfedo took advantage of the creature's divided attention. He sloshed through the water, grabbing hold on the hilt of his sword as it remained stuck in the serpent's neck. He waited for the living fire to garb him again, then drawing with all his strength and summoning the powers in the sword, he ripped the blade up the serpent's gullet. A shower of blue blood rained on him. The serpent's scream was cut short. Its house-sized head bombed into the sea.

Ilfedo held up his blade, and the water stormed past him. The water divided around him as if avoiding the sword's power. When the sea calmed, he walked ashore. The five sisters stood there, sober despite the victory.

When Ilfedo reached the sand and sheathed his sword, he heard a low rumble of voices and looked up at the multitude of awed faces. The people sent up cheers that shivered up his spine. At the sound, the sisters standing beside him turned to look at the crowd.

Joining in with the masses, Ombre first, then Honer and Ganning, raised their voices in celebration. Ombre lifted his fists into the air and shook them.

Suddenly the people grew quiet. Whispers raced through their midst. A chant began.

"Hail! Hail Ilfedo, master of all swordsmen! Hail! Hail the women who stand with him. Hail the Lord Warrior and his Warrioresses!" When the chant ceased the people grew quiet. Then, one by one, with solemn, eager faces, the men knelt on one knee and bowed their heads toward him. The women fell to both knees, heads lowered.

The sky paled to orange, and the dead serpent king washed onto the shore.

Ilfedo cringed as the people bowed to him. Obeisance. He did not want it.

His discomfort changed to horror when, beside him, the five sisters—his Warrioresses—started to bow. And Ombre, with a broad smile, knelt where he'd stood. Honer and Ganning also fell to their knees.

"No, my sisters!" He pulled them to their feet. "Never, I vow, will the blood-kin of my Love kneel before me."

Walking through the sand to his three childhood friends, he pulled them to their feet as well. "You will rise with me, my friends. Together we will build a great nation for our people. With you by my side, and only with you by my side, can I do this. Do not kneel to me."

"As you wish," Honer and Ganning replied in unison, standing.

Ombre rose too, dusted the sand from his pants. "Of course, Lord Ilfedo." There was no sarcasm in his statement, only a playful congratulation.

Turning to the people, Ilfedo bade them rise. He surveyed the sea of faces, knowing that this was a turning point for the Hemmed Land. Things would never be the same.

He would embrace his new role and use his influence as best he knew how. With a heavy sigh, he prayed to God for guidance, praying also that he would not let this newfound power lift him in pride's ugly hands.

He thought of his child and set his jaw firm. The Hemmed Land must be made strong to protect Oganna. She was all that he had left of Dantress. Her future was all that mattered to him now.

OF VIPERS AND DOVES

Ilfedo started to descend the stairs from his bedroom, wearing only his britches. Then he slapped his forehead and chuckled a bit. He did not want to make his new family members uncomfortable as they settled in to his home. Their home. He wanted this to be their home for as long as they wanted it to be. That was as Dantress would have wanted it, he was certain of that. Dantress had had the love of eons to spread over the people around her, and as much as was in his power Ilfedo intended to continue spreading that love to everyone he knew.

There was never too much good in the world. Always evil seemed to raise its ugly head as if guided by the corrupt spirit of the underworld himself. Thanks now to the dragon prophet's mighty gift of a fiery sword, Ilfedo had hope that he could bring peace to his world. Perhaps he was a fool to think so, but then again, when was the last time that the sea serpents had been decimated by a human? Never! Not in the short history of the Hemmed Land, nor that he could recall in the legendary texts of his ancestors.

The Hemmed Land was about to change and he was going to direct that change with his newfound influence.

He grabbed a shirt and slipped it on before heading back down the stairs. Usually baby Oganna would be sleeping in his room, but last night Evela had kindly asked to take a turn so that he could rest. She was kind and thoughtful. As Dantress had been.

Downstairs, the kitchen was a bustle of activity. He was getting used to this change. It was good to have so many willing, helpful hands, but sometimes he felt a bit lost in the midst of so many women. Caritha and Rozel were flipping pancakes, chatting softly to each other as they did so. Evela was lying in the living room on her stomach and swinging her bare feet over her back as she talked to baby Oganna. The baby was smiling back at her, fat little cheeks rosy with happiness.

Levena emerged from the back hallway to the other bedrooms and smiled at Ilfedo. "Do you want pancakes this morning?" she asked.

He smiled back and nodded at Laura, who was setting plates on the table.

"Sit down then and let us serve you," Laura said, gesturing to a chair. "You have a busy few days ahead. First the trip, and then with the gathering at Coral Haven. And then Ombre, Honer, and Ganning will be joining you, of course. Am I forgetting any-one?"

Ilfedo sat at the table and accepted a pile of pancakes, then he drained maple syrup over them. He had never taken the time to tap trees himself, but a bit east of his house an old trapper had broken his leg and decided to start a syrup business. So far, it had proven highly profitable for the old man. Good for him! The Hemmed Land needed such variety of industrious ideas.

Ilfedo enjoyed the next couple of hours. The sisters were a pleasure to be around. They lent his home the pleasant feminine touch that filled the void left by his wife. It did not fill the emptiness of his nights. It was then that he missed her most, when in the darkness and the quiet he reached out for her, then drew back and wept softly at her absence. But for the rest, the women were filling the gaps. They loved his child as if she were theirs, and that mattered most to him.

He spent some time that morning holding his daughter, marveling at the clarity of her eyes and the intelligence that he perceived behind them. He loved her more than anything. He would protect her until his dying breath from the horrors that he had wit-nessed.

Someone knocked firmly on the door and Caritha went to open it. She greeted someone in her gentle voice, then bowed away and ushered Ombre into the room. Ombre seemed not to notice Ilfedo at first. In low tones he conversed with Caritha as she politely responded, then he excused himself and walked into the living room. It was unlike Ombre, Ilfedo thought amusedly, to excuse himself away from someone.

"Today is the big day, brother," Ombre said as he clapped Ilfedo on the shoulder.

"Indeed it is," Ilfedo replied. He kissed his baby on her forehead and smiled as she cooed a response. Ombre's eyes locked on the child and she gurgled at him. Ilfedo placed her in Ombre's arms. "You had better spend a little time with her while I prepare for the trip."

Ombre sat on the floor and talked with the baby as if she was fully conversant. "Do you like your Uncle Ombre? Of course you do! We are going to become best friends. Hey, what can I say? I'm a somewhat likeable guy. You are beautiful like your momma. Do you know that?" As the baby cooed again, he said, "That's what I'm saying, little one. You will have to listen to me so that I can protect you from all the boys who'll be chasing you from here to Coral Haven. Don't you worry. Just stay close to Uncle Ombre."

As Ilfedo turned away to gather his things for the coming journey to the coast, he heard the baby burp. He turned in time to see that the baby had spit up down Ombre's shirt. Rozel's jaw hung open as she watched from the kitchen. Laura, Evela, and Levena looked ready to laugh. But Caritha was standing quietly in the corner of the room. She watched and Ombre's face spread into a grin as he tapped the baby's nose with his thumb. Ilfedo thought he detected a smile steal across Caritha's face before she knelt down and took the baby and helped Ombre dry his shirt.

Dantress would have done the same for Ilfedo, he knew. How he missed those little things. They should have been raising their daughter together.

He sighed and moved on upstairs to gather a few things. Coral Haven. He had not expected to return there so soon, but there was no better place to begin the work. A body of respected men was assembling there, leaders among the people of the Hemmed Land. Half of them had never met Ilfedo, but they knew of him and of his heritage. His family name of Matthaliah was respected as one of the oldest families in their tiny nation. If he was to unite them, then he would have to accept the mantle of politician as well as that of a warrior.

Ilfedo packed a few changes of clothes along with a small knife. Never knew when he would need that on hand. It was best to be prepared but to pack light. He slung the pack over his shoulder and moved to the stairs, but before setting foot on it he looked at the assortment of swords that he'd hung on his wall. He contemplated bringing a large throwing sword or the sword from his parents, but no that would not do. Politicians would need to take him seriously, not only as a worthy combatant but also as a man who outshone their finest.

Only one sword would do. The sword given to him by the great white dragon.

Ilfedo lifted it from the pegs on which it balanced in its sheath. He held it up for a moment, again marveling at how light it felt in his hand. Its exquisite craftsmanship did not rival all others. It put them to shame.

With the sword in hand he descended the stairs. Evela stood there waiting for him. She reached out and stroked back his hair, catching him by surprise. "You look regal," she whispered. Then she cleared her throat and raised her voice. "Be safe, my lord."

"And you," Rozel declared to Ombre as she thrust a pack into his arms, "guard the food. You're all going to get hungry so do share."

Ombre laughed and headed outside.

Caritha was right on his heels. She turned to her sisters as she left and said, "We will be home again soon." All except for Rozel gave Caritha hugs as she left.

Then Ilfedo kissed his child one more time and headed outside, closing the door behind him. On the lawn they were joined by Honer and Ganning, their horses prancing in the warm air. Ilfedo swung onto another horse that Ganning offered him, then he turned and helped Caritha up behind him. Ombre swung up behind Honer, and they all galloped eastward through the forest.

They alternated between riding and walking on their journey. There were a few points along the woodland paths that were still too narrow for a man to ride through. A few fallen trees, low-hanging branches over the path, and in some places muddy creeks to cross.

But Ombre remarked on the change that had come over the Hemmed Land in the past couple years. "Used to be that we would mark the trees along this route, otherwise strangers would get lost on their way home to the coastal towns."

"It is remarkable," Ilfedo said. "I marked these trees for Ramul a while back. Remember that? My first fight with the sea serpents and Ramul accompanied me from Coral Haven to home, then he followed the trails back on his own. I'll admit, a small part of me worried he'd get lost on his own. There was always that risk." He glanced behind them as they emerged into a meadow. "It used to be so easy to get lost on the return journey, but today look at it!" He pointed to the clearly worn path that they were following across the green grass. The trail had been beaten wider than ever before and it proceeded clearly eastward into the forest.

The Hemmed Land had changed much since his childhood. His father had blazed the trails into the wilderness, and now the population was growing. Over the course of a couple of days they followed the trails to the coast. Honer and Ganning had recently traveled this way for supplies, and they had befriended a couple of families along the route. They stopped to rest and refresh. Ilfedo's party was warmly received on both occasions. The fame of his battle with the serpent king had spread and it seemed that every father and son wanted to speak with him, and every woman and her daughter prayed blessings upon him.

When they emerged from the woodlands at last and looked out over the cornfields to Coral Haven, Ilfedo steeled himself for the coming days. From the north, small bands of people were marching on foot up to the town gates, and from the south flowed another, but this one an endless parade of men and women on horseback.

Honer drew his horse up beside Ilfedo. Ilfedo was standing on the ground, gazing out at the scene. "Word of what you have done to the sea serpents has reached every corner of the Hemmed Land," Honer said to him. "The towns northward are primarily reliant on hunting and farming, so they already respect the type of man you are. But they are neither the most populous, nor are they the wealthiest. You will need the support of the more powerful southern mayors if your claim to the title of Lord Warrior is to hold. I have visited a couple of their towns and they are growing into cities with high stone walls and small garrisons of swordsmen."

Ganning dismounted and limped up beside Ilfedo. He pointed at Coral Haven's southern gate. "That man riding out front there into the town is Vortain. See? He has the distinctive, long blond hair. He is a perfect example of his type. His town is called Gwensin and he treats it more like his personal kingdom, and no one dares tell him otherwise."

"How do you know about that man?" Ilfedo asked.

"Reputation, Ilfedo. Reputation." Ganning kicked a stone as he talked. "I heard about an excellent blacksmith a while back. Remember when my plow broke? Well, this blacksmith in Gwensin was the only one who was able to fix the cursed thing. My stay there was short, but I heard much. Gwensin is bursting with its growing population. The people are safe and, by and large, happy."

Ilfedo cleared his throat approvingly. "The people are safe and happy. That speaks well to Vortain's leadership."

"Perhaps," Ombre interjected. "Or he has good counselors. Such a wealthy man will resent the push to unite us all under another man. That is, under your leadership."

"And Vortain has been known to close his gates against those in need on several occasions," Ganning said.

Ilfedo glanced sharply at him, then waited for him to continue.

Ganning nodded, as if affirming his statement in stronger terms. "A while back there was a killer wolf holed up near Gwensin Town. It killed a farmer, and the farmer's widow carried her young child to the city gates. Vortain was on the wall, inspecting somewhat or other that evening. When he saw the wolf chasing the woman he ordered the gates barred against her. While the wolf mauled her and her child, Vortain's archers killed it from the safety of the ramparts. Only after the wolf lay still did the town open its gates. They rescued the woman but her child did not survive its wounds. I saw that woman. Her face is a ghastly testament to Vortain's selfishness."

Ilfedo frowned deeply and swung back onto his stallion in front of Caritha. He dug in his heels, renewed purpose filling his spirit. "Come," he called to his companions. "It is time to form a new authority, to bring peace and not fear to the people."

Ombre chuckled aloud. "I like the sound of that," he said. "We are with you, my brother. Let's go and show the lords of the Hemmed Land to whom their people want them to bend the knee."

As they rode, Caritha spoke into Ilfedo's ear, "I once read where a wise man said that when those in power gather, it is hard to discern the doves among the vipers. We should only trust those you know until these lords have proven themselves to you."

"This I know," Ilfedo shouted back against the

wind. "But thank you. Keep your eyes and ears open at this meeting. I will need all the information we can gather."

6

A NEW DAY IN THE HEMMED LAND

Ilfedo had never seen so many people before. The harvested cornfields around Coral Haven had filled overnight with hundreds of tents. It was a strange sight to his eyes. All of these people had gathered in one common interest, and he was that interest. All eyes were watching him, waiting to see what he would say and what he would do. He had stayed the night at the inn called The Wooden Mug. The innkeeper had insisted on not charging him or his guests, rather insisting what an honor it was to have the Lord Warrior stay at his humble lodging.

Now, with Ombre at his side, Caritha behind them, and Honer following closely with Ganning, Ilfedo walked out of town through the gate. He proceeded toward the center of the pitched tents, noting their wide range of sizes. Some could barely house two people, others were propped up with thick posts and could comfortably fit a hundred.

The air was still and humid. He wiped sweat from his forehead and came to a stop. Hundreds of people had gathered. No! There had to be a couple thousand! This was a historic day for the Hemmed Land. A gathering of this size had not happened in his lifetime.

The myriad of people who stood around him, filling the space around the tents for as far as the cornfields stretched, were silent. Men, women, and children watched him or waited to see him. But they did so without frustration, without anger. In fact, curiosity and hope were how he would describe their expressions. He nodded back at them, feeling the need to separate himself from them. They did not need to fear him, but he wanted their fealty and he needed the lords of the Hemmed Land to stand behind him without question.

Those who had gathered divided like grass before him, leaving a path through their midst that led all of the way to an imposing white tent trimmed in gold brocade. He followed the path toward the tent, and as he neared it a handful of figures became clear in front of its open door. The tent stood taller than any other, its center tapered to a point with a golden spike rising through it. The door flap was being held open by two broad men dressed in humble brown, whereas most of the men standing in front of the door were dressed in colorful clothes, some with jeweled daggers strapped to their waists.

He was within a hundred paces of the tent when he paused, looking around at the masses. Not long ago he was a mere hunter. A hunter with a reputation but not a leader among the people of the Hemmed Land. He knew that his attire was humble. It mirrored the clothes of the common man, but these people wanted him to be extraordinary, a pillar of hope rising far above them.

He offered nods to the people around him and their faces brightened. Parents whispered to their children, and the elderly nodded at one another in wordless communication. They all wanted the same thing as he did. Peace. Peace and security in their wild world. Perhaps they were waiting. Waiting for him to give them a sign that would demonstrate why he alone was worthy of being called Lord Warrior.

"Look well at him," Ilfedo heard one man say to his son as Ilfedo turned to resume his march. "This man will lead our people into an era of prosperity, and your generation will bless this day. For on this day the petty rulers of our towns will bow to one who is strong of mind, body, and character."

"Did he really take on the king of serpents all by himself?" the son asked. His eyes sparkled, as he kept his ear inclined toward his father and his gaze aimed upward to Ilfedo. He pointed with his little hand. "Is that the sword people say was given to him by a dragon?"

"He is looking at you, my son! Stand straight and smile. One day you will tell your children that this hero noticed you in the crowd today."

The boy stood stiff and grinned.

Ilfedo allowed himself a smile as he looked upon the boy. Then he rested his hand on the sword of the dragon and summoned its fire. The flames roared from the blade, covering him again in the armor of living fire. The crowd shouted out, falling backward a few paces, then erupted into cheers as Ilfedo strode boldly toward the lords of the Hemmed Land. His voice carried with power as he approached them. As he advanced the people fell to their knees all around him, bowing not in reverence but in relieved joy.

The line of finely-dressed lords in front of the tent fell apart before him. Their bravados humbled, their respect demanded by the people. One by one they knelt, heads bowed. One of them, Vortain, was the last to do so, but he did so nevertheless.

"Welcome," Ilfedo said to them. "I am pleased that you came, my lords. A new era is dawning for our people, for my people, and I would have you build our nation with me." The crowds thundered around him until he raised his flaming sword, then he said, "For too long we have lived divided. A nation of many voices with none to speak for all. I stand before you all to claim the title of Lord Warrior, a title of authority that will help me mold our nation into greatness. This is the beginning of a new era! Let us embrace hope, rather than fear. And if any creature or man seeks our destruction again then let him answer to me, and to the army of the Hemmed Land that will rise behind me!"

The people rose with one voice and began to chant his name, and the lords joined in, some of them sooner than others. It was a feeling akin to nothing

Ilfedo had ever experienced. His word would be law. He knew that and he knew that the people wanted it.

Ombre grinned at him. Caritha bowed slightly, but she looked pleased as well. Honer and Ganning stood beside him, watching the crowd as if they were his sworn bodyguards.

Ilfedo left that day with the pledges of lords, ladies, warriors, and commoners echoing into the forests. Over the next several months mayors and other representatives from all over the Hemmed Land sought Ilfedo out, pledging their support. A few men of evil intent came to him as well, but with his friends' help he saw through their facades, found out their corrupt states and replaced them with simpler, more honorable men.

By a nearly unanimous decision the inhabitants of the Hemmed Land accepted Ilfedo as the Lord Warrior. It was a title that had belonged to only one other man in recorded memory. Others may have existed before, but the recorded history was too fragmented and confused with myth to be certain.

Scrolls made of skins had been passed from generation to generation. Scrolls that gave them precious insights into their heritage, though not enough to solve the mystery of their origins. One man was spoken of in the scrolls, a man who'd held the title of Lord Warrior. It had been a Lord Warrior that had first brought their ancestors to the Hemmed Land.

The scrolls made it clear that this role not only carried with it the responsibility of safeguarding the people, but it also gave he who held it the final say in all matters of state. Pertaining to responsibility it nearly matched the position of a king, except that the Lord Warrior was obligated to put his life before those of his people. If he did not then another would rise to challenge him.

Most people considered the majority of the scrolls in which these things were written to be little more than fiction based on threads of fact that were so slight the truth could not be discerned from it. Compounding this belief was the fact that the scrolls had been scribed by a man known only as The Count. His writings were loved by all. However, the vast majority of the Hemmed Land's people laughed aside his fabled travels in which he always happened to fill a central role in the saving of a civilization, or the mediation of some territorial dispute, or some other such fantastic event.

The Count claimed in his writings that there had been many Lord Warriors. Some, he declared, purportedly built themselves winged craft to fly through the sky. At this juncture, people would smile and advise their children that this was nonsense. They would point out that the Count, having exaggerated the legends of their ancestors to such a gross extent, could not be wholly believed to have been telling the truth.

But the people embraced the idea of having a Lord Warrior again. Ilfedo fit the image that every child, parent and grandparent had pictured a Lord Warrior to be. He was tall, strong, sober, and his battles with the sea serpents, his hunt for the man-killing bears, and his duel with the serpent king had made him a living legend.

In Ilfedo they saw hope for the future and a land freed from the fear of monstrous beasts roaming at will. The Hemmed Land started to change under his leadership. Most thought it was for the better.

He ordered the building of roads to connect the towns and settlements along the shore of the Sea of Serpents, replacing the beaten trails. With travel quicker and easier between once-distanced centers of civilized living, the towns grew and the forest settlements cut down the trees in order to expand.

Perhaps it was the reduction of stress, perhaps it was the new ease of travel, but Ilfedo became aware that many more babies were being born than had been at any other time in his life. The next generation in the Hemmed Land would thrive. Of that he was beginning to feel extremely confident, and they would fill the land.

The five sisters had become legends in their own right. Wherever they went they were treated with admiration and honored. But too closely observed for their comfort. Keeping for the most part out of the public eye, they lived in the wilderness, caring for their deceased sister's daughter. Ilfedo allowed them that, as often as possible.

Peace and security had been established, but Ilfedo could not dismiss the feeling that an evil was creeping upon the Hemmed Land. He could not place it. But something nibbled at his confidence when he looked out over the Sea of Serpents, and when he journeyed to the deserts at the northern and southern borders. He gazed out over the vast stretches of lifeless sand and wondered what lay beyond.

THE SWORDSMITH'S ARRIVAL

Mick stood barefoot on the white sand, his legs spread wide in the manner of a sailor. For he was a fisherman and proud of the life he lived. A long life. Longer than many others. He had seen other ships drowned in the Sea of Serpents, some by storms and others by serpents of the deep. On the shore before him his crew was gathering the nets, muttering to one another as a misty rain seeped through their tunics. It seemed that the gray sky thickened with each sopping minute.

Mick scratched at his silvery beard and chuckled to himself. He had told his granddaughter that his hair was not silvered due to his age. Instead, he had told her, he was part nuvitor. She had looked skeptical and he had given her one of his warm hugs.

The sky lightened for an instant, or rather it flashed. Young and old faces turned upward, blinking back the water that coursed down their skin. Chilled to the bone and weary after a most unprofitable day, they grunted and renewed their attention to their nets. As they stretched the nets on the shore and examined them for rips, a distant rumble made them stand upright.

Mick looked out to sea, that old Sea of Serpents, expecting lightning to flash. Instead a dull boom echoed from the east above the frothing waves, and a bright object hurtled through the clouds, large and pulsing.

The fisherman let the slimy net slide through his fingers and fall to the white sand. He narrowed his eyes, inquiring of his neighbors with a glance before looking seaward.

Pulsing white light burned a determined path toward the shore. It descended rapidly. The rain thickened and evaporated into steam around it. At last it touched the tumultuous waves, sending a fresh cloud of steam upward as it buried itself in the sea.

"Piece of the sky has fallen," the grizzly-bearded fellow grunted to the others. Mick returned to his net and began mending a tear. His friends joined him, picking up the work they'd neglected.

Absorbed in his task, the fisherman let time fly around him. The rain lessened, the clouds thinned, and thinned some more, until moderate sunlight warmed his shoulders. It had to be at least an hour later.

"Yimshi's light is burning today," one of the fishermen admitted, glancing at his reddened shoulders. He rolled his net into his wood boat and jogged into the surf.

"Yeah, 'nuff work for now!" another man said, loosening his tunic and joining the first. "I can use a cool swim."

The remaining fishermen stampeded into the water, grins brightening their tanned faces. Mick laughed as he watched them, but remained by his net. He finished mending the tear and slung one corner of the tri-sided net over the bow of his single-masted fishing vessel. The prow of his boat rested solidly on the white sand while the seawater lapped at the stern. He held the rail and let his knees buckle, hanging on as his weight stretched his stiff back muscles.

Something knocked into his knee, and he glanced down to find a ghostly-white face glaring up at him. "Shivering timbers!" he exclaimed as he jumped back. The other fishermen sloshed out of the water and stood in a half-circle behind him. He knelt and waved his hand across the face of the individual before him. The new arrival's eyes seemed frozen open and his shoulder-length white hair pulsed in sync with the incoming seawater.

"Who is he?" someone asked.

Mick shrugged. "How should I know?"

A stocky man leaned close and whistled. "Would you look at those eyes! I thank God I don't have eyes like that."

"Yeah, Bartholemew, would be a bit embarrassing. Girlish, even," Mick said.

Bartholemew ignored him and remarked, "Big fellow, though. I wouldn't have wanted to cross him when he was alive. Wonder where he came from."

Mick scratched his grizzly beard again, then he flipped their white-haired guest onto his stomach and pounded his fists into the man's back.

Bile and water spewed from the new arrival's mouth, and he coughed. When he could breathe freely, he rose to his feet and faced the assemblage of humble laborers. His pink—almost white—eyes made him seem soft and childlike. That is, until he spoke in a voice deeper than any present. "My gratitude to you all. You have, perhaps, preserved my life. Tell me now! What part of the world is this?"

Mick stood wide in front of him. He crossed his arms over his chest and eyed the white-haired man up and down.

No shirt, only loose-fitting blue-gray pants made of coarse fabric, but around his waist a belt of hammered steel. An assortment of heavy tools hung from it including an anvil no bigger than a large man's fists, tongs, a long narrow file, and a curious hammer with a wooden handle and shiny silver head. It was a miracle the stranger had washed ashore with those heavy items attached. They should have drowned him in the depths of the sea.

"Before answering your questions," the grizzly-bearded fisherman held up his forefinger, "how about answering a few of my own?"

For a moment the man's pink eyes flared, then he gently nodded his head.

Mick said, "Good, then what is your name?"

"I am Linsair, a swordsmith. My origin is harmless, though none of your affair, and I speak without guile. So you need not fear me."

The grizzly-bearded fellow unfolded his very large arms and leaned against his vessel. "Smoothly spoken, Linsair the swordsmith, but we know not you not of you. And what cause would make you hide your origin? That concerns me. Well, rather, it concerns us?" He paused.

"Yes," his fellow fishermen declared.

"So you see, Linsair, I do not desire to make an enemy of you, and I am not forbidding your entry onto our soil. Ilfedo the Lord Warrior himself welcomes travelers who bear us goodwill. It is part of this process of growing many settlements and towns into a strong nation." He cleared his throat as the other men lent him a short cheer, for he thought he'd handled that phraseology rather fine. Though there was a lack of truth in his statement concerning travelers to the Hemmed Land. To his knowledge, the Hemmed Land had not been visited by a foreign human in his generation. Well, other than the arrival of the Warrioresses.

"I am not a suspicious old sea lubber," Mick said. "But I do find the timing of your arrival a bit strange. Never have I heard of a stranger coming to us from the Sea of Serpents. Did you fall from the heavens on the back of a star?"

"You have deduced correctly." Linsair bowed to the grizzlybearded man and walked barefooted toward the coastal town of Coral Haven with his head held high.

"It was a strange encounter by all counts," the fisherman muttered to his neighbors. Some thought they should stop the stranger and moved as if to follow. But Mick the fisherman held them back. "Let him go where he will. He seemed to be an honest fellow, even if a bit waterlogged. 'Fallen on the back of a star' indeed! Preposterous! And yet he may prove useful to the Lord Warrior."

* * *

Linsair left the shore in peace and, arriving in town, found the sign of The Wooden Mug. He tried to blend in with the townsfolk. But two men who had too much to drink harassed the proprietor. Linsair bade them go home and consider God's ways. "Are they not the chief of all ways?" he asked them. "He gave you breath and life. Should we not honor such a glorious master?"

One of the men hiccupped. "Look, Smithy, you're in the wrong part of town." He took another swig from his mug and put it back on the table, gazing into Linsair's pinkish eyes. "Take your preaching to Brother Hersis where it'll be appreciated."

Linsair overturned the table and growled with such force that he might as well have been a creature instead of a man. The inn quieted around him as he strode to the door and onto the cobblestone street.

8

A Sorcerer in the Hemmed Land

In the depth of evening's light, Auron stood in the midst of a desert. This was not a vast desert, not compared to others he had visited. He grinned to himself as he thought on that. A thousand years and more. He had lived a thousand years and more. He had seen more deserts between the various lands of this world than most men could remember in their lifetime.

He pulled the cowl of his black cloak over his head and strode forth with his staff in hand. The desert hereabouts was littered with stones. It had that distinctive aura of death and he knew that is was a true aura. Vipers and scorpions abounded here. Their combined venom could kill an army, but that was of no concern to him. The scorpions were insects that could be avoided or killed, but the vipers were intelligent. Auron's new master, Razes, had discovered that long ago.

Razes. The very name of Auron's new master sent daggers of fear through his skin. He absently touched his fingers to his face, tracing the scars that spiderwebbed across it. Razes knew how to motivate his student, and Auron felt like a different man than when he had first met the giant wizard. Each lesson, whether in failure or success, Razes had taught Auron true brutality and how to use it to subject others to his will.

Now the vile desert vipers served at Letrias's pleasure. Even this far from the Valley of Death, Letrias was exerting his growing power. Auron had been humbled as he witnessed conquest after conquest in the wizard's name. Nostravium had fallen. Burloi had fallen. Others were in their death throws. Letrias's reach would soon know no limits. There were no kingdoms strong enough to resist him, that is, no kingdoms of men. The old kingdoms of Subterran must have fallen long ago, during the thousand years of Auron's wanderings. The great white dragon and his prophet allies remained silent and hidden, or they had died.

Letrias had expressed concern over one nation that he could not yet conquer, but that was a land of dragons, not of humanity. The dragons were secure behind their mountains. The land of Etina stood strong. They were strongly governed by one dragon lord, a beast named Venom-fier. One day soon Letrias would be ready to bring even that proud race to its bellies. Auron did not relish the prospect of fighting a thousand and more vicious dragons, but he knew that if Letrias called for his participation then he would have to obey.

As he crossed the desert the moon rose on the horizon, and by its light a dozen Art'en flew out and over Auron's head. They circled him, screeching like birds of prey. He raised his staff above his head and they dropped to the desert floor ahead of him. They folded their dark feathered wings to their backs and waited until he caught up with them.

"Master," one of them said as he bowed to Auron.

Auron smirked. Letrias had done something right. Razes had trained Auron well, for these creatures feared him. 'Master.' It boosted his pride to hear this recognition of his growing status among the wizards.

The other Art'en all dipped their boney faces in Auron's direction, waiting on his instructions. They were his bodyguards, assigned by Razes himself. Auron motioned for the creatures to follow him. Their tall, lanky frames moved in sync with his quickening pace.

At last the desert gave way to a line of trees in the distance and as they approached the thick forests of the Hemmed Land. Auron knew little of this place. Razes had said that it was a small nation of men, inconsequential really. But Letrias had said that nowhere could be neutral in the war to come, and he wanted an understanding of all potential threats and assets to his cause.

Auron reached the trees and he turned to the Art'en. "Fan out! Search until you find signs of habitation, and when you do return to me," he said.

The creatures spread their wings and leapt

into the trees, quickly vanishing in several directions. Auron waited for a long while. When the first Art'en loped back through the trees and stood in front of him, it grinned and Auron grinned back. He felt a kinship with these creatures. They enjoyed the darkness and dark deeds as much as he did. Heaven help the prophets! For if heaven did not, Auron would help Letrias bring hell upon them. If only the proud Xavion could have lived long enough to see Auron now! He would kneel at Auron's feet and confess his inferiority.

Auron waited until the rest of his scouts had returned, then he led them off through the forest. They arrived at a large grassy clearing. A long cabin of logs had been built in the midst of it and lantern light warmed the single window in its walls. Auron started forward, crossing the clearing, but his knee caught on a tree stump. He stumbled to the ground, cursing aloud both God and the prophets.

The cabin door opened and a tall woman peered out, holding a lantern out into the night. She screamed as the moonlight fell upon the dozen winged men creeping toward her door. Auron stood in the midst of the creatures and threw back his hood, cursing loudly as his bruised shin shot pain through his leg. The woman slammed the door shut and a commotion of voices rose from inside the cabin.

The door opened again and this time a broad man and his son charged outside. Auron channeled his pain into hateful rage. He sneered at the man and his boy, "You will invite me inside, else I'm gonna kill you."

The man and his son drew bows and arrows,

training them on Auron. In the moonlight Auron could read deep confusion on the man's face . . . and fear.

The Art'en creatures spread their wings and flew at the pair. But Auron twirled his staff expertly around his body and spun into the creatures. "You will not spoil my fun unless I say so!" he screamed at his bodyguards, and the Art'en fell away from him, bruised and humbled. Auron turned toward the cabin and grinned again. He charged the man and his son, pointing the dark orb atop his staff at them. He latched his sick mind onto theirs through the dark powers he had learned, confusing them long enough to close the distance.

Auron halted in front of them, spun, and bashed in the man's face with the head of his staff. As the father's blood splattered across the boy's face, Auron kicked the boy in his chest, sending him crashing through the cabin door. Auron leapt after him into the cabin and speared him through the stomach with the other end of his staff. The boy went limp on the floor beneath Auron as he crouched like a maniac over him. Then the wizard turned his gaze around the cabin. The woman stood by the fireplace, clutching two small children to her skirts. Her eyes were fixated on him and her open mouth refused to utter a sound.

She was rather pretty, Auron mused. Mid-thirties, with nut-brown hair and green eyes. He stood and approached her, whipping a dagger from his belt and then she screamed.

That night the wizard and his Art'en minions visited several other cabins along the Hemmed Land's border, sowing terror in the hearts of the few who survived their attacks. When Auron led them back into the desert, he wiped the blood of the innocent from his face and laughed. Razes would be pleased with him for his work this night, and Auron would send the Art'en back to this place to ensure that the terror of the wizards subjugated the Hemmed Land before ever a battle was fought.

A GAME OF CHRONICLERS

With a mug of grape juice in his hand, Ilfedo sat at the table and glanced at the lantern set in its midst. Evening was in full effect outside, ushering in a moonless night. Beside the lantern light a bed of coals glowed from the fireplace. He sipped the juice as the five sisters pulled out their chairs and sat. They moved with gentle grace, except for Rozel as she slammed the chair back and plopped into the seat. Laura slapped her on the arm.

"Hey!" Rozel started to say.

But Laura held up a finger. "If you utter one more word of complaint, we will all put you outside for the night. I'm serious! Evela just put the baby to sleep. With your ruckus you're going to wake her."

Rozel grumbled an apology and Ilfedo chuckled.

There was a knock on the front door and

Caritha rose to answer it. Ilfedo could hear the pleasant welcome in her voice as she ushered Ombre inside. Ombre and her spoke in low tones to each other, seeming to share things they did not need the others to participate in. Ombre was carrying an oblong wooden box under his arm. As he approached the table he smiled around at Ilfedo and then at the rest of the Warrioresses. "Ladies," he began, "this game was my father's. He crafted the board himself and collected the cards from the finest artists in the Hemmed Land. And tonight, you are all going to discover its magic!"

With near-reverence Ombre laid the box on the table. He waited as Caritha sat down. "May I?" he asked her, indicating the empty seat beside her.

She nodded silently as he sat in the chair.

Everyone stared at the game's box. It had been carved from mahogany and oak. The corners had been rounded slightly and small bronze tacks had been hammered along its edges. *Chroniclers* was spelled out in narrow letters that had been inlaid on the case, both on the top and on the sides, each of them meticulously carved from a piece of ivory. The box had been stained in an alternating dark cherry and white pine finish. The waxed wood gleamed from decades of handling.

Caritha ran her fingers along the wood and traced the ivory letters. "Your father had a talent for this."

"He did," Ombre uttered softly. He paused to allow everyone a longer look, then he lifted the top off the box.

Ilfedo left the table for long enough to fetch

another lantern. He lit its wick and set it on the other side of the table so that they would have ample light.

By the lantern light the box's contents were revealed. A long, narrow playing board lay folded on one side, and on the other were three rectangular compartments. There were two decks of cards, one red and one blue. The third compartment held a handful of playing pieces. Ombre dealt out five cards to each player, then gave them a quick summary of the game. "One card deck has attack values. One has defense values."

Ilfedo unfolded the playing board on the table as Ombre explained the nature of the game. Evela was sitting closest to him. She leaned closer to the board, the soft curve of her lips betraying her curiosity and pleasure at doing something purely for the fun of it. Ilfedo wondered in that moment when was the last time she had been afforded the opportunity. For him, slowing life for these simple moments was essential to his happiness. Otherwise the stresses of life diminished him as a man. Life had to be balanced.

He smiled at her and she laughed softly as she returned his look. He pointed to the board. "It is a map, as you can see," he said. "You choose a playing piece. Everyone starts at the same position, and everyone journeys across the board."

"So," she mused as she looked it over, "if I reach the end first?"

"Then you wait for the rest of us to join you before everyone counts their points," he said. "Each round you will draw as many cards as it takes to restore your hand to five cards. The attack and defense cards are all mixed, so the only indicator that any other player has of what you can do is the color shown on the back sides of your cards. You are trying to collect points for creatures captured and places explored. The player with the most points at the game's conclusion wins."

Suddenly realizing that everyone else was quiet, he glanced around and found everyone staring at him and Evela. Ombre cleared his throat. "Ahem. If you two are ready to play, let us know."

Evela blushed as she sat back, staring at the cards in her hands.

"Everyone understands the basics already?" Ilfedo asked.

"No!" Ombre laughed. "But you two were so absorbed I figured we had better bring you back so that she didn't miss anything important."

Ilfedo reached over and punched him on the shoulder, grinning. "Let's get to it then."

They selected their playing pieces, set them at the start position, and began to play. They were so wrapped up in the game that time lost all meaning to them, and it was a beautiful thing. They teased one another, discussed little things, conversed about their day, speculated on the future, and sighed when Ombre beat Levena in the first card battle. For his trouble Ombre captured a sea serpent worth fifteen points and the look on his face betrayed his glee.

Later that night the clock chimed midnight. Ilfedo glanced at it. It was a tabletop piece with a glass face that he had purchased from a wandering trader. A simple device whose workings were beyond his understanding.

Everyone at the table glanced at the clock,

then at each other, and Ombre shrugged his shoulders. "We should finish what we started," he said, indicating the board.

Caritha elbowed his side and laughed as he cringed. "You are confident of winning this round. I can tell."

"Hey, what of it?" he replied with a smirk. "It's only fitting that I win. It is your first time playing, after all."

The game resumed and Laura let out a whoop as she won a hand against Ilfedo, wresting away his only explored territory card.

Just then someone pounded on the front door. Everyone gave a start. Everyone except for Ilfedo. He pushed back his chair and walked over to answer it.

Ilfedo opened the door to a sight that he would never forget. A black-bearded frontiersman stood there with trails of dried blood down his face and neck. He was a head shorter than Ilfedo, wearing a coonskin cap. The lantern light from inside washed over the man's form, revealing a child lain across his arms. "Hello, stranger, what brings you at this late hour," Ilfedo said cautiously.

"Are you the Lord Warrior?" the man demanded in a husky voice.

"I am," said Ilfedo.

"Then you will hear me out!" the man said as he barreled passed Ilfedo.

The Warrioresses rose from the table and formed a half-circle in front of the man as Ombre took station by the fireplace. "Wrong house to force your way in," Ombre uttered as he regarded the man. He pointed at the sisters, each of them with a look of cold steel in their eyes.

Ilfedo continued to hold the door open as he watched the man. He didn't perceive any threat from the stranger, just anger. And anger directed not at Ilfedo, but elsewhere. The man knelt and set the child carefully on the floor. He began to weep uncontrollably as he stroked the child's red hair back, revealing the beautiful but cold dead face of a girl no older than seven. Ilfedo closed the door, noting how Ombre's expression turned to confusion at the stranger's tears.

Evela knelt in front of the man and the child. She stared into his bearded face, then turned her dark eyes up to Ilfedo. In the lamplight the red tinge in her dark hair was fully evident. She was waiting, as were the rest of them, to see how he would react.

But Ilfedo did not move. He stood by the door, staring down at the bereaved intruder.

At last the stranger gained his voice again and glanced over his shoulder up at Ilfedo. "I pray you forgive my manners tonight, my lord, for I have traveled far and the days were hard. Up north they call me Brandon. I hunt, trap, make a fine living off of the land that our fathers left us. The forests north are almost as wild as these and I have lived there my whole life. But the rest of the Hemmed Land pays us no mind."

Ilfedo frowned a bit at this. "You mind yourselves and few care to venture up there. There is not much in that region, except for a hunter such as yourself," he said. "I understand. Perhaps I understand better than you think. But I never casted blame on the rest of the Hemmed Land for the tragedies the wilderness brought to me. Is this what you are trying to do?"

"She was not killed by some wild animal!" Brandon nearly shouted as he pointed at the child. "Something else has entered the Hemmed Land. Something unlike we have ever known."

"Go on," Ilfedo said, and he caught a look of morbid curiosity pass over Ombre's face as the man continued.

Brandon took off his coonskin cap and clutched it in his calloused hands. "I would have attributed what I am about to tell you to hearsay, except that the last time it wasn't. I saw it! I saw them. I saw him. Other than the wild animals we have no enemies, but something came by night from the northern desert. One of them is a man, and not just a man but a wizard out of our nightmares." Brandon shook his head and said, "There's something else with him. Giant bird men that sound like eagles in night."

Ilfedo walked around the man and stared into his eyes. Then he glanced at Ombre and the Warrioresses. He read the truth of it in their eyes. The stranger was being sincere. A wizard had entered the Hemmed Land.

That night Ilfedo heard a tale of horrors visited upon the humble homes of his people along the northern border, and a rage grew inside of him. First the sea serpents and now this. This enemy was coming at them unprovoked, seeming to enjoy carnage for its own sake rather than for some purpose. The wizard had been seen only a couple of times during the night attacks, but the survivors had corroborated their descriptions of him adequately. The threat was real and it must be dealt with swiftly.

When morning arrived, Ilfedo sent Ombre and the Warrioresses to the east and the south with a command. "Bring me five hundred warriors of the highest merit. Meet me at Coral Haven in five days and we will march into the north." Ilfedo watched them leave and sent Seivar and Hasselpatch with word of the mission to Honer and Ganning. Before the noon hour, while he cuddled with baby Oganna in a chair on the porch in the warm air, watching the beautiful day unfold, Honer and Ganning rode out of the forest. Direct on their heels rode Eva, Honer's wife. She took the baby in her arms and cooed to her, then rode off in the direction of her own home.

"I have strange news," Ilfedo said to Honer and Ganning. When he had told them of the northern attacks, the three of them set off through the forests of the Hemmed Land, riding for the town of Coral Haven once again.

THE NORTHERN THREAT

On the Hemmed Land's northern border, Ilfedo camped his makeshift army of five hundred men in the shade of the trees. He spread them thin so as to cover as much territory as possible. If the sorcerer and his minions returned through the desert tonight, Ilfedo's warriors would meet them.

As evening fell he stood between a pair of sturdy trees, stabbing his gaze northward into the stone-strewn desert. Some kind of creature had been reported to come from that desert. On three separate incidents, it had slain people. A few men and a couple of children dwelling along this stretch of the Hemmed Land's border. All attacks had reportedly occurred in the dead of night.

The wind howled over the desert and whistled into the forest. Ilfedo fingered the hilt of the sword of the dragon. People in his territory had taken to calling it the Sword of Ilfedo. But for him it remained the Sword of the Dragon.

He wondered how well his baby had fallen asleep tonight. So delicate, so precious. The sisters had returned home to care for her, so he did not doubt that she was safe. Someday this land would fall to her as an inheritance. He had heard the term Princess being passed around among the people when he had stopped in Coral Haven and spoken to the men who had answered his call. As far as his people were concerned, Ilfedo was founding a dynasty to protect them and Oganna was the next link in that chain. He did not doubt, that with her mother's dragon blood flowing through her veins, his daughter could become a strong ruler. But what of her character? Power should not be lightly handed to a youth. The Warrioresses would not spoil her. He felt certain of that. They would keep her safe, too.

"Dantress, why oh why? If you were here now our child would grow in your footsteps. Play with your skirt, learn from your voice, and smile at your love," he whispered. "Oh, I want that. I want that more than anything."

Someone's sword clinked against a nearby tree, and Ilfedo retreated into a deeper shadow. No one must see him like this. He would show himself strong at all times for his departed wife. She had sacrificed herself so that their child could grow. How could he let his people perceive his still-grieving heart and expect them to focus on a bright future?

A breeze bent the short stalks of grass on the forest floor. He could see for a long distance through the trees as long as he kept his gaze near the desert where the trees thinned. First one of his shadowed warriors stepped toward the dry, stone-strewn landscape, then another beyond him sixty paces farther. Soon a substantial force marched in a line from the forest. Even in the darkness Ilfedo could see that they all kept their faces toward the desert, and their hands on the hilts of their swords.

None of this would be happening if his life had followed a different course. If Dantress were still alive things would be different. He sighed and leaned his shoulder against a nearby oak tree. The hard bark released some of the tension in his muscles. Every day her death returned to his heart as potent as that fateful morning.

"Release me from this world, dear God," he whispered through the shadows. "I want my heavenly rest in her bosom."

"Your time is not yet, my love." Dantress's voice wafted so gently into his mind that he almost believed she was really there, standing beside him in the tree's deepening shadows. "You and you alone must protect our offspring. She is the hope of your people. Stay for the fruit of my womb to blossom." The voice faded.

"If only you were here, Dantress. If only." Ilfedo turned toward the heart of the forest and walked into the darkness. The fleeting shadow of a woman slipped deeper into the woods and vanished. He froze, wondering for a moment if somehow Dantress had really spoken to him from beyond the grave. The darkened floor of the forest offered him no reply. A breeze rustled the leaves, an owl hooted above him. Ilfedo shook his head and skirted behind the treeline, checking on the warriors as they waited in the shadows.

A long while later, Ilfedo stood again looking out over the desert. A cloudless sky allowed the starlight to illuminate the rock-strewn sand. Nothing had come from the desert so far as he could tell. And nothing indicated anything would come. The sands remained settled on the cool desert floor. The rocks seemed frozen in its midst.

A swordsman crept toward him. The man twisted to glance out at the desert. Another warrior knelt behind a bush nearby and rested his longbow on the ground, peering through the trees at the barren landscape.

Slowly Ilfedo walked to the edge of the forest. He stood gazing across the desert for a few minutes more, then he strode along the tree line.

Four of his armor-clad men emerged from the trees ahead of him and fell in alongside him. "My lord, we have seen nothing yet to indicate if any enemies have crossed the desert."

"Remain at your posts until I give you leave," Ilfedo said. He waved them back and issued the same command, as every fifty paces he came upon another group of men. He glanced over his shoulder as the soldiers obediently shrank back into the forest. They would await his command as they always would.

Facing west, he made his way up a steep incline to a thick group of trees. Behind them the ground descended gradually into a large valley where a hundred canvas tents dotted the grass. Not a single tree grew in the valley but a line of oaks ringed its rim, rising like mighty sentries in the night.

From the midst of the camp a group of lightly-armed men rose from around their campfire and wove their way between the tents. As they approached, Ilfedo smiled at their commander. "Ombre," Ilfedo said.

"How's the first watch coming?" Ombre asked as he slapped him on the shoulder. "If you need a better set of eyes on the ground, I'll be more than happy to take your place!"

Ilfedo shook his head. "I want you to rouse Honer and Ganning." He stood at the valley's crest and pointed briefly out over the desert. "If something is out there I want it found before it harms anyone else."

"We could continue waiting, Ilfedo. You haven't given it all that much time," Ombre said.

"We could. You are right," Ilfedo replied. "But I want whatever is out there, if it is out there, found. Rouse however many men you need and form search parties. Just make sure that Honer and Ganning are in on it."

"Too bad you didn't bring Seivar." Ombre cleared his throat and grinned. "I told you that bird would be handy out here."

Too bad, indeed, Ilfedo acknowledged to himself. The nuvitor's eyes would have offered a welcome expansion of his army's scouting efforts. He left the valley, keeping inside of the tree line as he made his way back to his post. Once again the men hiding in the shadows acknowledged him as he passed, but he beckoned them to remain in their positions.

He had laid the trap for whatever or whoever the inhabitants of this part of his country had encountered. Now, if they came at all, the creatures would have to come to him. If not, perhaps the search parties would find something.

That night passed without any signs of an enemy on the desert border. Ilfedo took a couple of hours to sleep, and the next morning Honer and Ganning reported to him. They had braved the desert cold with a hundred men. "There's nothing out there save for lizards and rodents' tracks," Ganning said. "If there are winged creatures out there then perhaps they stay in the air until they land in the Hemmed Land. Otherwise, they could be hidden somewhere in our own forests. Biding their time, perhaps. But then there's that troubling matter of the wizard, or whatever he is. Maybe he isn't going to return. We could wait forever and learn nothing."

"True," Honer added. "Ilfedo, it is entirely possible that the wizard was a figment of the locals' nightmares. Otherwise, where did he come from?"

Ilfedo frowned at that. He had considered the possibilities. Considered them and discarded the possibility that the wizard did not exist. There had been too many people murdered in this region, too many for a random attack. "He is out there. Somewhere," Ilfedo murmured.

That afternoon a messenger rode into the camp. He dismounted from his black stallion and bowed to Ilfedo. "Word of your efforts here for the people in the north has spread among the towns. I was sent ahead of another five hundred men who have volunteered their swords and their bows to the Lord Warrior's new army. Our men will arrive later today and are eager to serve you, my lord."

Ilfedo clapped his hands on the man's shoulders and grinned. The people of the Hemmed Land were rising, like a brightening star in a dark time.

When evening cast its shadows across the forests again, Ilfedo commanded the watch to continue while he went in search of one of the recent victim's cabins. Brandon had sent him with instructions on how to find it. Trust a frontiersman to know the lay of the land.

Ilfedo found it tucked into the edge of a small meadow. The grass there grew peculiar, for its blue stalks glowed in the darkness. He paused at the meadow's edge to marvel. It was unlike anything he'd ever seen. He remembered his mother telling him a fairytale when he was only a child. A tale of a princess who had been lost in the Hemmed Land, far from her own people. When she had died, her blue hair had lingered in the ground and sprouted blue grass that glowed at night, to remind the world of her sorrow.

He ran his fingers along one of the stalks and found it soft as a rabbit's fur. He had thought the blue grass was only a myth, but apparently the fairytale had its roots in some truth.

At the far side of the clearing a single lantern shone from one of five small windows in the cabin. The place sported a second floor, which was unusual this far from the coastal towns. But the lantern provided the only evidence of habitation.

The grass shimmered around him. It stood up to his waist and when he looked down, deeper blue hues were rippling around him. He watched the ripples expand to the edge of the meadow and then he headed for the cabin. The grass continued to shimmer in the starlight. Despite the dampening air, he felt incredibly warm.

The cabin door eased open a crack, and a woman's sharp voice rang out. "Who's there? Tell me now or else I shoot!" A round woman of no mean size slammed the door open the rest of the way. She leveled a crossbow at him.

Ilfedo raised his arms and said, "There is no need for that, madam! It is I, your Lord Warrior."

The crossbow clicked as the woman locked her arrow in position. "If you really are who you claim to be, my lord, I need you to stand where you are so that you can prove your identity to me."

"Very well, madam." Ilfedo stood still and crossed his arms. "How shall we proceed?"

"I . . . I . . . I hadn't thought about that, my lord." The woman shrugged her shoulders. Two children emerged from behind her, clinging with tiny fists to her skirt. She tightened her tone and said, "How do I know you are the Lord Warrior? You could be that thing come back to take another of my babies. I will not allow it! You will pay for that, you blood-thirsty coward. Murderer!"

Whether she had intended to or not, the woman released her projectile. Ilfedo heard the arrow zing through the air. It struck his right shoulder and the force of the blow spun him around. He gritted his teeth as he fell.

"Curse you, woman," he muttered. "I have a child, too!"

She must have heard him, for as he looked at

the shaft of the arrow sticking through his shoulder, she came running. Kneeling down she clasped her hands over her mouth. "I am so sorry! When you said that you, too, have a child, I knew it must be you. Oh, what have I done?"

A screech rent the air, like a woman's cry and an eagle's scream blended into one.

Ilfedo struggled to his feet as the woman barreled through the glowing grass back to her cabin. She screamed, "No!" and tackled a shadowy figure darting toward her door. The children froze as their mother fought their would-be kidnapper.

The creature! It had returned as he had suspected it would.

Ilfedo's useless right arm hung at his side. When it came to swordplay, his left hand was nearly useless. He left the sword of the dragon in its sheath, ignored the pain stabbing across his chest, and ran to the cabin. The glowing grass illuminated the woman as she tangled with a creature. It appeared to be a humanoid with feathered wings.

Ilfedo swung his boot into the side of its head with all his might. The creature screamed. Two more like it leapt from the roof. The impact twisted the arrow inside Ilfedo's shoulder. But he raised his hand and faced the creatures. They were attacking him without weapons. He swung his fist at one creature, then another. Every blow he delivered seemed to bounce off a leather-clad muscle in their bodies.

In a blur of movement, the thickest creature punched at him. He ducked, and his foot struck a rock. He picked up the stone, and battered the creatures mercilessly on each of their gaunt manly faces. They fled into the trees. The remaining creature turned away from the frenzied mother. Dropping to its hands, it raised its legs and kicked the stone out of Ilfedo's hand. Then it stood and screeched birdlike at the trees.

Four other creatures glided from the branches and landed in the meadow behind Ilfedo. He regarded them wearily. He had lost a lot of blood from his wounded shoulder and he was growing weak.

The big woman stumbled into her cabin and closed the door. Now the only light that remained for him to see by emanated from the blue grass.

His vision wavered in and out of darkness and then he collapsed. Again the grass seemed to warm him. The creatures cackled, and one of them walked up to the cabin and leapt through a window. Glass rained around Ilfedo. The woman and her children screamed.

"I won't let this happen!" Ilfedo screamed and his left hand found the hilt of his sword. He struggled to draw his weapon. One of the creatures, a sort of man it seemed, held him back and yanked the sword from his grasp.

It screeched and smiled at its fellows. They cackled and pinned Ilfedo to the ground.

Raising the sword, the creature stabbed it at Ilfedo's heart. Living fire sprouted from the blade of its own accord. The hilt ripped itself out of the creature's hand, twisting as it did so to cut off a couple of fingers. The blade hovered in the air and angled at the creature, blazing with glorious light. Ilfedo felt a surge of impending victory.

The creature spread its wings and raced into

the trees. Just as the creature seemed to have escaped, the sword of the dragon speared through the air and pierced its back. Its light illuminated the scene in the midst of the dark trees. The living fire engulfed the creature from head to toe, burning the body to ashes that rained on the dry leaves of the forest floor and formed a heap.

The sword floated over the remains and stabbed itself into the midst of the ashes. A voice spoke from its blade. "As spoken by his holy prophet, I am living fire. From the hand of God I came and if ever used for evil I will, of my own accord, turn upon the wicked one."

The remaining winged men stumbled over each other as they fled into the forest.

Ilfedo could hear the woman inside of the cabin fighting for her life with the one who had crashed through the window. But he could not find the strength to move. "I am coming home to you, my love!" he cried to the starry sky.

"Not so soon, my friend," Ombre cried as he crashed out of the woods and stood over him. A contingent of soldiers swept from behind him and into the cabin.

The winged man stumbled out of the window, desperately seeking a retreat from the soldiers' revenge. A couple of his fellows swooped in and carried him into the darkness.

Ilfedo lost consciousness.

* * *

Ombre darted to the heap of ashes. It was all that remained of the winged man that had been burned by the sword. He wrapped his fingers around the cold blade of the sword of the dragon and carefully pulled it out of the dirt. He waited, half-expecting the frightening weapon to blaze anew. But it did not. He walked back to Ilfedo, knelt, and placed the sword in Ilfedo's hand. The Lord Warrior's wounds were beyond a quick fix. But Ombre had seen the sword destroy an enemy by its own power and of its own accord. Surely this mighty gift, if it truly came from a prophet of God, could help his friend.

Light radiated from the sword, and the blue grass in its immediate vicinity died. The arrow that protruded from Ilfedo's shoulder burst into flames and vanished. Blinding light sprouted from the blade in tendrils that latched onto the Lord Warrior's wounds.

Ombre stepped back and closed his eyes. "Dear God, let him live," he said. Footsteps scuffled beside him. He opened his eyes to find the woman of the cabin with her two children kneeling beside Ilfedo's prone form. His helmed men came out the cabin door, lowering their swords. More soldiers darted from the forest, all of them gazing upon the awesome sight as the sword continued to keep Ilfedo alive. They shook their heads in amazement, then fanned out to search the forest for the escapees. Some of the soldiers remained and faced the forest with drawn swords. They kept their wary eyes on the trees.

Ilfedo gagged as the sword inundated him with energy and Ombre glanced back at him. Fire burned dully on the blade as it lay on Ilfedo's chest. Beside Ombre the woman's frizzy, red-headed children had their heads bowed and their tiny hands, though bruised and bloody, they had folded in prayer.

Humbled by their display, Ombre fell to his knees as well. He poured his pleas to heaven, and when he opened his eyes the sword was sheathed at Ilfedo's side. Nothing remained of Ilfedo's near fatal encounter apart from his torn clothing. His chest heaved steady and strong.

Ombre stood and smiled down at the boy and the girl. They returned his gaze with weary curiosity. "The faith of the young is strongest of all, apparently," Ombre said as he helped the woman to her feet. "You need not worry about those winged creatures. They will not return. Five hundred men are encamped two miles north of here and another five hundred are combing the woodland. They will be found. In the meantime, I suggest you get these little treasures to bed. They well deserve it." He patted the woman's shoulder and summoned four of his men. "You will keep watch here tonight," he told them. "If the creatures return then send for me. Reinforcements will not be long in coming."

"My Lord Ombre." One of the men cleared his throat. "The main body of our forces are spread too thin to effectively cover the entire border—"

Ombre clapped him on the back. "Yes, but not for long. Lord Ilfedo already sent a courier requesting additional men. We are going to thoroughly sweep the forests for these creatures until we find them. Also, a fort will be established in the valley along the border. When we are done, this area will be as secure as any in the Hemmed Land."

Ganning limped out of the trees over to Ombre and shook his hand. "I heard what happened," he said. "How is he?" He glanced at Ilfedo.

"Fortunate to be alive," Ombre declared. "You'll not believe it, Ganning, but that marvelous sword of his actually cauterized his wounds."

Ganning grinned from ear to ear. "And I thought you were going to claim an angel came down and saved him. Was she a handsome brunette with long wavy hair and eyes the hue of summer clover?"

Ombre shook his head. Perhaps it was his own fault for being a jokester in his youth and allowing it carry over into adulthood. Why couldn't he always be sober like Ilfedo? People always took Ilfedo seriously and believed what he said. Perhaps, in time, people would take him as seriously. Ombre hoped so. There was a certain young lady whose affection he desperately hoped to win. She was always on his mind.

"Let's get him up and back to camp," Ganning said as he limped over to Ilfedo and shook him out of a deep slumber.

Ombre obliged, putting Caritha out of his mind to focus on the task at hand.

AMONG THE LORD WARRIOR'S TROOPS

Caritha turned her back to the fireplace's warmth and brushed back her hair, opening the door to Ilfedo's house. Cool, damp night air rushed in from outside. Ilfedo had been gone for weeks trying to find the mysterious enemy in the north. He had returned once, briefly, after he had nearly been killed by those winged creatures. She suspected from his description of them that they were Art'en, the same species she and her sisters had dealt with at the temple of Al'un Dai. Somewhere out there Ilfedo was fighting for his people. Selflessly seeking the good of others before his own. He was a worthy man to serve, and he had surrounded himself with others of notable character. Before she and her sisters had left Coral Haven, after the first five hundred men had assembled to fight for Ilfedo, she had seen messengers sent to every corner of the Hemmed Land. The people were behind their Lord Warrior's every command and they were going beyond his command, building for him an army far greater than he had asked for. Five hundred had turned into a thousand, and now many more were assembling inland. Ilfedo would soon have an army that would make any enemy hesitate.

"Don't leave that door open," Rozel said rather sharply.

Caritha glanced over her shoulder with a knowing smile.

Her tallest sister pulled a blanket around her body and lowered herself into the hammock. "You . . . you'll wake the baby," Rozel said as she glanced at the floor. Then she pointed at the crib on the hearth next to Evela.

"The baby is fine, Rozel. And haven't you used that excuse a couple times too many by now." Laura put a dish under the water pump, washed it, and handed it off to Levena. Leaning against the counter, Levena took the dish and dried it as she whistled a soft tune.

Evela was sitting on the hearth. A contented smile warmed her face as she peered into the short wooden crib. She sighed. "I don't think any baby could be more content or secure than this one feels right now, surrounded by all of us. Rain usually calls for gloominess, but look at her. She sleeps as if there is not a thing in all of Subterran for which she'd stir."

Rozel rolled her eyes. She often treated these sentimental moments as trivialities. But Caritha laughed, for Rozel's eyes hesitated upon seeing the head of the bear Ilfedo had killed, hung above the mantle. She harrumphed her disapproval and shook her head.

Caritha slipped outside and eased the door closed. She walked along the stone patio to the newly constructed outdoor fireplace. A scrap of flint lay on top of the fireplace. After throwing in a few scraps of dry wood, she sparked a flame that soon crackled warmly across the logs. An overhang made of skins and canvas kept the rainwater running away from the patio. Ilfedo had made a few modifications to the house before his departure to the Hemmed Land's boundary with the northern desert. Including bringing the bear's head back inside. According to him Dantress had removed it from the house and he had stowed it in the stable. He had been inclined to get rid of it permanently, but for now he was using it as a reminder. A reminder of the dangers that such creatures posed to his people.

For an hour or more the fire warmed her while she sat on a bench looking down the grassy clearing. A few bugs fought through the raindrops until the downpour lessened to a drizzle. A rabbit hopped out of the forest to nibble on the grass.

From the tallest tree in sight, Seivar glided to the patio and swooped under its roof, perching in front of the open fire. "Mistress, mind if I share the fire with you?" the bird asked.

"Of course not," Caritha said. "I will be happy for the company. My sisters have been a little distracted of late. The young princess has won their attention more often than I."

Seivar fluffed his feathers and raked his silver talons through them.

Caritha gazed around the rest of the clearing.

"Where is Hasselpatch? I have not seen her today."

Seivar blinked his silvery eyes at her. "Does Mistress desire me to find her?"

"No. No, that will not be necessary." She petted the bird's wet back and added, "I only wondered."

The rain continued to fall. The clouds thickened, then thinned and thickened again. The rabbit hopped back into the forest.

As Caritha and the nuvitor sat enjoying the warmth of the fire, a curious sound caught her ear. A distinct cough that could have belonged to a very small person. She glanced about the patio and there, on the lowest step, stood Miverē the fairy.

Seivar lunged toward him with beak open, but Caritha caught the bird's tail feathers. "No! This is a friend." She knelt and held out her hand to the fairy. She had not seen him for a long time. Not since she had last been in her father's palace in Emperia.

Miverē used his silver wand as a cane and teetered into her palm. "Hi," he managed. But his voice sounded hoarse.

"You poor thing," she offered. "Have you caught a cold?"

In answer the fairy sneezed and hoarsely replied, "Yes." He jabbed a slender finger at his throat. "I have laryngitis."

She hurried him inside where all the sisters could help. They decided first to get him warm by the fire and then to give him a bath. He didn't protest. Levena carried the hot water from the fireplace to the kitchen, and they filled a bowl for him.

He held on to Laura's pinky, and she lowered him toward the water. As soon as his miniature toes dipped in, he shot out as quick as an arrow from a taut bow. His little body turned red to match his hair. They added some cold water and convinced him to try again. This time the temperature suited him fine.

If allowed, he would have remained in the bath for a long while, but Caritha pulled him out and insisted he get good and dry. He wrapped himself in a dishcloth and tapped his head with his wand. Every hair hissed, steam rose until his head dried, and his tiny quill formed out of thin air and stuck itself behind his ear. Pulling it out he smoothed the feather with tender care, then tucked it in place atop his head.

That evening he said not a single word. He sat wrapped in the dishcloth on Evela's shoulder the whole time, coughing and gazing into the crib. Caritha could tell he wanted to say things, but his voice wouldn't allow it. So he stared and occasionally a silvery tear rolled down his cheek.

Clearly the fairy missed his beloved friend, Dantress. He missed her a very great deal. Caritha wondered if that was why he had come. To see the infant for whom Dantress had sacrificed her life.

"Is anyone hungry?" Rozel asked. She held her stomach and it growled. "I am. Very!"

Laura and Caritha prepared a soup. Dantress's former garden had yielded a generous variety of vegetables. They sliced potatoes, red onions, and mushrooms into the pot. Rozel muttered to herself as she walked to the back of the kitchen and opened the trap door to the root cellar. She vanished into the darkness and returned with a jar filled with a brown liquid. "Here." She handed it to Caritha and shuffled back to the fireplace.

Caritha poured the broth in and before long everyone was enjoying a bowl of steaming vegetable soup in front of the fireplace. For Miverē they filled a small measuring cup. He sipped the soup for a long while, still staring at the baby.

"It is good to be with you, daughters of the great dragon," he said at last.

"Your voice is back," Evela said as she smiled down at him.

He sniffled and coughed, but nodded his head.

The hour grew late. The sisters rose to go to their chambers, but Caritha remained by the fireplace as goodnights were said. "I'll put the baby to bed," she said as her sisters stepped out. She stood and watched the bedroom doors at the other end of the house close.

The fairy slipped out of the dishcloth and flitted onto the baby's stomach. "'Twas your fate to die, fairest of the dragon's daughters, and now I have come to give what gift I can to preserve your child," he said.

Caritha knelt beside the crib. "She really is beautiful, isn't she?"

"Yes, fair daughter of the dragon. But too young to play with me," he said.

Caritha studied his troubled face for a long moment. At last she spoke. "Miverē, why have you come?"

The fairy glanced up at her with his green eyes, as if concerned that she might send him back to Emperia.

"You would be welcome to stay here, but I

don't think Ilfedo should see you," Caritha said. "He doesn't need to know that fairies exist, too. Not now when he has so much weighing upon his spirit. And he'd want to know where you come from." She frowned. "Emperia must remain hidden from this world and unknown to its people. There is evil on the rise. I can feel it growing as the months pass. Something ancient is stirring malice in its heart. This place, this land, and this child's father are a beacon of hope."

Three tears rolled down the fairy's face. "Maybe I can give her little life a silvery lining, a gift from us fairy folk to honor the fairest of the dragon's daughters." Thus saying, he sniffed back a sob, drew his little wand, caught one of his silvery tears on its tip, and suspended it over Oganna's clenched baby fist. The tear fell from the wand and splattered against her skin.

Miverē opened the baby's hand and plucked a long red hair from his head. He used his wand for a needle, sowed the hair through her palm, and then did the same to her other hand. He hovered over Oganna's forehead and kissed it. A warm glow briefly passed from the fairy's lips over the baby's skin. The fairy's hairs in each of Oganna's small palms glowed for an instant beneath the skin, then faded.

Miverē stayed that night in Ilfedo's house. He slept in the upstairs bedroom with Caritha and Oganna while the nuvitors watched over them. Caritha lay in Ilfedo's bed, rocking the cradle next to it, and the fairy lay on the pillow. In the morning he left just as unexpectedly as he'd arrived. Caritha said nothing to her sisters of the fairy's strange gift to Oganna. She turned over the baby's hands and could see no sign of the red hairs sown beneath the skin.

She went about her morning as if nothing had happened. Breakfast was served, the baby fed. Later Honer's wife Eva arrived to care for Oganna. Her three children ran into the Warrioresses' arms, peppering them with kisses before darting into the house. Seivar made a discreet getaway out the kitchen window.

The sisters had dressed in their familiar purple garments. They tied white sashes around their waists and marched eastward through the forest. A couple of hours later they crested a hill and stood there, looking out over the land ahead of them. The trees here had been thinned, and a clearing half a mile wide and as great in length spread before them.

Caritha parted the fold in her skirt and drew her rusted sword from its sheath. Five hundred white tents had been pitched on the cleared ground and in the shelter of the bordering trees.

A horn sounded from the far side of the camp. The flaps of the arrayed tents flipped open and a thousand men marched forth. They filed into perfect lines and waited in disciplined silence as the Warrioresses descended the hill. Caritha could feel the anticipation rising in the men. Out of several thousand original volunteers to recently join the Lord Warrior's army these men had been selected for their aptitude to sword fighting and put under the Warrioresses' supervision.

A heavy-set man barreled out of the largest tent. A breeze caught the bearskin cape on his back, and it billowed behind him as he stomped up to meet

Caritha. With a quick bow and a smile, he chinked his sword against the chain mail covering his chest. "We are at your service, my lady!"

"Commander Veil, this armor of yours." She stared at the intricate chain mail adorning his chest. Never had she seen anything like it in the Hemmed Land. Back home in Emperia yes, but not in the Hemmed Land.

"A masterful piece, don't you think?" Commander Veil said as he again smote it with the pommel of his sword. "An enemy would need a spear to pierce that. I got it from this fellow down on the coast. He's a new arrival. Strange looking fellow with white hair. Calls himself Linsair the swordsmith. And the best part is I didn't have to pay him anything for it. He just made me promise a donation to the monk's parish."

Caritha did not answer him. It seemed a strange thing for a craftsman to give such a beautiful gift in exchange for a charitable donation to a parish. She knew of only one parish on the coast. She'd visited it a couple of times for prayer. The monk there was young but zealous. When first she'd met him, she had thought he could have passed for a jovial brother to Patient the shepherd. He was pious and wise despite his meager experience.

"I hope your donation was generous," Rozel commented as she stepped forward. She looked down at the man's mail. "It is a magnificent piece."

"Oh, I was generous. Always try to be. They do serve God after all!" Commander Veil laughed. "Enough about me, the men are eager to begin again. Yesterday's challenge is still ringing in their ears, I daresay."

He led them down the line of men to the arena at the center of the clearing. One by one the men came forward and mock-dueled with a Warrioress. By Veil's command the men left their swords sheathed and used wooden ones instead. The challenge was simple. Not a single blow could they land on the sisters. The Warrioresses evaded their attacks with the practiced ease of dancers and always touched their wooden blades lightly on some vital part of the warriors' bodies to end the duels.

This went on for several hours until Veil ordered the Warrioresses to stand aside and let him take a turn in the arena. He did not move with the swiftness or lightness of foot that the sisters had. Instead of avoiding thrusting wooden swords, he struck back with his own, laying wood against wood until he wore down his opponent. Several times he welcomed two men to combine in their efforts to defeat him. Eventually a couple of them succeeded.

Veil bowed to each of them and yielded the arena. The pair of victors now faced their fellow trainees by pairs. The afternoon wore on in this manner and the sweating swordsmen became an unpleasant aroma. Wooden swords met blow for blow as they honed their skills. They were the Elite Thousand and, when the Warrioresses declared them ready, these men would look for the approval of their Lord Warrior.

Caritha stepped back into the arena with her sisters. The men about them effected deep bows and then angled their swords defensively. The sisters darted into their midst, working as one unit. Their swords struck swifter than arrows against the fifty warriors assailing them.

One day soon, Caritha vowed, these men would be worthy of fighting alongside of Ilfedo. They would become the cornerstone upon which Ilfedo could build a capable army.

# Linsair's Silver Hammer

As the shadows under the trees lengthened and the sky paled, Ilfedo leaned against a tree. He wiped his sleeve across his sweaty forehead and undid the sling supporting his arm. The soreness of the wound was tolerable enough now to do without it. Laughter flowed from his home. The door slammed open and Honer's son ran outside and around the house, then reentered.

The sisters of his wife filed into the clearing. From their slow walk he knew they must be tired from a long day with the trainees.

"Ilfedo, is that you?" Evela stepped toward him and laid a hand on his arm. His skin tingled where she'd touched him, like it used to for Dantress, and he pulled back. "You are injured again," she whispered.

"No," he said. "It is the former injury from

the arrow. It feels sore and a little stiff. But I have been healed."

Rozel grunted. "You're fortunate that woman's arrow did not strike your heart. You could just as easily have been killed by leaving yourself so unprotected."

He looked into her eyes. "Ombre believes that it was a direct intervention by the Creator's hand. An answer to the prayers of little children spoken on my behalf that night at the northern cabin."

Caritha, Rozel, Laura, and Levena strolled back to the house. Evela delayed for a long moment. She glanced up at him and smiled softly. "Anything is possible, even an angel from heaven. I think Dantress would have taken Ombre at his word. Now come!" She guided him to the house. "You must be tired."

That evening his baby girl laughed in her crib, holding his pinky as he smiled down at her. The blackened wood in the fireplace crackled while the sisters sat around the hearth drinking tea. He ran his hand down the length of the sword of the dragon's scabbard which lay across his knees. Such a magnificent weapon.

"The swordsmen are becoming more skilled with each day under Commander Veil's training," Caritha said as she sipped from a cup of tea. Then she told him all that had happened in his absence.

"That is what I have been waiting to hear." He glanced into the crib. "Ah, Oganna is asleep." He pulled his pinky out of the baby's fist and drew the sword a few inches out of its scabbard. Flames coiled beneath the glassy surface of the blade. It seemed he could look through it at another world. A world of silver and blue, deep and vast.

Glancing up at the sisters he told them what had transpired in the north. They listened with rapt attention as he described his fight with the winged men and then of his defeat. "I recall losing consciousness and waking to find Ganning staring down at me." He chuckled. "Ombre won't let up about the incident. He has told everyone that God healed my wounds and used the sword to preserve my life. He makes it a fascinating tale."

He smiled. "Only God and Ombre know what really happened. I'm just fortunate to come back and see my child again." Ilfedo slid the sword back into the scabbard. "So," he said, "what are your thoughts on this incident? I know that you have seen some stranger things than I have."

The sisters' mouths gaped and their eyes widened.

He held up his hand. "You are all a mystery to me. I am still in the dark about many things. But from time to time my wife did mention things from her past. A few strange things that did not make sense to me. Now, if you know anything that might help in this strange situation I am asking you to share it."

Caritha glanced at her sisters, and they put their heads together in whispered conference. What things were they hiding from him, and why? Someday, perhaps, whatever prevented them from sharing everything with him would be removed. Finally, Rozel grunted and the sisters faced him.

"These creatures you spoke of." Caritha cleared her throat. "We have dealt with them before. They can be ruthless and vicious in an almost animal way. Our father told us that the winged men are called Art'en and the winged women are called It'ren."

Ilfedo frowned. "The white dragon told you this?"

"You must be very careful, brother. The Art'en have been known to ally themselves with the vilest of men, especially powerful sorcerers." Laura folded her hands. "It seems that as long as their master is strong, they flock to him and do his bidding."

"Do you know of any tactics that might prove useful against them?" Ilfedo asked.

The sisters shook their heads. Their dark eyes bored into his as Caritha spoke for them. "Only a warrior with superior hand-to-hand combat training would be a match. Go for the wings before using that." She pointed at his sword.

What memories or knowledge she had drawn upon for this information, Ilfedo could not even guess. Nor did he ask her to explain. The sisters guarded their past with a veil of mystery impossibly thick. Perhaps someday he would discover their mysteries. But not tonight.

He thanked them for their insight and picked up the crib with Oganna nestled inside. It was just a little crib, small enough to set comfortably on the hearth stones.

Caritha grasped his shoulder. "One more thing, Ilfedo."

"Yes, Commander Veil has a new piece of armor," Laura said.

"Yeah," Rozel interrupted. "Some stranger is working as a swordsmith on the coast and asking nothing in return for his labor. Well, almost nothing.

His customers have to make a donation to the local parish."

Caritha set down her tea. "I think it warrants investigating. At the very least, his work is unparalleled in the Hemmed Land. If you take my advice, you will employ his services to equip your men."

Ilfedo lowered his voice and pulled the crib closer to his face. "What sort of armor are we talking about?"

"Chain mail. Very finely constructed chain mail. I haven't seen armor like that in a long while," she replied.

Laura sipped at her tea. "We could use a skilled craftsman to equip the Elite Thousand."

Caritha nodded solemnly and said, "He is associated with a monk on the coast. In Coral Haven, if Commander Veil's information is still accurate. If you want to find him, find the monk known as Brother Hersis."

"I'll look into it the day after tomorrow. For now, I need a little rest." He wished them goodnight and climbed the stairs to his bedroom.

Gently he rested the cradle on the floor. Seivar and Hasselpatch flitted onto the bed and nuzzled him with their silvery beaks. He kissed Hasselpatch on her soft head and stroked Seivar's chest. The nuvitors cooed in response.

Undressing, he opened the roof panels and laid in his bed. Home again! He hated popping in and out as he had been doing for the past few months, but things needed his supervision and he felt that his daughter's future depended on his actions. He watched the stars twinkle for a long while, then closed his eyes and heaved a deep breath. The nuvi-tors nestled under his arms and cooed him to sleep.

* * *

The coastal town that Ilfedo had first saved from the sea serpents welcomed him a few days later. He met with the mayor of Coral Haven but when the opportunity presented itself, he discretely slipped into a black hooded cape and wandered through the town. No one recognized him.

He asked directions of a hulking fisherman at the market who reeked of the sea, and he questioned several farmers who were carting heaps of corn through the town gates. But none could help him. Finally an elderly woman with a red shawl wrapped around her face stepped up with a grin that encom-passed her entire face, and pointed him in the right direction.

Ilfedo followed a narrow cobbled street to a fishing equipment shop. Beside it stood a log chapel. The humblest structure that he had seen in the entire town. There was a blacksmith's shop on the other side of the chapel, but someone had built a white post fence around the chapel, separating its grounds from nearby structures. He entered via a gate that stood as high as his waist and followed a narrow dirt path to the chapel's double doors.

Inside the chapel he entered a long room with benches flanking a narrow aisle up to a wooden altar. The floor and the benches had been painted white. The walls and doors remained brown except for the back wall that had also been accented in white. A round window of green and blue stained glass had been inserted near the top of the white wall.

What really caught Ilfedo's eye were the paintings. Colorful canvases hung from the high walls. Four on the left and four on the right. He stepped closer to the nearest one and studied the image of a dark-skinned woman in prayer, her eyes closed, a lifeless baby in her arms, and a tear rolling down her cheek. Above her, a white-robed man placed a baby full of life into an enormous hand that reached out of a cloud.

"This is of a bereaved mother who lost her young child," a gentle manly voice said from behind him.

Without turning to see who was speaking to him, Ilfedo gazed at the enormous hand in the picture. Was it the hand of Creator God?

"The innocent child is given into the hand of its Maker while the mother grieves for her loss," the man said, as if reading his thoughts. "All the woman can see is her dead child. God sees another life delivered into His hand."

"Are you Brother Hersis?" Ilfedo turned to study the white-robed monk.

The man nodded back up at him. His beady eyes flicked to the next painting. Yimshi's rays poured through the colored window panes, playing on his shoulder-length black hair. His shoulders spread too broad for his height, and his fingers engulfed Ilfedo's as they shook hands. "Blessings be given to you on this glorious morning, stranger. I am Brother Hersis. God is my witness, savior, and judge. Can you say the same?"

Ilfedo laughed. "Yes, I believe I can." He wrenched his hand from the shorter man's iron grip and turned back to the paintings. "Whose work is this?"

"Does the artist deserve the credit for the work he does? Or is the praise due to the Artist who designed the artist and who gave him the inspiration to paint?" Brother Hersis asked.

"I'll take that to mean that you painted them," Ilfedo said as he strode to the next image. In this one an elderly couple smiled down at a man lying on his bed. In the background the Grim Reaper stood inside the doorway, but a man robed in white held the Reaper back.

Ilfedo cocked an eyebrow and continued to walk along the gallery. "What do these pictures portray?"

The monk followed him and waved his hand at each painting before explaining each of his pieces. "Sometimes God takes away, as you saw in the first painting. But in this one he sends his angel and restores the sick man to his father and mother."

Ilfedo walked to the next one. Here a man in rich, frilly clothing stood in the midst of a street. Beggars reached out to him while he clung to his bag of gold. Lacerations scored the man's back and behind him stood a fierce angel with a whip in its hand.

"Pity that soul," Brother Hersis said. "God gave him much, and he hoarded it. Now his end will be bitter. The scourge of the Lord will follow him to death and beyond."

"I don't need you to explain this next one," Ilfedo said as he looked at the fourth painting. A man dressed in rags knelt on a cobblestone street to wrap a starving child in his only coat. He offered a slice of bread in his other. A great tear fell from an empty sky with an angel inside of it. "This is the man with whom God is pleased."

"Indeed." Brother Hersis smiled and led him across the room. "These other paintings are not lessons, just reminders of what we who follow God should become."

Brother Hersis had painted a soldier on the field of battle, standing over his wounded king. Lightning zipped from black clouds overhead. A path of escape lay through the enemy, but he stood over the king, sword drawn, while blood ran down his armor.

The next painting depicted a woman washing the feet of her weary husband. Another showed a family on a woodland picnic. In the last painting, a beautiful young woman knelt in prayer, a serene smile on her face.

Putting an arm around Ilfedo's shoulders, the monk led him into an adjacent room. "Allow me to show you the painting I am currently working on." His white habit swept the floor as he moved an easel, rotating it toward Ilfedo. Two children knelt in prayer beside a fallen warrior while a glowing angel holding a partially-painted sword rose over him. "I have still to finish the sword. And, as you can see, I have not painted in the mother, yet."

After gazing upon the painting for a long, quiet moment, Ilfedo walked with the monk out of the room and into the parish. Ilfedo lowered his hood and draped the black cloak over a chair.

"Ah, so it is you! Word of God's intervention on your behalf spread quickly over these last days." Brother Hersis folded his hands and grinned. "We must offer praise to Him for your escape from death, my lord. Such an event has not happened in our recorded history. It will be remembered, embodied in the painting for everyone to consider."

Ilfedo raised his hand. "Just don't raise me on a pedestal in the eyes of your parishioners. Be very careful that does not happen. Understood?"

The monk bowed. "Of course. Now, if it please you, tell me why you have come. I did not expect the Lord of the Hemmed Land to ever visit my humble parish."

"I need you to introduce me to someone who, as I understand it, you met recently." Ilfedo crossed his arms and gazed at the man. "I'm looking for the swordsmith, Linsair."

"Ah! Linsair. Well, I cannot say as that surprises me. It has been an honor to host that stranger. But his skills qualify him for many other things." Brother Hersis heaved a sigh. "In times like these our nation needs men like him. Men who will proclaim truth unabashedly and without fear, even with boldness, and men working diligently with their hands in the cause of the innocent." The monk led him outside and around the back where a few shacks lined a vibrant green lawn. Monks walked to and fro between the cottages, tending small gardens and gathering carrots, lettuce, and potatoes from the ground.

One man loomed out of the monks' midst, hulking over them. He left a basket of carrots in the garden and met them.

"This is the swordsmith you inquired of," Brother Hersis said.

Ilfedo looked up at the man and marveled

at the broadness of his shoulders and the thickness of his arms. His legs were hidden beneath the white habit of a monk.

"It is an honor to welcome you to my humble abode, Lord Warrior," Linsair said. He bowed and his white hair fell around his face. He straightened, unsmiling. "I assume that you have seen my handiwork and wish to enlist my aid in forging swords and more armor."

"Yes," Ilfedo admitted. He craned his neck to look deep into the man's pink eyes. It felt strange to gaze up instead of at eye level or below. He couldn't help but feel a bit threatened by the man's size and strength. Yet there was something in Linsair's eyes that conveyed honesty. Something about this man struck him as familiar.

Linsair rolled his shoulders and took off his monk's habit. His every muscle stood out hard and strong. "I am a valuable addition to your forces, yet I sense that you desire to know more about me. My place of origin, perhaps?"

Ilfedo wanted to ask. He wanted to know. "You came from the Sea of Serpents," he stated instead.

"That is correct," Linsair said quietly. "I washed ashore and made my home among your people."

"Can you tell me anything about the strange coinciding of your arrival with that of the star that reportedly crashed into the sea just prior to your appearance on my shores?" Ilfedo studied the man for any wavering of eyes or body that would indicate deception.

Linsair's eyes flared. "No. I cannot."

Ilfedo narrowed his eyes. "Are you willing to tell me how you came here?"

"Know this, Lord Ilfedo." Linsair rolled his shoulders again, and every muscle rippled. "I came not to harm thee or thy people. My service I now offer, my skills are at your disposal. If you fear or distrust me, then accept not my offer. However, if your heart tells you that I am to be trusted, accept me as a blessing from the hand of the Creator."

Ilfedo did trust Linsair. He wondered if he shouldn't, but he felt a kinship with the man's soul. A purity unparalleled by any he knew. Linsair would reveal nothing, apparently, but at least he was honest about that. Sometimes he struggled to understand his wife's sisters as much. They spoke in riddles but tried to pretend that they were being as honest as they could be. At least Linsair did not feign openness about things that he did not wish to share. Ilfedo smiled grimly and shook the man's hand, cringing in the other's powerful grip. There was a sober honesty in his new ally's face.

"Brother Hersis, my thanks for your gracious hospitality," Linsair said as he embraced the monk. "God will bless thee for all you are doing. Keep the faith."

"Farewell for now, Linsair." Brother Hersis slapped him on the chest. "When you return this way, pay me a visit."

Linsair heaved a sigh. "I'm afraid such will never be, my friend. But I wish you well." Then he fetched his tools from one of the shacks and followed Ilfedo into the street.

They made their way out of town. On every hand the people of Coral Haven whispered as Linsair passed them by, but they kept out of his path. The two men reached the forest and journeyed on until they came to Commander Veil's encampment further inland.

At their hail, Veil barreled out of his tent, the noon sun glistening off his chain mail like millions of diamonds. "Form up!" he ordered, and the men marched into parallel lines straight as two arrows.

With a deep bow Commander Veil greeted Ilfedo and then grinned up at Linsair.

"Commander," Ilfedo said. "Give this man whatever he requires."

Linsair ignored Commander Veil and strode down the long lines of men. Every twenty feet he paused to stare into the soldiers' faces. The men held formation with rigid formality. The swordsmith returned to Ilfedo, and his huge chest heaved as he drew in a mighty breath. "The construction of their weapons is inadequate."

"Inadequate how?" Ilfedo asked.

Linsair rumbled in his throat and, turning to one of the men, commanded, "Hand me thy blade!"

The soldier glanced at Ilfedo and rested his hand on the pommel of his sheathed weapon.

"What are you waiting for, soldier?" Ilfedo pointed at the man's weapon. "I brought this man here for a reason. Weapons are his specialty, so do as he asks."

The man drew his sword with grace and speed. He laid it in Linsair's hands and stood at attention.

Facing Ilfedo, Linsair grasped the weapon

by its handle and poised it above his head, its blade aimed at the sky. "Draw thy weapon, Lord of the Hemmed Land," said the swordsmith.

Commander Veil's eyes widened and he frowned. He stood in Linsair's path, his hand clawing at the pommel of his own sword.

The swordsmith's shoulders relaxed. "I do not intend harm. But this weapon's blade must be tested against the best before it is committed to battle. And your blade is the best."

Ilfedo drew the sword of the dragon and widened his stance as flames covered his body. He laid a hand on Veil's shoulder, and the man looked back at him. "Step aside commander," Ilfedo said.

Veil nodded, still wearing a frown, and stepped out of his path.

The albino man came at Ilfedo like a bear, and their swords clashed with such force that sparks flew. Ilfedo grasped his sword with both hands. The impact of Linsair's attack left his hands stinging. Nevertheless he advanced. As the larger, more powerful man attacked, Ilfedo grimaced.

Linsair's blade struck with great force, but the metal cracked and the blade broke in two.

Sheathing the sword of the dragon, Ilfedo shook his head. The swordsmith had made his point. The soldier's blade now lay in the dust divided in halves.

Commander Veil stared aghast. "Oh my."

Ilfedo looked up at Linsair. Those pink eyes stared back. "Do what you must," Ilfedo said. "I will see to it that you are well-paid for your work."

"Payment." The man growled. "Did I ask you

for that? My services are free. I do not want payment. Simply require your men to follow my instructions so that I may prepare them for the battles to come."

"So be it." Ilfedo summoned two men and placed them at the swordsmith's disposal. Linsair led them to one of the tents and ordered them to pull it down.

Then he spun about and returned to Ilfedo. His hand clawed toward the sword of the dragon, and he drew it from the sheath.

"Step back! How dare you draw the Lord Warrior's blade without permission," Veil cried as he drew his own sword. He charged the large man, and swung for Linsair's sword arm.

Living fire sprang from the sword of the dragon, enveloping Linsair instantly, and armor grew over his body like dragon scales. Yet the flames did not subside as they had on Ilfedo. They burned on.

Commander Veil slashed with his blade but Linsair turned so that Veil's blade glanced harmlessly off of his scale-armor. Veil struck again, but Linsair parried with the sword of the dragon. The man's pink eyes flared as the blade of Ilfedo's sword pulsed white light. Its flaming blade made contact with Veil's sword and cut effortlessly through it.

Veil stepped back as the shard of his sword clattered to the ground. He stared at the sword's handle, with the jagged remains of the blade stabbing out of its hilt. He shook his head as he gazed upon it. "Well, I guess I can't use this one anymore." He picked up the severed shard, turning it in his hand.

The armor vanished from Linsair's body, and he held the flaming sword before his face.

Ilfedo held up a hand, staying Veil with a sober glance. The squat man dropped the hilt of his broken weapon, and his hands hung limp at his sides.

Linsair stared unblinkingly at the sword of the dragon and nodded, as if thinking aloud. "Only dragon blood could create weapons suitable for the battles your men will face, Lord Ilfedo. A thousand swords I will make for thy men. A thousand blades strong enough to defend the helpless in a manner similar to this blade of yours."

"Dragon blood?" Ilfedo frowned as a chill breeze struck his back. "What do you know about dragon blood?" He remembered Dantress and the passion with which she had loved and the joy she had been in his life. He remembered also that her veins had flowed, not with human blood, but that of her dragon father. Her life was in her blood, and she had given it to their daughter.

"It is ancient knowledge that the life of a dragon can be, quite literally, in their blood." Linsair lowered his voice, drew near, and thrust the sword of the dragon back into Ilfedo's sheath. "If a dragon sacrificed a drop of blood—sacrificed willingly and knowingly—one drop for me to blend with each sword I forge for these, thy men, then I would create beautiful weapons of light. They would be superior to other blades, though not as magnificent as your own."

Ilfedo gazed beyond the man to the trainees. Many of them were younger men. Too young to die on the field of battle. But what battle? The Hemmed Land was at war with no one. Well, there were the sea serpents, and the Art'en creatures attacking the northern boundary. But were they a nuisance, or an indicator of a broader struggle to come? And what of the wizard? He must be found. He must be dealt with.

"Darkness always comes before the dawn, thou Lord of the Hemmed Land," Linsair said. "Do not permit it to linger through your inaction."

"You speak as a prophet would, swordsmith," Ilfedo replied.

"If you hear wisdom then pay heed to me. If I speak falsely, then reject my counsel. But dark days do lie ahead. Of this I feel sure." Linsair stepped back and his eyes shifted to look past him. "Ah, so these are the famed Warrioresses of whom the people speak so highly."

Ilfedo turned to find the sisters in a half-circle behind him. They stared at Linsair without speaking. "My sisters," Ilfedo said. "This is the swordsmith, Linsair." Still, the sisters said nothing.

"Commander Veil." Ilfedo waved his hand at the waiting soldiers. "They are dismissed for today."

The commander bowed and walked between the rows of warriors, sending them to various tasks. Most of the men trooped to the makeshift arenas, challenging one another to improve their swordsmanship.

"Forgive us, Linsair." Caritha curtsied and swept her hand toward her sisters. "You remind us of someone."

Linsair bowed. "Then I hope that someone is a person you respected and loved."

"He was," Caritha said. She introduced each of her sisters by name and then greeted Ilfedo. "You are heading back north, aren't you?"

"Yes. There is more to those attacks and I intend to hunt down the perpetrators." He turned to Linsair and shook the man's massive hand.

Linsair made a slight bow.

Ilfedo nodded back. "When you have outfitted all of these men, you will have my thanks and that of your adoptive homeland."

"And that will be enough for me," Linsair said. He stepped back as Commander Veil walked up to him, tilting his head to look at his face.

The shorter man cleared his throat as if to gather his wits upon facing so imposing a man. Ilfedo smiled to himself at that. Veil was a man to be trusted, and in this situation his frank manner would prove an asset. From Linsair's interactions so far, Ilfedo judged that he would appreciate an honest man.

Evela rushed forward and planted a kiss on Ilfedo's cheek. Stunned, he looked down at her and held her away from him. He could see embarrassment in the other sisters' eyes, yet none said a word. Tears welled in Evela's eyes. She sniffed and said, "Don't stay away too long, my lord. Remember that you have a child to raise."

Ilfedo left as quickly as possible. He stopped on the brow of a hill and glanced back at the encampment. Inside of an open tent Linsair set down his anvil and shouted for someone to help him build a forge. A dozen men answered his call. In the arenas, the sisters raised their swords and commenced combat with the warriors. He turned to the forest and set off to the north. Now to deal with the Art'en that were haunting the Hemmed Land's border. He found himself confused by Evela's affection. Not resentful, to be sure. A kind woman's affection was not something to rebuff. But he was confused. And so he set his mind and committed his sword to the north.

SWORDS OF LIGHT

Ombre ignored the sweat that was dripping down his face and gripped his sword with a vengeance. Moonlight filtered through the trees in front of him onto the winged man who was thrashing on the ground. "Why did you come here?" Ombre shouted.

The creature shrieked and rolled in the leaves.

Ombre stepped closer. "Tell me what I want to know and I will spare your life."

A laugh erupted from the creature, a laugh that turned into a cackle. It stumbled to its feet and grabbed at him.

Ombre poised his sword toward its chest, preparing to strike the fatal blow. Suddenly the forest erupted around him. Three more creatures springing out of the shadows with unsettling screeches. Two more dropped out of the trees above him. They landed on him and he rolled to the ground, forced down by their weight but keeping his balance. He backrolled, came up on his knees, and thrust out his sword, cutting one creature's boney face. The being screamed with unadulterated hatred and rushed upon him with a spinning kick that forced him to roll to the side.

Ombre took a deep breath and called into the night. "I need reinforcement!" The Art'en assailed him with blinding speed, but he had grown more proficient with a sword. They fought like beasts, yet without weapons. Their kicks bruised his side, and their fists opened bleeding splits on his face and arms. But he inflicted an equal number of wounds on them.

Mere moments passed, and where the moonbeams cut through the forest and painted the ground, a line of shadows emerged from the trees. They approached in silence, catching the Art'en by complete surprise. A few men leveled spears and ran the creatures through, while other warriors jumped forward with brandished swords.

Ombre whooped and grimly set about taking advantage of his men's arrival. As a few of the Art'en succumbed to death's spasms, more screeches sounded in the night. Art'en wings spread across the moon and fresh members of their species dove upon the scene. They fought like animals, quickly dropping Ombre's men to the forest floor.

"No!" Ombre grunted as several creatures beset upon him, driving him to his knees with a kick in his side. "Oh you had better get back from me," he screamed at them. "You don't realize the enemy you are making here! Those men you killed were friends of mine and friends of my friends." They swung their fists at him, the lot of them closing a circle around him, and he impaled another of them on his sword.

As he drew the blade from his opponent, a whinny rang through the trees, and a white stallion burst into the fight. Its silvery mane flew behind it as it reared and kicked one of the creatures in the head. It landed on its forefeet and kicked its hind hooves into another's chest, crashing the Art'en against a tree. Silver flecks flew off its hooves. It moved with the speed of lightning.

"My champion." Ombre rose as the animal rampaged through the winged men. It wheeled close to him, and he swung his leg over its back. The white, silver-maned stallion raced him to a hill and dumped him. Ombre sat on the ground, breathing in the free air. The stallion pranced around him, flaring its nostrils in the direction it had come. Its silvery-blue eyes watched the shadows. Then it reared, thrashing its silver hooves at the moon and screamed with such rage that the sound echoed in the forest.

"Whoa there, boy. Take it easy. They aren't even close to us anymore." Ombre stood and sheathed his sword. He approached and stroked the wild animal's moist neck. "You were magnificent! This is why we call your species Evenshadow. After the glorious twilight hours." He chuckled. "Perhaps it is not only us humans that are fed up with these creepy attackers in our land, huh?"

The stallion blew its nostrils, and suddenly Ombre knew that they were not alone. He glanced over his shoulder and three white mares crested the hill, whinnying to the stallion. The moonbeams reflected off of their silvery manes, tails, hooves, and eyes. The grass glowed blue around their feet.

Ombre walked to the mares and stretched out his hands. "You are all Evenshadows." They nuzzled him as if he were an old friend. He stroked their velvety muzzles and glanced at the forest from which he'd come.

A winged man sprinted from the shadows at the base of the hill. Ombre slipped his hand to the hilt of his sword. The villain dropped to all fours and raced up the hill.

But then the forest erupted with blinding white light and a torrent of flames ripped through the trees behind the winged man. The Evenshadow stallion wheeled and fled into the forest with the mares racing after him, silver flakes glowed on the ground in their wake.

On the other side of the hill Ombre watched half-a-dozen winged men fly from the trees. The moonlight revealed their startled faces. They screeched and their companion on the hill sprang into the air after them.

* * *

The sword of the dragon blazed in Ilfedo's hands. His body shone in the darkness with blinding brilliance. He saw the Art'en creature on the hill. It had been running toward Ombre but had turned to flee. Ilfedo ran forward and pointed the blade at the winged man. Flames leapt from the blade, wove through the air, and engulfed the creature. It screamed and crashed into the trees as it burned alive.

The others had flown beyond the sword's

reach, but Ilfedo cupped his hands around his mouth and yelled into the forest, "Archers!" Arrows broke through the trees. They soared like an avenging rain into the fleeing creatures' midst. The Art'en floundered, and the arrows peppered them until they too fell.

Ilfedo climbed the hill and sheathed his sword. The living fire pulled away from his body, the armor vanished, and the flames withdrew into the magnificent blade. He grasped Ombre's arm and pulled him to his feet. "Are you hurt, my brother?"

Ombre shook his head. "Thank God you came now. They slew the other men who stood with me." He pointed at the sheathed sword at Ilfedo's side. "Every time I think you've proven the limits of that weapon, I am overcome with amazement and humbled."

"It is the power in the sword. I cannot call it my own strength. The Creator has given me a great gift." Ilfedo grasped the sword's handle for an instant and the living fire sprang forth. He released it and the flames subsided. "But it is a magnificent weapon, to be sure."

Together they returned to the valley by the desert, and the men celebrated the victory around roaring fires. But Ilfedo summoned a dozen of his choice men and rolled out a map. "My lords and captains," he said, standing before them. "Consider the future of our land as laid out on this skin. In ten years' time the Hemmed Land will become an effective nation with an organized military and an established government."

He waved his hand over the map. Laid out

for all to see were the three known borders of the Hemmed Land. "To the south of our land is an uncharted desert, to the east lies the Sea of Serpents, and here in the north the way is again cut off by desert. To the west is the Western Wood and beyond that we know not what. Our recent clash with this race of winged men, called the Art'en, has made us all realize how vulnerable we are to the unknown territories beyond our borders. Therefore we will secure the exposed northern, southern and eastern borders with three forts. And within the Hemmed Land we will establish walled towns." He tapped his finger on the map. "Here, in this valley, the first fort must be built."

That night he deliberated with his captains and reveled in their enthusiasm. The land would be secured and their wives and children would sleep soundly knowing that a wall of soldiers watched over them. Ilfedo wondered briefly what progress his new recruit, the swordsmith Linsair, was making in his absence.

* * *

"Peace! All I require is a place to work in peace!" Linsair loomed before Caritha while her sisters fidgeted behind her in the tent's shade.

The crowd of soldiers milling around outside the tent grew as the swordsmith struck his hammer against the anvil. Linsair spun and threw the hammer into a heap of unfinished swords at the tent's rear. The neatly stacked blades clattered to the bare damp ground and the smith faced Caritha again.

"I cannot work under these conditions. Too many people are watching, and my forge is open to the elements. I would that this task was completed.

Already a cycle of the moon has passed and not half of the swords I promised Ilfedo are forged. Therefore I have something to show thee." He crouched near the swords, fished out his hammer, and stuck it in his belt before rising. With long strides he led her out of the tent and into the forest in the general direction of Ilfedo's property. The rest of her sisters fell in line behind her, as did a few of the Elite. Linsair roared at them, "This business is between the Warrioresses and I. Do not follow us!" Stiffly bowing, the men returned to camp, some of them exchanging amused smiles.

It was a long hike up trails and through the forests before Linsair halted them at a stony place. Here there were broad trees that had grown between numerous boulders that had been strewn over a small hill in the forest.

Rozel leaned against a tree and crossed her arms. "We followed, swordsmith. Now, pray tell us what in Subterran you've brought us here for."

"We are near Matthaliah Hollow," Evela said as she pointed to the northwest. "Ilfedo's parents died not far from here when he was a younger man. I wonder how well the cabin is holding up. I think he's not been out here for a long time."

Linsair used his foot to clear fallen branches off a stone. Then he bent over the boulder and dug his arms around it, rolling it out of the ground. In the boulder's place a hole no more than two feet across stabbed deep into the earth. An iron grating spanned its mouth, alleviating Caritha's fears that a person or animal might break their leg falling inside.

"Follow me." The swordsmith barreled downhill through thick bushes. Caritha and her sisters swept after him until he paused by another boulder and stepped behind it, out of sight.

Caritha stepped over a dead branch. Her skirt caught, and she knelt to free it.

"Caritha," Laura whispered as she crouched next to her. "He reminds me of Father."

"You mean Linsair?" Caritha asked.

Laura nodded vigorously.

"Yes," Caritha admitted. She freed her skirt and stood, placing a hand on her sister's arm with a smile. "But Father is a good deal larger than any man."

Everyone laughed except for Rozel. She rolled her eyes and trudged around the boulder.

Caritha followed to the mouth of a deep cave. Large torches lined the long tunnel that descended under the hill. Their flames spread a warm orange glow down the passageway, and at their end stood Linsair with a blazing torch held in his fist.

Rozel trudged forward, neither glancing to the right nor to the left. She stood next to the sword-smith, unsmiling.

"What delayed you?" the man demanded of the lagging sisters.

Caritha gazed around the cave's interior. It was a circular chamber of considerable size. The walls were of solid stone and arched behind the swordsmith to an orifice at its center some fifteen feet above her head. Directly beneath it on the floor stood an enormous forge on tri-sided legs of hammered iron. "Linsair, what is this place?" she asked.

The smith strode to the forge and ignited its

wood with his torch. The flames ripped through the dry bark, chasing the shadows farther from the smith. Next to the forge sat an anvil much larger than the one Linsair kept in Commander Veil's camp.

"My work will continue in secret," Linsair said. "Here, away from the noise and disturbance, I will create weapons for your lord's army." He set his silver hammer on the anvil. "The people of this land will know misery before they know a time of peace. I would that their passage through that misery be eased."

Laura frowned. "We don't understand. Is there something you need us to do?"

"I can fashion swords that are lightweight and strong, Warrioresses. Yet, if I had one—" He held up his index finger. "If I had only one drop of your dragon blood to use with each sword, I could create weapons that would array their bearers in light. On the field of battle, when darkness falls, the bearers of those swords would shine like stars on Subterran." His pink eyes flared as if with fire. He pulled a sword out of a dark corner and buried its blade in the forge. When he withdrew it, the blade glowed white-hot. "Give me only one drop. Sacrifice it willingly for the soldier who will one day wield it."

Evela narrowed her eyes. "How does he know these things?" she hissed to Caritha.

"Yes. How does a swordsmith know that we are of dragon blood?" Caritha drew her sword and Laura did the same. "Speak, Linsair. We want to know the truth."

He regarded them with steady eyes. "Put down your weapons."

Evela drew her rusted blade. "Answer my sister's question."

"So be it." Linsair heaved a sigh and shook his head. "As you may have guessed by now, I am also of dragon blood. Remember how Lord Ilfedo's sword responded to my touch. Unlike you, I know both the limits and the extent of my abilities. Therefore the sword of the dragon will not ignite if one of you were to use it."

"Ah," Evela said. "You are mistaken. Lord Ilfedo is not of dragon blood."

Caritha smiled. Surely the swordsmith had cornered himself.

But the man laughed. He laughed long and loud with amusement. "Thou art so innocent of that weapon's true nature," he said. "It is a weapon of Living Fire, not of dragon blood. The difference is vast, yet you cannot begin to understand. I could not explain it to you and if I tried, I would likely fail. For the time being it must be enough that I do understand, that the sword of Ilfedo covered me in living fire, and that I have the knowledge to use your gift for the good of mankind."

He frowned and swung the white-hot blade to point at them. "Do you believe I am a deceiver? Or have you any cause to think that I mean harm to the people of this land? And what of my faith in your cause? Do you find it in your hearts to raise obstacles for me while I seek your benefit?"

The sisters regarded him in silence. One by one they lowered their blades.

"Surely thou hast seen purity in my heart. Otherwise I would not still be standing," Linsair said as he relaxed his frown. "Trust me, dragon daughters, I intend only good for everyone that you care about."

Caritha sheathed her sword and nodded for the others to follow her lead. "Forgive us, Linsair. It is only . . . that we have lost so much, and we have grown cautious."

"You are deceiving thyself, Warrioress. It is not caution which compels you." The smith lowered the sword, resting it on the anvil. "It is fear," he said as he glanced from one face to the next. "Now, who will sacrifice a drop to empower this weapon?"

For a long while no one answered his request. Then Rozel stepped forward, drew a dagger from her belt, and pricked her finger. A single crimson drop splashed onto the sword. The metal strummed as if it were the bass string on a harp. The blade glowed pure white, and Linsair beat it with his silver hammer. Sparks flew in every direction, and he smiled down at Rozel. Flipping the blade on his anvil, he beat it with such rapid strokes that Caritha could not distinguish one strike from another.

Linsair plunged the sword into a water barrel. The water sizzled, steam rose in billowing clouds. Linsair held forth the sword, and it radiated with white light. "Now you can see that my promise is true," he said as he smiled again.

Caritha took a step forward. "Very well, Linsair, your point is well made." She swallowed and glanced at her remaining sisters. "We will contribute a thousand drops of blood to be used in the creation of swords of light for the Elite warriors among Ilfedo's army."

He nodded and resumed his work on the anvil. She glanced at the floor and walked up to him, putting her mouth close to his ear. His arm froze in place as he leaned down and listened. He said nothing as she whispered in his ear. "Later I have a favor to ask of you, swordsmith."

GRANDDAUGHTER OF THE DRAGON

In the heat of the afternoon sun two dozen men strained at the ropes, raising the final wall in Fort North. The high, log wall had been built on the ground and then the ropes had been attached via pullies. Slowly the wall rose into position between the even taller guard houses that had been positioned at intervals around the fort. The guard houses had taken the most labor, requiring stone masons in addition to carpenters, but it had been worth it. The time invested was producing a site of strength from which the Hemmed Land's northern border could be guarded by a small garrison.

Ombre, Honer, and Ganning mingled with the laborers as the wall stood in place. One man slipped in the dirt and fell, letting loose his rope. The wall leaned toward him, threatening to fall.

"Ah no, it doesn't!" Ganning called as he

limped up and grabbed the loose rope. He threw his weight into the task and growled up at the teetering wall. "Stay where you are."

The wall groaned and Ganning slipped, but Ombre and Honer ran up, whipping off their shirts. They grabbed onto his rope and hauled on it. Finally the wall stood in place and Ombre nodded through his gritted teeth to the carpenters up on the guard towers to both sides of him. They acknowledged him by raising their mallets and hammering large pegs through the wall and into the towers.

Fifty paces back from the scene, Ilfedo stood with a contingent of his officers watching the construction. At last this project was about to be finished! He had waited six years for this day. Six years! He exhaled with relief, but apparently he had allowed himself to relax too soon, for the wall groaned and started to fall back toward the ground and the men.

Ilfedo glanced over his shoulder at his officers. "Get over there and lend them a hand," he said.

"Aye, my lord." The officers stripped off their shirts and weapons and ran to the tilting wall. Soon the barrier stood straight and firm. The carpenters pegged and nailed it as needed and then gave the signal for the ropes to be released. As the wall stood on its own between the guard towers five hundred men cheered, clapped each other on the back, and marched onto the parade grounds in Fort North.

Ilfedo's officers slipped out of the crowd, donned their shirts, and belted their swords to their sides. They lined up behind him, and he led them between the ranks of smiling faces to the fort's central structure. It was a sizeable building made of thick logs with rooms for officers and common soldiers alike. A short flight of stairs allowed access to the long porch that had been built along the length of the building. He climbed the short flight of stairs and stood on the building's porch, turning to look upon his men.

Down on the parade ground the men gazed back at him. Honer strode through their ranks, then up the stairs to stand beside him. Ganning limped up after him, leaning on the porch rail. Ombre walked through the crowd. The men stepped out of his path, acknowledging his passage with slight, respectful bows. At last, he too made his way up the steps and smiled at Ilfedo.

Ilfedo smiled back and faced his soldiers. Six years of hard labor had paid off. The fort filled the valley where once his men had encamped to repel the Art'en threat. Today log walls encircled the valley at its crest, and the trees camouflaged them from prying eyes.

"Today," he shouted, "thanks to your hard work, the citizens of the Hemmed Land know a lasting peace. Peace from the strange creatures that would hunt us from without and from within our borders. The land has been tamed, and some of our towns are growing into cities." He frowned. "Where once a young man could lose his father and mother in a single night to a wilderness beast, today those beasts have been hunted down. Where once the sea serpents haunted our shores and waylaid our fishing ships, now coastal towns prosper. And where the Art'en flew into our northern forests, we have erect-ed a fort."

The men cheered upon hearing him. They cheered strong and long, and that night they feasted together. Ilfedo slipped away from the milling crowd with Ombre. "I'm going home to see my little girl. It has been too long."

Ombre raised a mug and smiled. "Safe journey, Lord of the Hemmed Land!" Ilfedo turned to go, but Ombre laid a hand on his shoulder and said, "I almost forgot." He set his mug on the ground and dug into his pocket before putting something small into Ilfedo's hand. "Please give this to her." He picked up the mug and walked off, eyes fastened on his cup.

Ilfedo watched him go, watched him mingle with the crowd. He shook his head. Ombre wanted a family badly, and he probably would have had one by now if he didn't have his eye on a certain woman. He had risen in the eyes of the people, risen with Ilfedo. He was now numbered among the most influential figures in the Hemmed Land, and many a woman would have gladly tied the knot with him. But he had eyes for one woman and Ilfedo knew it. It seemed that in the last few years Caritha rarely let down her guard in Ombre's presence. Perhaps she sensed Ombre's interest as strongly as Ilfedo saw it. Perhaps she did not want to die in childbirth, as Dantress had.

Little Oganna had filled the void in Ombre's heart that a family of his own would have filled. "Someday, Ilfedo. Someday I'll have a little angel of my own," his friend would often say when he spoke of Oganna. And Ilfedo hoped that someday it would be so. Ombre deserved that much. He would make a wonderful father and a loyal husband.

Ilfedo tucked the gift into his pocket and

tightened his backpack's straps. A long hike lay ahead of him, and Linsair had sent word that he'd completed the swords for the Elite Thousand. That alone would have been enough to bring Ilfedo home, but the thought of his daughter quickened his steps.

The forest swallowed Ilfedo in its lonely embrace. He left the sword of the dragon in its scabbard, preferring anonymity over the bright light of living fire. He journeyed well into the night, preferring to walk in the scant moonbeams that strayed through the forest onto the path. He listened for a while to the hoots of owls in the forest, and the occasional squealing of mice as the owls caught them. At one point a vixen raced through the bushes along the trail, barking at her three pups as they stopped to stare curiously up at him, their eyes silver orbs reflecting the moonlight. They nipped at each other's ears, played with one another's tails, and rolled in the leaves until the vixen's insistent calls drew them back into the forest.

The path was broad and skirted a pond and continued south toward home. The moon was a thin cresent low in the sky that night, and soon the depths of the forest grew too dark for him to see the path where it passed beneath overarching trees. Drawing the sword of the dragon from its sheath he let the living fire clothe him in armor of light. The brightness obscured his surroundings, and he closed his eyes, hoping to somehow dim the light through will-power. When he looked, the blade no longer sprayed harsh light into the forest but glowed instead, gently illuminating every stone, tree, and creature in his path.

Deep in the forest he found a log cabin, shockingly with its door open to the night. He smiled. A few years ago no one would have even considered leaving their door open at night.

Weary from his trek, Ilfedo stopped, sheathed his sword, and knocked on the doorframe. But he felt foolish for doing so, for almost immediately the interior of the cabin was open to him. A few rough tables had been set in the middle of the room, and a long bar stood at the back of it. Wooden mugs and glasses for drinking were neatly stacked on both ends of it. There was but one customer, a stocky fellow with a frizzy yellow beard. He didn't even glance up as Ilfedo stepped through the door, instead he stared into his mug, blinking his eyes wearily.

"Welcome, welcome to my inn!" called a woman as she emerged from a side room. She stood there smiling at him as she wiped her hands on her apron. She was a stunningly beautiful brunette with shoulder-length, fine hair. Her eyes were as green as summer grass.

Ilfedo returned her smile and gave a slight bow. It seemed the right thing to do. "Good evening. I did not realize that we had any inns along this route."

"We didn't until I bought this cabin," she said with a soft laugh. "It is just me and my son running it, but we'll make a success of it. The soldiers going to and from the new fort along the northern border will surely provide enough business."

Ilfedo nodded, suppressing the instinct to question her further. He found her almost irresistible and that admission felt almost like a betrayal of his deceased wife.

"Would you like a room for the night?" the woman asked. She had misinterpreted his silence for tiredness.

"I would. Thank you." He pulled a silver coin out of his pocket and handed it to her.

She almost blushed as their hands touched. Or, perhaps that was his imagination. He followed her to the room where she wished him a good night and left him with the promise of a hot breakfast.

Ilfedo rose with the dawn and left the bed chamber. He found himself looking forward to seeing his hostess again. She was there in the main room, patting the bearded fellow on his back as he buried his face in his hands. There was a palpable sorrow about the fellow.

"Morning," she said as she turned to Ilfedo.

He managed a smile. "I will recommend this place to others," he said. "You will have plenty of business, just as you hoped. You have my word on that."

She blushed and said, "You never did give me your name last night. I don't mean to sound ungrateful, but are you a man of influence to promise me something like that?"

Ilfedo smiled broadly. "Some smitten soldiers are going to try and win your heart, my lady. That's another promise."

"My lady?" she said and shook her head. "You are a gentleman, sir. My husband was one as well. I recognize character when I see it, and I do not say that lightly."

Ilfedo sat down and ate a hot breakfast. He didn't see the woman's son until he finished eating.

The boy was no more than ten years of age with bright eyes and an eager manner. He took Ilfedo's dishes and brought them to the counter for cleaning without any urging from his mother. She patted the lad on his head and then followed Ilfedo to the door.

"I hope," she offered tentatively, "that you will visit us again."

He turned to her, gazing into her lovely green eyes. She was a beautiful woman. Maybe he should point Ombre in her direction. But he chastised himself at the thought. He should pursue something with her himself. He had a daughter. She had a son. Both of them were without a partner.

Dantress's face came to his mind and he cleared his throat. "I wish you the best success here," he said, then turned to leave.

She touched his arm and he hesitated as she stared at the sword belted to his side. She curtsied low to the ground, very gracefully, and met his gaze with her lovely eyes. "I recognize you now. My name is Allison, my lord, and I pray your journey goes well."

He thanked her before tearing himself away and heading down the trail again.

Without stopping to rest, he pressed on. The prospect of seeing his daughter was foremost on his mind. A few hours later the trail broadened greatly and crossed wide-open fields. Yimshi's rays split the sky with full daylight and a rooster crowed in the distance, a reminder that the wilderness had been tamed. He shook his head. If only it had never been tamed. He preferred the wild, untamed land of his childhood. But that sort of land was not a place to raise his only child.

When he finally arrived home the smell of onion soup greeted him. He opened the door and immediately his daughter ran to him.

"Father!" Oganna was six now. He spread his arms wide and dropped to his knees, letting a relieved smile play across his face. She raced from the kitchen, radiant with childish joy. Her blond tresses were so fair that they could have been woven from gold. Her gold-blue eyes sparkled, and she giggled before throwing herself into his arms, pressing her cheek against his, and grabbing his hair in her small hands.

Evela stood from beside the fireplace, resting her hand on the mantel. Her eyes shone almost as brightly as his daughter's upon seeing him.

"How is my little angel?" He kissed his child's forehead and lifted her off the floor, holding her at arms' length. "My goodness, have you grown in this past month?"

She laughed as he set her down. "Look what Rozel made for me." She twirled, permitting him a full evaluation of the purple dress fashioned in the manner of the Warrioresses . . . and of the one that Dantress used to wear.

"It is beautiful," he said. He kissed her forehead again and strode to the fireplace.

With a long wooden spoon Evela stirred the contents of the pot hanging over the flames. "Are you hungry, my lord?"

"Truly starved." He kissed her hand, immediately regretting it as her cheeks flushed. Over the past years her actions had told him that she held a romantic place for him in her heart. He sighed and turned to Oganna. "How would you like to take a walk after breakfast? Just the two of us."

She jumped up and down. "Oh yes! I would, I would!" Then she stopped and curtsied, glancing up at Evela. "I mean, of course I would love to, Father."

"Then we shall," he said as he glanced around the room. "Is anyone else home?"

"Aunt Caritha was gone when I woke up. I know Rozel and Aunt Levena went berry-picking." The child stuck her finger between her teeth and looked at the ceiling. "I don't know what happened to Aunt Laura."

Evela stopped stirring and pulled the spoon out of the soup. She dabbed her finger in the pot and licked it. "Laura will be back soon. She's checking the garden for tomatoes." She ran her tongue over her lips. "Perfect."

"Oganna." Ilfedo dug into his pocket and lowered his voice. "I need a few minutes alone with your aunt, so I'd like you to go outside. Can you do that for me?"

Her smile melted, and she turned away. He grabbed her shoulder. "Hold a second, my little one. Ombre gave me . . . Well, I'm not sure what it is, but I have something here for you." Pulling Ombre's gift from his pocket he placed it in her outstretched hands. The firelight revealed a wooden wolf, finely carved. Ombre must have spent hours making it for her.

Oganna's face lit up, and she bounded to her bedroom at the opposite side of the house, closing the door after her.

"That was nice of him," Evela said. She stopped stirring and sat on the hearth, gazing up at

Ilfedo.

Clearing his throat he sat next to her. How should he do this? She was one of the kindest souls he had ever known, and her beauty could make any man's heart leap into his throat. He didn't want to hurt her feelings, but he needed to be honest with her.

"Ilfedo, what's wrong?" She slipped her hand into his, her dark eyes earnestly searching his.

He felt awful, yet he had to do it. He pulled his hand gently away from hers. "Evela, I can see that you have feelings for me," he said at last. "These past few years it has become more and more apparent to me and to those around me."

"Ilfedo, what are you saying?" she interjected, her expression sobering.

"Please, please let me finish. This is not easy for me to speak of," he whispered. Then he swallowed. "It has taken me a long time to work up the nerve to approach you about this."

He hesitated, and in that moment she smiled shyly, lowering her gaze. "Then you feel something for me?" she asked.

"My mind is so conflicted right now," he said. "I am torn between the love I had and the life that I now have. A part of me wants to move on, but the past still holds me. It has never let go. If I have feelings for you then they are buried under all of the emotions that I struggle with every day. I can't give to another woman what I gave to Dantress. My heart is fragmented now between life with my daughter, and a desire to die and be with Dantress again." He watched Evela's gentle dark eyes well with tears. How heavy his heart felt. But she deserved the truth from him. "Honestly, sometimes I think maybe I do feel that for you. But I still see Dantress in every woman's eyes. It happens to me all of the time, and it is especially difficult with you. She imprinted on my soul and I do not want to let her go, even though she is gone." He touched her hand, and she glanced down at it. A few of her tears splashed onto his skin. "You deserve someone who will focus their love on you," he said. "Not a man who cannot let go of the dead."

Evela dabbed at her eyes with a handkerchief. "Ilfedo," she whispered, "I ask you for nothing. But if ever you feel differently, I will still be here." He opened his mouth to interject, but she shook her head and spoke in a stronger tone. "And do not dare tell me that I shouldn't wait for you. I may, or I may not. But that is my choice, and I have made it. I will take no other man."

She forced a smile as she stood. She gazed down into his eyes and Ilfedo felt his heart splinter as if it would break into even smaller pieces. She took a step toward the kitchen, but he grabbed her hand.

"Please understand," he said quietly, and he took great care with his choice of words. "The problem lies with me, not with you. I know that I am a fool for not taking you as my new wife. My little girl looks up to and adores you, and I—"

Evela's eyes brightened somewhat as he continued.

"I adore you as well. I admit it. But I cannot go beyond that. Not now, or possibly ever. My fear is that you will hold out hope when it is unlikely that anything will ever happen between us." He sighed and released her hand. "For me there was and always will be my great love for Dantress. I loved her with all that I had. My heart is and always will remain empty where she once filled it. I do not want to deny you happiness, but neither will I deceive you. I am still grieving for your sister. And my grief is as fresh—as painful—as the day she died."

Suddenly the memories of Dantress flooded his mind, and his heart ached. He bent over in pain, weeping as he clutched his chest. Tears spilled from his eyes, and every tear spawned a new pain in his body until he felt small and childlike.

Tears ran down Evela's face as she sobbed with him. "I have not hidden it, I guess, which is why you knew. Y . . . yes, I do love you. But you cannot see and cannot allow me to love you because you are unwilling to let go of your pain. You are unwilling to heal. I pity us the joy we will never know because of your scars." With that she kissed his cheek and ran her soft hand down his face.

He instinctively closed his eyes. Her hand comforted him and he had to resist the urge to take her into his arms and kiss her on the mouth.

She withdrew her hand, cupping her hands over her face, and fled out the front door sobbing.

Ilfedo's heart sank even lower as the door closed behind Evela. He could feel misery standing in the room with him, as if Misery was a real person and not an emotion. Misery. He had brought it on himself this time. Worse, he had spread it to one that he loved. Evela did not deserve this. She deserved his heart, too, as he had given it to Dantress. But he could just as easily have pursued a relationship with that beautiful innkeeper. She deserved to be loved as well. To be cherished and protected. Why could he not be like most other men? Why could he not release the dead and be thankful for new love that fell into his arms?

Against his better judgment he started to cry.

Across the house the door to Oganna's bedroom swung open. Oganna skipped across the room and hugged him. "Father? You are crying," she said as she buried her head in his chest.

Such tenderness washed over him. He clutched her to himself, wishing somehow that the pain would vanish. He felt as small as an ant that ate the crumbs off his floor. When he thought his sobbing had ended, Ilfedo released his daughter. He looked upon her, little beauty that she was. So like her mother in many ways. His heart pained him again and tears flowed down his cheeks.

"Father, what is wrong? Did something bad happen?" Oganna stared into his eyes and clutched his shirt with her hands. As he sobbed, he saw her chest heave, too. His tears slowed, and instead he saw tears flow from her eyes. Oganna clutched her own chest, and Ilfedo's pain vanished. With a startled cry she fainted in his arms.

Ilfedo darted to the door. His pain had disappeared and his tears had stopped flowing, but he could not rouse his daughter. "Help! Someone help me," he screamed out of the door. Then he looked down at his sweet child's face. "No! I will not lose you, too," he whispered.

From the forest a figure emerged in answer to his call, and he glanced up as Evela ran toward him. Of course, he thought, she would be the first to come to him when he needed it. Even after he had ripped her heart from her breast. He cursed himself and asked the Creator to bless Evela, and to spare his daughter's life.

LINSAIR'S PARTING ADMONITION

Caritha watched Linsair drop his silver-headed hammer on the broad side of the blade of a long sword. White-hot sparks splintered from the metal, and a wave of heat washed over her. Caritha was sweating beads down her face, but the large man before her was not. He focused on his work and his skin did not even glisten with a hint of moisture. In the light of the forge Linsair's belt of hammered steel gleamed.

The walls of the deep underground cave where the smith worked had been hardened and singed by his tireless forging. He'd forbidden anyone else to enter the cave save for she, Ilfedo, and her sisters.

She gazed into the dark recesses of the cave as the firelight flared, and she caught a glimpse of many swords bundled into sheaves that had been leaned against the stone walls. There were a thousand of those swords, all of them identical to each other and prepared by Linsair with the blood of the Warrioresses to empower them. She held her skirt off the dirt floor and moved toward the weapons, bending low to keep from hitting her head on the sloping ceiling. Reaching out she traced her fingers along the engraved flame in the hilt of one of them, then followed the thin metal vine that wove down its hilt and around the arms of its guard. The blade was about three feet in length with a broad side that mirrored her surroundings on either side of a thin fuller. To each of these swords she or one of her sisters had sacrificed a drop of their dragon blood.

The hammer rang against the sword again, and she retreated to the smith's forge to study his work. She pulled out a handkerchief and wiped the sweat from her face.

Linsair's biceps rippled under his rolled up sleeves as he clanged the silver hammer against the flat of the sword's blade. The blade bent, and he flipped it, struck the other side, and flipped it again. The man cleared his throat, though she thought it sounded more like a growl. She fastened her eyes on his face.

"It is time, young one," he said. His pink eyes gazed back at her without blinking, and his chest heaved a deep breath.

She stepped deeper into the scalding air. The forge burned hotter. She wondered that the smith did not flinch in its heat. To her it was tortuous. But she had come to deliver a gift. One final gift in the arming of Ilfedo's men.

She extended her arm and hovered her wrist over the sword. Linsair's last and best creation. Then she spoke to him. "Should I do this one the same way that I did with the other swords?"

Linsair nodded, his eyes studying her as if looking for a deeper understanding of her desires.

"But I want this weapon to be special." She pulled back her hand to wipe the sweat from her eyes. "I want Ombre to have a superior sword, something that will preserve his life as the sword of living fire has preserved Ilfedo."

"Thou art certain of your decision then?" Linsair asked as he furrowed his brow. "In order for this to be done, thou must be willing to give up part of your gift, part of the life that is in thy blood."

Her mind flashed back to a moment not long ago when Ombre happened upon her alone in the forest. She'd tripped and he had caught her. Her cheeks flushed at the memory. "Linsair, I do know what it is I am asking you to do."

"Then so shall it be!" Linsair grabbed her hand in his enormous one and said, "Brace yourself, child. This is going to hurt as if your arm was bathed in fire." Then he forced her wrist against the searing-hot metal.

She screamed in pain and tears streamed down her face, but through her tears she saw the smith raise her skin away from the blade. Large drops of her dragon blood remained on the blade and the sword began to glow with pure white light. Linsair released his hold, took up his hammer, and beat the blade with renewed vigor. A smile spread across his face and his pink eyes sparkled.

Caritha wept in the agony of her wound. She felt weak. Too weak to use the power in her blood to attempt a healing. Instead she drowned her arm in the smith's barrel of water. When the pain eased a bit and she drew out her arm, she regarded the criss-crossing scars which remained. As she twisted her wrist, pain knifed up her arm.

The smith plunged the sword into the water. Steam rose in clouds around him. He reached out and caressed her wound. From his touch, a sensation of coolness spread through her arm. The scars vanished, and then they reappeared on Linsair's arm. She looked up into his eyes with sudden recognition as her scars transferred to his body and her arm was left healed. "It is you!" she said.

Footfalls sounded in the cave. Though she peered into every corner she saw no one. Then a voice spoke from the cave entrance. "Hurry, my master, the child has collapsed."

Linsair dropped his work. "Did you not watch over her as I instructed?" he asked.

"Indeed," the voice of the other man said. "It was not within my power to prevent. Her father returned home and Evela—"

"Say no more, Specter," Linsair commanded. "Return to the woodland hollow and wait for me there."

In the dimness a gray-robed figure congealed and bowed in Linsair's direction. Caritha thought her eyes were deceiving her, for the figure held a scythe blade in his hand. The figure vanished, and Linsair rushed out of the cave.

"Wait! Where are you going?" Caritha raced

after him and up the slope, through the forest in the direction of home. She stumbled on a stone, and he did not stop to help her. He raced on ahead of her, flitting over bushes and around trees.

Not wishing to lose him now and eager to know what had caused him to act this way, Caritha picked up her skirt and ran with all her strength. Before long her breaths came with difficulty, yet she kept him in sight.

The swordsmith slipped into the clearing in front of Ilfedo's house and ran to the door.

* * *

Ilfedo and Evela hovered over Oganna. The child was breathing but unresponsive to them when they tried to rouse her. "I am a curse upon my own family," Ilfedo said as he fought the urge to weep again.

But Evela looked at him and angrily slapped his face. Stunned, Ilfedo stared back at her.

"This isn't about us," Evela said. "Stop focusing on you and get back to being the pillar of strength that my sister married. Really, Ilfedo! I am sorry for hitting you, but I am not! What happened is not important. We can discuss that later, but for now we need to hope and pray that she wakes up soon."

Ilfedo could have kissed her at that moment. Her words gave him a clarity that he hadn't had for a long time. Instead he whispered, "Thank you. I needed to hear that."

Evela laid a warm, wet cloth on Oganna's forehead. "Sweetie, wake up now and show us that you are all right. Please, Oganna, you have the same dragon blood as I. Call it forth and rely on that strength that God has given you."

The front door crashed open and Ilfedo looked up. Linsair stood on the threshold, his countenance grim and a fury burning in his pink eyes. The swordsmith glanced around the house, then his eyes rested on Oganna. He ripped the hammock off the post, making a direct path to her. He glared at Ilfedo. "What hast thou done?" Linsair's pink eyes flared as he pulled the child from Ilfedo's grasp and tenderly laid her on the hearth. "Tell me now, thou Lord of the Hemmed Land. What have you done?"

Such fury burned in the smith's eyes that Ilfedo shrank back. "I . . . I was distraught, and she came to me." He strengthened his voice. "The next moment she collapsed, and I no longer had any tears."

"Fool! Thy daughter's veins are mixed with the blood of humanity and dragonkind. Your need called out to her, and her dragon side answered." Linsair rubbed Oganna's chest and closed his eyes, whispering a prayer as he did so. "Father, holy Father tend now this child I pray. Father, heavenly Father now our fears allay."

At that moment, Caritha burst into the room. Her hair was askew. Uttering a startled cry, she knelt next to Oganna. "Ilfedo, what has happened to her? Did she fall?" Linsair glanced at her with sharp eyes, silencing her.

"Too young. She is too young to manifest these abilities," Linsair said, and again his lips moved in prayer.

Someone put their hand on Ilfedo's back, and he glanced over to find it was Evela. She half-smiled as if to encourage him, then she closed her eyes, murmuring a prayer of her own for Oganna.

Ilfedo closed his eyes and sent up his own plea for his daughter's life. Had he broken Evela's heart and slain his own child in the process? He opened his eyes and found Linsair gazing back at him. "What did I do?" he asked the strange man.

"You did nothing except to plead for an easement of thine own suffering, Lord Ilfedo," the swordsmith said. "The power in thy child's blood is beginning to manifest itself. It is apparent to me that when she touched you, she took on your pain. She absorbed your sorrow, your grief, and your tears. They all became hers. But it was too great for her tiny body to handle. And now I must take the portion of thy suffering that she has taken, or I risk losing her."

The man's pink eyes brimmed with tears, and his chest quaked. He sobbed and wept until his tears sizzled on the hearth. Oganna sat up and her skin had a ruddy glow. A smile appeared on her face as she watched her rescuer. Linsair continued to weep. He caressed Oganna's face and smiled through his tears, then glanced at Ilfedo. "How truly deep, how truly vast is thy love for both the dead and the living," he said. Then he rose and looked down at Caritha. Tears had formed in her eyes as well, and her lips started to form a word. Linsair touched the side of her head. "Remember no more what thou sawest in me. Remember only my craftsmanship and this deed of healing. Pass this to thy sisters for me so that they will remember no more." He withdrew his hand. "Farewell, child."

Without another word Linsair strode out of the house, closing the door firmly behind him.

* * *

Ilfedo didn't know what to think of the man's charge to Caritha. He clutched his child to his chest and laid kisses all over her head until she giggled and begged him to stop.

"Caritha, you look confused. Are you all right?" Ilfedo watched the eldest sister rise to her feet.

"I think so," she said.

Evela stood also. She stepped over to her sister and looked on her with concern. Caritha reached out and touched Evela's hand. "I ran all the way here," Caritha said. "I do feel quite exhausted. Both emotionally and physically."

He frowned. "What did Linsair mean by all that?"

Caritha furrowed her brow, and pulled a handkerchief from her skirt. "What are you talking about?" she asked as she wiped sweat from her forehead.

"He told you to 'remember no more,'" Ilfedo said.

She sat on the floor, shaking her head. "Honestly, brother, I have no memory of that."

THE GHOST OF MATTHALIAH HOLLOW

The shadows deepened under the tall trees, and a gentle, warm breeze rustled the leaves. Dry leaves of red and brown crunched under the feet of a young girl as she skipped through the forest. An owl hooted in the darkness. The breeze strengthened, swirling the leaves around her legs, then weakened, allowing them to settle back on the ground.

Oganna glanced over her shoulder, watching the glowing windows of her father's house. She was ten years old now. Old enough to let her curiosity pull her outside but young enough to dismiss all fear of the mysterious shadows of evening. No one knew she'd snuck away. Aunt Caritha had been the last one awake, cleaning the kitchen. Her father was taking a deserved nap by the fireplace, swinging in his hammock with Seivar nestled under his arm.

She looked into the darkening woods. For the

past several months something had felt amiss. Even when she had been left alone in the house, she had sensed someone else nearby. When she shared that feeling with her nuvitor companions, Seivar and Hasselpatch, both of them had agreed that sometimes, when only they and Oganna remained at home, something felt downright spooky. As if an extra set of eyes gazed upon them at all hours.

This evening she had been standing by the window, watching darkness fall beneath the forest branches. A chill had coursed through her body. She hadn't known why. That is, until a cloaked human figure coalesced in the trees and then vanished again.

Now she turned away from the house and stretched her hand toward the forest, trying to sense that other presence. But she did not know how to find it. She knew that her dragon blood could search for her, but she knew not how. If only there was a way to send her mind out into the woodland to search for another intelligent being. She focused on that thought and suddenly her hand glowed. She let out a little cry, quickly clapping her hands over her mouth and glancing back at the house. The door remained closed and the house silent.

Breathing a sigh of relief, she bit her lip and stretched out her hand again. It did not glow. But this time she felt a mental pull. Something was drawing her into the forest toward Matthaliah Hollow.

For over a year now, a few of her friends had spread the superstition which maintained that Matthaliah Hollow was haunted. That isolated narrow valley was part of Ilfedo's generous property. Actually it bordered the old cabin site where his parents had been killed. In recent months long blue stalks had grown in Matthaliah Hollow, stalks that glowed at night. Her father had called it Night Grass, but its appearance in the hollow only seemed to confirm the local children's suspicions. Her father had not visited the hollow himself. Not in a very long time.

"Those memories are best left buried for now," her father had told her when she had asked.

It took Oganna a while to reach the hollow, but when she stood at the forest's edge, looking down into the meadow with its patches of glowing blue grass, she saw a shadow race to the opposite side and halt. Total darkness fell. She glanced up at the clouds which were covering most of the stars. The moon had risen as a bright glow behind the trees. The shadow, if she had really seen one, blended into the larger, darker shadows.

She hesitated. Fear should give her caution, shouldn't it? There was no such thing as a haunted hollow, was there? But then a hooded figure glowed into existence in front of her, as if waiting for her. A scythe rested in the figure's hands. No, that could not be. The Grim Reaper was only a myth! But there he stood in glowing gray garb. She blinked, trying to see if he was an illusion. Unless she was experiencing a dream. Had she fallen asleep in her bed and never left the house?

She pinched her cheek, cringed at the self-inflicted pain, and then panicked. He was real! The reaper of death himself was standing before her. She turned, prepared to run, but her face bounced on someone's belly.

"Slow down, my child," a familiar voice rumbled. "There is nothing to fear here while I am with you."

She craned her neck to see into the pink eyes of a man who, for the life of her, she could not name. Yet somehow, he was a friend. A long lost friend. "Sir, I . . . I think I should go home now."

The man knelt in front of her and smiled gently. He looked like a ghost, too. His skin was so pale and his hair was so white. "Do you not remember me, my dear child?" he asked.

Her eyes felt like they were going to pop out of their sockets as realization dawned on her. "Linsair!" She leaped into his arms and giggled as he laughed with her. The memory of him, which had seemed buried, came back in a blizzard of knowledge awakened. He had worked for so long for her father and then, after saving her life, he'd left. No one had been able to venture a guess as to where he'd gone.

He was the grandfather she wanted to know, not like her actual grandfather. No one interacted with the dragon father of her mother. Few knew of him and still fewer had met him. Linsair was different. Every memory involving him spoke of kindness—at least to her. Toward others he had sometimes displayed a coldness, an austerity.

Linsair stood, raising her off the ground, holding her away from him. His grin encompassed every corner of his face. "How you have grown, my child! God has been good to you. Oh, and I have missed you."

"Linsair, where have you been? Father and Aunt Caritha and Rozel . . . they wanted to know why you left."

"My task for your father was done," he interjected. "And, child, I had other things to attend to. But," he carried her down into the hollow and nodded at the Grim Reaper, "I always kept a watchful eye on you through my friend."

She shook with fear, seeing the scythe blade with greater clarity. The long shiny blade seemed poised to slit someone's throat. Thankfully the cavernous hood hid the immortal face of Death from sight. She clung to Linsair, wishing he would turn her away from the horrible scene.

"Oganna," Linsair said and she glanced into his gentle face. "*Do not fear him,*" his voice said in her mind. "*This is not the Reaper, but a friend and an ally in whom I trust.*"

She opened her mouth in astonishment. He had spoken into her mind! She could hear his words but not with her ears. It was the strangest sensation, yet comforting coming from him.

Linsair looked at the cloaked figure and growled like a lion. "Specter, cannot you see that the child is afraid of thee?" He set her on the ground and crossed his arms, looming beside her. "Remove your hood and set aside your weapon!"

"Of course, my master. Forgive me. I had not realized." The hood slipped off the man's head, revealing his handsome features, albeit his sober face.

"Specter." Oganna repeated the man's name cautiously. She bit her lower lip and then took a step forward, dipping a curtsy in her nightgown. If Linsair said this was not the Reaper then she would trust this man.

The man leaned his scythe against a nearby

rock face and bowed to her. "At your service, princess. I have watched you all your life, and I continue to do so. Today, I'm afraid, you discovered me against my strongest attempts to hide myself."

"I do not think," she said as she cleared her throat and held her head high. "I do not think I understand."

The swordsmith's pink eyes mirrored the moonlight, sparkling in its radiance. "My child, you are special to me, and so I have given you into Specter's charge until the day that you are able to stand on your own. Until the day that you surpass your aunts in mastering the power in your dragon blood and until you can nearly match your father's skill with a sword."

"Does father know?" she asked as she pointed a finger at Specter.

"No. And you must not tell him," Linsair said.

She frowned. Linsair would have to give an awfully good reason if he wanted her to keep this from her father. She shared everything with him. He trusted her to do that so that he could protect her and guide her as she grew.

"Listen to me, my child," Linsair whispered. He knelt in the wet grass. "The death of your mother broke your father's heart, resulting in a fear that threatens thy future. You must be safeguarded from all that would harm thee, but not sheltered from the storms that will come against you. Specter is my loyal and trustworthy friend. He once saved your life, and he may yet do so again."

She shook her head. "I know that Father trusted you, Linsair, but that is not a good reason for me to keep this secret. I have to tell him."

Linsair growled and stood back. "You are strong like your mother, little one. I shall have to convince you in another manner." Then his skin glowed pure white and hardened. Scales grew over every inch of his body. His arms and legs thickened and he grew. His head elongated, his neck lengthened, and a fin cut through the clothing on his neck while horns grew from his head. Suddenly there he stood in full majestic power, and she knew him for what and who he was.

Her father had told her the story of Albino: "A magnificent creature and the father of your mother." Oganna clapped her hands and laughed as the creature towered above her.

"Now you know me, child. The command that I now give you I charge thee to keep. Specter is a friend to you and me. I appeared to your father and to his people in human form to prepare them for things that will soon come. Tell no one of Linsair's true identity and keep thy hidden guardian a secret. Both of these things are for thy benefit and security."

Soberly she nodded and, just as she thought of hugging the dragon's leg, he sprang into the air, his wings beating wind into her face. She fell against Specter, and he held her steady until Albino shot westward into the night sky.

Cold air filled the hollow, and the clouds thinned. Stars multiplied in the heavens. "Come, princess," Specter said as he took her hand and led her to the rock face close by. He held aside some wet vines and waved her into a dark cave chamber.

"I . . . I can't see." Her hands glowed momentarily, but the light lasted only an instant.

A torch blazed out of the darkness in Specter's hand. He smiled down at her and seemed to relax as he led her slowly down into the cave. The cave opened into a chamber some thirty paces wide. He stooped where the portions of ceiling dipped low and let go of her hand when they reached a dry section of stone. A heap of sand formed an upgrade in the floor.

He stood to the side and motioned for her to step up beside him. As she did, a shaft of moonlight blazed through a hole in the ceiling and spotlighted a sword that was leaning against the stone in front of her. She caught her breath. The blade had rusted, perhaps from sitting in the moist cave, and the leather along the handle appeared to be peeling. She reached out and touched the blade. It glowed rusty-orange for as long as her skin made contact with it.

Something else lay half-buried in the dirt next to the sword, and she dusted away the dirt with her hand, uncovering a boomerang made of some sort of crystal. The elbow had been fashioned like a handle, yet the wings had been honed to sharp edges.

"Whoa there," Specter said, placing his hand gently on her shoulder. "Be careful now." He sighed and his eyes filled with tears that would not spill.

"Are these weapons yours?" she asked. She gazed into his face, wondering what brought about such sorrow in this man.

"The sword was mine," he admitted. "Though that was a very, very long time ago." He stood and forced a smile. "But now it will belong to you."

She jumped up and down. What a gift! But

the man laid a hand on her shoulder and guided her toward the cave's exit point. "The dragon said that one day you will have need of a sword, and when that day comes, you may return to this place and claim it."

"I want to show it to everyone!" she said.

"Now, now." He raised his pointer finger. "Tonight's events are a secret between you and I. No one, and I mean no one, must know of my presence here. Do you understand, little one?"

She nodded, realizing even as she did so how hard it was going to be to keep such a thing from her father and her aunts. It would be hard to keep this a secret, yet the dragon had said it must be kept. She would not let him down.

"Come," Specter said, and he walked her out of the cave and retrieved his scythe. "I will escort you home. And please, Oganna, don't try to find me again. After tonight I believe you have the ability to render me visible whenever you wish. I won't pretend to know how. I only ask that you never do so again. I must remain your secret guardian."

She hung her head, unsure if guilt or elation was the proper emotion at that moment. "I promise," she said.

With Specter at her side, she treaded over the leaf-strewn floor of the dark forest until they reached the trees bordering her father's clearing. Then she turned away, determined to put her adventure out of mind, and slipped unnoticed into the house.

* * *

Specter watched the dragon's offspring close the door to Ilfedo's house. An otherworldly cold seized his body, and he fell to his knees. A force seized his chest, constricting him until he could not breathe. He gasped, praying to God for instant help. He could not move.

Voices whispered in evil undertones from the darkened forest. Voices that sounded all too familiar. He remembered the battle in Al'un Dai and the demonic hands that had clawed at him, as if dragging him into their accursed abode.

But why and how had those haunting spirits found him here? This place was so very far from the Eiderveis River and no one in the Hemmed Land worshipped the evil spirits. At least not to his knowledge. So who had called them to this place?

Humanoid figures dropped from the trees and spread their feathered wings. Art'en! Eight of them! They chortled like birds and crouched, ready to spring on him.

Wisps of thick blackness rose from the grass in the clearing before him. They curved swiftly upward, and a skeletal hand coalesced, reaching toward him. The Grim Reaper congealed in all his awful potency, his deadly fingers clattering against the handle of his scythe, as if anticipating Specter's death. The serrated blade drew back and then swung toward Specter's head.

Unable to move, unable to scream, Specter closed his eyes. The Creator's will be done.

One of the Art'en shook its wild, lengthy hair and screamed long and loud into the darkness. The other creatures bounded to their fellow and covered his mouth. Apparently they did not want their presence revealed. The Grim Reaper turned toward Ilfedo's house as if sensing someone else approaching.

Its cloaked form began dissolving into smoke.

In the doorway stood the Lord Warrior of the Hemmed Land. In his hand the flaming sword of the dragon burned. Someone had heard the Art'en's cry.

* * *

Ilfedo rushed toward the smoking figure in the clearing. The living fire enveloped his body. The darkness raced away from him, and over a dozen winged men became visible. They appeared to be standing in a circle, though he could see nothing in their midst.

The Grim Reaper floated there in dreadful clarity. His body kept turning into smoke and solidifying as if something prevented him from escaping. Ilfedo tried to breathe slowly, but every moment he gazed upon Death, fear drove deeper into his body, making him shake as never before. The Reaper turned to face him with eyeless sockets and a blackened skull. The jaws moved yet uttered no words. Instead the teeth clacked against each other in a hollow sort of way.

May God help him, what horror was this? Had the very specter of Death come to his lands? Even so, he would drive this creature out of this land, and forever the Art'en would fear Ilfedo and the sword he bore.

Suddenly invisible bands forced his arms to his sides. Darkness swirled from the Reaper's hand, like a tornado around his feet. He could not move. Death floated closer to him and pointed to the ground with a finger of blackened bone. Every muscle in Ilfedo's body fought to keep him standing, yet inch by inch he fell to his knees. His hand still held the sword, but its flames sputtered.

The door of his home flew open, and a small figure stepped into the moist night. "Father!"

Several Art'en bounded toward her, shrieking with freakish fury. Two of them brought her to the ground as she screamed and cried. "Father!" It seemed to be the only word she was capable of uttering.

"Let . . . her . . . go!" Ilfedo drew upon his rage and felt his connection to the sword reestablish. Voices whispered in the trees, and the screams of men and women echoed all around him. Darkness crept toward him, constricting the sword's circle of light.

The Grim Reaper approached him, but the living fire poured strength into Ilfedo's muscles. He laughed and rose, snapping the invisible bands that held him in place. He raised the sword of the dragon, stepped forward, and drove the flaming blade into the Reaper's skull.

Death fell back but slashed back with its scythe.

Ilfedo brought the sword down upon the scythe's broad side, forcing it to the ground. The curved blade bent. With a yell of victory, he reached under the Reaper's tattered hood. His fingers found a vertebrate in Death's neck. Raising the sword, he smashed its pommel into the Reaper's forehead.

The Grim Reaper fell to the ground, its jaws opening in a soundless cry.

Oganna screamed. She collapsed, eyes closed. An Art'en scooped her up, turned toward the trees with her in its arms. But Caritha charged out the front door and jumped on its back, driving her rusted blade into its neck. Rozel followed, driving her sword into the Art'en's head. Evela joined them and snatched the child from its arms, ducking to avoid another of the creatures.

Levena and Laura darted outside and wrestled the Art'en nearest the house to the ground before slaying it. Seivar and Hasselpatch streaked into the fray, digging their silver talons into the assailants' backs, ripping at their wings, and viciously stabbing their beaks into the Art'en's bodies.

Swaying to its feet, the Grim Reaper evaporated in a cloud of dark smoke that shot toward the sky. Ilfedo gritted his teeth. He needed to keep it from getting away. Holding his sword with all his strength and pointing its blade at the ground, he willed it to flame. The sword blasted fire at the ground, launching him into the air. He reached into the Reaper's smoky essence, hoping that the sword would force the being back into skeletal human form.

The Reaper's body begin to take shape again. Ilfedo's hand closed on one skeletal arm. But his upward momentum had slowed and his fingers slipped. He started to fall away from the Reaper, but he cried out, "I am taking payment, you foul creature. Remember me when you think of returning to his land!" As he fell he held on to the creature's arm and hacked at it with the sword of the dragon. The Reaper's bones snapped under the pressure and Ilfedo ripped the arm completely off.

As Ilfedo crashed to the ground, he stared at the Reaper's startled face. The Reaper wisped from its bodily form into black smoke. Ilfedo looked down at Death's severed arm imprisoned in his fist. As he struggled to his feet, he dropped it, then raced into the forest after the surviving Art'en. How had these cursed creatures come so far south?

His every sense seemed enhanced. He hunted the winged men with ease, finding several hiding in the trees. Enflamed by the sword's strength, he climbed the trees faster than the creatures could escape. None of the Art'en survived the night. The Warrioresses combed the forest floor, and the nuvitors soared overhead.

A couple of hours later Ilfedo counted twenty-three dead Art'en. Oganna woke with a headache and said that she'd been knocked in the head by one of them. At first he thought she was trying to show that she did not fear the creatures. He shook his head and told Evela to put her to bed. But the child walked to the midst of the clearing, bent down, and picked up the skeletal arm.

With a smile on her face she handed it to him and kissed his cheek. "I love you, Father." There was no fear in her bluegold eyes, only gratitude.

He felt her head but found only a bruise, so he put her into Caritha's bed that night, more for his own peace of mind than for hers. "This attack," he said in a hushed voice, sitting on the edge of the bed and gazing into Caritha's sober face, "did you sense where it was directed?"

"How do you mean, brother?" she whispered.

The other sisters filtered into the little room, standing against the walls. Laura, Evela, and Levena were brushing out their long, thick hair. Caritha had already cleaned up. Rozel's hair remained askew, and her gaze refused to leave Oganna. Evela offered her brush to Rozel. "You need it."

"Keep it for yourself!" Rozel said. Evela's eyes widened, and she retreated a step. Rozel offered no apology. Her gaze remained on the sleeping child.

Ilfedo half-smiled, then he said, "I sensed the Reaper's focus. All it wanted during the struggle was my child. It wanted Oganna."

"But why?" Caritha looked at Oganna and lightly stroked the girl's blond locks.

Ilfedo shook his head. That he did not know.

For a long while everyone was silent. Then Caritha, gazing into each of her sisters' dark eyes, said, "The dragon promised you that dark times lie ahead. Perhaps it is time to begin teaching Oganna what we know. We can teach her how to fight and how to exercise the power in her dragon blood."

"She is my baby girl," Ilfedo started to say.

"A dragon's offspring, nevertheless, brother. It is time you see that for what it is." Caritha frowned deeply. "Untrained, she is helpless, but with our instruction she can be as strong as any of us. Her mother was the best among us, and I do not doubt that she can be as well."

Ilfedo paced to the door and back. Oganna was so young, so innocent. Must she be condemned to endure horrors in her youth, as he had? As hard as it was to admit, though, Caritha was right about her dragon blood. The dragon's sword afforded him great power in battle. He would have died tonight without it. But he knew nothing of the mysterious power inside his daughter. If only the swordsmith had remained with them, Ilfedo would have gladly given Oganna into his tutelage. Without Linsair, he'd need to rely on the sisters. "You may train her," he said at last.

Caritha smiled at him and nodded. He read gratitude in her eyes and excitement for the coming task.

"However, you must not bring her with you on any combative mission. Perform what training exercises you must, but perform them here in the heart of the Hemmed Land." As the sister started to object, he raised his hand to silence her. "These are my terms. My child's safety is my first concern, and if it is not yours also, then I cannot give her into your instruction. I lost her mother. I will not lose her."

"And if your fear leaves her less capable of defending herself in a desperate moment?" Evela interjected.

"I will protect her," he replied, and he noted that he did not refer to her as 'sister.' For now that term seemed inappropriate for her. He stood and then bent down to kiss his child's cheek. "Goodnight." With that he trudged upstairs and lay in his bed. Seivar and Hasselpatch flew after him, nestling on the blankets beside him. "My dear, trusted companions," he whispered, and they cooed as they rubbed against him. He brought them downstairs and washed them in the sink. Then he trundled them into bed, leaned the sword of the dragon against the wall nearby, and fell into deep sleep.

* * *

Sitting against a tree, Specter spat blood from his mouth and laughed. He looked at the sky. The Grim Reaper had shot like a black comet into the east. "You fled like the snake you are!" And he laughed again.

He still felt winded from the attack. But the thrill of watching the man defend his child, and the ferocity of Ilfedo's attack made the humility of the dark being's defeat sweeter than honey in his stomach.

How swift and sudden was the Reaper's humiliation. How unexpected and glorious! The evil spirits had fled as well. Peace reigned where terror had intended to take root. A moist cold wind tossed the hood off his head and forced tears from his eyes.

Specter stood and smiled. He could sense the strength that now emanated from Ilfedo's house, and it had been a long time since he'd felt such security. In truth, he had not felt such strength in a very long time. Carrying his scythe on his shoulders, he strode into the depths of the forest. Hope seemed to shine from heaven, as the favor of God upon Specter's young ward.

ONE THOUSAND SWORDS OF LIGHT

As Ilfedo led his daughter through the crowds that thronged the streets, he held her hand firmly in his own. She was ten years of age now. My how these years had flown by. In some ways it felt as if Dantress had been alive only yesterday, but when he looked upon his child it seemed a lifetime ago. A dream caught and then lost to the winter wind.

Stirred dust tickled his nostrils and clouded his path. He wrinkled his nose at the strong odor of lye coming from the wash hung between the small houses on either side of the street. Ignoring the stares and the hushed voices that followed him, he made his way to the stockade fort at the street's end.

How strange that this place had arisen out of the forest so near his woodland home. It had begun with the training of the Elite Thousand, and perhaps he had underestimated the local impact that would have. It was regrettable in his mind. Regrettable that he had not thought to move the training grounds farther east. He could have put them near the sea. Either that or he could have sent them into the south near the border to the desert there.

But, no, he had committed himself to this project and as he gazed around at the town that had sprung up to support the warriors, he could not regret it. People felt safe. The residents here were, in large part, the families of his finest warriors. They deserved to be here. This had been a mature forest for as far as his eye could see, but now a large number of stumps and a few dozen oak trees dotted the rolling landscape. The town had remained unnamed, as of yet, though he thought wryly that they ought to call it Roughshod Hills, or Mishmash Town. The houses and businesses had been built hurriedly and it showed in their rough appearances.

He was leading Oganna along the streets past the houses and businesses. Ombre was trailing them, acting as a rear guard in case some crazy fool tried to hurt them. A short distance farther on these dwelling gave way to wide open ground that had been hammered hard by the feet of men in training. Beyond that, in the midst of the training fields stood the wooden fort that Ombre and Commander Veil had ordered constructed for the Elite Thousand.

"Father," Oganna whispered as she tugged at his sleeve with her free hand. "Everyone is staring at us."

Ilfedo grinned down at her, and continued to walk. "Yes they are, my little one," he said. "But do not mind them. Today we have important business at the fort with Commander Veil."

Oganna kept her gaze fixed on the dusty street for a short while, then she glanced up and around again. "Father, they are still staring at us? Why don't they look at someone else instead?"

Ilfedo crouched beside her and brushed a strand of loose golden hair from her forehead. He'd found himself wondering of late when she would ask a question he could not answer. As with most children, she was full of questions. "You and I are important to these people, Oganna. I am their lord and you are their princess. That carries with it an unavoidable privilege that makes them curious about me and about you. Someday you may be the most important person in this whole land. Everyone will know your name, and it will be between you and God as to how you use that influence. You can either do great evil with that influence or great good."

The child frowned, then she turned to point behind them at Ombre. He was following ten paces distant with his hand on the hilt of his sheathed sword. "They do not stare at him, and he has great influence, too," Oganna whispered.

Ombre was wearing the distinctive wolfskin as a cape, with the wolf's vicious head thrown over his back. His attire had evolved with his rise in the public eye. Instead of his rough woodsman clothes and frequently grimy appearance, now he shaved his face clean and wore a gray tunic and pants that matched. Over the tunic he wore a chain mail coat and his sword's gold-studded scabbard glinted in the sunlight. He had become a military leader that enjoyed the respect and love of Ilfedo's growing armies.

"I think they do stare," Ilfedo said to this daughter. He lowered his voice conspiritorially. "It's just that they have seen him before. And Uncle Ombre scares them a little so they try not to stare at him. We, on the other hand." He smiled as he spread his arms wide. He could see by the look in her eyes that she was mulling deeply on his words.

A breeze caught her golden hair and flung it across her face. She brushed it aside and returned the crowd's gaze. Her eyes bore a startling severity, and Ilfedo observed that many of the bystanders were more than a little taken with her.

Ilfedo let out a long, slow breath, remembering when the people of the Hemmed Land had wanted him to become their Lord Warrior. That mantle of authority would pass, upon his death, to his daughter. The princess, as people called her now. He stood and led her on by the hand. His position had enabled him to work for the greater good, not just for the safety of his little family. Oganna had a future worth fighting for.

The past six months had seen no more Art'en appearances. The latest incident had inspired Ombre to order a thorough combing of the nation's forests. No more of the creatures had been found. Ilfedo had chosen to keep the Reaper's involvement a secret. Some would have called him a fool for claiming the Specter of Death really existed. Some would have called him proud for assuming it would be interested in visiting death particularly upon him and his household.

Come what may, he was confident of the future and he had reason to be. Ombre had taken charge of forming the military with a zeal equaled by none. Honer was organizing centers of learning and overseeing the building of a national archive to preserve the ancient scrolls and texts that had been passed on from their forefathers. Besides this, Ganning now oversaw the local governments and ensured that they executed justice with mercy.

In the past many people had been executed after controversial verdicts in cases of theft and bigotry. With his three friends aiding him, Ilfedo had strengthened the trust and loyalty of the people.

As Ilfedo left the makeshift town, the buildings gave way to white military tents pitched for as far as he could see. He crossed the training grounds through the tents, the chaos of noise in the town faded behind him. He approached the fort and several sentries acknowledged him with salutes from the tall guard towers. He approached the gate, looked up at the sentries and commanded them to open it to him. Wood creaked and an out-of-sight latch was lifted. The oversized double doors opened outward, and he slipped inside, pulling Oganna with him. He relaxed into a wide stance as he gazed around the fort's courtyard. A handful of horses were tied to posts, whinnying softly to one another, and a few men were standing outside of the fort's command center. They glanced up, recognized him in an instant, and brought their fists to their breastplates in salute.

At the gate behind him there was a commotion as a fist pounded on it. Ilfedo turned as the sentries atop the wall signaled to the guards on the ground. The guards swung the gate open again and Ombre stepped through. "The next time you shut the doors on me it will be your captain that you answer to," Ombre shouted. Then he shook his fist at the guards until they closed the gate and cowered away from him.

"My apologies, brother!" Ilfedo said with a laugh.

Ombre was dusting off his pants as if cleansing them from a discourtesy. He shook his head and said, "Don't mind all of that. They closed the door on me. You didn't!" He waved his hand, indicating the interior of the wood structure. "What do you think of all this? Quite the change from the woodland camp we started with." He finished dusting off his pants and grinned down at little Oganna before continuing with Ilfedo. "The first few families lived here in tents, but Veil quickly realized that would not be sustainable as other families moved closer to the training grounds. They chopped down enough trees to build all of this and many of the buildings in our makeshift town. Not bad for a thrown-together effort."

"The walls look sturdy," Ilfedo said. He gazed around at the broad courtyard. "The parade grounds are more than adequate." He followed the smell of musty hay to one side of the central building. It was long and low with barred windows open to the elements. "The stables?" he asked.

"Oh yes," Ombre affirmed. "I have more to show you in there when you are ready."

To Ilfedo's right stood a two-story log structure. A sort of barracks for the officers. The command center was the central building. It had been placed between the barracks and the stables with a short wood ramp permitting access to the front door.

The door to the command center opened and Commander Veil strutted out. "At your service, my lord," he said as he looked up at Ilfedo and saluted with his fist to his chest. Then, as an afterthought he maintained his salute and smiled down at Oganna. "At your service, little lady! My, but you look pretty today."

Oganna giggled and spun around. She glanced up at her father and Ilfedo smiled back at her.

"Commander Veil is living up to his reputation as one of our best officers," Ombre said. He stepped next to the broad man and grasped his shoulder. "There is hardly another man in our army whom I would trust as easily to safeguard our interests."

"You flatter me, my lord," Commander Veil said with a bow in Ombre's direction. The fine chain mail he wore glittered in the warm sunlight. "I simply follow the orders of my lords, trusting them to do what is best for our people."

Ombre slapped the man congenially then directed his attention to Ilfedo. "Veil has been assisting me with a personal endeavor here at the fort." He led Ilfedo to the stable, opening the wide doors to permit Yimshi's light inside. Fifty stalls flanked a broad aisle down the center. At least half the stalls appeared occupied. Whinnies filled the air, mingled with a few snorts.

Ombre proceeded half-way down the aisle and opened a stall door. Ilfedo peered inside. The dim, dusty interior made it necessary to wait for his eyes to adjust to the light. A white stallion pawed the straw floor, spraying silver flakes from its hoof. Its mane appeared equally silver, glittering even. It was a magnificent creature. A paradigm of the Evenshadow breed.

"You caught him?" Ilfedo asked, and Ombre nodded solemnly. Ilfedo chuckled and let his gaze rove over the stallion. "He is magnificent, my friend. Honer will probably want to breed his Evenshadow mare with this fine stud. Imagine the strong offspring they would produce."

The stallion shoved its muzzle toward Ombre as the man reached out to it. Ombre stroked the creature and it blew out its nostrils with pleasure. "Honer was the first to capture one of these fine animals, and his is a fine mare to be sure," he said. "But as to this strong fellow, I did not have to hunt him down. After he saved me from the Art'en creatures that attacked me up north, I assumed I would never see him again. But this stallion found me on my return journey home and he has not left me since. I cannot explain it, brother, but we have a bond that seems unbreakable. You would think from his easy manner that I have tamed him at the least, or even had broken him, but it is not the case."

"What happened?" Ilfedo asked.

Ombre opened the stable door and stepped into the stall. The stallion flared its nostrils at Ilfedo, but it nuzzled Ombre as if it had known him forever and the man wrapped his arms around its neck. "This magnificent creature has not left me since that day," he said. "I was walking along the road, heading home, when this stallion trots into the path ahead of me. At first I stood still, worried that he would bolt if I moved toward him. But he just stood there and I walked up and stroked his muzzle for the first time." Ombre stared hard into Ilfedo's eyes. "And then I tried the craziest thing. I walked to his side, grabbed his mane, and swung atop his bare back."

Ilfedo raised his eyebrows, astounded. To touch one of these creatures was a miracle on its own, a story that a man could tell that few people in the Hemmed Land would believe. But for one of the wild and rare Evenshadow stallions to invite a human to ride it? It seemed impossible.

"Believe it," Ombre said, and he patted the horse's shoulder. Then he stepped out of the stall and closed the door. "Come on, my brother. I am not yet finished surprising you today."

Little Oganna took an eager step toward the stallion, reaching up as if to climb the stall door. Ilfedo held her back and said, "Follow your Uncle Ombre. He is full of surprises for us today."

Ombre glanced back and saw the disappointment on the child's face. He squatted down and kissed her on the forehead. He reached out with his arms and she held out her own as he picked her up. He stood again and strolled to the next stall, then rested his hand on the half-door. Another white horse poked its head through and Ombre ran his fingers through its silvery mane while Oganna reached out with her small hand. Her fingers stroked the Evenshadow's muzzle and she laughed lightly.

Ilfedo's mouth gaped. "You have not one but two of them? How is this possible? Is that Honer's mare?"

"Nope!" Ombre grinned as three more Evenshadows jutted their heads over the stall doors. Then he pointed dramatically at the horse farthest from him. "That one is Honer's mare. These other three followed my stallion as calmly as if I had tamed them, too. They are beautiful, aren't they?"

"No one could say otherwise," Ilfedo said as he reached out to stroke one of the animals. He expected the mare to pull back from him. One would expect that from a wild animal, but instead it held still and his fingers brushed her warm, wet nose.

"These horses are impossible to forget," Ombre said in a reverent tone. "They are like bits of magic that dropped out of heaven when God created the world. They were magnificent in the wild, and they are easy to ride. They are stronger and more intelligent than ordinary horse breeds, and I believe they will be a pivotal asset in the development of our national army."

Ombre stroked another mare's face and she snorted, then turned away. He led Ilfedo out of the stables, still carrying Oganna. "How is my favorite little lady?" he asked the child as he closed the stable doors behind them. He bounced Oganna in his arms, wrapping her in a bearish hug, and she wrapped her arms around his neck, a smile filling her face. Then he set her, still smiling, on the ground.

"Can I ride one of your horses, Uncle Ombre? Please!" she exclaimed.

Ombre glanced up at Ilfedo. "That is okay by me, but it will be up to your father."

A fly buzzed in Ilfedo's face and he swatted it away. "You are certain they are safe for a child to ride?" he asked Ombre.

"The mares? No. But the stallion rides gentler than a nuvitor in flight. I'm breeding them. The mares are more free-spirited than the stallion, surprisingly." Ombre patted Oganna's back. "She'd be safe on that horse with me."

Ilfedo looked at his little girl's beautiful face. She wasn't begging, wasn't manipulating, but her desire to ride filled her bluegold eyes. "You said you are breeding them?" he asked Ombre.

"Evenshadow stallions would make invaluable mounts for the army officers, Ilfedo. I've tested these animals and their strength and stamina is superior to ordinary horses."

Ilfedo nodded. He'd heard that Commander Veil had an affinity for horses. "So you and Veil are looking to train young stallions for potential battles."

"If all works as I hope it will," Ombre said. He stood and tousled Oganna's blond hair. "What do you say I take her for a ride? The training fields are occupied at the moment, but I could take her down a woodland path I know of."

At that moment Caritha entered the fort. As the great doors shut behind her, she strode toward Ilfedo. He kissed Oganna's forehead and shooed her toward Ombre. "Have fun, but be careful, my daughter. And, Ombre, take care of her." Then he turned to greet Caritha.

"The Elite Thousand are ready," she said to him, while casting a subtle glance in Ombre's direction. "My sisters and I have taught them everything they are capable of learning. It is time to begin instructing our new pupil."

He steered her toward the gates with his arm around her shoulders. "First, I want to see what the

Elite are capable of. Then we can discuss Oganna's future."

Commander Veil joined them at Ilfedo's request. The three of them left the fort and walked onto the training fields. Veil preceded them onto the grounds, his orders ringing out as he passed each captain. There were ten of them. One captain to each hundred men. "Assemble your troops on the main training field!" Veil commanded them. "Tell your men that the day has come for them to prove their worth to become an Elite. Every soldier, to a man, fall into line!"

The lines hastily formed with a precision Veil could be proud of. The afternoon sun left few shadows, and the dirt crunched dryly under Ilfedo's boots. Veil led him around the fort to its opposite end. As he stood outside the fort walls, looking out over the vast clearing that was the primary training field, he felt a swell of confidence building in his chest. Line upon line the Elite marched onto the field from both sides. The only weapons they carried were their swords, masterfully crafted by Linsair before his disappearance. The swords were belted to their sides in brown leather scabbards that had been subtly accented with silver studs.

One thousand swordsmen stood line upon line before him. Ten lines. Ten captains. A thousand men waiting on his word. Ilfedo drew the sword of the dragon from his side. Every soldier turned their gaze upon him, emotionless.

As the living flames sprang from his blade, Ilfedo fondled the crystalline handle. It felt incredibly smooth, even soft. "One by one Commander Veil will call you forward," he called out to the men within reach of his voice, and his captains relayed it to all. The fiery armor solidified on his body, rippling with light that challenged the day. "Those of you who are called forward will individually step onto the training ground with me and demonstrate to me that you are capable, of not only wielding your weapon, but that you know how to defend yourself from fire by using your sword's power."

Unrolling a freshly inked scroll and holding it before his face, Commander Veil called out the first name. "Ezekiel Madon!"

A burly, short fellow stepped from the ranks and marched between them to face Ilfedo. He was garbed in nothing more than a long-sleeved black shirt, gray pants, and leather shoes. But he drew his blade from its sheath with great speed. Light flashed from his sword, and his body glowed for a moment, covering his other clothing with white armor. A metallic breastplate grew over him, and greaves, and white leather garments underneath. A white helm adorned his head. His sword never ceased to glow with white light.

Ilfedo took aim with his weapon and sent flames from its blade. The fire raged toward Ezekiel Madon but funneled into the man's Sword of Light, leaving him unburned.

Running forward, Ilfedo struck Ezekiel's blade with his own. The elite warrior struck back, holding his own. For several long minutes Ilfedo beat on the man's sword until, satisfied it would not break and the man could hold his own, he stepped back and bowed to him. "Return to your place in line, Ezekiel

Madon. You have passed the final test."

Striking his chest with the pommel of his sword, the man sheathed his weapon, the armor vanished from his body, and he marched back into line.

"Benediah Hilthan!" Commander Veil called out.

And so the afternoon progressed. Every man merited Ilfedo's sincerest respect. When evening came and Yimshi settled behind the hills, the Elite Thousand drew their swords against the darkness, and the plain in which they stood radiated with ethereal light.

Ilfedo stood apart from them and exhaled slowly. "Magnificent," he whispered, and then Caritha stepped up beside him. He looked down at her but she watched the Elite with sober vigilance.

Commander Veil saluted the troops and shouted out for all to hear, and the warriors of light responded in kind. They spoke an oath. They recited a vow.

"I will bear the sword of light with wisdom, so that I will live to serve justice. I will die to protect the innocent. I will die to protect my brethren. I live to serve justice, and I am committed to showing mercy rather than vengeance. This say we all!"

THE DRAGON'S EYE DIAMOND

Oganna was grinning up at Uncle Ombre, and his eyes twinkled back at her. She trusted him as she trusted few other adults, with the exception of her father, of course. She loved her aunts, but with Ombre she had something special. Some adults made her feel that she could not act like a child, like they expected a maturity from her that was too far beyond her years. Ombre's projected lack of expectation affected the way she felt now. There was no pressure from this gentle man. Only kindness.

"Are you ready to go on a ride with me, little one?" He knelt in front of her, poked her in the stomach, and hopped to his feet again. "You know what?" he said. "Someday I hope to have a little girl just like you."

She was all smiles as she replied, "You do?"

Ombre patted her head but his gaze wandered

elsewhere. He watched Caritha as she walked alongside of Ilfedo toward the fort's gate. The pair was heading for the training fields. It would be the final test for the Elite Thousand, Oganna knew. She did not understand all that was happening. Why did her father want so many men at arms? Was it necessary? She imagined it must be. Her father was not one to waste his energy or the efforts of those closest to him on inconsequential matters. He had a plan and she was just too young to fully grasp it yet.

Uncle Ombre's eyes were still following Caritha as she left the fort. "Unless your aunt softens toward me, it will never happen," he said so softly that she almost didn't hear him. "A man needs a good woman to return his love if they are to have a child."

Oganna grinned anew. He did not realize that she had overheard that last part. The admission of a lonely, love-sick heart. She did not understand what all of that meant either, but she thought that she grasped enough to know one thing. Ombre would never let anything bad happen to her aunt. He cared for her, too. "I like you, Uncle Ombre," she said.

With a smile of his own, Ombre broke out of his musing. "And I like you, little one." He bobbed his head toward the stable. "Now, are you ready to ride one of those beautiful horses?"

She jumped, and he caught her, swinging her legs over his strong shoulders. He glided into the stable, ducking once to keep her from hitting her head on the doorframe. But the door was quite high enough for horses, so his gesture was appreciated but unnecessary. The Evenshadow stallion whinnied and kicked the stall door. "Anxious, aren't you, Midnight?" Ombre spoke to the animal.

"Is that his name?" Oganna asked.

Ombre chuckled as he opened the stall door and lifted her off of his shoulders, then he set her astride the magnificent creature. "Yes, my little princess. I have named him Midnight to remind me of the first time I saw him. Now, I want you to grab a fistful of his mane to keep your balance. Do you understand?"

Oganna's legs barely held on to the animal's shoulders. She almost slipped off, but grabbed the stallion's mane and pulled herself barely back into balance. It reminded her of a time when she had tried to sit on a log in the river, rolling beneath her at unpredictable moments. The stallion snorted in protest as she held his mane tighter, but otherwise he held still.

Ombre patted the Evenshadow's shoulder and stroked its neck before slipping a bridle over its ears. He swung up behind Oganna, his knees gripping Midnight's sides. The stallion's body quivered, and its muscles rippled beneath them. Ombre held her firm with one arm while managing the reins of their mount with the other.

He leaned forward. "Fill your hands with his mane, Oganna."

She grabbed larger handfuls of the long silvery hairs and tightened her fists. Midnight lunged out the door, and she felt as if she'd left her breath in his stall as he raced through the courtyard.

"Open the gates!" Ombre called.

Four swordsmen put their bodies against the doors, forcing them open ever so slowly. Midnight screamed. He darted through the narrow opening between the gates. He wove through the rows of white tents that stood outside of the fort, heading away from the town. At last they left civilization and raced through the fields. The rush of air cooled her face, startled birds flew past her head, and Yimshi's rays turned the greenery into gold hues.

Midnight's hooves beat methodically, pulling and driving him forward until he came to the forest's edge. The horse did not slow its pace. Reaching the tree line the stallion slipped between the trunks and fled over the forest floor.

Ombre leaned over Oganna, and his body pressed her against the stallion's neck until silvery hairs whipped around her head. He pulled the stallion's head to the side, guiding it around a large tree. Another tree, but a fallen one, lay across their path at eye-level, and she ducked her head until they passed beneath it.

As they passed beyond the fallen tree Oganna raised her head again. Twenty paces ahead of them the underbrush grew too thickly to let them pass, but Ombre steered Midnight through at breakneck speed. She buried her nose in the flailing strands of mane. The horse's hair was not harsh, but soft and comforting, and she leaned forward.

Ombre wheeled the stallion around another tree and brought him to a halt. Golden beams streamed through the branches above, and vibrant green grass shivered in the meadow that now lay before them. Small patches of blue grass had grown in the midst of the green, scattered around the meadow.

He threw his leg over the stallion's side, dropping nimbly to the ground. Then he turned and lifted Oganna down. As she set her feet in the grass, tiny clouds of pollen stirred into the air. The fragrance of wildflowers filled her nostrils. She bent down, pulled up a clump of blue grass by the roots, and ran her fingertips over the fuzzy blades. At night the blades would glow. She had seen it happen.

"Beautiful, is it not?" Ombre remarked.

She nodded and swatted a mosquito with her free hand.

"That stuff used to be a rarity," Ombre said. "However, it has been spreading across the land these past years. Some people say that your father's magic sword is spreading healing energy throughout the land and that the blue grass is a byproduct of that."

Replacing the grass in the dirt, Oganna nodded vigorously. "Father told me that some people are purposefully transplanting it. He said they want it to spread because it is so pretty."

"Like a beacon of hope after our lost and fragmented histories." He smiled and patted Midnight's glistening coat. The stallion blew through its nostrils and galloped into the forest. "He'll be back after he finds a cold stream to satisfy his thirst," Ombre said as he gazed after his mount. Then he waved his hand toward the curious patch of plucked grass. "People want to spread this stuff for two reasons, not just for its visual appeal. They are anxious about the Art'en creatures. They think that by spreading this weed around the floors of our forests they can illuminate the shadows of night, thus keeping those winged men from sneaking upon them. And perhaps there is wisdom in that. It makes some sense to me."

Oganna sat in the grass and shivered at the memory of the Art'en attack on her father's home. Across the clearing a rabbit dove under a bush, crying out as it did so. She could have sworn it said, "Yipes!" but that seemed strange for a rabbit. Oganna glanced back up at Ombre and said, "Do you think that the winged men are all gone now? Forever?"

"Now that is impossible to say," Ombre sat beside her and crossed his legs, patting her head. "Did they frighten you the other night?"

With a nod, she glanced at a goldfinch perched at the meadow's edge. The songbird shook its tiny head and sneezed. She was sure that she had seen it sneeze. But did birds sneeze? She didn't think they did. "Achoo!" the sound came again, and again she shook her head, trying to clear the sound from her mind.

"Are you all right?" Ombre frowned down at her and felt her forehead. "You haven't been having bad dreams or anything like that, have you?"

"Oh no, Uncle Ombre, I never have bad dreams," she said.

He chuckled and shook his head. "You can't fool me. Even I had my share of nightmares as a child. Used to be bears in my dreams. Bears as big as a house."

"Uncle Ombre?" she asked.

"Hmm?" he replied as he twirled a lock of her hair around his finger. He glanced at the sky, shading his eyes with his hand.

She sighed and gazed up at him. "I really have never had a bad dream. Believe me, please. I'm not lying to you."

Returning her gaze he seemed to search her heart for a moment. His eyes widened and his brow rose. "Well," he said, "that is not natural." He stroked his jaw with his thumb. "You always have good dreams? Never a hint of a bad one?"

Soberly, she fingered the clump of night grass in front of her. Should she tell him what was on her mind? He wouldn't believe her. Of that she was certain. But what if she could share the experience with him?

Ombre stood and took her hand in his. He walked her into the forest where bees buzzed past their heads and clamored over the blue and yellow flowers that carpeted the ground. Butterflies of extraordinary variety flitted to more distant purple and white petals, keeping just out of reach. Yimshi's rays pierced the woods, spotlighting a pool of water surrounded by bright moss. A small rainbow graced it where a light mist rose from the water's surface.

They sat cross-legged on a moss-covered stone. Oganna watched the scenery for a long while, drinking in creation's glory. Then a strange voice entered her mind. "Fat, lazy humans . . . blurp! I wish they'd just leave." The only things in sight were the butterflies and bees. Oh, and one bullfrog spying from the opposite side of the pool, only its bulbous eyes visible in the mud.

"Uncle Ombre," she said, turning to him and frowning. "Would you think me silly if I told you a strange secret?"

"A strange secret?" he asked.

"Yes. It is something I have not told anyone else. I know that people would laugh at me for saying it." She suddenly jerked her head as another sound caught her ear. "I think I can hear the frogs talking."

He knit his brow, skepticism filling his eyes. "Talking frogs?"

"Never mind," she said and she turned away, wishing she hadn't told him. And why should he believe her? It sounded very silly, even to her. Then his hand grasped her shoulder.

"Forgive me, little one. I should not doubt you," he said, then he sighed. "Please, go on. Tell me everything and I promise that I will listen with an open mind."

A second bullfrog joined the first, and they hopped onto lily pads. One croaked, and she again heard something, though this time she could not discern what had been said. She waited a moment, and then the croaking resumed. An entire conversation entered her mind. Not understanding why, she reached up, touched Ombre's forehead, and listened to the bullfrogs. Their words formed in her mind, and she felt that he could now hear them too. Ombre's eyes grew big, and his jaw dropped in astonishment.

"Do you hear them, Uncle Ombre?" she asked.

In a hushed tone he replied, "I do. I hear the bullfrogs talking! But that's crazy, right?"

For several minutes they listened together. Oganna maintained her touch on his forehead. The bullfrogs boasted to one another of their underwater homes and of how many tadpoles they had raised. They talked about the weather and complained about their neighbors. All in all, it sounded very much like a conversation between two people. Except of course that they spoke of the most distasteful things for supper and of mannerisms that, to a human, were very strange.

Oganna dropped her hand from his forehead. "Sometimes," she said, "I can hear other creatures talking too, and I—" She hesitated again.

Ombre urged her to continue. "Go on, little one. Tell me what's on your mind."

"Some of the wild animals come when I think of them." Silence followed her claim. She rose and closed her eyes to focus her thoughts on a buck, nearby in the forest's undergrowth. She could feel it respond to her call, and she heard it walk up behind her. A cool breeze rustled the leaves as the buck nuzzled her neck, then plucked a flower with its teeth and set it in her hand.

Ombre looked up at her with mouth agape again, but his eyes were shining. "I never," he started to say.

She petted the buck until it meandered back into the forest.

"Little one." Ombre gazed into her eyes. "I won't pretend to know how you do these things, but from now on I promise you can tell me anything, and I will believe you. You are special, Oganna. Like your mother, you are unique."

She smiled back at him and spoke in soft tones. "You know what is really strange?" She giggled as she mulled over her thoughts. "I don't think that all of the animals can speak. Only some of them, and I cannot imagine why. Why would one pond of frogs sound like intelligent creatures, and another seem like simple animals? One deer is a mere animal with no mind of its own, but another can speak like you and I."

They remained by the pond for a little longer, but daylight was falling into late afternoon.

"Are you ready to go?" Uncle Ombre threw her over his shoulder like he would have carried a sack of potatoes, and returned to the clearing. She laughed the whole way until he set her in the grass. Midnight lifted his head from his grazing, whinnied, and trotted up to them. Silver flaked off his hoofs as he moved, leaving glowing chips on the ground.

"Up we go," Ombre said as he set her in front of him on the Evenshadow, and they rode back to the fort.

When they had passed through the gates and entered the stable, Ombre put Midnight in his stall and removed the bridle. He spoke softly to the handsome creature, patting its neck and stroking its head.

Commander Veil barreled into the stable. "Princess," he asked, "how would you like a tour of our little town?" He looked at Ombre for permission.

Ombre considered for a moment, then he spoke. "I will tell Ilfedo where you have taken her, and I will follow shortly. Keep a close eye on her and on those around her."

"Of course, my lord!" Veil leaned down and grinned. "What do you say, Princess?"

She smiled back and gave him her hand. "I've always wanted to see the market."

"As you wish," he said with a bow, and she giggled.

Ombre chuckled. "Beat it, you two, and have

a good time."

If Oganna had chosen one word to describe Commander Veil, that word would have been warm. As he led her out of the fort and across the surrounding fields toward the town, a small crowd gathered. The voices of the people were a low, curious murmur in her ears as she approached. She wanted to shrink out of sight as their eyes riveted on her, but Commander Veil raised his fist and four swordsmen broke from the crowd and surrounded her.

"Do not worry, my princess," Veil said as he led her down the street between the rough-hewn buildings. "The people here want to see you. They want to be able to tell their relatives and friends that they were this close." He held up his hand as if pinching something together without quite touching his fingers together. "This close to you, the future ruler of the Hemmed Land and the daughter of the mighty Lord Warrior. Our guards will keep them at a distance for your safety while you survey the town. Come!" He turned and walked her up an adjoining street toward a torrent of sounds. "The market is this way," he said.

She followed him closely, yet could not hide the wonder in her eyes. This town was a strange place. A jumble of friendly and severe faces, of shoppers and merchants flashing their wares. Farmers had brought carts of animals to the market, and sacks of potatoes. One man sold apples and pears under a canvas tent. Oddly enough, though his tent was filled with fruit, he was lofting a bundle of carrots in his hand as he called out to passersby, but his words were drowned out by a sheep bleating nearby.

Oganna had seen a market before, but none so diverse as this.

A tall man with deeply-tanned skin guarded one shop, and it was a shop. Not a ramshackle building or a tent like many of the others, but a storefront that stood out from the rest. Commander Veil chuckled when he saw her eyeing the place.

"Not everyone who does business here is a simple farmer or tradesman," he said. As he spoke the shop's door opened and Oganna glimpsed a gayly dressed fellow inside with a counter covered in precious stones. Behind the fellow stood two men in dark red robes, nearly concealed in the shadowy recesses of the shop. Seeing her interest, Commander Veil led Oganna inside and stood back as she examined the stones.

The fellow selling the precious stones smiled down at her from across the counter. The robed figures behind him stayed as still as the stones he was displaying and she did not doubt that they were heavily armed. The fellow was a round sort of man with a bald head that glistened with sweat in the warm building. Low over his head hung an iron lantern the size of a birdcage. "Come, child," he said in a raspy voice. "I have rubies, and emeralds, even a few diamonds from across the Sea of Serpents." He picked up a diamond that was about the size of her thumb, balanced it in on his palm, and held it out to her. Unlike any other diamond that Oganna had seen, this one was as red as blood. "This is the rarest type of diamond in the world," said the fellow. "The traveler that sold me this particular gemstone told me that it has a history. It was found buried in the skull of an ancient dragon and given to a prince of some faraway land. Now it happened that the prince had become infatuated with the beautiful daughter of a carpenter, but being of noble blood he knew that he would never be allowed to marry her. So one night he bribed the carpenter with the dragon's eye diamond to buy one night with the beautiful daughter. But during the night, while the couple still lay in bed, the stone began to glow and it transformed into the real eye of the dragon. Some say that the dragon's breath erupted from the stone and consumed the young couple, flesh and bone. Other versions of the story maintain that the prince burned the bed himself to deceive the carpenter and the nobles, and fled that night with the girl. But he left the gemstone, which was just an ordinary diamond, for the girl's father to find." The merchant's eyes danced as he told the tale, and Oganna found that her own delight mirrored his own.

But Commander Veil grasped her by the shoulder and started to guide her out of the shop. "Perhaps you should be more careful who you tell your tall tales to," he said to the fellow. "Her father is the Lord Warrior. I wonder but that you would not change your pretty story if he was standing here now."

Instead of looking horrified, the fellow beckoned Oganna back to his counter. Reluctantly Veil let her go and she found herself again looking upon The Dragon's Eye. "The story is more than likely true," he rasped out to her. "This is a unique diamond and one that holds very high value. I have never found another like it." He looked up meaningfully at Commander Veil. "It is a beautiful diamond, after all. And red diamonds are exceedingly precious!" Then he watched Oganna's eyes and smiled. "There is something equally magical about you, Princess. I am a common man, but you will achieve greatness. I can see it in your eyes. What remarkable eyes! Both gold and blue. Never have I seen the like. Your eyes are unique, just like some of my precious stones."

Then the fellow did something that quite stunned Oganna. He reached out and opened her hand, then he set The Dragon's Eye on her palm. The diamond felt warm to the touch.

"A gift for you," the fellow said. "It would surprise me if I ever again meet someone as unique as you in this world. Take it, and do with it whatever your heart desires."

Oganna did not know what to say. She stared at him, then at the diamond in her palm. Commander Veil was speechless, and the fellow behind the counter laughed and waved them off. Finally, as she left the shop, Oganna turned and graciously thanked him.

The fellow sobered, then bowed to her. "May it bring many good things at your bidding," he said.

Veil guided her out of the shop. "I daresay that man has a tongue more valuable than his gems," Veil said. "Still, that was a costly gift. I never would have taken that man for a benefactor. But come along, there is more to see and evening will soon be upon us."

Within a short while the hubbub of the market diminished. It was as if someone had thrown a blanket over the scene. The sky dimmed. A quiet settled over the area, and the shoppers left for other parts of town as the merchants closed their stalls.

As she followed Veil out of the marketplace she passed a white picket fence and peered through it. A shepherd boy no older than she, was herding a small flock of sheep out of a side gate. A man and a woman stopped to look at the sheep and immediately a thick farmer barreled past the shepherd boy. He stepped around the pen, grinning as he let his potential customers touch the wool draped over his arms.

Oganna turned away from the sight and was almost knocked down by a passing hunter. He was short and carrying a stack of raccoon pelts over his shoulder. Under his other arm he had rolled a deerskin.

"Hey! Watch out there before I skewer you on my sword," Veil said hotly.

The hunter apologized with a curse, then walked on as if nothing had happened.

"Forgive his rudeness, my lady," Commander Veil said to Oganna. "These people are hard at work and their minds are filled with the duties they must perform in order to fill their bellies and care for their families." He shot a glance at the departing hunter. "Though it seems that men of certain professions are more susceptible to rudeness than others are."

Oganna knew from things that her father had told her that occasionally a farmer's crops produced insufficient return, and he would find himself without the means to provide for his family. Sometimes a hunter would have an off-season and would find himself without the means to trade for that which he needed. These people had come to the market as well and tried to barter as best they could for what they needed. But these unfortunate few had little if anything worth bartering for.

She saw one such man that evening. He was speaking with a merchant as she passed by. "I don't have anything to trade, good sir," she overheard him say. "But I'm an honest man. I will pay you back double. Just as soon as I'm able."

"Sorry, mister." The merchant held up his hand as if to protect his produce. "I can't be giving handouts, or I'll end up in the ruts too. Now move along! Come back when you have something substantial to offer."

The farmer hung his head as he turned away.

"Stop!" Oganna broke free of Veil's grip. She ran to the farmer and gazed up at him. A small crowd gathered as she reached into her dress pocket and drew out The Dragon's Eye diamond. She did not hesitate, but smiled up at the farmer. "A long time ago this diamond was found in a dead dragon's skull." Then she launched into a retelling of the tale of the prince who slept with the daughter of the carpenter.

The farmer's eyes widened as she told the story, and there were gasps from the onlookers.

"Use this to buy what you need," Oganna said. "But spend it with someone who will value it and pass along its story. Let it be a blessing to you, and also to others."

"Child, you are too kind. But I cannot take this. Times will favor me again," he said.

Confused by his refusal, she backed away. Then seeing he was embarrassed by his need, she spoke again. "I have no use for a diamond. Take it. Take it and spend it on what you need." Then she beamed as she said, "Or try to find out the truth of it, and see if the prince and the carpenter's daughter are alive or dead."

Commander Veil lumbered up from behind her and put both hands on Oganna's shoulders. "Do not refuse the future queen's gift," he said gently to the farmer.

"Princess!" The farmer fell to his knees. "Forgive me. I did not realize. Certainly I will not accept. Especially knowing now who you are!"

Another voice interrupted him. "And yet, for the future queen, to foster generosity in her heart and kindness toward her people is among the highest virtues. Would you not agree?" The crowd parted. Ilfedo stepped through with Ombre following. The people bowed and made room for him. "Oganna will one day rule over your children. Do not deny her this simple deed, for in the performance of such things her heart will be encouraged to do good rather than evil." He addressed Veil. "See to it that this man and his family are given what they need." He picked up Oganna and kissed her forehead.

Holding on to her father with one hand, she held out The Dragon's Eye and smiled at the farmer. "Please hold out your hand," she said.

The farmer's eyes sparkled as she rolled the diamond into his open palm. "Thank you, sweet child. One day you will make a fine queen, and on that day I will serve you well."

Oganna nodded her head slightly, Ilfedo turned away, and they returned to the fort. Once inside, her father set her at a wooden table in the command center. An array of weapons decorated the walls. There was a wide variety of swords, as well as some spears, and a few shields.

"The Elite Thousand are prepared," Ilfedo said as Ombre and Commander Veil took seats. A fly buzzed by and landed on the table before him. With a deft motion he brought his hand down and squashed it. "Little is left to do as far as building the army is concerned and, thankfully, no military challenges have presented themselves. I suggest that, for the time being, we keep the army busy by using it to construct roads and bridges."

"We should consider forming a few more patrols to cover the northern border," Ombre said as he leaned back in his chair. He crossed his arms behind his head and glanced sideways at Oganna. "I'd hate to see any more Art'en sneak across the border without our realizing it."

At that moment Caritha walked gracefully into the room and addressed Ilfedo. "Now the first task is complete," she said. "The Elite Thousand are ready to be incorporated into your growing army." She shifted her focus to Oganna and smiled gently, still speaking to Ilfedo. "With your permission, my brother, my sisters and I are ready to begin training Oganna."

Ilfedo closed his eyes for a moment, deep in thought. When he opened them, he stepped over to his daughter and stroked her blond hair. There was a resignation in his movements that told Oganna he was not thrilled with the idea, but nevertheless he felt it was the right course to take. "Very well," he said to Caritha. "When do you wish to begin?"

OGANNA'S TEST

Oganna parried her aunt's sword thrust with ease, then she rolled on the ground and came up behind her. The strength of her youth was reaching its peak now, for she had passed her seventeenth birthday. She slipped her blade around the woman's neck and held it gently against the jugular. "Will you finally surrender this match?" she asked.

"Most definitely," Laura said. She backed away with a bow, turning her sword hilt-first toward Oganna.

It was the traditional move in the Hemmed Land by which one relinquished to the greater swordsman, and Oganna smiled with her victory.

"You did very well this time." Caritha stepped from the ring of trees that formed the natural arena in which they were training. "Not meaning you, of course," she said as she shook her head at Laura and softly chuckled.

"Oh?" Laura asked with a note of challenge in her voice. "Sometimes you act rather cocky, Caritha. But if you are that confident of your talent, or skill, or whatever you want to call it, why don't you try to best her?"

Oganna smiled but remained quiet as she ran the flat of her sword's blade along her white glove. The metal zinged as she did so, and Yimshi's light caught its shining edge, casting rivulets of metallic radiance against the surrounding trees. Finally, she spoke in a casual tone. "Aunt Caritha, you aren't afraid I'll win, are you?"

"Well look who has grown up and is ready to conquer the world!" Caritha crossed her arms across her breasts, though her expression was not as severe as her words. "How long have you trained with us?" Caritha asked.

Oganna knew that Caritha did not expect an answer. Who could forget? These past seven years these kind women had helped her mature from an innocent child to a cunning woman. Her mother was long dead, but in her place the five Warrioresses had invested their all into her. Through their training she had discovered that she had an affinity for swordplay. Perhaps some of that affinity came from her mother, but she thought most of it came from her father. He could best anyone with a sword. Anyone.

No other woman in the Hemmed Land could cross blades with her and emerge the victor. She felt confident of that, and doubted not that many a man would now find her more than their equal in that regard. Ilfedo was still far her superior in swordsmanship, but she was able to hold her own for short rounds with him. Not an easy feat, especially with his superior size and strength. He always subdued her eventually though.

Of the Warrioresses, only Caritha had never tested herself against Oganna in one-on-one swordplay. Honer's wife Eva had recently expressed the opinion that Caritha was as good, if not better than Oganna. Oganna had asked Uncle Ombre his opinion but he had remained non-committal on the matter.

"Your aunt is a fine woman, and a fine fighter," he had said with a faraway look in his eye. "You are getting better, Oganna. Just don't try to pull your roots out of the ground before the tree is fully mature."

No wonder that Oganna felt deep in her instinctive gut that many people were simply flattering her. Flattering her because of her youth. They believed that Caritha was the better swordsman, didn't they! She longed to finally challenge herself against Caritha. What better way to determine if her training had come along as well as she believed it had?

Caritha took a step toward her, studying Oganna's eyes, then she pointed at her. "You have been under our instruction since you were a little girl, and we have trained you in sword combat for these last seven years. Now that you are seventeen, you wish to challenge me?"

Oganna twirled where she stood, then laughed a bit. "Why not?" she said. "Father and I have challenged each other on numerous occasions."

Amusement twitched the corners of Caritha's

lips as she replied, "Oganna, your father has his own way of fighting, and he is formidable with a sword. But he has strength on his side and size, advantages that give his technique more brutishness than finess. Whereas he drives his blade like a hammer at his opponent, I must rely on my speed and accuracy. Beyond that, I rely a good deal on the intuitive power of my dragon blood. In the past you have won duels against my sisters, but you have not truly been victorious. Yes, you are skilled with a sword, but you have not learned to pair that skill with the power in your dragon blood. That is what any Warrioress will admit to you. That she held back her dragon blood in order to train you first with the sword. If you want to challenge me then you will first need to master your dragon half, for I will not hold back."

Levena and Evela emerged from the encircling trees and sat on a log. Rozel followed them but leaned against a tree instead of sitting. She crossed her arms and rolled her eyes. "Humph! Caritha, stop this foolishness. You have put off Oganna's challenges for too long. I for one would like to see her prove herself. Her father does not utilize all his skills against her, either, and among us you are the quickest with a blade. Give Oganna a challenge."

"I agree," Laura said.

Levena raised her eyebrows at Caritha. "Are you worried that our pupil has grown stronger than you?"

"Nonsense," Caritha replied. "Why are you all encouraging this?"

Evela waved her arm in a generous manner. "Then let us see the teacher and the student test themselves against one another," she said. "I have done my part in Oganna's sword training, as have the rest of us. Caritha, you often enough stand back and suggest improvements to her technique. Now it is time you actively participate. If Oganna is to become the best, as well she should, then we need to give her our all."

Caritha shook her head and faced Oganna. "Step out out of the ring, everyone," she commanded. Then she leaned down to part the fold in her skirt where she had concealed the rusted sword of the Six. Her gaze fastened on Oganna. "Tell me what conditions you would like to lay down for this match, because if you lay down none then you will certainly be defeated."

"No conditions," a male voice said from the trees. Ombre stepped out, grinning from ear to ear. "Let's see Caritha use everything available to her! That would give me a personal thrill, and I am sure that Oganna could benefit from the experience."

Caritha looked at him out of the corner of her eye and picked at the ground with her blade. "You want me to use everything available to me?" she asked softly.

"Yes," Oganna agreed with a grin. "Use everything you can."

"Oganna, you have not yet learned the true power of dragon blood. But that is my greatest defense. Without it you haven't a chance in this world of beating me," Caritha said.

There was a thick chuckle from Ombre when he heard that, and Oganna glanced at him. She remembered her horse ride with him all those years ago. He knew better than the Warrioresses that she had gained an inate connection to her dragon blood. For her sake, she hoped that he could keep that knowledge a secret for a little longer. She watched him move to Caritha's side.

"How about we agree upon a little bet?" Ombre said. His nose brushed against her cheek as he spoke, and she blushed. "You say that Oganna has no chance against you, but I think you are wrong. Dead, dead, dead wrong." He took a step back.

Caritha cleared her throat. "Oh, and what stakes did you have in mind?"

He leaned over and whispered something in her ear. Color mounted to her cheeks again. When he backed away, she glanced about the clearing at everyone's faces. "Well, Caritha?" Ombre asked. He chuckled, and Oganna thought he sounded hopeful.

Slowly, Caritha nodded her head. Whatever the wager, Ombre seemed happy about it. He walked away, sat on a tree stump, and waited for the match to commence.

Oganna had observed that many opponents tended to circle each other, evaluating one another before joining in combat. She chose a different approach, preferring to strike immediately and thus force her opponents to respond on the defensive. One could learn a lot from their opponent by the way that they responded to each attack.

She stood straight, letting her bluegold eyes stare blankly ahead as she relied on another sense. Deep within her being she had long ago discovered a source of inhuman strength and drive that she could explain only as dragon power. There were things she could do that were not possible unless she searched for that something within her. Things she could feel and things she knew that no one suspected she could do.

Even now she felt the power growing inside of her, filling her, and branching out. But she held it back. She would only using her sword to block Caritha's attack. The first strikes, she was determined, would not be won by magic. No, they would depend on her skill with a blade.

She rolled forward, coming up in front of her aunt, and they both swung their blades simultaneously. Metal clashed with metal, and such was the force of their attack that they both reeled backward.

The observing Warrioresses gasped. Even Ombre with his tendency to treat events lightly narrowed his eyes. Perhaps he had assumed that a 'friendly' bout would mean an easy one. But this was her chance to prove her worth in battle.

Caritha swung her rusted blade, and Oganna blocked with her own sword. The force of the rusted weapon buffeted her. It might as well have been her father wielding the sword of the dragon against her. She fell to the ground and rolled to the side, rising again to her feet.

Again Caritha struck, and once more Oganna fell back. Caritha struck at her with rapid strokes, ringing metal against metal until Oganna's wrists ached. She closed her eyes and let her senses dig deep into that reservoir of energy she'd discovered in her blood. Strength flowed into her arms and her wrists. She opened her eyes and smiled up as her aunt darted to the side and swung her sword for another strike.

This time Oganna had no difficulty absorbing the impact. She swung her weapon up and stood. Their blades clashed, and this time Oganna sensed an extra force behind her aunt's blade, something strengthening the older woman's arms and steadying her weapon. But now Oganna's power matched her aunt's. Their blades locked against one another, neither giving way.

Gazing between the swords, Oganna met the woman's eye and laughed. Caritha's eyes widened, and she gritted her teeth. Oganna spun, freeing her blade from the stalemate. She came around and rained blows like hail against the rusty sword. Her breaths came easily, yet she maintained a speed to her movement that was unrivaled by either the Warrioresses or her father. She knew it. She could feel it, and she could see it in Caritha's narrowed eyes.

Beneath the relentless barrage of blows that Oganna dealt with her sword, Caritha's hand weakened a bit. Oganna charged, but Caritha rolled out of her path. Turning, Oganna saw her aunt facing her with her outstretched hands, palms up. Suddenly the tree branches around the clearing grew toward her. From over Caritha's head they extended to the ground in front of Oganna.

"Caritha!" Rozel cried out, and Oganna knew that her aunt was as surprised as she was by this particular use of the dragon blood. Perhaps she had never seen Caritha do this before.

The branches left no room for Oganna to slip through. She could hack the branches but would only waste precious time as Caritha recouped her energy. She bit her upper lip. The barrier presented a new challenge of a sort she'd secretly played with on a few occasions.

She reached out with her mind until the trees' essence reached her subconscious. Her vision darkened, and in place of the normal world she saw the root systems of every tree and the skeletal forms of her aunts and Ombre. For a moment the comical appearance of things made her want to laugh. Then she reached out with her hand and pulled at the tree roots with her mind.

The roots stabbed out of the ground, wrapped around Caritha's feet, and grew six feet high. She held her palm toward the branches, willing them to return to their lofty abodes. The branches shrank away from the ground. Oganna closed her eyes and held the back of her neck. A feeling of weightlessness washed over her for an instant. When it passed she blinked open her eyes to find Caritha suspended in the air, the roots holding her up by her feet.

"You were harder than I thought you would be," Oganna said as she curtsied to the disheveled woman. "Are you ready for me to let you down?"

For a moment it seemed that Caritha would admit defeat. Then Ombre stepped closer with a smug grin on his face. "Well, my lady, it looks like you will have to live up to your end of our bargain!"

Caritha grunted, struggling to free her feet. She shook her head. "Not yet, Oganna. I'm not finished yet."

Oganna's strange perception faded. People were no longer skeletons. Sizzling purple energy appeared on Caritha's body. It wove around her in a web of sparkling light, and the tree roots started to recede. Oganna walked up to the roots. Her hand glowed blue as she touched the forest growth. Her soft blue light spread up the roots. Her vision returned to that of an ordinary person. The tree roots spread around Caritha's ankles, then her legs.

Caritha's struggle resulted in a partial release from the branches. One of her feet fell loose and dangled in a most undignified position.

The woman was strong, Oganna was forced to admit. She could feel Caritha's resistance through the roots. She held one of the roots, reaching deeper, manipulating the trees and using their direct contact with her aunt to read her intentions.

Shocks of energy coursed from Caritha into the roots. But Oganna cancelled the attacks with her own power. The trees shook violently as if unable to contain the powers that were struggling to control them. Cracks appeared in the bark. Water failed to feed the leaves. No longer could the plants function as a whole. The pressure was too great. The green leaves browned, the bark burned, and large sections of the trees splintered.

Her powers were coursing through them. Oganna could feel it happening. It coursed through them, over them, and at last her dragon blood overwhelmed Caritha's resistance. The branches exploded, and the woman dropped to the earth.

The alarmed observers hastened to remove the debris. "Caritha, are you all right?" Laura asked as she felt for a pulse. She heaved a sigh of relief. "Thank heaven! I thought you'd killed yourself with that display."

Caritha sat up, sputtering dirt out of her

mouth. Dirt had covered her from her long dark hair to her leather boots. She flipped her sword, holding it pommel-first toward Oganna. "Well done, student," she smiled. "You have defeated me."

Oganna sat beside her in the grass. All around them lay splintered and smoking wood. "I must admit you put up quite a fight. I had no idea that you knew how to manipulate trees," she said.

Caritha looked both pleased and bewildered. "And I had no idea you could use your powers yet, at least not with such control. Oganna, we did not teach you these things. So who did?"

"No one," Oganna replied with a shrug, and she meant it honestly. Her connection to her dragon blood was almost as natural as breathing to her. How could she not have developed control in these past years?

This reply did not appear to satisfy her aunts. Standing, Caritha glanced doubtfully at her and said, "It is impossible to learn how to use the power in dragon blood without an instructor. Responsibly, that is."

Oganna did not know how to reply. How could she deny the woman's wisdom and yet maintain the truth of what experience had proved? Albino had taught the Warrioresses the use of their powers, yet she had discovered them herself. "I've been tinkering with my abilities ever since I discovered that some creatures talk," she said.

Evela gasped and covered her mouth with her hand. She glanced at Caritha. "An affinity for intelligent animals. Just like Dantress!"

"Oganna is only half-dragon, Evela. The rest

of her blood is human," Caritha said. "I'm only assuming, but doesn't that mean she does not have the same potential as we do? Dantress caught on more quickly than the rest of us. Her ability to manipulate her dragon powers was beyond anything we are able to do, so I suppose that is in Oganna's favor. Yet the extent of her power cannot be any greater than ours. It may be less, but not more."

"Humph! You say that after she soundly thrashed you in fair combat," Rozel said. She waved her hand in dismissal and walked off. "Don't feel so certain of yourself, Caritha. I for one think my niece has great potential to outshine even you." She looked over her shoulder and winked at Oganna.

Oganna smiled back. "Thank you, Aunt Rozel."

Ombre grasped Caritha's shoulders and gently turned her to face him. "I do believe this settles our little wager, my lady. Are you going to honor our agreement?"

"Rozel, where are you going?" Laura called after her.

"Humph! Where do you think?" Rozel replied.

"Oh! I almost forgot. Come along everyone," Laura said. "We should return to town and get these two cleaned up before dinner."

Oganna grimaced. "Ugh! I hate state banquets."

"No, you don't," Ombre said.

The tallest sister laughed as she stopped in mid-stride. Rozel spun to glance at him. "Oh yes, she does."

He furrowed his brow. "What makes you say that?"

She raised her eyebrows knowingly, then said, "One word of explanation, my dear friend."

Oganna watched Rozel's amused expression, for Ombre was twiddling his thumbs as he waited for her to finish. "And, and," he demanded. "What word are you talking about?"

"Men," Rozel said.

"Men?" He looked confused. "Men aren't a problem. They love her."

Rozel nodded and said, "Then let me be more precise. Young men are a problem for her."

"Nonsense!" He rested a hand on Oganna's shoulder. "Oganna, if any of the young men behave improperly, just slap them in the face." He raised his eyebrows. "But if you do happen to find one of them appealing, then treat him nicely and just flash your eyes in his direction from time to time."

"Ombre!" Caritha scolded. "That would be no way for the future queen to behave."

But Oganna smiled to herself, amused. She mulled it over and pictured the consequence of such an action. Ombre winked at her, and she winked back. Though she loved her aunts, Uncle Ombre was closer to her than they. Even though she was not his blood relative, she knew that she had adopted a few of his mannerisms.

"Come now, everyone," Evela said. "The mayor of Gwensin will be looking for us at the table, and we mustn't keep Ilfedo waiting."

# Like a Second Father

Oganna emerged from the tall trees and stared out across the fields that ended at the white stone walls of Gwensin City. This former town was the fastest growing center of civilization in the Hemmed Land. Somewhat centrally located, but to the south of Ilfedo's house in the west and of Coral Haven to the east. It stood on its own, grander than the other towns, and had been designated the new national capital. She followed Ombre and her aunts along one of the broad dirt roads that led past prospering farms to the city itself. Rows of corn stood guard on either side, waving their long leafs in the wind as if in respectful acknowledgement of her passage.

Ahead, rose the tall stone structures of Gwensin. Spacious homes and businesses had been painted shades of blue and some of white. At the city's center lay the castle-like residence of the mayor. She turned a corner onto the main street. Cheering people lined the way, waving streamers and shouting to her and her companions. She quickened her pace and shielded herself between Evela and Levena.

They turned to her quizzically, and she put a finger to her lips. "A princess must never appear in public when she is filthy," Oganna whispered. They smiled a bit at her excuse, but nonetheless they kept pace, shielding her from the crowds' stares. In truth, she was still quite dusty from her duel with Caritha.

The roadway was cobbled up to the open iron gates of the mayor's residence. Passing through the gates, Oganna was struck by the manicured flower gardens. They were beautiful, broad, and disappeared around the building's solid corners as if they circled the entire mansion. Stone pathways formed a maze through them, with intermittent fountains and iron benches placed along the way.

The front entrance sported a pair of tall wooden doors, which a butler now opened for her. She noted his yellow and black suit as well as his tall black hat. "Welcome to the State House," the butler said.

Oganna offered him a gentle smile.

"If you will follow me, Princess?" He led her away from her companions up one of the wooden stairways that flanked the wide open foyer. He took her to a large bedroom where he introduced her to three maids. "These girls will tend to your needs," he said.

She thanked him, then greeted her assigned

helpers as he departed. "You work for the mayor and his wife?" she asked.

"Yes, my lady. We serve Master Vortain and his lady," one of them replied, dipping a low curtsy. The other girls followed her example.

"Um, no. I will have none of that," Oganna said. "I do not keep servants, and I do not approve of servants."

"But, my lady, that is what we are," one of them protested.

She chuckled a bit at that. She had heard of Vortain's struggle for mastery over other men. Apparently his desire for power spread to the common folk as well, and she despised that. Perhaps she was too young to understand his reasoning, but on the other hand, how would Vortain like to be treated as a servant?

At last she looked at the maids again and said, "Every one of us is a servant to a lesser or a greater degree. Maybe you were, but you are no longer. The mayor knows I do not approve of servitude, and if he did not realize that then he should have. I will see to it that your jobs are kept for you, and that you are given wages for your services. Understood?" They nodded, but they still looked confused. She opened a nearby closet and surveyed the elaborate dresses that had been arrayed along the wall hooks. A delightful idea popped into her brain, and she stifled a laugh.

"Please," she said to the girls, "go tell the staff that I said to set three more places at the table for this evening's meal." The maids left to carry out her instructions and when they had gone, she laid several elaborate dresses on the bed. "Now let me see," she said to herself. "Which four shall I choose?" The dresses were quite beautiful. Oganna doubted that she would wear another as fine in the near future.

At the sound of a knock on her open door, she turned.

"May I enter?" Ilfedo asked. Then he stepped in, dressed smartly, with the mighty sword swinging from his belt. His pleated white pants were tucked into his freshly-shined black boots. He wore a black shirt embroidered with gold, and long white gloves were on his hands.

After an affectionate embrace, he pointed at the dresses on the bed. "Having trouble deciding which one to wear?" he asked.

"Not at all, Father. I think I'll use the crimson-and-white one," she said.

He furrowed his brow. "Then why the mess? Dinner will be ready soon."

She rolled her eyes. "The mayor assigned three maidservants to me—"

Ilfedo put a cautious hand on her shoulder. "Do not do anything to embarrass our host. You may not agree with Vortain keeping servants, but he does them no wrong and they remained here of their own free will. He did not snatch them off of the streets and press them into service. He signed a contract with them."

"And he does well by fulfilling those contracts. I know," she said. "But, you have told me time and time again not to worry what other people think, but to do what I think is right. Someday the practice of servitude must be abolished. No one should have the freedom to exercise that power over another human being, unless over criminals." She flashed him a smile. "Don't worry, I won't embarrass him too thoroughly. I'll just make him rethink his practices, and let him know that I do not approve of keeping servants."

"Very well." He pecked her on the cheek. "I'll see you at dinner."

As he left the room, the maids slipped back through the door. "We did as you told us," they said to Oganna.

One of them came close. She had a pretty, dimpled face, and long red hair. With some hesitancy she said, "We'd heard rumors, my lady, that you disapprove of lords keeping servants. Is it true?"

Oganna ran her fingers like a spider down a strip of lace. It was strong but light. A very nice example of the lace art. Absently, she replied to the girl, "It most certainly is true."

"But this is how we earn our livings. We're indentured for ten years. There is nothing we can do about it," the girl said.

Oganna held one of the dresses she'd chosen up to the girl's shoulders. "Mm hmm . . . now, take this into the washroom and put it on."

The girl's dimples deepened and she gasped, "My lady, I dare not!"

"You dare not do otherwise," Oganna said. "We are all servants, in a way. Even Vortain serves at another's pleasure. To deny me this little delight is to deny your master's master." She smiled at the stunned stares on the girls' faces, then she gave the dimpled one a gentle push and glanced at the others. "Now I don't want you two thinking you are getting out of this. I have picked dresses for you as well."

They opened their mouths to protest, but she shook her head. "It would be not be wise for you to deny me in this. My father may tolerate some things that his men of state do, even if he questions them. Keeping servants is one such tolerated thing. However, one day I will be queen and I have vowed servitude will end. You are young. You need to be ready for the future. Fair wages must be paid for fair work." Her warning seemed to drown out their protests. She saw to it that they changed, then slipped into her crimson dress. It fit the gentle curves of her body perfectly.

When the maids had finished dressing, they returned to the room and fought over the mirrors. When they saw Oganna in her dress, they put their hands over their mouths and squealed with delight. "You will drive the lads crazy with that!" said the dimpled one.

"I hope not," Oganna replied, then she eyed the others up and down. She let out a soft whistle. "Thanks to you, the lads' eyes will be divided among the four of us. Just look at yourselves. You will attract suitors from every station of life."

They looked horrified. "Our lady, we cannot go to the banquet with you."

She listened for a time as they raised objections but in the end she waved them aside and shooed them ahead of her through the door. "There will be many eligible young bachelors at this party, and they will have to be fools to pass up you three."

"No one will have us," one protested. "We are mere maids."

Oganna shook her head and said, "Nonsense! The honorable young men may be fewer than the fools, but the honorable ones will not care about your social standing. And those who do, cannot help but notice that you enter with the Lord Warrior's daughter."

"But we don't know anyone—" the dimpled one said.

Oganna sped toward the dining hall. "Don't worry. Stay with me and I will introduce you to those of consequence." The great double doors were opened by two men in black and yellow livery and she led the girls inside.

Under the vaulted ceiling of the dining hall stood a hefty table carved from mahogany. Its eight thick legs curled up from the floor, shaped to spiral to the tabletop. Oganna guessed it was just over forty feet long. Finely dressed gentlemen and ladies rose from their chairs as she entered, and she spotted her father at the table's far end. He looked so regal that it put her instantly at ease, despite the many admiring eyes that now turned to her.

The mayor's wife frowned at the maids, and Vortain himself followed his wife's example. He ran his fingers through his long blond hair until Oganna caught his eye and nodded. He relaxed his shoulders and bowed as she sidled up to him.

"I do not need more servants, Vortain," she whispered in his ear. "But I do appreciate your hospitality."

When his gaze returned to the maids and their fidgetting fingers, she smiled. "What sort of a queen do you desire to have? I could have a retinue. Indeed your own daughter might become my servant. Or shall I make peace with all that I meet and treat them as equals?"

"If I may speak with all honesty, princess." He folded his hands behind his back and scowled. "To build a kingdom requires strength of arm. Your diplomacy endears you to all you meet. But when you are queen, no one will be your true equal. If you lead this nation into a glorious future it will be your name that is remembered, and none other."

She bowed and gazed up into his eyes. "Without the hearts and minds of the people, Vortain, where is our strength?"

His face relaxed, and the hint of a smile touched his mouth as he dipped and kissed her hand. "Truly you will make a great and memorable queen, my lady. We shall continue this debate at another time?"

She pulled back her hand with a nod and gestured at the maids. "These are lovely young ladies, and I hope you will extend to them the same courtesy that you have to me and the rest of my father's guests."

"As you wish, Princess." He managed a smile in the direction of the maids. "Your word, as it always shall be, is my command."

Nodding gracefully to the other guests, Oganna bade them, "Good evening," and sat beside her father, indicating that the three girls were to sit on her other side.

Ilfedo put his arm around her shoulder, pulled her close, and whispered in her ear, "There's a rumor circulating that you bested Caritha in a sword match."

Catching the praise in his voice, she kissed his cheek.

He chuckled. "Well done, my daughter. Well done."

They greeted Laura, Evela, Levena, and Rozel as they arrived. Honer and his wife Eva came next. The woman paused by Oganna's seat. Oganna took her hand, squeezed it affectionately, and Eva returned it with a squeeze of her own. Shortly thereafter Ganning limped in with his wife on his arm. Now only two seats remained empty, one for Ombre and one for Caritha.

As the moments passed and neither showed, Oganna wondered where they had gone. "Father, do you know if Uncle Ombre and—" She hushed as Ilfedo's eyes looked past her to the entry doors. Ombre marched across the polished floorboards in a green dress coat and white trousers. His black boots shone, and his sword swung in its sheath at his side.

Caritha, her face slightly flushed, was holding his arm. She was arrayed in a fine dress of lavender, and her hair had been brushed until it shone like the still surface of a dark lake. She was wearing twin ruby earrings that glinted in the lamplight, and a necklace of miniscule jewels adorned her neck. Her feet were bare. As she followed her escort to her seat, she allowed him to seat her before he settled himself beside her.

Their entrance created no small stir. Oganna saw people whispering to each other and she could well imagine the questions they were asking. She couldn't help wondering herself. Was this the beginning of a permanent relationship? The answers were nobody's business. Not even hers. Nevertheless it pleased her greatly. No two people deserved each other more and she wished them only happiness. She would have to wait to see how events unfolded.

Later that evening, as the guests filtered outside into the flower gardens, Oganna followed, stopping on one of the stone porches. The cool night air smelled of perfume and a lone cloud drifted across the sky. Ombre and Caritha walked along a path toward one of the fountains.

"Keeping an eye on our lovebirds?" Laura asked as she came up behind her.

Oganna had been resting her hands on the deck railing. Now she turned to reply. "If I hadn't seen them walk into the dining hall together, I wouldn't have believed it."

"Don't get your hopes up that it is permanent," Laura said. She nodded toward the couple. "Caritha is probably just fulfilling her end of that little bet she made with him earlier today. Still, I suppose if she didn't have an attraction to him, then she wouldn't have made that bet in the first place."

Oganna crossed her arms. "I hope there is more to it than simply keeping her word. They are two of a kind. A very special kind."

A moment's silence passed before Laura spoke again. "Don't rest hope on it, child. A union between them could never be. If they were to consummate then it would result in a child . . . and that would be the end of her. I do not think Caritha would make that choice."

At first Oganna felt like laughing her aunt's statement aside, but there was something cold about the way Laura had said it, as if she spoke from a deeply rooted conviction. "Why? Why would you say that?" she asked.

Laura shook her head and sighed. But words seemed to have left her.

"Does this have something to do with what happened to my mother? Are you saying she would have lived had I not been born?" As Oganna asked the question a tear fled her eye, running down her cheek.

"I'm sorry," Laura said, and wiped away the tear with her sleeve. Then she sighed again and gazed after the couple. "Your father never told you how and why your mother died, did he?"

"No. He hasn't," Oganna admitted with a touch of bitterness.

"Have you asked him about it?" Laura said.

Oganna nodded, but there was little conviction in her admission. Her father had loved her mother more than life itself, and that was no exaggeration. She could see it in his eyes each time Dantress's name was mentioned, but always he grew quiet. Like the memories were his treasures alone, and no one else could share them. "She died giving birth to me. What more is there to know?"

Laura gazed back at her and tears formed in her eyes until they shone. "Giving birth, for a dragon's daughter, is always her last deed in the land of the living. Your mother knew that she would die, the day that she found out she was pregnant. She fought to live, but ultimately the power in her blood had to be given to you. Otherwise you would have died. So, you see, it was and was not by her choice." She swept her hand in a circle. "And the same is true of Levena, Rozel, Evela, myself, and—yes—even Caritha. Ombre may want her fiercely and she may want him, but they could never be together."

Their conversation was interrupted as Rozel joined them. She was frowning down at her dress. "Tore the fabric on that wicked chair," she muttered.

They were interrupted then by a young man in a long suit jacket, who swaggered toward them with his eyes fixated on Oganna. "Hi there," he said to her. He excused his way between Laura and Rozel. "I am Faynor," he said.

After Laura's revelation, Oganna was not feeling social, and Faynor's manners lacked discretion, so she excused herself and moved toward the garden. The young man followed several paces behind. Perhaps he had mistaken her departure for an invitation. "Faynor," she said, turning to face him, "I am not interested in your advances. If you wish to be a gentleman, you will leave me be."

He smiled in a foolish way and proffered his arm. "Later there will be dancing."

"Thank you for your offer, but I am not interested." She left him and wandered alone through the gardens.

To her delight she stumbled upon the maids who'd been assigned to her. Three dark-haired young men accompanied them. Each of the youths bowed to Oganna and politely moved aside. The girls' faces were no less than radiant. These youths were not farmers, or woodsmen. They were not servants of Vortain, but the sons of a prominent merchant who had come from Coral Haven to join the feast. Oganna slipped past them, smiling encouragement and nodding as each girl lipped a "thank you."

Oganna found a quiet spot on a bench surrounded by petunias, and settled back. Nearby, hidden somewhere behind a shrub, she could just make out Ombre talking with Caritha. His words were too soft for her to pick out, and she was glad, for if he wanted her to know what he spoke about, he would tell her. She was content to sit on the bench where her presence would not disturb them while she listened to the rhythm of their conversation.

Laura's words rang in her mind, but her aunt's fears seemed misplaced. The revelation about Oganna's mother dying to give birth to her was both painful and glorious at the same time. What greater love could a mother have for her child than to be willing to give up one life to bring the other into the world?

As the low sounds of Ombre and Caritha's conversation reached her ears again, Oganna felt contented. Aunt Laura was wrong in one respect. It was better to fear that Caritha would say no to Ombre, not the other way around. Better that they have a short, glorious happiness than that they should live long lives alone. If Caritha were wise then she would see through the choice and judge Ombre's love more valuable than her life. Oganna smiled to herself. Yes, and that is what her mother would have taught her, or had taught her by making such a sacrifice on her behalf. True love would pay any price.

Above her the sky filled with stars. Tonight was the time of new moon, the darkest night of the month. The constellations decorated the heavens. She picked out her favorite. The Fire Tree constellation. It lay near the celestial pole, its imaginary branches marked by a plethora of bright star clusters and gas clouds. Below the Fire Tree stretched the Blood Sword. Eight emerald stars formed its handle, six gold stars represented the sword's guard, and twenty brilliant ruby stars made up the blade. To the west a tiny comet blazed its steady trail of white across the heavens, and overhead a great fireball suddenly burst, lighting the ground in one flash as it burned through the atmosphere and burst apart without a sound.

She recalled speaking with an astronomer on the coast. An astronomer who also wore a monk's habit. He had an observatory north of Coral Haven that had been built on a great stone overlooking the sea and the coast, and the forests west. It was a glorious view nearly from horizon to horizon. The monk had spent many evenings studying the heavens, and her father had once brought the man home for a visit to share his knowledge with Oganna. That night had been similar to this one. Moonless with clear skies. A fireball had burst in the heavens, and she had gasped at the beautiful display.

But the monk had frowned as he watched the fireball. "It is odd," he had said.

She turned to gaze at his face. "What is?"

"Child," he said, "if something as large as that apparently is, exploded in the sky, you would expect to hear an explosion, even if it were only a faint one. Would you not?" He had shaken his head, still staring skyward. "It is as if something keeps the sound from reaching our ears. I wonder . . . I wonder if the Creator means for us to find out why."

Oganna sighed at the recollection. The world was beautiful, life was good, and she was content. Beside her an invisible foot left an imprint in the soft garden ground, and she slid to the opposite end of the bench. The seat creaked as someone unseen sat down.

"I was impressed with your duel today," the man's voice said. "It is most incredible how quickly your powers are manifesting themselves."

"No one is around," she said to the empty seat. She pleaded with her eyes. "Can you simply talk with me face to face? I need the company right now, and I think only yours will do."

Specter's hood fell away from his smiling face. He looked down at her and rendered his whole body visible, then stretched his arm along the backside of the bench. He had grown fond of her and she of him, he was like another uncle to her. "I overheard your conversation with Laura," he said, and his face sobered. "Are you all right?" With a sigh that told him she was content, she slid next to him and let him put his arm around her shoulders. "Specter, my dear silent guardian, my mother was blessed to have you watching over her. And now I am as well."

"Ah, your mother was a wonderful young woman." He exhaled slowly and gazed at the stars. "Your father was, I truly believe, the luckiest man on Subterran when it came to his wife. She was strong and beautiful, and you are like her."

"Don't disappear again for a little while. Please stay with me. You know you are like a second father to me."

A soft laugh escaped him, and he leaned his scythe over the back of the bench. "More like a long-lost great, great grandfather?"

She smiled up at him and warmth spread

through her body upon seeing the softness of his gaze. "Tell me more about my mother," she said. "Please?"

INCURSIONS

With each plod of the creature's feet, shivers ran down Garner's spine. He crouched lower to the dirt and stayed hidden behind a shipping barrel. The ground shook again as the creature loped between the darkened buildings that were the general store and the local brewery. Garner looked around at the destruction the creature had brought upon his town and he wanted to weep.

Bordelin was the only town along the Hemmed Land's southern border for several miles. Not as many people had been interested in settling this close to the desert, as they had been in moving inland or living along the coast of the Sea of Serpents. Garner reckoned that after tonight, no one would want to live in Bordelin. Not even the survivors if there were any.

It was too dark for him to see clearly, but he peeked from his place of concealment. In the middle of the road lined with rubble, he spotted the creature's enormous form outlined against the horizon of stars. Glowing yellow vapors emanated from the creature's nostrils and Garner trembled.

Sweat dripped down his forehead. He reached up to wipe it away, but a woman's scream stopped him. It had been impossible for the people to defend themselves, but apparently the creature hadn't found everyone and some had hidden. Garner wasn't alone! The frantic cry had come from a house by the bridge. Casting off consideration for his own safety he darted across the bridge and entered the front door. A roar sounded, and in that instant the creature smashed its tail through the wall, turning the house into an impossible maze of fallen beams and broken glass.

Garner did not dare look up through the gaping hole in the wall as the creature looked about. He swallowed his fear and clambered over a broken couch and looked about. The woman who had screamed was pinned to the floor by a fallen rafter. By itself the rafter would not have been too heavy for one man to lift, but jammed as it was from the floor to the ceiling it was carrying an impossible amount weight. Garner knew the woman. She was his neighbor and had been a kind friend to his wife. He had seen her at the market the day before. She'd bought a loaf of bread and a bag of lemons. She loved to share her lemonade.

Again the creature roared and spurted flames from its long mouth, setting what remained of the roof ablaze. The woman's leg, glistening red with blood, protruded from under the wooden beam. Her face was turning white.

The creature's hand smashed into the wreckage, sending rubble flying in all directions. Garner moved to cover his face with his arms, but a beam struck him and threw him out of the building onto the bridge. Pain shot through his leg and he looked down. A large shard of glass had lodged in his calf, and his blood was pooling on the bridge. He grasped his leg with both hands, ripping his belt off and tying it just below his knee. The bleeding slowed, but he knew that unless he received help soon he would die.

The house walls had fallen outward, as if the creature had pulled them down. The creature's long, tooth-ridden snout poked over the wreckage and the woman screamed again. This time the creature blew a stream of vapors into the house. Its victim's cries broke off into a spasm of coughing, then ceased as she died. Garner grit his teeth and clenched his fists. The tears streamed down his face. That woman was one of his neighbors, a good friend, and a good soul. Was there no pity in this creature's heart? Was there no shred of remorse for this senseless murder?

Several enraged townsfolk suddenly appeared from their hiding places inside of nearby buildings. Unheeding of their own peril, they stabbed pitchforks into the creature's thick hide. But the beast seemed unfazed. It turned toward them and continued to pour vapors from its nostrils upon them. The townsfolk grabbed at their throats, dropped their makeshift weapons, and stumbled to the ground. As they fell the creature tossed their bodies into the town well.

Garner remained out of sight, biting back

the tears of helplessness that stung his eyes. Then he scrambled out of town. Reaching the shelter of the forest, he grasped a treetrunk for support before glancing back to let another tear hide the carnage from his eye.

Through the darkness he stumbled northward until he came to a woodcutter's secluded home. He beat on the door until it opened. Weakened from loss of blood, he fell forward on the floor. Excruciating pain shot through his body, and he cried out, "Please, send for help." He could not go on.

The woodcutter and another man came into the room, cleared the table, and lifted him onto it. They tended to his leg and gave him liquor to numb the pain. "That's the limit of my knowledge," the woodcutter said. "This man needs a doctor." He grabbed a lantern and barreled outside.

Garner felt weak. He was weak. As the door closed, he blacked out. When he awoke, light was coming through a small window. He was lying in a comfortable, clean bed, and a woman was dressing his leg.

"You've been out for a while," she said, putting a hand to his forehead. "How do you feel?"

He breathed deeply. "Much better."

"Good," she said as she turned away, but he caught her sleeve.

"Must not let that creature get away!" He spoke through clenched teeth. "Send help to my town. My people are dead, but some might still be alive."

"Your town?" she asked.

"Town of Bordelin," he managed to say.

Then a wave of exhaustion swept over him, his vision blurred, and he lost consciousness again.

* * *

It had been an eventful morning for Ilfedo. A messenger had arrived from Fort North where Ombre was reviewing their troops there. Ombre's message cast a palor over Ilfedo's heart, for it bore a troubled report of a new threat. Now he was sitting on a chair on his porch, soaking in the momentary peace of a quiet afternoon. But another messenger ran out of the treeline and breathlessly stood in front of him, making a hasty bow. He was a lean-muscled fellow with a small leather pack thrown over his shoulder. But it was his eyes that caught Ilfedo's interest the most. The irises were as black as the depths of night itself. "My Lord, I have troubling news from the southern border." He proceeded to tell of the unidentified creature's attack on the town of Bordelin. "Several smaller settlements along that stretch of territory were also decimated in the last few days," he said as he drew an envelope from his pack. He extended the message toward Ilfedo. "People are panicking," the messenger said. "Many have fled the southern border towns and are moving inland."

After the courier had delivered the sealed dispatch, he left with the same speed with which he had arrived.

Returning indoors, Ilfedo sat at the table and opened the envelope. He drew out the paper inside and unfolded it. Laura and Caritha had been cooking dinner, but they paused and glanced over at him.

"What do you have there?" Laura asked.

"Trouble, I am sorry to say." He laid out the

skin and read aloud:

To the Lord Warrior:

Greetings from your faithful subjects. May God bring you health and prosperity all of your days.

With high consideration to your many duties, we request your attention to a matter that has presented itself among us. A creature of formidable strength has, in a single night, destroyed the town of Bordelin. Many of the town's inhabitants were slain, but a privileged few escaped the monster's clutches to tell us their tale.

All the reports gathered from survivors were consistent with each other, so we sent warriors and hunters to find the creature. They followed its tracks into the southern desert, but none of them has returned, and no word of their whereabouts has been received. We fear that the worst has befallen them and that our lives may still be in danger.

The survivors have stated that the creature stands on six legs and exhales poisonous vapors from its nostrils. Some say that it breathes fire as well. Reports indicate that the creature's hide is too thick to be penetrated by a spear and that it stands about ten feet high at the shoulders.

We are at a loss what to do unless a champion is sent to our aid. Please come and avenge the innocents whose lives were so brutally taken. One of the survivors of Bordelin was treated by a local doctor from the village of Harpen. Please come and speak with him. The survivor's name is Garner Nimmit. Please, help us.

We are respectfully,
Your humble subjects of the Hemmed Land's South-ern Border

The letter ended with a list of signatures. Mayor Grenenwill, Mayor Bart Timson, a few tradesmen, and several others who wanted to speed his response. Ilfedo set the letter down, rose, and walked to the fireplace. This was supposed to be a short vacation for him, yet this report was the second he had received today. He couldn't decide if he found this new report or Ombre's earlier one more disturbing.

For the last couple months Ilfedo had received disturbing reports that vipers were venturing out of the northern desert under cover of darkness and poisoning people along the Hemmed Land's border. A dozen people had died in their sleep, and he had sent Ombre to assess the situation from the safety of Fort North.

Caritha interrupted his thoughts. "You look perplexed," she said.

"I am, or at least I am torn between two issues," he said. "This problem is along the southern border, and I already sent word to Ombre that I will meet him at Fort North within the next few days. I need to make certain the Art'en are not behind the viper problem. My previous struggles with them focused on the northern border. If the Art'en have returned, then Ombre will need my help in dealing with them."

The sound of footsteps alerted him to the other sisters' presence. Rozel, Evela, and Levena came from their bedrooms.

"Well, that cuts our vacation short," Caritha said with a sigh. "Say no more, Ilfedo. We will deal with this situation in the south while you head north.

And we will do so gladly."

Rozel huffed in a very loud manner and placed her hands on her hips. "Like he didn't know that you would volunteer our services."

He returned her accusation with a smile. "Whom else can I rely on to truly get the job done? I could send soldiers, but they would not be as efficient. I can't send the Elite Thousand because they are deployed along the northern border. I can't send Ombre because he is also engaged at Fort North." He shook his head. "Of course, you don't have to go."

Drawing her rusty sword from the fold in her garment, Caritha spoke soberly. "We will reap vengeance on the creature. Its blood will be spilled in payment for the innocent blood it has shed." Her hands glowed, and her sword's blade gave out a steady reddish light as she spoke.

The others followed her lead, but they laughed at each other as they raised their swords. They formed a circle and touched their blades together dramatically. Then they pulled their swords back and Rozel said with a smile, "Wow, we must look amazing pulling these theatrics."

"Caritha, you really are dramatic," Laura said. "You do know that, don't you? Glowing your sword now, inside of the house, was unnecessary but showy."

"You are the five who become one," Ilfedo murmured. "The hunt that you are setting out on will not be an easy one. Take care how you proceed, and may your swords execute justice for the Hemmed Land."

Putting away her sword, Evela cleared her throat then looked at him. "Actually, we are hesitant to say this, but there is one more blade that we would like to add to our party."

He narrowed his eyes, "Oh?"

"Oganna is ready, Ilfedo. In fact, she can stand among us as an equal," Evela said.

The others nodded their approval. Caritha spoke up. "She has the makings of a cunning fighter, Ilfedo. Let her come with us. There is nothing like experience to prove a warrior's value."

"No," Ilfedo said. "I will not consent to that. She is too young."

"Only in your mind, my brother." Caritha laid her hand on the table. "Did she not prove herself capable when she bested me?"

He shook his head, determined not to concede the issue. "Continue to train her in your ways, if you must. But I am content that she knows how to defend herself. Do not permit her to become involved in potentially lethal situations. If and when I feel that she is ready to handle herself against true threats, then I will let you know."

"You send us into 'potentially lethal' situations with far less concern than that," Laura said. He could tell she regretted saying it as soon as the words left her mouth. She hastily apologized and asked his forgiveness.

But he waved the matter aside and put a hand on her shoulder. "I will think on the things you have said, and I am pleased that you hold Oganna in such high esteem. However, as her father I am saying that I do not believe she is ready. She is too young."

THE BLADE AND BOOMERANG

Standing outside on the porch, Oganna had heard the majority of the conversation through the partially open window. She was both saddened and hurt by her father's apparent lack of confidence in her. Evela was right. She was ready. Why could he not see that? Was he letting his fears interfere with his judgment in this matter? Regardless of the reason, she reached a decision of her own, but she went indoors and made no indication of what she'd heard.

Later, when night had fallen and everyone slept soundly, Oganna slipped a robe over her silky nightgown and pulled on wool slippers. She quietly opened her bedroom door, and peered around the kitchen and living room areas. Embers glowed in the fireplace, casting flickering light around the room.

She tiptoed into the kitchen and opened an upper cabinet. It was too dark to see what lay on the top shelf, but she knew what she was looking for. Her fingers found a large iron lantern. She pulled it down and set it on the counter. Then she slid open one of the drawers by the sink and plucked out a small tin of matches. Closing the drawer and the cabinet door, she tightened the cord around her robe and opened the house door.

Chill air blasted her, and the coals in the fireplace flared. But she closed the door and lit the lantern. Overhead a blanket of clouds blocked most of the stars, and no moonlight warmed the forest. She ran into the woods following a familiar, albeit unmarked trail beneath the high trees.

Owls hooted from every direction, and a possum skittered out of her path. At last she stopped at the crest of Matthaliah Hollow and gazed down, reaching out her senses to determine if Specter was nearby. Blue grass pretty much filled the hollow and outlined the cave entrance.

"Specter!" A gust of wind stole her voice, and she ran to the cave entrance, shivering. If he was there, she could not sense him. "Are you here?" she called as she walked into the cave's main chamber. But it was empty except for the old sword and crystalline boomerang. She drew in her breath slowly, then knelt in front of the weapons and reached out to at last take her sword.

"Oganna, why have you come to me at this hour?" Specter coalesced beside her, his face buried in the depths of his hood. His hand held the black-handled scythe. Its blade glistened as she set her lantern on the cave floor.

Craning her neck to look up at him, she

smiled. "The time has come for me to take my place among the dragon's daughters. Father is sending the Warrioresses into the southern desert to find a creature that raided our border towns. It is the mission that I was born to begin, Specter. I know it in the deepest reaches of my soul."

"Does your father know of this?" he asked solemnly.

"No. And for the time-being I do not wish him to," she said. "He still grieves for my mother and it has become an obstacle that he must be forced to surmount, otherwise I will forever be a prisoner of his fear."

Specter reached for his hood with his free hand and slipped it off his head. As his hand dropped back to his side she noticed for the first time the extent of his old burns. Without thinking she reached out and touched his injuries. Immediately the power in her dragon blood boiled forth, her hand glowed blue, and when she withdrew it, Specter's hand had been healed.

His mouth startled open. He brought his hand up and examined it for several long moments. "Strange, someone else tried to heal those wounds when you were very young, and I objected. I told him that I was proud to bear those scars because they had been inflicted while saving an innocent life. You have a strange effect on me, child. I feel . . . grateful . . . and I thought I would resent it."

"I . . . I don't know how or why," she said, looking down at her hand and turning it over. "I just reached out, and it happened."

"You are growing very strong, child. I think

even the dragon's daughters underestimate your potential. You have the strength of your father and the compassion and purity of your mother. A potent mix." He laughed and held up his once-burned hand. "The innocent life I once saved when I received this injury was your life."

"Mine?" She frowned. Why would he have received an injury saving her life before she could remember? "How did it happen?" she asked.

He let her words hang in the air and merely smiled. She sighed, knowing that the secrets this man harbored would take a lifetime to dredge up. Facing the sword and the boomerang, she sighed again. "Now that I am here, I'm not sure what to do with them."

Specter stood as still as a statue.

"This sword looks similar to those my aunts are carrying. And its blade is rusted also, yet not so extensively, and the blade is longer than theirs." She reached out, grasping the handle that she'd been forbidden to take and that she had not touched in all these years. The blade glowed ruby red and the crystalline handle shone white, then dimmed.

She released her hold and pulled Specter out of the cave. He appeared confused, as she expected him to be. She took his scythe from his hand and began harvesting the glowing blades of nightgrass and kicking them into heaps. Before long she had mowed down the majority of the beautiful growth. She smiled however, for the blades that she had severed continued to glow.

After dropping the scythe, she filled her arms with the glowing grass and grinned at Specter as she re-entered the cave. "Do not come in. Whatever you do, stay out there," she said.

"W . . . what? But why?" he asked.

"Just do as I ask. Please," she begged him. Again and again she filled her arms, then heaped the grass inside the cave. Its glow, as that of many flickering blue candles, dimly illuminated the cave's interior. When she finished, she sat on the moist floor and centered herself, meditating. Yes, there it was! Energy, a source of fresh power, radiating from the blue blades. It was a power source that she could draw on. Just as her father had drawn it with his sword, she fed on it with the power in her dragon blood.

Rising, she found Specter's stash of dry kindling and dead logs. Although she doubted he'd ever lived in this cave, she knew he frequented it, and the dampness was enough to make anyone desire a fire's warmth. She tossed the wood onto the glowing grass and then dropped to her hands and knees. Carefully she arranged some wood on a dryer section of the cave floor. Then she used a match to start a blaze.

When the little fire ran its course the dirt beneath it had dried somewhat. She stood back several feet, held her hand palm toward the ashes, and squinted her eyes. If only she could clear the dirt away from the stone beneath. As the thought passed through her mind, her hand glowed. White energy blasted from her hand, and she gasped. The energy impacted the dirt, sending it flying in all directions, including onto her face.

She wiped the dirt off and smiled to herself. The floor ahead had been cleared of all dirt. Only flat, shining stone remained.

Oganna knelt and ran her hand over the stone, feeling every imperfection. Then she folded her hands and pictured the creator on his throne. "God, you know what is in my heart," she prayed quietly. "You know how many people have suffered and how some have even died for my sake. I have an opportunity now to use my unique heritage to help others. Now, in my time of need, grant me a weapon that my dragon powers will feed. Grant me a weapon to defend my people. And please give me wisdom to exercise strength with humility."

So saying she rose and, stretching forth her hands with palms facing one another, she waited as crackling energy spiked from one hand to the other. A ball of light spun into existence, pulsating blinding white light that forced her to avert her gaze. Then she threw the energy with great force into the pile of night grass and sticks, engulfing it in flames.

The heat of the fire built until steam rose along the cave walls. Specter raced back into the cave and opened his mouth in horror. "What are you doing? Get out of there!" He raised his arm, shielding his face from the waves of heat rolling toward the cave entrance. "Oganna, get out of there before you kill yourself!"

But she formed another ball of light and threw it into the blaze. The flames rose to the ceiling, sweeping toward the exit. She cried out, "I told you to stay outside!" She could feel the heat building and she knew that it would harm her invisible guardian. She spun on Specter and held out her hand, letting a portion of her inner energy blast in his direction, pushing him out of the cave. A second later flames roiled into the space he had filled.

Her robe burst into flames and she screamed momentarily, expecting her face and hair to combust next. But though the fire disintegrated her robe and burned off her gown and slippers as well, she was left naked and unharmed. She touched her arms and breasts, stunned. The flames filled the cave, cloaking her nude form from even her own eyes. She turned victoriously upon the inferno, and repeatedly blasted it with white energy thrown from her hands. The energy welled inside of her and she expended it through her fingers until the stone walls arching above her began to melt and fall apart.

Fire consumed the pile in its entirety, leaving a seething mass of molten liquid on the cave floor. While the cave continued to burn, she knelt and held one finger in the molten mass. A thrill passed through her when she pulled it out, white-hot like an iron poker! With this finger she carved two impressions in the stone floor— that of a new sword and the form also of a boomerang. She took great care in designing the sword as she envisioned it should be and not as it currently was.

When the impressions were complete, she grabbed the sword and the boomerang from their places. First she laid the boomerang in the impression. It fit perfectly. Then she balanced the sword in both hands and sadness filled her for a moment. A tear fell onto the old rusted blade and, as it ran down the blade, crimson rivulets ran out of the metal. Was that blood?

Stunned, she dropped the weapon and watched. The blood ran off the blade's tip and pooled in the impression she had carved for the sword. It formed into a sphere and held its place at the end of the handle, like a liquid jewel ready for placement.

The heat intensified again, and now sweat poured from her body. The sweltering air drove the oxygen from her lungs. She had remained too long. Grabbing the sword, she positioned it in its mold and raced out of the cave.

On her way out she ran into Specter. In the light of the star-studded sky now visible through the thinned clouds, his face appeared fearful. She was suddenly very aware of her exposed skin. He narrowed his eyes and wrapped his cloak around her. "You have done enough for tonight. Come!" He caught her arm. "I'm taking you home."

"This thing that I am doing, I cannot stop now!" She desperately tried to shake him off, but his arms felt solid as iron. "Let me go. I will free myself by other means if you do not."

But he dragged her toward the edge of the clearing.

With her free hand she reached up and touched the side of his face. "I'm sorry, my dear guardian. But this task I have set myself to complete," she said. His eyes closed as she transferred a shred of her energy into his mind, and he collapsed to the ground.

She covered him with his hooded cloak and then patted it with her hand. The fabric rendered him invisible, and she sped northward deeper into the hollow. As she ran her naked skin felt every slap of each branch that she passed, and her feet grew numb as she stepped on stones and dirt alike. There in the hollow she found the dilapidated ruin of the cabin her grandparents had died in, and near the cabin she spotted their old well.

Leaning over the well's lip, she drew up the old bucket by its chain. The water felt as cold as ice and she shivered. But her mind was not on clothing, her focus was on crafting the best weapons that she could. She ran the bucket of water back to the cave, sped inside, and cast the water over the molten forms of the sword and boomerang. A blast of steam flooded her nostrils and stung her face. She ran outside, not stopping until she was a safe distance from the cave's entrance.

Daring to look back, she saw beams of light radiate from inside. Grazing deer scurried away, their white tails flashing as warning flags in the darkness. The cave blew up, and the ground shook beneath her feet. She raised her hand to shield her eyes from the blinding flashes.

There was another explosion, dazzling and more forceful than the previous eruptions. A beam of light blasted from the roof of the cave and shot into the sky. It traveled unhindered, thundering through the air, and then it lost momentum and fell back to the cave with a resounding *Crack!* Its impact knocked her legs from under her, and she fell.

She could feel the power within her growing in magnitude until she feared she would burst. Her hands glowed, and the grass around her fingers steamed as though it would catch fire. The energy surged through her one final time from her feet, ending at her finger tips. She shook her head to clear it and looked toward the cave.

A woman stood there, her body blazing with

fire, blocking Oganna's way. "Steady yourself, my child," the woman said. "You have had a busy night." She extended her arm and pulled Oganna to her feet. The stranger's clothes were blazing fiercely with red and orange flames, yet they were not consumed. Her dress was crimson, and she wore a belt of silver and gold. Her hands were gloved, and the material appeared to be woven of silver. Her long, dark, wavy hair was held back with a silver strand. Flames obscured her face.

The woman produced a white dress and helped Oganna slip it on. When Oganna's nakedness was covered, the woman rested a hand on her shoulder and spoke to her in the kindest voice that ever a person could hear. "Use your powers for good, Oganna, and do not be corrupted by the lust to control others." The woman lowered her arm and walked away.

"Wait!" Oganna said as she held up a hand. "Who are you?"

But the woman retreated, wrapping herself in flames, and vanished.

A tornado of air whipped through the clearing, and a shadow obscured the stars. Leathern wings snapped against the wind, and great claws dug into the ground in front of Oganna. Towering into the night was the great white dragon. Oganna caught her breath and eyed his tremendous form, strong yet agile.

Bowing low, she spoke in near reverence. "To what do I owe this honor?"

His elegant head dipped lower as he replied. "I have watched you from afar, Oganna. You are still young and somewhat impulsive. However, thy heart is full of compassion, and you hate evil as I do." He paused and held out one of his hands. A sphere of white light formed and hovered above his claws. "There are precious few in this world who wield power with wisdom, yet I pray you will be one of them."

She gazed up at him in all his potency. That time as a little girl when he had first revealed himself to her, she had wanted to embrace him as the grandfather she never knew. But at the moment fear of him felt more appropriate. He was capable of terrible things, yet he seemed concerned for the good of all. He was such a noble creature. How could she deny this dragon? "I will do my best," she promised.

A smile creased his scaly face. "That is all I ask of you. Remember Starfire's words: 'Use your powers for good and do not be corrupted.' There will come a time when you will be tempted to turn against the good and follow the easier path. Evil men will seek to corrupt you and use you for their own purposes. Oganna, you must not let them!"

"Starfire?" Oganna said in a hushed voice. "Is she the woman that I just met?"

"Indeed she is," the dragon rumbled. "Listen to what she told you. Always use the weapons you have created for good. Defend the helpless and exercise judgment with wisdom."

Oganna gave a sincere nod of her head.

The dragon shook his body, twisted his neck to look at the sky, and spoke in a low rumble. "I do believe that you will not fail me." Then he spread his wings and flew into the night sky.

The wind buffeted her for a moment after he'd gone. She braced herself until it had passed and then looked to the cave. She neared it, wondering if her labors had been fruitful. The explosion had more or less split it apart, shedding dirt and stones in a circular pattern and leaving the cave floor exposed. A thick, transparent, crystal-like substance had covered it. She chipped away the cooled crystal from her molds and examined the results.

Her hands trembled with excitement as she lifted the sword and the boomerang from the floor. They were both composed of identical transparent crystal and the slightest flicker of light danced on them like stardust. The top of the sword's handle, where the blood had collected, now held a transparent ruby of enormous size.

She stood to her feet and held the sword in one hand and the boomerang in her other. A feeling of satisfaction welled up inside of her like warm water filling her soul, coursing through her, and driving all doubt of her abilities from her mind. She laughed to the sky and threw out the boomerang in a long arc. Its transparency was so absolute that it was rendered invisible. Gentle as a feather, it returned to her hand. She raised her sword. Its blade turned crimson, and the crystal handle pulsed with light. Luminescent silver grew from the sword to cover her arm. It spread, coating her body and leaving her outfitted in a flattering dress of woven silver. The stars reflected on her garment as if in a mirror, causing it to shimmer in the darkness.

"Now," she said, "I am ready!" She slid the sword under her belt, and the silver garments disappeared. Its unguarded blade rested against her side, and so perfect was its cold crystal that it was hardly visible. She tucked the boomerang under the belt's other end, over her hip.

Invisible weapons. Ingenious! She whistled a soft, cheerful tune as a wind kicked up and she turned toward home. Specter stood before her.

At first she feared his anger, then she saw the spark of hope in his eyes and when she smiled he returned it with one of his own. "Go, dragon's offspring! God speed you on your journey, and I will follow, always, to watch over and protect you as I did for your mother."

She flung her straying blond hair over her shoulders, left the area, and passed swiftly through the forest toward home. Cool moisture was settling in the air. A testament to the late hour. A mouse darted past, stirring the leaves at her feet. She heard the beat of an owl's wings as it dropped from its perch and caught the protesting rodent in its talons.

Oganna felt for her sword's pommel. The sword was a weapon to defend the innocent and to destroy the wicked. A saver of lives, and a destroyer of lives. "All things that begin must someday end, little mouse," she whispered into the night. "All things eventually end."

* * *

The soft patter of rain on the roof greeted Oganna the morning after her encounter with Albino. In order to avoid questions she hid her blade and her boomerang under her bed and joined her father and aunts for breakfast.

Ilfedo stirred his raisin oatmeal for a couple

minutes, glancing from time to time at the sisters. "Oganna," he said, "an urgent matter has come up, and I must leave again."

She dabbed at the corner of her mouth with a napkin. "When do you leave?"

"I am sorry to say it must happen quickly. This morning," he said as he stared at her.

She knew he was waiting to see if she would ask to go along with him. She smiled inwardly, but kept a disinterested expression on her face. It would be amusing to watch his reaction when she didn't, and it amused her to surprise him. She nodded to her aunts as if in resignation. "Are you going to leave with him?" she said.

Caritha shook her head and said, "Not this time. There is another matter that requires our immediate attention." She told her of the reported creature along the southern border, and then Ilfedo related Ombre's report.

Oganna momentarily nodded again. "That's nice."

Ilfedo raised his eyebrows. Either he was relieved that she wasn't pestering him, or he was confused by her detached attitude. Maybe it was a little of both. She laughed inwardly, amused by their confusion and enjoying every minute of it. If only they knew what she had been up to whilst they slept last night, then they would have guessed her intentions.

"You will not be alone, my daughter," Ilfedo said. "Both Seivar and Hasselpatch will keep you company, and if you need to communicate with me they will fly any message to me that you like."

About mid-morning, Ilfedo bade everyone

farewell and left for the northern border. A little later her aunts set out to the south, waving goodbye as she wished them Godspeed. As soon as they were out of sight, she raced indoors, grabbed her weapons and one of her father's hunting packs, filled it with food and clothes, and set out with determination to track her aunts. Seivar and Hasselpatch cawed after her, but she waved to the beloved birds and ordered them to stay behind. She hiked the pack higher on her shoulders and faced the forest trails. "Path into the unknown, here I come," she said with a grin.

TOKEN OF A PROMISE

Caritha stretched her hands toward the blazing fire and craned her neck to look at the night sky. The air felt cool and damp, reminiscent of her days in the cave when she and her sisters had resided in the forests west of the Hemmed Land. She threw another log on the fire. The flames licked around it, curling yellow and orange tongues along the bark.

"Just about done," Evela said from the opposite side of the blaze.

"Good." Caritha rose to watch her sisters finish setting up the tent.

Rozel, wielding a wooden mallet in one hand and holding a stubborn stake in her other, harrumphed. Her blows stabbed it into the ground at last. "Now stay put you stupid thing!" She straightened and kicked at the stake before wrapping a tent rope around it. She pulled the rope, stretching the tent over its frame.

Caritha smirked. "Having trouble with that?" she asked.

"Some sisters don't know when to hold their tongues and when to pitch in," Rozel muttered under her breath. She pounded the stake's head with the mallet, driving it deeper into the ground. This time she applied too much force. The stake split and the near corner of the tent collapsed. "That's it! I'm not wasting any more time on this nonsense." She dropped the mallet, stormed off several paces, and pointed at Caritha. "I've been at this for almost half an hour. If you feel so smart, then why don't you try it?"

"Don't take things so hard," Caritha said as she picked up the mallet and chose a new stake. "Patience is required when setting up one of these contraptions."

Standing near her shoulder with arms crossed, Rozel huffed. "I still don't see why we couldn't just lay out our mats and sleep under the stars."

Caritha wrapped the rope around the stake, pulled it taut, and drove the stake into the ground. It held firm, and the tent walls straightened. "See? With a little patience the task is done."

"You want to know something, sister?" Rozel placed her hands on her hips. "Sometimes you can be the cockiest, most arrogant—"

Laura, Evela, and Levena threw their bedrolls into the open end of the tent and lay down. "Come on," Levena said. She crossed her arms and rested her chin on them. "We all need our rest."

Rozel relaxed her arms and went inside.

Caritha started to follow, but as she entered the tent her ear caught the faint snap of a stick. She stopped and looked outside at the dark trees.

"Is anything wrong?" Evela asked, raising her head.

Caritha let her gaze rove over the dark shadows in the forest. "I thought I heard a twig snap. Like someone stepped on it." But nothing moved in the shadows, so she shook her head. "I must be more tired than I realized." She rolled out her bedding and lay down.

The wind outside their shelter howled through the trees and the light of their fire flickered. Laura fell asleep as did Evela and Levena. Rozel's soft snoring followed.

With a last glance at her sisters, Caritha made certain they were really asleep before pulling a small object out of her pocket. She held it up and looked at it in the shielding dimness. If her sisters knew what she was considering, they would most likely try to dissuade her. She felt the smooth gold band in her fingers. The small diamond cradling its surface sparkled.

She sighed and closed her hands over it. "I don't know what holds you back," Ombre had said. "But I do know that I will never love another as I love you." He had pressed the ring into her hand. "I had hoped you would accept this tonight, but I want you to do what is best for you." He had stroked her hair and looked fondly into her eyes. "Keep this and when you are ready to be mine, put it on. I will wait until my eyes can no longer see, and the hairs on my head have turned gray."

Oh, how she had longed to say yes right there, right then. But for all his love, Ombre could not understand what held her back. She had seen what had happened to Dantress, and she knew that as the daughter of the dragon, she too bore the gifts and the curse. Was a year of love worth the sacrifice of a lifetime? She envied Dantress. Envied her certainty, her courage, and the life she'd brought into the world. But she had also seen what Dantress's death had done to Ilfedo. She had seen how it hurt him, and she could not bear to leave Ombre in the same way. Something deep inside told her not to worry about it, that Ombre was cut from a different mold than Ilfedo and his life would go on.

Feeling sorrowful, she shook her head. No, she could not bear to wound Ombre. She put the ring back in her pocket, rolled on her side, saw his caring face in her mind, and silently wept. She craved his love, craved his embrace, and yet feared the consequences. With a full heart she closed her eyes. Morning would bring a string of activities to keep her mind busy.

* * *

The next morning Caritha led her sisters southward to the village of Harpen. The buildings here rose suddenly out of the forest and the streets were narrow, the buildings being in close proximity to one another. The sunlit streets were thronging with people. Many appeared to be refugees from other southern towns, trudging through the dusty streets with their possession on their backs and in horse-drawn carts.

Caritha let the flow of people bring her through the town until she located a large inn. It was a long, single-storied structure with a white porch fronting it. A fresh coat of yellow paint on the building's walls ensured that it stood out from the other buildings on that dusty street. The passersby crowded past her, but Caritha wedged herself between two broad men and stepped out of the street onto the inn's porch. Her sisters were right behind her. Evela and Levena made a point of beating dust off their skirts before following her inside.

The main room of the inn was sizeable and at least a dozen men were sitting around drinking and eating at its various dining tables. But the room also had a strangely low ceiling. Caritha stepped up to the counter and politely asked the innkeeper if he knew about the attack on Bordelin.

"Who aint?" the innkeeper growled. He was a tall fellow with curly blond hair, and a dimple of a chin that bounced around as he talked. "I'm not one to complain about an influx of business. But someone has got to get these refugees out of here before they run out of money to pay for all their sleepin' and eatin'."

Caritha pushed past the man's gripe by asking, "There is a doctor around here who cared for a survivor from the Bordelin attack. Do you know where can we find them?"

"Follow the main road west," a burly man spoke up from a nearby dining table. He raised a mug to her as she glanced over at him. "The doctor lives at the very edge of town in a fine, two-story brick house. It's the last on the right. You will have no trouble finding it."

She thanked him for his help, then turned to her sisters. "Did you—?"

"Wait a minute," the curly-haired innkeeper said. He jumped over the counter and stood over her, grinning down as if he was a schoolboy. "Aren't you the Warrioresses?"

A small crowd of mug-holding men rose from the dining tables and gathered around the sisters.

Caritha dropped her voice and whispered in Levena's ear, "Get out of here and meet me at the doctor's house. I'll keep these people distracted long enough to keep them out of our way." Her sisters filtered out of the door, and Caritha faced the friendly faces with a charming smile. "Yes, I am a Warrioress."

The men came in closer, some shaking her hand, some trying to kiss it. She turned to the burly fellow who'd given her directions and played at being shy. "I need to find a ladies' room," she whispered.

He puffed out his chest and boomed orders to the crowd. "Make way for the lady!"

She strode into the restroom at the back of the inn and locked the door behind her. A couple of windows, built half-way up the wall to let in fresh air, offered her the perfect escape route. She sprang up, grasped one of the sills, vaulted through the window, and landed in a crouch on the dirt in a back alley. Keeping to back streets, she made her way to the western side of town.

The last building on the right hand side of the main road was a two-story brick house. Her sisters were waiting for her in front of it. Laura beckoned with her hand and said, "Come along, and quickly. We were just starting to wonder if we were going to have to go back and check if those men had let you go."

"Well, I got away rather quickly, but I wanted to make sure I wasn't seen," Caritha said. She ran her hand through her hair and dusted off her skirt.

Laura went up to the front door and knocked. A tall, tanned woman, wearing a bright yellow dress opened the door.

Caritha stepped forward. "Ma'am, we seek information—"

"Are you the Warrioresses?" the woman gasped.

"Yes. Lord Ilfedo sent us to—" Caritha started to respond.

But the woman nearly tripped over her threshold as she stepped outside and held the door wide open. "Please, please. Do come in. I am Doctor Malinda."

"Thank you," Caritha replied as she stepped inside.

The lady doctor was all smiles as she showed them into her cozy parlor. Long, lace curtains decorated the high windows. Plush, green carpeting covered the floor. Three portraits adorned one wall, a grandfather clock chimed in the corner of another, and two couches layered with animal furs formed an L around an oval, knee-high table in the room's center.

"My husband is gone for the week. Oh, he'll wish he hadn't been! If we had known that the Lord

Warrior would send you, we could have arranged a more fitting welcome," she said. She invited them to sit, then served them tea, and sat with them.

"You will understand," Caritha said, "that we cannot stay long. Lord Ilfedo sent us to find the creature that attacked the town of Bordelin."

Laura smiled at the doctor and held her gaze. "We were told that you cared for a survivor from Bordelin, and we were hoping you could tell us where to find him."

"Well, I can't say for certain." The doctor combed her fingers through her long blond hair. "However, the last time I saw him he had decided to stay for a while at the house of the woodcutter that saved his life." She leaned back. "Their house is southwest of here in the forest."

Caritha stood. "Can you show us?"

"Oh, I had hoped you'd stay a while," Malinda said. She rose, wrapping a white shawl around her shoulders. "But I do understand. The creature needs to be found before it can return. Come with me and I will take you there." Malinda let them out her door and escorted them out of town, and down a forest trail. About mid-afternoon, after trekking a few miles through the woods, they came to a little house set by itself in a small clearing. Beds of flowers lay on either side of the front door. "That is the place," Malinda said, grasping each of them by the hand. "I will say good day to you now. But if you come by my way again, please stop in. My husband and I would love the opportunity to host you in our town."

As the doctor disappeared back down the trail, Caritha approached the house and knocked. A pale man with splints on his legs and bandages on his arms and neck opened the door. Hobbling on crutches, he brought them inside where he could answer their questions. "Garner is the name," he said, as he sat at the dining room table and invited them to do the same. "Thank you so much for coming."

Leaning forward, Caritha folded her hands. "We have a few questions for you, sir. Then we must be on our way."

"I will answer what I can," Garner said.

She and the other sisters questioned him for at least an hour. For the most part, their inquiries revolved around what little he had been able to see of the creature. What he reported disturbed them. Never before had they heard of a creature that could exhale poisonous vapors from its nostrils. The survivor recollected how he'd tried to save the injured woman and how she'd choked and coughed on the foul air until she died. His eyes moistened at the telling of it.

"Thank you. You have been most helpful," Caritha said. She grasped his shoulder gently and held his gaze. "We will deal with the creature. Your loss will be avenged. We will see to it."

As they rose to go, Laura asked him to point them in the direction of Bordelin.

He pulled himself to a standing position and flinched. "Go due south through the forest along the broadest trail, and you will find it on the edge of the desert." He sighed and closed his eyes, then he quietly said, "It used to be a beautiful place."

"We will find the creature. You get your rest," Evela said. She touched his shoulder and smiled at him. Garner beamed back, then he cleared his throat and his eyes wandered up and down the length of her. "I'll be here if you have any more questions."

Evela's face flushed. She slapped his cheek, glanced at the floor and stepped outside.

"Wow. I meant that in a kind way," Garner said. He swallowed and gazed after her before glancing at Caritha. "Let her know that I think she is beautiful and spirited. She is welcome to visit me any time, and I am not some creep. Ask around and you will hear that from people who know me."

"Goodness. Give me a break!" Rozel exclaimed. She rolled her eyes, and followed Evela outside.

Caritha nodded her thanks to Garner then stepped outside, closing the door behind her. She had to shake the image that lingered in her mind of his crestfallen face as she turned to proceed back onto the trail. But she almost knocked into Evela.

"I am so ashamed of myself," Evela said. "Do you think I should apologize to him? He was just trying to be kind. I think he really meant it."

"Don't tell him that, not at the moment anyway." Caritha chuckled and walked into the forest. "That man seemed taken with you, Evela."

"Him? I doubt it," Evela said. They set off down the broad trail. Evela stayed quiet for a time, then she kicked a stone. "Did he say something about me? To you, I mean. After I walked out?"

Caritha laughed and shook her head. "You are a hopeless case. Yes, he thinks you are beautiful and spirited, and he'd love to see you again."

"He would?" Evela said under her breath.

The other sisters joined Caritha in a hearty

laugh, and Evela even joined in. Her embarrassment would pass, but Garner's flattery would linger with her. The sisters knew that. Although, Caritha thought that Evela whispered something about Ilfedo immediately afterwards. She tried to understand but it eluded her, and she passed it off as a wayward thought. After all, Evela didn't feel that way about Ilfedo. Dantress had.

It did not take long to follow the trail out of the forest. Garner had not lied. The path was as broad as the main street in Gwensin City. Caritha and her sisters stood at the edge of an expanse of open grassland. Smoke rose from the blackened buildings that had formed the town of Bordelin. A few dozen men and women wandered through a maze of collapsed structural beams, broken furniture, and upturned boulders. Some of the people wore bandages around their heads, others had their arms supported in slings. Many had lacerations on either their faces, necks, or arms.

Caritha wandered along the town's perimeter, exploring until she found the graveyard. Seven men were busily digging rectangular graves in the brown earth, and a smattering of others were parading linen-wrapped bodies out of the town, carrying them into the graveyard. Three grizzly-bearded old men lowered one body into one of the fresh graves, and their grim faces were red from the tears they had shed. Flowers had been strewn on the ground, probably in an attempt to subdue the stench of death in the air. New stones lay on the ground next to unfilled holes, some with half-completed epitaphs chiseled on their faces.

"One creature did all of this?" Rozel growled. "Just wait until I get my sword in range of its throat. If it is an intelligent beast, it will wish it had never touched this place."

The creature's clawed footprints were deep and they were everywhere in Bordelin. The sisters searched until they found the claws pointing away from the town, and then they followed the tracks through a large flat field to where they ended at the sands of the southern desert. Caritha looked back at Bordelin, as did her sisters. What was left of the town nestled at the very edge of the Hemmed Land's forests.

Caritha pointed to the desert and said, "It could not be any clearer, could it? The beast, whatever kind of creature it is, headed out across the sand. I guess that is where we will have go."

"Hmm," Rozel grunted. Then she pointed out across the desert. "Its tracks are not as clear out there, but I can still see them. If we wait then the wind might bury them with sand, but for now I think we can catch the beast."

"We should first take stock of our supplies," Levena said. "It may be a long trip, and we don't want to run out of food and water. Or shelter for that matter. We should return to Harpen for supplies, then come back here tomorrow morning."

Caritha agreed and together they set their steps back to Harpen. As they neared the town they happened upon Doctor Malinda as she returned home through the forest. "I am so sorry for abandoning you earlier," she said. "I was almost home when I realized that I should have introduced you to

Garner. So I went back and checked on him. Did you find the border town?"

"That, and the tracks of the creature that caused the chaos," Caritha said.

Rozel laughed harshly. "And it is a disaster," she said.

"We will be making a trip through the desert tomorrow, but first we'll need to rest," Caritha continued.

They emerged from the forest and into an open field leading up to the town. Malinda pointed out her house on the edge of the rows of homes and businesses. "I have several guest rooms upstairs that you are more than welcome to use. I insist, you must spend the night in my home. And tomorrow morning I will have breakfast ready bright and early so that you can be on your way."

Nodding a thank you, Caritha instructed her sisters. "As soon as we get into town, buy the things we need. We cannot have any delay but must leave early on the morrow."

Much to Caritha's relief, the doctor accompanied them into the stores. The woman was very friendly but she also had a forceful nature that seemed to drive away the crowds of onlookers. Quit staring," she would call to her fellow townsfolk. "You are making our guests uncomfortable!"

That night the doctor cooked them a nice meal, then showed them to their rooms. "If you need anything," she said, "just knock on my door. It's the one at the end of the hall."

When she had been left by herself, Caritha sat on the bed and then felt in her pocket for the ring that Ombre had given her. It was a thing of comfort. A sense of security that she could not explain. Night fell fully on the town and it quieted outside, and in her bed Caritha fell asleep clutching the ring to her breast.

The next morning dawned humid. A thick fog rolled through the forest before Yimshi's rays dispersed it. Caritha brushed her hair, then pulled out her rusted sword. Its blade had killed before, and if they found the creature, she suspected her weapon would have to do so again. Her hand trembled as she remembered the purported size of the creature. If they found it and engaged it in combat, she did not know what she would do. What if the beast's hide proved too thick for her sword to penetrate? She put the blade back in the fold of her skirt and closed the fabric over it.

Opening the bedroom door, she followed the greasy scent of frying bacon downstairs to the dining room. In keeping with the doctor's expensive taste, the table was set with silverware and wooden plates carved in the likeness of flowers and butterflies. She picked up one of the napkins. Silk.

Laura and Levena swept in and raised their eyebrows at the arrangement. They took their seats, and soon Rozel and Evela came in too. Rozel stopped, shook her head, and spoke only loud enough for them to hear her. "What foolishness to waste one's time on such frivolities. A plain and simple table is more than adequate."

Evela elbowed her. "Exercise some of those manners Elsie tried to burn into you as a little girl. I, for one, enjoy eating in a more formal manner."

She neatly unfolded her napkin, laid it in her lap, and sat ramrod straight. "Setting a table like this requires thought and preparation, which I appreciate."

"Oh well, la-de-da!" Rozel said with a scowl.

"I hope you all slept well?" the doctor asked as she emerged from the kitchen, balancing a silver tray loaded with bacon in one hand and a large bowl of scrambled eggs in her other. Rozel forced a smile.

The doctor was beaming, and Caritha made sure to compliment her on her beautiful table and the tempting smells that had drawn them downstairs. She chuckled to herself when Rozel went to greater lengths of eloquent praise.

"I get company so infrequently," the doctor said as she set down the food and turned to go back to her kitchen,"that I decided to go all out for you. After all, it isn't every woman that gets to entertain the Warrioresses." She disappeared into the other room and returned with a bowl generously heaped with freshly cut fruit.

Caritha ate until her stomach couldn't fit any more. Each of her sisters had pushed aside their plates, mostly scraped clean. Feeling the need to be on their way, they thanked their new friend, gathered their things, and left the house. "Come back any time,"Malinda said. "I have enjoyed your visit."

"You have been more than generous to us," Caritha replied as she stepped into the street. "Thank you again. Thank you for everything."

Many townspeople were already up and about, even though the sun had risen not an hour before. The sisters had walked a hundred paces down the street when Laura stopped and searched the milling people with her gaze. Her gaze sharpened.

Caritha eased up next to her. "Is something wrong?" she asked.

"I thought . . ." Laura shook her head. "I thought I saw Oganna in the crowd."

"Oganna? Here?" Caritha said. She let her eyes roam the faces of the townsfolk. But no one even resembling Oganna caught her eye. She shrugged and turned to go. Her hand slipped into her pocket, and she reached for the ring. It was gone! Frantic, she looked at the ground, trying not to let her sisters see the fear in her eyes. "Go on ahead," she said. "I forgot something back at the house."

"You forgot what?" Rozel asked, crossing her arms. "Come on, Caritha, I want to get this hunt over with."

Caritha waved a hand at them and ran back to the doctor's house, shouting, "I'll catch up with you!" As she raised her hand to knock on the front door, Malinda opened it.

"Thank goodness you haven't gone yet," Malinda said with a twinkle in her eye. "Did you drop this?" She held out her hand, and the sunlight danced off the diamond in Ombre's ring.

Caritha took it, trying not to let the tears of relief show. "You have no idea how much this means to me," she said, and she put it back in her pocket and tied it securely in place. "Thank you."

With a departing wave, Caritha raced after her sisters. It was all she could do to keep her joy to herself as she joined with them.

Laura turned to her with a curious expression. "Find what you were looking for?"

"Yes," Caritha said, ignoring the insistence of Laura's gaze. "Yes, I found it."

ADVENT OF THE MEGATRATHS

Wasteland, that's all the southern desert was. A barren stretch of white sand that extended to the flat horizon. Ilfedo had told Caritha that the Hemmed Land had been designated "hemmed" because of its geographical isolation. Its eastern border ended at the Sea of Serpents. According to a couple of adventurers who had ventured west, a vast swamp cut off the Western Wood and an active volcano lay beyond it. And both the southern and northern forests bordered vast, uncharted deserts. In a manner of speaking the Hemmed Land was an oasis.

Ilfedo had said that his ancestors came from an ancient civilization in the distant southwest that, for some unknown reason, fell apart. According to legend, these ancestors harnessed the power of sunlight and made machines to carry them into the sky.

But that was so long ago that no one could be certain if the stories were true. Caritha had heard many a resident of the Hemmed Land call such claims myth.

She squared her shoulders, breathing deeply of the forest air before heading into the hot, dry desert. The stinging wind threw salty sand in her face as if forbidding her passage. She spun around to face her sisters. "Are you ready?" she asked.

Rozel grimaced and said, "Ready."

Bending down to look at one of the creature's large footprints, Laura picked at at it with a twig. She could have curled up and fit her body in the impression. Her blade sifted the dirt and sand. She held up her sword, flipped it in the air, and raised it level in both hands. Her eyes scanned the blade.

"What are you doing?" Caritha asked.

"I was thinking that the creature, especially being so large, must leave skin samples wherever it steps," Laura said. She pointed into the desert. "The wind could easily obscure the creature's tracks, but I think I can tune my sword to detect the residue in the sand so that we won't lose the trail."

"Really?" Caritha said, and when Laura looked up at her, Caritha continued. "The idea is logical enough, but how will you do that?"

Laura shrugged her shoulders. "I'm following my instinct on this. My dragon blood connected to that of my sword should allow the weapon to act as a magnet to what it last touched. To be honest, if you ask me how confident I am of making it work, then I will not be able to give you a straight answer."

"If you can make it work then go ahead with it," Caritha said.

Laura pricked her finger on the tip of her rusted sword, frowning as she did so. "I feel something. Almost the sort of feeling you might expect to find if a strange skin were to touch the blade." She half-closed her eyes and her blade glowed, then she stood and shrugged her shoulders. "Hopefully that will do the trick if we need to find the tracks again," she said.

Caritha didn't know what to think. Perhaps Laura was on to something with this sword divining. Then again, perhaps not. Turning, Caritha followed the creature's tracks into the desert. The creature's tracks followed a straight line, leading to the south but at a decidedly western vector.

That night they set up their tent and tried to sleep. Their canvas walls protested as stiff winds buffeted them, and finer sand sifted through the seams. When Caritha at last dozed off, her slumber was restless.

In her dreams she saw herself and her sisters standing on the strange shore of an inlet, surrounded by mountains of ice. Clouds overshadowed the sky, and the air was frigid. Beyond the inlet lay a deep blue sea that stretched to the horizon.

The sandy ground trembled, and a long-necked creature rose before them. She gazed up and quailed in fear, for the creature's size dwarfed even that of her dragon father. It smashed its fore-flippers together and addressed them in a masculine voice that rang around them. "You have fought worthy of a Water Skeel." Then the creature lowered its neck so that she found herself staring into his enormous mouth arrayed with needlelike teeth. "But you are no match for me!" he said.

Caritha felt exhausted. She tried to summon her powers but found only hints of strength. Her reservoirs had been depleted, but how? She looked to her sisters for help, but their faces froze in terror. The creature pulled back his head, and a geyser of water issued from his nostrils. It slammed into her chest, drove the oxygen from her lungs, and threw her against a large boulder on the shore. She felt as if every bone in her body was bending and every organ had been bruised.

On either side of her, the sisters were trying to rise from beneath the creature's deluge of water. She raised her sword. "Join with me, my sisters!" Their blades met, and sent a wall of energy surging against the water, turning it away before it could do further harm.

The creature laughed and bore down upon them. His gargantuan body slammed into the beach and his flippers smote them. "Your puny powers cannot compare to the might I wield!" He dug his flippers into the inlet and plucked, as it were, large cubes of ice from the water. These he chucked effortlessly in the sisters' direction. Caritha felt a stabbing pain as the cubes neared, and the magic within her was stifled and confined. Her body temperature dropped. She was freezing though she remained alive!

Suddenly she sat bolt upright in the tent. Sweat had soaked her clothes, and her breathing was irregular. Laura woke up with a scream, and the others started from their sleep. They looked at one another, and then at Caritha. Their eyes were wide with horror.

"I was dreaming," Rozel gasped. "A night-mare of ice and an enormous white monster."

The others glanced at her, then at Caritha. Piece by piece they revealed to each other the details of the dreams they had had. But the details that they shared were not unique. They had each shared the same dream. The same nightmare of ice and terror. It didn't seem possible, but they had. Caritha shud-dered inwardly. Had they received a warning of some kind? Or, was it a mere coincidence?

She raised her hand, silencing her sisters' chatter. "We are the daughters of the dragon. We do not fear fate, and we will not let doubt cloud our way. If this was a shadow of something to come, then we will face it as we face everything else. With vigilance and determination."

Evela swallowed hard, then forced a smile. "You are right, Caritha. We must not let this over-shadow the task at hand."

Everyone else lay back down. Their eyes, how-ever, remained open for a while. Caritha lay down too, forbidding the fear to get a hold on her heart. She felt inside her pocket for the ring. With its comforting smooth surface between her fingers she closed her eyes with thoughts of Ombre, and let her body rest for the day ahead.

* * *

The following morning the desert wind fanned them like a hot breath and drove them to con-tinue their journey with haste. As the day progressed the wind grew in intensity. Small whirlwinds wavered between dunes, throwing clouds of sand in all direc-tions.

Shielding her face with her arm, Caritha spread her legs to steady herself. "We need to find shelter," she called through the building storm.

Laura laughed sardonically and said, "Oh, sure. As soon as you see a tree or a house for us to hide in, just let me know."

Visibility decreased with alarming swiftness. Though Caritha knew that Yimshi was shining, she found it difficult to see more than a few feet in any direction because clouds of sand swirled through the air. She was about to call a halt when her foot caught on a buried stone and she tumbled forward. Cringing, she waited to hit her head on some unseen protrusion. Instead she felt herself falling farther, as if the ground before her had given way. When she landed it was rather softer than she'd expected.

She rolled to the side just as Laura, Evela, Rozel, and Levena all fell in the hole behind her. She glanced around and found herself in a subterranean cavern. A dozen feet above her head the desert sand swirled over the hole through which they'd fallen.

"Oh this is much better," Rozel said. She punched the ground with her fist. "Now how are we going to find that creature after this? Its tracks will certainly be buried by the time this storm stops."

"I don't think we'll have to follow the tracks," Evela said. The others looked puzzled. "It seems to me that desert inhabitants would have to travel the most direct route possible in order to conserve water and strength. If we continue in the direction we know it took, we should eventually stumble upon its destination."

Laura lowered her eyes. "You're right," she

said. "And we don't really have another choice because I tested my sword theory earlier today, and it won't find the creature's footprints."

The storm abated a few hours later, and the sisters looked for a way to get out of their hole. Above them the cavern ceiling was a mixture of sand, dirt, and red stone.

"Why don't we just blow up the ceiling of this chamber?" Rozel asked. "If we take out one corner, the amount of dirt that is above it should be enough to raise the floor so that we can climb out."

The sisters pointed their swords toward the far corner of the cavern and touched the blades together. A blue flame ignited between the tips, then shot out and struck the stone ceiling. The hole through which they had fallen, widened. The stones crumbled, then collapsed in a heap tall enough for them to climb up to the desert floor.

As they emerged back into daylight they grew silent, for an unearthly calm reigned over the desert. Not even the slightest breeze troubled the sand, and the sunlight fell oppressively hot on their skin. "Come on," Caritha urged, and she walked a few hundred paces. The ground gave way beneath her again, and as she fell into another subterranean cavern her sisters tumbled in after her.

This was not so deep a hole and she climbed out with relative ease, then turned and offered her assistance to her sisters.

"I don't know about the rest of you," Rozel said as she grabbed onto Caritha's arm and clambered back out of the pit. "But I think we should take greater care where we are stepping out here."

"Agreed," Caritha said. She took off her shoe and held it upside down, draining it of sand. The others clambered up behind her. "We should thank the Creator that this pit wasn't a good deal deeper. We could have broken our legs. Or, worse yet, in a large cavern we could have broken our necks. As Rozel has pointed out, we will have to be more cautious moving forward.

She set out again, this time drawing her sword and using it to stab the ground ahead before proceeding. It was a good thing she did, for she discovered that the region was pocketed with numerous caverns just waiting for the unwitting traveler to step into them. Night fell and the moonless sky grew cloudy, impeding their progress further.

"Maybe we should camp in one of the caverns," Laura suggested. "It would offer us shelter from any more sandstorms. I know I will sleep better if I'm not worried that my tent will blow away in the middle of the night."

Everyone nodded, and Caritha peered into one of the nearby holes. "This one has a bit of a slope to its opening. Should be a lot easier to get out again." She descended first, sliding somewhat on the sloping sand.

Rozel slid down beside her and laid out a bedroll several paces deeper into the cavern. "Yep, I approve! This is much better," she said.

"Better, yes," Levena said as she looked around at the strangely formed walls. "It's still not to my liking."

Rozel scratched her head. "What *would* be to your liking? An inn out here in the desert?"

"Home would be preferable," Levena said.

Rozel clacked her tongue. "Tut tut, living at Ilfedo's house has made you soft!"

At last the sisters settled in, and the night passed without incident. In the morning everyone confirmed that their dreams had been pleasant, with the exception of Rozel. "I'm not saying I had nightmares but they did border on that," she said. But they all agreed that they felt relieved not to have had more visions of massive swimming creatures pummeling them with ice.

They ate dried biscuits for breakfast and pulled themselves out of the cavern. There was no breeze, thankfully, so no sand whipping about. Once on the desert floor, they used Yimshi's rising disc as a frame of reference and continued their pursuit of the creature.

Several days passed, and they had about given up hope of ever finding the beast. But a wind kicked up, and when it stopped, they saw the creature's tracks clearly imprinted straight ahead of them and continuing on to the horizon.

"That is amazing," Evela murmured. "To have come this far and end up right behind the creature. I would have thought we would have strayed off of its trail by at least several hundred paces by now."

They all agreed with her. It bordered on miraculous but also bolstered their confidence in their tracking skills. Perhaps living with the skilled hunters of the Hemmed Land for all these years had sharpened their talents in this regard. They followed the beast's tracks for an hour or so and then stopped, for ahead of them the desert floor was cut off by a massive wall. As far as Caritha could see in either direction, the vertical wall of solid yellow stone rose from the desert floor. A natural hinderance to any invader of this baren desert.

The barrier stood over a couple hundred feet high, and its smooth face was unbroken except in one place. About two thirds of the way up the wall a large opening cut into the rock, most likely a cave. Deep claw marks marred the rock face beneath the opening where the beast had made its way up the wall and into the cave.

Caritha bit her lip, contemplating what they should do next. The creature had the higher ground. By a large margin, too. If it was up in that cave watching them then they might as well turn around and head home.

Rozel let out a long whistle. "Now that is something incredible. How can a creature that large climb that? Why, it is almost vertical. Do you realize what it would take to pull that much fat up that? I don't know about the rest of you, but I'm duly impressed."

Gritting her teeth, Caritha tied back her hair and stepped up to the wall. She gathered her skirt, hiking it above her knees and tying it in place. Fortunately the fabric was airy and light, making it easy to manipulate. She gazed up at the desert wall and felt the ground turn beneath her feet, but then she fought back the dizziness and gathered her willpower. Rozel was right. The rock rose from the desert floor at a near-vertical angle. Grabbing hold of a crevice in the rock face, she pulled herself up and set her foot on the slightest excuse for a ledge.

Repeating these steps, she soon reached a place some twenty feet above. Careful not to undo her balance, she glanced under her arm to see her sisters below. "What are you all doing standing there? Climb, ladies. Climb!"

The stone under her hand crumbled, forcing her to grab another handhold. The climb demanded all her attention. She lost track of time. When she was within a dozen feet of the cave opening, she dared to look down. First she noticed her sisters making their way up the rock face behind her, then her gaze wandered out to the desert and, for an instant, she thought she saw another human figure on the horizon.

"Is someone following us?" Caritha asked.

Rozel closed the distance between them. "For all that is holy! Move along Caritha. I can't climb over you, you know." She grunted, pulling herself higher. "This isn't so easy in a dress. Now quit staring out there. It's probably a mirage."

Taking one last look into the desert, Caritha had to admit a mirage sounded plausible. Heat waves created several images of people in pursuit, but one by one they vanished. She put her attention back where it should be and led her sisters the rest of the way up the daunting rock face. Upon reaching the ledge of the cave, she pulled herself in, sat near the opening, and breathed a deep sigh of relief.

She leaned over the edge and extended her arm to Rozel, helping her into the cave. Then she reached down to help Laura up. "Here give me your hand," she said.

"No thank you!" Laura pulled herself up, and

the others soon followed.

They gathered on the ledge, looking at the desert below. At last Caritha drew her sword and scraped it along a deep claw mark in the floor. Grimly she turned away from the blinding brilliance of the desert scene and faced the cave's dark interior. It took her eyes a little while to adjust. They did but they ached all the while.

Caritha moved her finger to her lips and then said, "Let us proceed with care. We should stay as quiet as possible. This is the creature's domain, not ours." She pointed to her sword, signifying that her sisters should produce their weapons. From their skirts they drew their rusted blades and held them at arm's length as they followed her into the darkness.

"Shine, oh my sword," she whispered. Her command could not affect the weapon, but saying it aloud and willing it in her mind somehow steadied her, and immediately her blade glowed with a brownish-red color.

The others followed suit, murmuring, "Shine." One after the other their blades illuminated the area, albeit dimly. Caritha moved ahead into the pitch-black chamber. So dim was the light from the swords that she had to call a halt until her eyes adjusted to the darkness and she could better see the path ahead. Gradually the floor and walls became distinguishable, and she walked on.

At the rear of the chamber, Caritha found a tunnel of great size that led downward at a steep pitch. The tunnel's stone floor and walls were covered in deep gashes, a crosshatching of marks that the creature's claws had left behind. She placed her feet in those grooves and used them to navigate her way safely down the tunnel.

The descent was long and the way difficult, but at last the tunnel leveled out. She stood up and stretched her aching limbs. The tunnel's ceiling angled upward into the underground chamber. It angled so high that the light of her sword could not touch the darkness and she had no way of knowing how high the cavern was.

To either side the walls curved into shadows too deep for her to see through. Caritha strained to see into the darkness. The light of the swords revealed a flat floor of stone, worn and polished by usage. Whichever direction she walked there was no end in sight.

Laura laid a hand on her shoulder and whispered, "I hope you are thinking caution is in order here, Caritha. You do realize this could be the creature's lair. For all we know, this could be some kind of massive nest." Something thumped in the darkness somewhere ahead and Caritha stopped. Her heart pounded in her ears as she waited, every nerve on edge.

A rumbling voice penetrated the stillness. "Who are you that dares enter this dark dwelling, and what right have you to disturb Vectra?"

"We come on an errand from the north in search of the beast that has murdered the inhabitants of our land. We come at the request of that land's Lord, whom we serve," Caritha said, and she managed to keep the trembling out of her voice. She grasped her sword with both hands and waved it from side to side, searching the darkness for the beast. "Are you responsible for killing those people, or was it another?"

A mocking laugh preceded the creature's retort. "You actually came all this way from that weak land. Flattered I am and, if you want to fight me, then I welcome it! Come to me."

Cautiously, she led her sisters in the voice's direction. The light of their swords revealed a small area of stone around them, but nothing more. An enormous, clawed hand slashed at them out of the darkness, nicking Caritha on the neck. She rolled to the side as another hand came at her from the other direction. She stabbed it with the point of her sword and the creature pulled back. She could hear it lick its hand as it stood back a safe distance.

Another voice suddenly rumbled out of the darkness, this time from above them. "Loos, stop immediately!" it said. The creature that had attacked them grumbled assent and remained out of sight. The new voice spoke again. "Loos, what have you down there?" There was agitation in the tone and a sharpness to the question.

The attacker was quick to respond. "They are intruders, Vectra! They were going to kill us in our sleep."

A long silence ensued before the creature above continued. "Harm them no further. Start up the firelights so that I may see clearly."

Their attacker grumbled as he moved farther into the cavern. Behind Caritha her sisters whispered to one another, doubtless their minds were filling with as many questions as her own. What kind of creature were they dealing with? Obviously not some brute beast, but something intelligent. Did this other voice belong to another member of the same species?

A flame broke the surrounding darkness and sparked its way along a channel in the rock. A strong smell of burning oil filled the stagnant air as the flame spread, igniting the oil in long channels that burned around the cavern. Each channel of oil fed the next, and soon filled the cavern with glowing firelight.

Chiseled designs had been carved into the walls. They were quite ornate, following geometrical patterns. Caritha and her sisters were standing in what appeared to be the main chamber. Its height was undeterminable because the firelights did not reach high enough to see its apex. Hundreds of tunnels branched off from the chamber, some gargantuan and others of various smaller dimensions. Deep cuts crisscrossed the cavern's rock walls, leading to countless caves high above the sisters' heads.

The creature that had attacked them stood near the far wall. Caritha felt a lump build in her throat. Loos, as the creature had been called, was truly a monster! He took a few steps in their direction, his muscular body supported on four tree-size legs only slightly smaller than his two forearms. A layer of dark gray scales covered his back and all six of his limbs. His underbelly was armorplated too, though with creamy white scales instead of gray. He swung a heavy reptilian tail, not as long as a dragon's, but tapered to a bony point.

At sight of his crocodilian head riddled with sharp teeth, Caritha shivered. The creature's forearms had five fingers, and as he flexed them, long claws slid out of each. A cold sweat broke out on Caritha's forehead, for she could now see several dozen of the creatures. Their heads peered out from the openings of their cave dwellings high in the walls. How many of these creatures were they dealing with? As she gripped the sword tighter, its leather handle slipped under her sweaty fingers. She and her sisters were outmatched this time, and she knew it beyond a doubt.

One of the creatures slid down the wall, its claws sparking along the rocks. It landed on the cavern's floor, shaking its heavy hide, much as a dog shakes its wet coat, and the scales along its back knocked off their dust. "Loos," the creature rumbled, "your forays into unknown lands have given me trouble before. Am I to believe that you do not deserve my wrath, and that these small creatures are laying false accusations against you?"

Something about the creature's manner of speaking and the tone it used, made Caritha realize that it was female. She looked at the creature that was called Loos. He had hunkered down a bit, and his dark eyes looked at the floor as if concocting a falsehood.

"If you cannot speak forthrightly then keep silent!" the female screamed, filling the cavern with her voice. The sound forced Caritha and her sisters to cover their ears or go deaf.

Loos cringed and skirted the chamber. He ventured a step closer to the female and raised his eyes, but the other raced forward, swung her tail in a tight circle, and sent him crashing into the wall with one thwack.

As Loos crashed to the ground, the creature turned away from him and faced Caritha and her sisters. It lumbered in her direction with powerful strides. It raised a clawed hand, retracted its claws, and dipped its head ever so slightly to stare down at them. "I am Vectra," the creature rumbled. "You need not fear now, for this is my realm and I welcome you to it." She sat back on her rear legs and gestured with her heavy hand. "Now, state your errand. Why have you come here?"

Caritha bowed to the creature. "Our quarrel is not with you. We have come at the bidding of Lord Ilfedo, the ruler of the Hemmed Land." Then, feeling emboldened by Vectra's inquiry, she pointed her sword at Loos. "We have come to deal with this murderer, for he came by night into our land and slew our people, burning them in their homes and pouring his poisonous vapors upon them until they died."

Laura moved to stand next to her and bowed as well. "We are messengers of death sent at the behest of our lord, Ilfedo, to stop the wicked in their tracks. When a creature threatens the Hemmed Land, we are sometimes called upon to seek it out," she said. "We cannot overlook rampant murder and this one you call Loos is guilty of that."

Approving rumbles resonated from the creatures that observed from their caves.

Vectra cocked her head to one side and looked up at her companions. "You speak with uncommon strength for members of your race," she said. She swiveled her massive head to gaze upon the Warrioresses. "It is a rare thing to find such strength in your weaker species, especially a strength that gains the praise of my brethren."

Caritha lowered her blade. "Humanity, compared with you, is weak. At least, that is, if you are speaking of physical strength. But my strength and that of these, my sisters, is born of another race and our roots are not as they appear."

"Hmm, your speech is a riddle." Vectra dipped her head. "Far be it from me to unmask your secrets. I enjoy the manner of your speech."

Long moments of silence passed during which Vectra seemed to contemplate her next words. When she spoke again, it was gentler, yet firm. "You need not fear me," she said. "I also seek justice. If Loos has indeed slain the innocent people of your land, he will pay at your hands for his wickedness."

Caritha relaxed, but the creature raised a cautionary finger and a long retractable claw slid out of it.

"However, his condemnation must be according to the laws of my domain, not according to yours," Vectra said. "If you do not abide by our laws then I will be forced to execute you instead. Loos must be proven guilty either by his own admission or by the testimony of no less than three witnesses. If this proof is not obtained then the accusers, in this case you, have the right to duel him in our great arena. Secondly, it is permitted under our law that if his guilt is in question, he has the right to procure aid in the duel from his relations and friends. If he wins against you through combat, his record is cleared. If you defeat him, your actions are approved, and his destruction is declared just in the eyes of all megatraths." Her dark round eyes bored into Caritha's.

"Have you come with proof, or a mere accusation?"

"The proof lies in the distant border of our land, in the blood spilled that lies there, and in the destroyed habitations of our people," Caritha said, and she felt despair creeping over her. Was Vectra mocking her by making these demands? She could see it in the creature's eyes. A look that told her that Vectra knew Loos was in fact guilty. "How can we possibly offer three witnesses? They are severely injured, some are near death! Do we drag them here to prove Loos's guilt?"

"Nevertheless, it is our law and you must abide by it," Vectra said. She turned to the accused. "Answer me truly, Loos, or I will see to it that your lies are bared before your brethren." She stood on all six legs and punched her foot into the stone floor. "Answer their accusation!"

He dipped his head to her and replied, "Among your servants I am faithful above many. My conduct both near and far has always, and always will be, honorable among megatraths. It grieves me that these vermin have even dared to accuse me of these deeds." His gaze shifted to the Warrioresses. "Let me clear myself in the arena!"

"Presumptuous fool!" Vectra threw him again and spat upon him. "The great arena is the purest test of the heart. By your own words I believe you are guilty, and I will soon be proven right when these humans stand over your corpse." She pulled him to his feet and drove him out of the cavern, yelling after him as he ran into a tunnel. "Choose those who will stand with you. The duel will begin within the hour."

Vectra turned and ran back to the Warrioresses, her feet sounding like thunder in the cavern. Her eyes were so fierce that they would have driven many a warrior to their knees. "I see the purity in your hearts," she said. "Do not fear the duel, for the wicked never win a battle in our arena. Win this fight, and you will have proved me right."

Caritha glanced over her shoulder at her sisters. Rozel lipped four words: "Lose, and we're dead."

"Come," Vectra growled. She pivoted and stomped deeper into the cavern. "This tunnel leads to the arena."

They entered the dark passageway, and the stone floor shook repeatedly behind them as the creatures climbed down the walls. They thudded their mighty bulks to the floor, and followed their leader. Caritha tensed her arms and raised her chin. "Walk proud, my sisters. Remember our father, and fight as he would fight."

"Oh quit talking. Humph!" Rozel strutted onward with her arms hung stiffly at her sides. "You're making me even more nervous than I already am."

Vectra led them out of the darkness into blinding daylight. Enormous stones ringed a flat section of desert ahead of them. The creatures congregated to the stones from tunnels along the solid stone hill that rose behind them.

"God help us," Laura said. "What are we going to do? The spectators are gathering to watch our duel. We cannot do this! One on one we are no match for these creatures."

Levena glanced down at her sword, gathering herself. "It won't be only one of us," she said. "Be encouraged, sister. Loos will have to take on all five of us, and I say that gives us a significant advantage over him. We can attack him from all sides and one of us will slit his throat."

They were now standing at the arena's far end. Yimshi's rays beat down on them without mercy. The movement of the surrounding creatures in the stone grandstands stirred a canopy of dust.

"Prepare yourselves!" Caritha cried as she loosened her sword arm, swinging it in small arcs in front of her. A breeze kicked sand into her face. The dust stung her eyes, making it difficult to keep them open.

A loud commotion came from the tunnel through which they had entered. The sisters turned toward the sound as Loos and three other members of his species exploded into the arena.

"Great, so we won't be fighting just one of them," Evela said. "Do you have a plan that will get us out of this, Caritha? A plan that will keep us alive?" She steadied herself by grasping Laura's shoulder.

"Now we have to take on four of them?" Levena gasped.

Laura bit her lip. "It certainly looks that way."

"Silence!" Caritha scolded. "The time for doubts is long past. You've grown soft in the Hemmed Land, my little sister. Remember how you acquitted yourself against the Sea Serpents?"

Evela laughed nervously. "I've tried to forget."

"Focus! Only our combined powers and skills with a sword can bring us home in one piece. Do you want to die out here?" Caritha said.

"Of course not!" Evela's eyes flared, and she

pointed her blade at Caritha's face. "Now stop haranguing me! I'm going to fight."

They raised their swords in unison, but Caritha felt doubt growing in her heart. The creatures charged toward them, hints of yellow vapor in their nostrils. The sisters widened their stances, and tendrils of energy accumulated between their joined swordtips. A ball of electricity formed there, radiating a bluish-white light as it grew in size. In a deft move, Caritha reached under the ball, plucked it off the blades, pulled her arm back, and threw the projectile at Loos. It struck him squarely in the chest.

He stumbled, collapsing to his six knees. His companions closed in, surrounded the sisters, and blew clouds of vapors upon them. Gasping for breath, Caritha reached out with her mind, using her dragon blood to draw energy through the air. A stiff wind blew from the north, dispersing the vapors harmlessly into the arena's stony grandstands.

Still, she could not catch enough fresh air to purify her lungs. Her strength seeped from her arms as the megatraths exhaled fresh vapors upon her and her sisters. She dropped her sword and grabbed her burning throat. Through the stirred dust she caught a glimpse of Laura dropping her weapon as well. One by one the remaining sisters fell to the desert floor. The whites of their eyes showed, and then their eyelids closed.

"No . . . no!" Caritha cried out as she fought to remain conscious. With trembling arms, she grasped for her sword. All she needed was a few moments longer. But her fingers did not find the hilt of her weapon. Instead they skipped over it and clutched sand. The light of day was veiled to her as the poison deprived her of oxygen. She could feel death closing in on her.

sand. The light of day was veiled to her as the poison deprived her of oxygen. She could feel death closing in on her.

REDEEMING THE FALLEN

The seemingly endless natural wall of stone lay in the distance ahead of Oganna. She watched as the five human figures began to climb toward the opening high in the rock. Suddenly one of the women hesitated.

"Fool," Oganna chided herself. "They probably spotted you!"

She laid flat on the desert sand, and waved her hand in an arc, feeding the already hot air with her energy. The already present heatwaves intensified in front of her, creating a curtain of illusion between herself and the Warrioresses. If all went as she hoped, the sisters would see a few mirages and then dismiss their doubts.

Within moments her aunts resumed climbing the desert wall. Oganna remained on the ground, shielding herself from any prying eyes with more heatwaves. The sisters filtered into the cave and disappeared within its dark recesses. She rose, shook the sand from her loose golden hair, and raced to the wall.

She had never climbed a cliff before, but there seemed no better time to learn than the present. Reaching over her head she grasped a crag and pulled herself up. The pack on her back offset her balance, making her task more difficult, but she made steady progress until she was a few feet from the cave. She grabbed a loose stone and almost lost her balance when it broke free in her hand. Regaining a secure handhold she continued up until she stood within the safety of the cave.

She licked her parched lips, pulled out her water canteen, and drank two long draughts. The straps of her pack bit into her shoulders so she hefted it down and leaned it against the cave wall. Her shoulders ached. She stretched her arms and twisted around to loosen her back muscles.

Then she drew her sword and waited as the silver dress grew from it to cover her body. The crimson blade provided more than adequate lighting to reveal the cave's interior. She looked down the tunnel that opened in the cave's rear wall and glanced back at her pack. If she encountered the creature that inhabited this place she would want to face it unencumbered. Thus decided, she left the pack and climbed down the tunnel. In the darkness her silver garb emitted a faint glow, giving her a ghostly appearance.

The descent was not easy but when she reached the tunnel's end and stood in the creature's underground home, she looked around. The ground shook, and she flattened herself against the tunnel wall. A stampede of terrible creatures passed by, racing into a tunnel at the cavern's opposite end. She made a quick evaluation, noting the creatures' crocodile-like heads and their thick hides. Many of the creatures stood over ten feet tall. She complimented herself on her success. She had found a nest of the species that had destroyed Bordelin. This was the right place, but where had the sisters gone?

As soon as all of the creatures had thundered by, she followed them. Sounds of battle came from up ahead and blinding sunlight spilled toward her, drawing her to a tunnel that led back to the desert floor on the opposite side of the natural wall. She walked through and halted at the tunnel's end to peer outside. It took long moments for her eyes to readjust to the brilliant light of day. Enormous stones ringed a parcel of flat land ahead of her. The creatures were, for the most part, lying on the stones. Their dark eyes gazed at the arena floor. Four of their species were blowing concentrated clouds of yellow vapor upon an unidentifiable target.

A wind blew through the arena, dispersing the vapors and revealing the target of the creatures' assault. It was the Warrioresses! Oganna's heart filled with rage at the sight. She spun her crimson blade in her hand as the last sister collapsed to the desert floor. She kept a firm grip on its handle. "Desist!" she screamed as she took a bold step into the arena.

One of the creatures turned toward her and snarled.

But Oganna raised her voice again. "You

scum of Subterran. You wicked creatures! Have you no honor? Are you afraid of these women? Come! Let us see if you dare to face my wrath." Sober and fearless, she strode forward, holding the crystalline sword before her with both hands. Its blade rose like a hovering spire of blood.

"Loos," one of the creatures called from the stadium, "your quarrel is not with the younger human."

The creature disregarded the other and ambled toward Oganna, his lizardian head skimming the sand. "Come near, human, and I will show you how a megatrath deals with threats. I will crush you as we have crushed our other enemies—"

In the midst of his sentence, Oganna reached for her blade boomerang. She spun around, and sent it spinning through the air. Her aim was perfect. The sharp crystal passed through his open mouth and severed his tongue. As the wiggling tongue fell to the sand, the arena went silent.

Loos's companions glanced at the tongue and took a couple of steps back. Oganna nodded to them and caught the returning boomerang in her left hand, holding it up for all to see. "Do any more of you have a word to share with me?" When the attackers didn't respond, she continued. "The next time I hear a tongue utter an ill, it too will fall."

From the horde a rumble could be heard, and Oganna thought it sounded like approval or respect. Meanwhile the megatraths in the arena shoved aside the unconscious sisters and charged toward her. Oganna firmed her hold on the sword. She closed her eyes, letting the rage within her burn through her blood, and then she poured it into the sword. When she was ready, she opened her eyes. "Give me fire, my sword," she whispered. "Give me a flame to scald the wicked." Flames sprouted from her blade, covered it, and shot out from its point.

The creature nearest her hunkered to avoid the inferno as it ran, while another opened its mouth to expose rows of teeth. She faced them, a new confidence arising within and driving out all uncertainty. With a piercing yell, she sprang onto the head of the nearest creature and drove the burning blade into its eye. It screamed in pain as she pulled the white-hot metal from its socket. Red blood spurted from the creature's wound as she dropped to the ground. An inferno of flames rolled from the other three creatures' mouths. They closed in around her. But her sword fed off their fire, absorbing and collecting their flames, then enveloping her in a bubble of energy.

Tongue-less Loos poured vapors from his nostrils. She choked a bit, but recovered long enough to jump again and stab out his eye. He flung her from his head, smashing her into the ground. He reached for her and with his large hands began to squeeze.

As her breath left her, she flipped her sword and stabbed it with all her strength into his wrist. Loos pulled away from her blade and reared into the air, making a horrible sound that probably would have been a scream if he had still possessed a tongue.

Oganna gasped for air. Her knees felt weak. She knelt on the ground. Yellow clouds covered her, cutting her off from the world of the living. Her shoulders drooped, the sword fell from her grasp, and she felt her eyes rolling to the back of her head.

* * *

"Rise, my daughter," said Albino, and his pink eyes were filled with love. His gaze was soft, and he reached out with a strong hand to steady her.

Caritha looked around, confused. She was in his throne room back at Shizar Palace. After all these years she was home. "Father?" Her lungs burned, and she coughed a vaporous ring of yellow out of her mouth.

"Breathe deeply, my daughter. Drink in the fresh air. Let it fill you with life anew." The dragon heaved in, expanded his chest, then let it all out in a plume of fire. A smile curled his mouth.

She shook her head. "How . . . what . . . how did I get here?"

"I brought you back." He slapped his tail against the marble floor. "And it's a good thing I did, too. Your life would have been lost."

Warm, clean air cleansed her body. Caritha stood straighter and looked to the side at a large stained glass window. "Why am I here?" she asked.

He lowered his head, drew her toward him, and looked into her eyes. "Oganna is making the ultimate sacrifice," he said. "She followed your path and now her life is on the line of death."

"Then you must send me back!" She trembled at the thought of her young charge facing all four of the terrible creatures alone. "She is not ready to fight on her own. You must let me return and help her."

"Caritha, my dear child, I would like nothing better. But if I restored you and your sisters to the arena, you would follow a very bitter path." He shook his head. "I have seen the future, Caritha, and it is littered with pain. If you go back, you will reap sorrow as if you are drinking the rivers of the world—"

"But isn't there joy along with the pain?" she asked. "Surely there is hope for the future."

"There is hope," he said, but his eyes emptied of emotion, and his wings flexed. "Even now one of my faithful warriors stands, though all of you have fallen. She is ready at this moment to give Oganna the moments she needs to survive this battle. You have lost one sister before. What if returning you to the arena will destroy those that remain with you? You do not know if you can defeat the creatures. What if you could avoid the pain ahead? Would you stay with me, or would you still wish to return?" He sighed. "I have seen things far more evil than a mere megatrath. I have battled the forces of darkness since long before you were hatched."

She reached out and caressed his scaly chin. "Father, do you fear the future?"

"No," he stated. "But do I dread it? Yes."

Caritha held her chin high. "If my life must be given in exchange for Oganna's, then so be it. I see in her the makings of a woman who can change the world. Her heart follows righteousness, and her will is governed by selflessness. My own pain is inconsequential compared to the gift that Oganna is to her people."

The great white dragon cocked his head to the side. "You have grown over the years, my daughter. Once you would have only concerned yourself with the welfare of yourself and your sisters. Living with your sister's husband has matured and changed you . . . for the better."

She reached both hands around his long neck as he embraced her.

"Now," he said, releasing her. "If you are convinced of your decision, then I will return you to the battle. Your sisters have been given the same choice as you." He grinned from horn to horn. "They all gave similar answers and will return with you."

The white and gold walls of the palace around her, along with the dragon's personage, began to fade. "I love you, Father," she called. She smiled as her sisters congealed around her and the desert sand reappeared under her feet. She and her sisters were truly one. One in purpose, one in motivation, and one in love. She ran her finger along her sword's rusted blade and laughed as it cut her finger. It was time to deal with these megatraths.

The sisters charged across the sandy expanse, closing the distance between them and Loos and his companions. They leapt on the creatures' backs, striking futilely at their hides. The megatraths rolled over on their backs to shake them off. They growled, rose, spun, and thwacked at the sisters with their tails. Laura, Evela, Levena, and Rozel were sent flying, but Caritha dodged the blows and remained on the offensive. "Is that all you've got?" she called.

Loos threw fire at her, and she noticed that Oganna had taken out his eye. Clever girl, she had aimed for the vulnerable spots instead of trying to take the creatures down all at once. She raced forward, holding back her sword until the last second. Loos's mouth opened to snap at her. She thrust with all her might, scraping her blade along the roof of his mouth. He stumbled, blood pouring onto the ground.

* * *

As the battle renewed and raged around her, Oganna heaved in breaths of clean air until the poison in her system lost its potency. Still, her strength refused to return, and she knew that she was not yet healed. What should she do? Her aunts were beginning to falter and the megatraths, though wounded, were still fierce opponents.

She picked up her sword, pointed it toward the sky, and called out, "Creator in heaven, I cannot rise. Will no one come to my side in this time? Will not a savior show himself?"

"Oganna, hold still," a soft voice said suddenly from behind her. "Let me draw the poison."

Turning, Oganna looked into the fiercely beautiful face before her. Starfire held out her hand, palm up. Strands of yellow curled out of Oganna's chest, gathering as a transparent sphere that floated above the fire lady's hand.

"There," Starfire said. "Rise now and fight!" Flames enveloped her and she vanished.

Oganna arose a new person, her spirits high and her confidence growing. She divided the air with her blade. "My sword, from this day forth you will be called the Avenger. Prove now your worth." She lifted it above her head and threw it straight as an arrow into Loos's remaining eye.

Now completely blinded, Loos opened his jaws wide in a roar of pain. Oganna sent her boomerang sailing into his open mouth. He clamped his jaws together, and the weapon's sharp edge sliced upward into his brain. He fell like a stone to the desert floor. The arena grew quiet. The Warrioresses and the remaining three megatraths stood still, staring at the grisly sight.

TOMB OF THE ANCIENTS

Standing over Loos's corpse, Oganna pulled Avenger's blade from his eye and used it to pry open his jaws. The boomerang had been lodged deep into his palate. She reached inside his mouth, feeling through the slimy saliva. When she found her weapon, she jerked it out. She pulled away her sword, and Loos's jaws snapped shut.

She gazed down on the carcass and shook her head. Slaying the creature should have brought some remorse to her heart, but though she tried to feel compassion or sorrow, she could not feel any for him. He had brought this end on himself by slaying the people of Bordelin. He was an unrepentant murderer, and she had been the agent of justice.

She waved a hand at Loos's companions. "It is over. He is dead. Get out of my sight before you meet similar fates." They dug their claws into the ground and bolted into the tunnel from whence they'd come.

Caritha ran toward her. "Oganna, are you all right?" Even as she asked the question, she was beaming with pride. "You have done well."

Oganna pointed at the creatures around the arena. "Will they give us trouble because I did that?"

"The megatraths? No, I don't believe they'll give us any trouble. Their leader, Vectra, seemed to sympathize with us and showed bold dislike for the creature you just slew," Caritha said.

One of the megatraths separated from the others, and began lumbering toward Oganna and the sisters. Oganna nodded her head in the direction of the approaching megatrath and raised an eyebrow. "Is that Vectra?" she asked.

Her aunt nodded and stepped out of the creature's path.

The megatrath was more than ten feet tall and walked with a confidence that seemed to frighten the sisters, but Oganna discerned admiration in the creature's eyes. Vectra neared her and snorted a flame, then spoke to Caritha. "Who are you? Never before have I seen humans fight with such ferocity."

Caritha bowed and gestured toward her sisters. "We are the Warrioresses—"

"Welcome to my domain, Warrioresses." Then Vectra turned to Oganna. She bowed in the young woman's direction. "And who is this?"

Oganna sheathed Avenger and tucked away her boomerang. Her silver dress vanished, and her aunts gasped. In the intensity of these last moments, they must have neglected to notice her new outfit. "I am honored to meet you," she said, wiping sweat from her forehead. She bowed low to the creature. "I am Oganna, princess of the Hemmed Land."

In a deep voice the creature said, "I am greatly honored by your presence here, Princess. My name is Vectra, and these are my people, the megatraths."

"I am sorry for this intrusion, but it was necessary," Caritha said.

Vectra shrugged, then she kicked Loos's carcass and returned her attention to Oganna. "Megatraths respect a valiant warrior who does not back down in the face of great odds. You have proved yourself to be most valiant and a superior combatant, unlike any human I have ever encountered. You have proved your worth to us today and have earned an eternal remembrance in our stories. From this day forward any megatrath that disgraces you or your subjects will bear generational shame. Please, accept my friendship and join me for my evening meal."

Caritha raised a hand. "Thank you for your generosity, but—"

But Oganna could see Vectra's expression changing from friendliness to disappointment, and she cut Caritha off immediately. "Your offer is kind, Vectra. We accept your invitation with gratitude."

The creature's lips opened to reveal a long row of teeth. Vectra lumbered back into the tunnel, her long thick legs quickly carrying her deeper into her subterranean habitat. She easily outdistanced Oganna, then glanced back as if realizing that she had left her guests behind. She reduced the length of her gait, allowing Oganna to catch up with her.

They followed the tunnel back into the main cavern, then passed through several adjoining chambers of lesser size. The firelight channels along the walls allowed Oganna to see almost every corner of the underground megatrath world, and it fascinated her. At some points she glimpsed megatraths high in their wall chambers, as if they lived in them. The creatures would poke out their long toothy snouts and quietly stare, but when they perceived Oganna gazing back up at them they offered her slight bows. They were certainly not unfriendly but definitely curious about the strange and weak human creatures walking along on only two legs behind their fearsome megatrath leader. Oganna wondered how many of them there were. They emerged from every tunnel and chamber that she encountered, and many more lumbered beyond her reach into the dark recesses of the adjoining caverns. She imagined that if these creatures were organized into a military force, they would be capable of incalculable destruction. They could probably tread entire forests, destroy fortresses, drink up rivers and, in the process, destroy nations.

As she walked on, she imagined hundreds of megatraths storming through the Hemmed Land and punching holes in her father's army. She shuddered at the thought. "It's a good thing that Vectra has taken a liking to us," she whispered to her aunts. "Otherwise she might pose a real threat to the Hemmed Land."

Laura pulled on her sleeve and said, "Oganna, what were you thinking in taking Vectra up on her offer? We don't know anything about these creatures."

"You are right." Oganna swallowed hard. "For all we know they might be planning to feast on us!"

Laura stared at the floor as she walked on, worry creasing her brow. Then she turned up her nose and looked sidelong at Oganna. "That was not funny, young one." She dropped behind and began to converse in a low voice with Rozel. Rozel looked relieved to have the opportunity to grunt out some of her own reservations.

The monstrous Vectra slowed as they entered one of the larger caverns. Glancing about, Oganna realized that she was standing opposite a monstrous stone slab about six feet tall and twice as wide, and nearly a hundred paces long. Vectra directed several megatraths to set another stone on one side of the table for her guests, then she lumbered around to sit at the table. "I apologize for the height of my furnishings," she said, "but we rarely receive human visitors." She waited for them to sit opposite her atop the stone.

When everyone had settled, another megatrath thrust its way through the other creatures that were milling around the table. Its enormous hands plunked massive stone bowls and platters onto the table. Desert fruits overflowed several of the bowls. The megatrath curled its lips up, showing its long rows of teeth as it plopped a stone platter in front of Oganna. A plump black fish of a variety unfamiliar to her, lay across the platter.

"I hope you will enjoy these." Vectra tapped the fish with the tip of her claw. "My cook snatched them from our underground rivers. Also try this." From a bowl she extracted an oblong orange fruit as long as Oganna's arm and cracked it on the table. Taking a small piece, Oganna tasted it. The creamy interior tasted like pears and, strangely enough, bore a hint of beef flavor. It should have been an awful combination, but it satisfied both the craving for sweet and for sustaining protein.

"This is delicious," she said as she smiled across at Vectra. "But we do not have these in my homeland. What do you call it?"

"Da'pra!" Vectra rumbled, and she licked her lips. Then she grabbed at several bowls, moving each aside until she picked one up and sniffed at it with her long snout. "Try this and let me know if it also pleases you."

Oganna stood on her stone seat to peer inside the bowl. Yellow leaves, brown grape-like things, and glowing red beans the size of carrots floated in a soupy mix. "I don't recognize any of these, either. What are the ingredients?"

Vectra rumbled in her chest for several minutes. At first Oganna thought she had inadvertently insulted the creature. But Vectra scratched her thick chin then scraped her claw on the tabletop. "I'm sincerely sorry, Princess. I have no idea how to describe this to you. It is construed of food indigenous to our underground realm."

Oganna dipped her fingers in the cold soup and slopped it in her mouth. Most of it tasted akin to grass. Not at all a pleasant flavor! But the strong aftertaste was even worse, almost forcing her to gag. Apparently the Creator had never intended for humans to consume some of the things eaten by these desert creatures.

During the meal an overwhelming sense of belonging filled Oganna. She had fallen upon her aunts' attackers with strength beyond her years, and she had triumphed. Her actions had saved their lives.

The sisters conversed with her in a manner that demonstrated their new respect for her. They responded when she spoke to them and even went out of their way to let her try the megatraths' food before they did. At last she had graduated from student to respected asset. Perhaps, in time, they would admit her into their group in the place that her mother had once filled.

Her thoughts then turned to her hostess. Vectra treated her as a hero and displayed confidence in her. Indeed, the other megatraths at their enormous table regarded her with near reverence. It was as if her victory over Loos had elevated her to a higher plane in their estimation than that of the Warrioresses.

Were they naïve enough to trust a complete stranger solely on the basis of that individual's combat skills? They seemed warlike and strong, yet maybe their culture was more vulnerable than it appeared. She imagined what would happen if a smooth-spoken warrior entered the megatrath realm and used deceit and subterfuge to bring about a war among them. They might easily be taken advantage of.

She focused her attention on Vectra, seeking to understand the megatraths and whether or not they would be inclined to form an alliance with the Hemmed Land. She told Vectra of her people's customs, such as turning one's sword handle to the victor in friendly contests. More than this, she elaborated on the layout of the land and the difficulties her father had encountered while securing peace.

Vectra found the stories of Ilfedo's encounters with the sea serpents of particular interest. "Your father sounds like a worthy leader," she said. She licked the food from one of her claws. "We megatraths respect one who proves his worth against such odds. I have never heard of a sea serpent before, but my people tell stories about the Sea of Serpents. Our ancestors said it is wild and untamable, with creatures that no being has dared disturb for two thousand years."

"I don't doubt it," Oganna said as she grabbed a sharp stone and carved into an apple that was the size of her head. "Among my people there are stories of men who have left our land in favor of crossing the Sea . . . never to return. Although none of my father's generation has attempted to cross, many of them now fish it, and some fishermen are venturing deeper into its uncharted waters where fish abound. Several of these braver fishermen have become rather prosperous."

The megatrath picked up a large basket of fruit, tilted it up against her open snout, and swallowed the contents in a single gulp. "We do not eat fish. The fruits of the desert and the water beneath it are all we require for sustenance."

"Have you ever tried fish?" Oganna asked.

"I haven't, but some megatraths did, and they died shortly afterward," Vectra said. "Though it is unclear whether or not it was the fish that killed them, we have determined that the spirit of fish was not intended for our consumption. Thus, we avoid it whenever possible."

Oganna nodded thoughtfully. "But you have served it today."

"Only when we have guests. Non-megatrath

guests, that is. The flesh of fish will not harm humans. Thus we serve it," Vectra said. "Just as our desert can kill you but will not harm us, so is the way of fish with humans." Vectra looked into another basket and pulled out an oblong fruit that was almost five feet in length. "This is Prapra, a delicacy among my species, but to humans it is deadly."

"Well, I find that curious," Oganna admitted, eying the exorbitantly large fruit. "How do you know it is poisonous to us?"

The megatrath grinned a toothy smile. "A human adventurer once came through this way and partook of my predecessor's hospitality. During the meal he was warned that the spirit of Prapra was poisonous to all except desert dwellers. As I'm sure you have figured out, he tried it anyway. Then," Vectra said as she snapped her enormous fingers, "he died."

It was a startling revelation to Oganna and she thought deeply on it for a time. A human had come here before her. A human who had managed to befriend these creatures, and yet through some unfortunate happenstance he had been poisoned by something he had eaten. But surely if he had been one of the Hemmed Land's people then she would have heard of him. There must be a trace. A story of a wannabe traveler who ventured into this desert and was never heard from again. Oganna looked into the megatrath's large dark eyes and asked the questions that burned in her imagination. "And who was this traveler? Do you know his name or where he came from?"

Vectra squinted at her and then cocked her head to the side. "Come, let me show you something," she said. Then she lumbered toward one of the tunnels and paused, glancing back to see if Oganna was following.

Oganna slapped Rozel on the shoulder and jumped to the cavern floor. "Don't worry about me, and do not stay up waiting for me," she reassured her aunts. "Get some rest, if you can. I am going to learn what I can from these creatures."

Caritha frowned at first and then nodded. "You may go," she said aloud, but her mouth formed more words, and Oganna read her lips. "You have your sword?"

Slipping her hand to her side, Oganna activated Avenger so that the blade glowed crimson. She turned away and followed Vectra down the tunnel.

* * *

In the dimness of that underground world, Oganna struggled to put one foot in front of the other without stumbling. Vectra had led her out of the megatraths' inhabited tunnels and caverns, and was now showing her even deeper places. Oganna drew her sword and used it and the glow of her silver dress to reveal the way ahead of her. The tunnel's stone walls were smooth and polished from centuries, perhaps even ages, of use. So much so that they could not have been smoother if an ocean had carved the passageway. She ran her hand along the stone as she walked, feeling every dip and rise in its cool surface.

Ahead of her Vectra spat a flame into a channel on the rock wall. It sparked in the oil and blazed, the flames spreading over a section of wall about twenty feet high and at least as many broad. The firelights helped illuminate the upper interior of the vast cavern into which they had walked, but the cavern floor fell away in front of her into the depths of an abyss that was cloaked in shadow. It was an abyss that prevented anyone from crossing to the other side of the shadowed cavern. How amazing that such a place existed. The air smelled damp, old, and somewhat stale. When Oganna gazed across the abyss, she glimpsed a sheer wall of impenetrable stone rising from the depths to a place out of sight far above. So far as she could tell there were no tunnels or caverns on that side of the abyss, but much of it was cloaked in shadow.

Vectra stopped and faced the abyss, her heavy body rigid, her head held high as she waited for something. From the dark abyss ahead of them a silver disc hovered into the air. It looked fluid, as if it was a disc of polished metal with oil running over its surface. It began to revolve clockwise, and various colors streamed from the disc's edges. The stone floor of the cavern under Oganna and Vectra radiated a soft glow and lines formed, as if some unseen being was drawing on the floor. The glowing lines painted a pink rose that shimmered beneath their feet.

From the shadows beside Oganna a voice chuckled softly enough for only her to hear, and Specter's voice said, "I think I'll wait back in the dining chamber with the dragon's daughters. You have good instincts, child. This creature is no threat. You will be safe with her."

Oganna grinned into the shadows. Specter! She should have known. He had followed her through the desert and probably watched her entire duel with the megatraths. She heard his cloak swish over the floor as he returned to the tunnel.

Vectra rumbled deep in her throat and knelt on all six of her legs. "We must respect the ancient spirit that guards this place, Princess. For it alone grants access to the Tomb of the Ancients."

Oganna stepped forward. "What is the," she started to ask. But she never finished her sentence.

"Look at the rose," Vectra growled as her tail twitched. "Read the marks upon its petals. Then follow my example, and bow to honor the dead."

The marks etched on the rose's petals were foreign letters. Oganna could not read them. She sheathed her sword, allowing her silver garb to dissipate. "I do not understand these runes," she said.

Vectra turned to her in surprise. "Surely you must, for this is the original script of the Common Tongue, which both you and I speak." After a pause, she snorted a yellow vapor. "You speak the truth, Oganna. I can see that. But," she pounded a fist on the floor. "But unless you come over here and kneel, the spirit will not open the tomb, and I will be unable to show you what we came here for."

Above the depths of the abyss the silver disc continued to hover in silence. Its lights mesmerized Oganna, and her curiosity grew. What was this strange contrivance? What was it guarding? At last she knelt on the rose. Then she waited.

"Princess, your head! Put it down," the megatrath grunted.

"My head?" Oganna looked with puzzlement at Vectra and observed that not only was the creature kneeling, she was bowing as well. Realizing her error, Oganna tipped her head forward.

She did so just in time. The silver disc had started to retreat into the depths, but when she bowed her head it stopped and then rose to its previous elevation, spinning erratically. Vectra's eyes remained lowered during the process. Oganna kept her head lowered, too, but she raised her eyes. The disc was beautiful, magical, but it was no spirit. There was nothing to fear from it.

Across the abyss the cavern wall began to transform. Its face of solid stone slid off like an incredible gate dropping into the darkness. Behind it lay the front of a building that had been carved in the stone with a white path leading up to it. Eight white pillars guarded a broad doorway that fronted the structure, and the pillars closest to the doorway radiated blinding white light, forcing her to turn her face away.

The blinding light diminished somewhat but the sound of metal grating on stone pulled her attention away from the abyss. She looked back at the tunnel through which she had come as a rusted iron door began to slide down, closing her off from the megatrath tunnels. The door had almost sealed the tunnel completely when the Warrioresses raced toward it from the far end, their glowing swords in hand. But they all slammed into an invisible barrier a few paces short of the door and fell, stunned, to the floor. Oganna smiled to reassure them, but she was too late. The door had sealed them out of sight.

She turned back to see the wondrous cavern and the building that it had hidden from her eyes. She was alone now with a megatrath, but she felt no need for concern. In fact, she felt as safe as she ever had at home and her craving to explore this strange world had grown. Vectra knew this place like the back of her massive, clawed hand, and remarkably she seemed eager to share it with Oganna. She was so busy looking up at the face of the building that she did not notice Vectra's silence until the megatrath spoke again.

"Princess, the Tomb of the Ancients awaits us." Vectra was floating over the abyss. The disc had vanished and she appeared to be standing where the disc had been. But no, as Oganna looked closer she realized that Vectra only had the appearance of floating. Just as the Warrioresses had bumped into an invisible barrier, so now there was an invisible walkway that stretched from her side of the cavern across the abyss to the building.

Taking a cautious step forward, Oganna set her foot upon the smooth, cool surface. Was it glass? She leaned down and tapped the surface with her fist. No, glass would feel firm, and this did not. She struck it but heard no resulting sound. It was as if it was there, yet not there. She stood, smiling reassurance to Vectra as she walked across the level surface toward the creature. The sensation felt odd. Surreal. Each step felt lighter, and each stride sped her passage across.

"Come," Vectra said. She plodded across the chasm on the smooth path, then stepped onto a path of white marble on the other side. She lumbered ahead of Oganna up the white path to the building's doorway. The megatrath growled and threw its weight against the hefty doors. The doors groaned inward, and Oganna breathed in sharply as she stepped inside the structure. In front of them lay an endless corridor. The floor was stone and the ceiling gleamed with an unearthly light emitted by innumerable crystals that studded its surface. Heavy wood beams crisscrossed high above, supporting the ceiling. This 'tomb' rivaled the splendor of a palace.

Oganna let out a low whistle as she pointed down the endless corridor. "How far back does this go?"

"I don't know. Some of us have tried to find out, but though we have walked for hours, we never even glimpsed its end," Vectra admitted. She pointed to an inscription on an overhead beam. "And that text says, 'Some secrets are best left hidden.' From this we have gathered that we must be content with the knowledge we have and not venture into the depths of this place. We must not offend the spirits that keep watch in this place."

Somehow, Oganna doubted the megatrath's understanding of the inscription. Doubtless the builders of this tomb had wanted their dead left undisturbed, but that did not mean that mystical spirits haunted it. She studied the structure, soaking in the grandeur of it all. Not in all of the Hemmed Land did there exist a structure to even hold a torch to this one. All others were but candles and this was a forest fire. The walls and columns had been etched, and even though she did not recognize the patterns, they felt somehow connected to her past. But that was foolish talk, wasn't it?

Oganna looked up at Vectra. The megatrath was gazing around the tomb as well, puffing its nostrils out with pride or satisfaction. Oganna suspected that not one, but both emotions were present. "Vectra, you said that this place is called the 'Tomb of the Ancients?' But why is that?"

Vectra grunted and said, "The runes that you cannot decipher were passed on to my people by the remnants of the ancient humanoid race that built this place. We know little about them, except that which has been passed down to us by our ancestors in the form of legends and myths. According to our stories, the Ancient Ones gave our ancestors this underground world as a reward for good deeds and taught them their language. As you entered this place, did you not see the writing above the doors?"

Oganna was forced to admit that she had not.

Vectra's long mouth curled into a grimace of a smile. "Above the entrance is an inscription that reads, 'Tomb of the Ancients.' On the doors are several lines of verse that I have committed to memory. The lines are:

> *Forever may the spirit of this tomb watch over these dead,*
> *And forever may they rest in the Master's peace.*
> *To those who come in hither,*
> *Pray that the spirit herein enchained will not awaken.*"

A shiver ran up Oganna's spine at the final line. "Sounds kind of creepy."

"And it should," Vectra said. "Our stories tell of an evil creature of great physical might who was pulled into the depths by a creature of great good. The evil one was chained in the darkness by the Ancient Ones. It is said that one day he will arise again and avenge himself on Subterran."

"Fascinating," Oganna whispered. "Who was this creature that brought him down? What was his name?"

Vectra sighed, her eyes moistened, and she smiled. "His name is too sacred for us to utter and too revered to be written."

Oganna inspected the tomb more closely. Numerous doorways flanked by marble pillars along the arching walls led from the endless corridor into darkness. No doubt the entombed remains of the ancient people that had built this place lay somewhere within the connecting chambers.

"Here, in this protected place, my ancestors have been buried along with anyone else whom we put to rest." Vectra's feet thudded on the stone floor as she turned to let her gaze rove over the high ceiling. "Beside this, you may have already guessed that the Tomb of the Ancients holds not only our remains, and those that we have buried here, but also those of the Ancients builders of this place." Ducking through one of the doorways, she led Oganna into another dark tunnel. Along the way, she blew flames from her mouth to ignite the many torches that nestled along the stone walls.

At the tunnel's end they arrived in a circular chamber. Vectra sat back on her haunches. "Notice that the floor is inscribed here as well. It says, 'Here lie strangers.' Observe that the room is nearly a perfect circle. And these tablets—" She indicated inscribed stones that had been set in the walls. "These mark the graves of the strangers that befriend us and die among us."

Oganna listened with rapt attention.

"Remember that adventurer I told you about?" Vectra asked as she continued. "The one that ate Da'pra?" She pointed a claw at one of the stone tablets. "Well, that is where we buried him."

"Really?" Oganna said reflectively.

Vectra spoke on. "We have reserved this particular chamber for those who are not megatrath and yet die among us. Here the adventurer will be preserved for all time by the spirit of this place." Vectra pressed the epitaph with her fist and it responded as if a spring had been loaded into the wall behind it. The stone slid out of the wall and behind it lay a peculiar sarcophagus coated in a translucent material. The sarcophagus had been laid on a stone slab that was connected to the epitaph stone. Clearly visible through the sarcophagus's convex surface was a middle-aged man, lying peacefully as if in sleep. A relaxed smile was on his face, and his body was clothed in a snow-white robe.

"In my homeland, when we bury our dead, they are sealed under layers of dirt and stone," Oganna said as she ran her hand over the sarcophagus. The sarcophagus was lukewarm to the touch and as abrasive as a fine sandpaper. "He does not even look dead. It's as if he is sleeping."

"I know what you mean, for I too have had that feeling. It does not matter who we bury in this place, or what their expression is at the moment of their death. When the spirit covers the body a smile lights the entombed one's face. All of the dead can be seen as whole as the day they were laid to rest. They are dressed in the same white apparel, and they have the same joyous expression. It is a mystery I do not pretend to understand."

"How many of your people have been buried here?" Oganna asked.

The creature shrugged. "The number is beyond reckoning. We are not even sure when the Ancient Ones gave this tomb to our forebearers. "Maybe a thousand years, maybe more."

Leading the way, Vectra returned to the endless corridor. She proceeded a couple dozen paces down the corridor, then turned to lumber through a larger doorway to the side. She spat flames against the walls and torches flashed to life, revealing a tunnel that was proportionally larger than the first one. It lead them into a vast room with walls that rose hundreds of feet high. Here the enshrined megatraths had been buried. Four circles inset in the imposing ceiling shone down pillars of light to illuminate the room.

Clearly the ancient architects had designed this chamber as a gift to their megatrath friends. Here the creatures' remains had not decayed. Within these walls they were safe. Here no tomb robber would dare enter to strip creatures of their dignity.

"Magnificent, isn't it?" Vectra scratched the floor then continued. "Someday I too will be buried here, but not until I have subjected all megatraths under my leadership and have led them to peace with one another. When my kingdom is greater than that of my forebearers, I will rest here among them."

Oganna folded her hands in front of her as she observed the megatrath burial chamber. What did Vectra mean by subjecting all megatraths under her leadership? Were the megatraths a race divided into nations that Vectra wished to conquer? Oganna decided to wait and ask the question later when Vectra was not so preoccupied with thoughts of the past.

"Well, Princess, now that I have shown you the Tomb of the Ancients, it is time to leave." The megatrath led the way out of the tomb and closed the doors behind them.

Oganna looked back at the doors. Yes, the inscription was there just as the megatrath said. She turned and briskly walked off the edge expecting that the invisible surface was still there . . . but she plunged foolishly into the dark abyss. Soon her fall slowed, and she ricocheted off an unseen force in the depths of the abyss. In an instant she found herself moved from the abyss and found herself again standing where she had been in front of the Tomb doors.

She looked up the path at Vectra. The creature slammed shut the heavy doors. Oganna about faced. Not ten feet in front of her she saw a duplicate of herself stepping toward the precipice. Oganna dashed forward, grabbing for her duplicate's shirt, but her other self plunged into the dark abyss. She looked back at her guide. The megatrath seemed oblivious to what had happened. Vectra loomed beside her and knelt, again awaiting the tomb's 'spirit.' Oganna glanced over the precipice into the deep shadows that played between barely visible cliffs and boulders. What had happened? Where had her other self fallen? Or had she somehow been thrown back several moments in time and placed safely again on the path? She shivered with the uncertainty of it and knelt beside Vectra. She'd had enough excitement for one day.

The silver disc rose out of the abyss, the lights shone, and once again Vectra and Oganna walked to the other side of the cavern on an invisible surface. Behind them a wall of stone slid back into place, sealing the tomb from view. The silver disc descended into the darkness, and the iron door that had blocked escape from the cavern now opened to reveal the tunnel behind it.

Oganna walked through the opened tunnel and greeted her aunts as they rushed toward her. They couldn't disguise their worry. Their foreheads were knit and their eyes were narrowed. Their hands sweated as they fingered their sheathed swords.

She wondered if she should tell them what she had seen. If she did would they believe her? She decided that, for the time being, she would sort out the mysteries of the Tomb in her own mind and tell them no more than necessary.

PART DRAGON

Oganna felt as though she had walked among gods and partaken of their former glory. Vivid recollections of her experience in the Tomb of the Ancients passed through her mind, and in her heart she understood more profoundly how little she really knew of the world. The Hemmed Land seemed such a small speck on a picture that had been drawn through the ages.

"This ancient race," Oganna said to Vectra as they walked alone through the cavernous depths later that day, "they taught your ancestors to read their language?"

"Yes. We are not certain why. Some of us believe they wanted to leave clues for us to follow, clues that could lead us to a greater, more meaningful existence. Others among us say that the Ancient Ones simply left it with us as a way to understand how to bury our dead in the tomb."

Oganna stood still and stared into another seemingly bottomless cavern. "What do you believe?"

The creature smiled and peered into the cavern along with her. "You are very inquisitive about us."

"I suppose I am," Oganna said, turning her bluegold eyes away from the depths and meeting the megatrath's gaze. "This language of the ancients. The script on the tomb and inside of it. Could you teach me to read it?"

"But you already speak it. Surely you are able to read it as well," Vectra said.

Oganna frowned a bit at that. "It is true that we speak the same language. However, I do not understand the ancient script. My people write very differently than your Ancient Ones did."

Vectra swatted the air. "Perhaps, then, you use a different set of runes. Maybe our runes are simply another characterization of that which you are used to." She brushed the dirt from a section of flat stone and scratched twenty-six figures into it. "This is the alphabet," she said, indicating the first figure. From that point on she recited the remainder of the alphabet for Oganna.

Beside the strange characters that Vectra had written, Oganna scratched the letters that were familiar to her. Vectra was right. They had the same alphabet, just different characters to represent each letter. The ancients had not written in a foreign tongue. They had likely created one alphabet or the other as a code to confuse their enemies. It was either that or the Ancient Ones' runes were the originals, and the people of the Hemmed Land were using a vastly modernized script.

A palm-sized granite stone lay nearby. Oganna picked it up and copied the cipher from the wall. It took a little while to accomplish, but Vectra patiently waited until she had finished. Oganna laughed as she held up the completed cipher for Vectra to inspect. "Now I can read the Ancient Ones' symbols and understand what they say just as you do." Then she slipped the stone into one of her pockets. "Vectra, what did you mean at the Tomb of the Ancients when you said that you will subjugate all megatraths under your leadership? Are there other megatrath nations with their own leaders?"

Vectra chuckled deep in her throat. "You are an inquisitive one, aren't you? You seem to remember every word I speak. And that is fine with me, in fact I welcome a keen mind such as yours." She paused before continuing. "There are several other underground megatrath nations, none of them equal in might to mine. They are scattered enough to make it difficult for me to reach them all. You see, in order to unite them I must prove myself to be the strongest in each of those nations, either by our nation conquering theirs in war or by taking on each of their leaders in ritual combat. This takes, as I am sure you can imagine, a very long time.

"These caverns in which we stand were once ruled by my great grandfather, an exceptionally powerful megatrath. He was the last in a long line of strong-willed leaders who held the many factions together as one nation. After his death there were five megatraths of equal strength who fought for the kingdom, but none of them could overcome the others. So an agreement was reached that allowed each of them to rule a portion of the kingdom so long as they left the others alone.

"My race was once mighty." She gave a toothy grin and ran her claws down the wall. "And we were feared by our enemies. Now we are divided and thus weakened. I intend to unite our factions once more and restore our former glory."

Oganna thought of her father and how he had taken the Hemmed Land's inhabitants from a loose network of vulnerable people to hope and unity. Vectra's desires seemed to be on the same, commendable path.

"No doubt you are curious as to what my motives are in this matter." Vectra scratched her side with her claws, then she said, "No doubt you must be wondering why I would care. Why not let each of the kingdoms rule itself, maintaining its own peace? But it is not for the glory of conquest that I want this, though I do enjoy a good fight! My kind have lived in the darkness for too long, and it has hardened us to the world above and to each other. It is time for the megatraths to follow me into a new era of peace that can only be achieved through conflict."

The possibility of forming an alliance with Vectra had been at the back of Oganna's mind ever since her visit to the tomb. With these desert monsters on her father's side, the Hemmed Land's southern border would no longer be a concern, and their assistance might prove helpful in Ilfedo's troubles with the desert north of the Hemmed Land. Had the time come to broach the subject, or should she wait?

A breath of damp air sent a shiver up her spine as she turned to gaze boldly into Vectra's eyes. "You and I have an opportunity here," she said. "To create an alliance between our two very different nations. Together we could change this part of Subterran by spreading civilized partnerships. Think of it! A human ally on your northern doorstep. What better way to strengthen your position in the eyes of your fellow megatraths? If your rivals make war upon you, we will aid you. If we are attacked, then you will come to our aid."

"Hmm." Vectra paced back and forth.

"Vectra, why not? Surely the rival megatraths will hear of how the Warrioresses and I slew Loos. If you ally yourself with us, strengthening the bond of trust between us, they will fear you more than ever."

Vectra remained silent, her monstrous face considering the proposal.

Oganna smiled. "By showing me the Tomb of the Ancients you have proved that you trust me. Tomorrow my aunts and I must return to our homeland. It is my sincere desire that you will accompany me so that I may return your hospitality and acquaint my people with your kind."

With a sigh, Vectra shook her great head. "Your people will remember my kind with bitterness forever because, though I did not wish it, one of my subjects invaded your territory and committed murder. His life has been justly extinguished, but his deed will forever haunt us."

"Then come with me to the Hemmed Land and prove the mercy of your horde. My father is facing a strange sort of threat on our northern border.

Winged men that fight like vultures have invaded our lands on occasion, and now it seems that desert vipers are going into our forests to slay people in their sleep. It shouldn't be happening. We have no enemies. If you were to come and assist him, the people would recognize the goodness in your heart, and you would earn their trust."

"I would be pleased to earn their trust," Vectra said as she rumbled in her throat long and low. "It has been many hundreds of years since we megatraths had peaceful and regular interaction with human nations. Not since the Ancient Ones has it been so, but it would be right to bring us back to that state of mind. Loos's deeds are a blot that I want to rectify. I favor an alliance with your people." She puffed out her chest and growled her resolution. "I rule here with absolute authority. I need the approval of none other! Let us today and now make a pact, between us alone, to stand by each other as friends even if everyone else stands against us. And let us bind ourselves to this friendship with an unbreakable oath."

Oganna relaxed and nodded. "Agreed."

"Come with me," Vectra urged. She knelt and invited Oganna to hop on her back to ride. "The place that I would like to take you to is a long run from here. It would be a rough walk for you but for me it is nothing."

Awkwardly Oganna swung her leg over the creature's back. Vectra's hide was rough and scaly, and as she stood on her six legs Oganna grimaced. She wasn't going to complain but Vectra swiveled her head around to look back her. "A ride on my back will not be the easiest on your body. Slide on up to my neck. It will be considerably easier on you."

Oganna pulled herself forward and tightened her legs around Vectra's neck. Here the scales were more flexible and they were covered with a layer of fuzz that kept her more comfortable. Vectra started to run down a narrow path that followed the inside walls of the cavern. It was a gradual but blindly swift descent. They spiraled down the narrow path until total darkness enveloped them. Only an occasional flash of fire from Vectra's mouth lighted the way.

Vectra reached the cavern's floor, slid on her rear legs to break her momentum, and skidded to a halt. "I used to come down here when I was a megling. The darkness hides these depths from the firelights above, and few megatraths ever venture down here. It is their loss, for I have found wonders that they have not imagined."

She tilted her head back, her sides billowing as her lungs sucked in air, then she snapped her head forward and let out a deafening roar. Her bellow resounded through the unexplored depths, daring any to stand in her way. As the last echoes died out, she repeated the roar, eerily bouncing it throughout the chasms, chambers, and tunnels. Satisfied, she walked forward with Oganna still clinging to her neck.

The megatrath spat a stream of fire ahead, revealing a tunnel straight ahead. It had a circular opening, and its floor sloped deeper underground. Large tiles covered the tunnel floor, but most of them had been broken. A statue had fallen across the floor. Large stone pieces that had once formed the image of a human. Male or female, Oganna could not tell, but the statue lay scattered around. The statue's base stood whole and a pair of stone-carved, sandaled human feet remained atop it, broken off at the ankles.

Vectra lumbered into the tunnel and stepped over the fallen statue.

"What is this place?" Oganna asked.

"Truthfully I do not really know," the creature said. She walked into the deep darkness, still descending. Oganna could feel Vectra's powerful feet thudding on the floor. "I really do not know the purpose of many of these ancient constructions," the megatrath admitted. "It is a pity. My race lives above all of this and we know so few of the secrets these places hold. We know the Tomb of the Ancients because it was a gift to the megatrath race. But beyond that there are unexplored depths. Depths in the darkest, deepest places. I know that the Ancients constructed this. All of this. Yet why and how is beyond my knowledge. I am now taking you to a place of solitude that I discovered as a megling. I believe it also was constructed by the Ancient Ones, and one of their spirits still resides there. He is a wise guiding spirit of great power, as you will soon discern. If we do not anger him, he will bear witness to our oath of alliance and ensure that we keep our oath."

"So, this spirit," Oganna said. "Is he someone you can see, or is he invisible?"

The megatrath barrelled forward. As the dark tunnel walls rushed past, Oganna cringed. She could only hope that Vectra wouldn't blindly knock her into a wall. She forced a smile, hoping it would influence her tone. She doubted very much this spirit that Vectra spoke of was real. "Vectra, have you ever touched this spirit? Like, is he able to physically manifest himself?"

The creature gasped. "Never! Once I tried to approach his form, but I will never do so again. He condemned my action, and my body suddenly felt as though it were boiling in lava. Fortunately I came to my senses and, in pardon, he permitted me to return from time to time to see his magnificence and hear his counsel."

Vectra rocked to a stop, and Oganna felt the mighty creature's body quiver. With excitement or uncertainty she could not tell.

A light shone on them from high above in the darkness. Its blinding radiance forced her to shield her face with her hand. She squinted between her fingers and perceived a cream-colored orb attached to the ceiling by a twisted iron elbow.

A voice spoke out, a confident male voice that filled the room. "Megatrath, welcome."

Oganna looked about at the brightly lit walls. They had been constructed of rectangular blocks of stone. But while Oganna studied her surroundings, Vectra kept her gaze to the floor. Oganna peered into the corners, trying to discern the voice's origin.

"What is your name megatrath?" the man asked.

"It is I, Vectra. And I bring a friend," the megatrath rumbled.

Oganna still could see nothing to indicate where the speaker came from. She glanced up at the orb. Was it possible that the speaker could see through that illumination device?

"I assume, Vectra, that you desire entry into the chamber for counsel," the voice offered.

Vectra bowed her head toward the far wall. "This human wishes to ally herself with me."

A long silence, then the light extinguished. Darkness flooded back into the chamber, and Oganna strained to make her eyes adjust. Another light blazed from overhead, shining in a narrow beam upon Oganna's head. The sudden brightness stung her eyes.

"Ah, yes. I had not noticed her," the voice said in a hushed tone. "She is human."

"She is also my friend," Vectra replied.

Oganna heard stones grating. The light shifted toward the far wall, shining upon a large square opening as if directing them to enter it. Vectra plodded through the opening and Oganna followed. Twenty paces inside the megatrath halted. The stones grated behind them as the entry resealed itself, leaving them in pitch blackness.

"Human, step forward," the voice demanded.

Oganna frowned. To what or to whom did the voice belong? She could hear Vectra lower her massive head to the floor as if in honor of the spirit, but Oganna felt tile under her shoes. She groped forward in the darkness in the direction of the voice. "Why?" Oganna called out.

She heard Vectra snort. The megatrath's voice hissed around her. "Do not anger the spirit!"

"I want to see what you look like, spirit. I want to see you for what you really are. Long ago you inflicted unnecessary pain on this megatrath," Oganna said as she dropped one hand to her side and curled her fingers around Avenger's crystalline hilt.

"Impudence!" the masculine voice shouted.

The chamber reverberated with the sound. "Submit to my will, human. If you choose to do otherwise then I will destroy you." Through the veiling blackness the ghostly image of a giant man strode toward her. In his hand he held a wicked-looking sword of enormous size, and a small helm crowned his head.

She drew Avenger from its sheath. Its crystal blade turned crimson, its power clothed her in silver, and she stood as an angel without fear. The light of her sword and garment lit the area. She stood in a room constructed of stone. The light revealed a small window set in the back wall. She glanced back at Vectra. The creature cowered on the floor, every muscle trembling. No doubt remembering the pain this 'spirit' had inflicted on her as a megling.

The man pointed his gloved hand at Oganna. Her joints ached, and then her skin warmed as if with a fever. But she set her face toward the small window. If the imposter had sequestered himself in there then she would expose him as the charlatan he was.

With a silent command, she doused the light of her sword and that of her clothing. She concealed herself in the shadows and ran along the wall, dragging her finger lightly over the stones until she found a deep notch. Carefully she spidered her fingers along the notch, tracing the rectangular outline. So, this was a small door. Tensing her arm, she pushed against the stone barrier. It swung inward without so much as a squeak, and she slipped inside.

To her right curved a long narrow room, dimly lighted by glowing ceiling panels only five feet above her head. She calmed her beating heart and walked around the curve. There, she stepped onto a grid of muted yellow lights that felt warm under her feet.

A grid of multi-colored buttons, along with a few levers, glowed on panels set in the walls. Green and blue strings stretched from the ceiling to the floor along the back wall. Each string pulsated with light, and a steady electric hum filled the room. A plate of glass three feet wide and two feet high leaned against one of the lighted panels. An image of Vectra, who was still cowering in the darkened chamber outside, appeared on the panel's face.

A bearded man stood on a white floor panel in front of the image display. He held the sword she had seen earlier in the ghostly image. But now both he and the sword were proportionally smaller. In fact, he stood a bit shorter than her father. The man scowled at the screen and muttered, "That little whelp. Where'd she go?"

Willing her sword to glow again, Oganna let it clothe her in the silver dress. The man spun and took a step back, eying her up and down.

"Despicable," she spat. She let her eyes bore into his. "It is hard for me to accept that some people are as cruel as you. How dare you torture a megatrath just to maintain this facade. You are no spirit!"

"What?" he cried out. "How did you find your way in here?"

"You are coming with me, sir." She raised Avenger and frowned. "I want you to tell these creatures that you are mere flesh and blood! And I want you to repent of this evil you have done. Deceiving these creatures with this ancient technology. That is what this is, is it not? Some advanced machinery that you have learned to manipulate?"

"I do not have to answer your questions, child." He flipped his sword in his hand and scraped its tip on the floor. "Treat me with respect, or I will soon show you that tricks are not my only talent." With a swift motion he brought his sword toward her throat. She ducked under it and shoved his blade aside with Avenger.

A smile curled his lips. His shoulder-length hair was gray, and his face was wrinkled, but he fought with great strength. Each time his sword smote hers she was forced to grip her hilt with both hands. He swung his sword in a V motion, always facing her, and steadily drove her back.

Beads of sweat moistened her forehead. She lost ground and struggled to keep her tired feet from slipping on the smooth panels. The recent journey through the desert and her encounter with Loos had drained her of energy. Her knees buckled, and she wavered in her defense.

"I am a spirit. You cannot win against a spirit," he said with a laugh. He held his sword in one hand and reached behind his back. Too late, she saw him slide out a second sword. He swung it like a club and smote her on the head. Stars danced through her vision and, as she fell, she heard him chuckle.

* * *

Bright green grass waved all around. Puffy white clouds dotted the blue sky overhead, and a gentle breeze moved the clean, warm air across Oganna's face. She blinked and raised her hand to her face. Yes, she had a welt where the pretender had hit her.

She shook her head. What had happened?

Where was she? The field she was lying in extended as far as her eyes could see on all sides. A shadow fell upon her from behind and she turned.

"Hello," said the stranger. He was a wrinkled man with a long white beard that nearly reached the ground. He sidled in front of her and offered a hand. He was barefooted, and his body was wrapped with a snow-white toga, while on his head he wore an equally white turban. "Are you lost, child?"

Without answering she accepted his hand and stood up. In her other hand the sword Avenger burned furiously, reflecting its red hues against her silver garment.

The elder who had helped her up was short. His turban didn't even reach her shoulder. His eyes were bright blue and, strangely, his ears were at least three times as large as her own. He eyed her weapon and vestments. "What is your name?" he asked.

Ignoring his question, she responded, "Where am I? What has happened?" She squinted her eyes, looking skyward, and recalled the duel with the stranger.

The little man stroked his beard, then looked up at her. "Thoughts. They are racing through your mind like a tangle of ridgeback rabbits." He reached up with his hand and touched her forehead. As he withdrew his hand, a web of light pulled out of her forehead. Instinct told her to stop him, but another conflicting sense restrained her. If he had wanted to harm her, he could have done so while she was lying in the field.

For a moment the man held the web of light in his hand and stared at it as it glowed. Then he closed his fingers over his palm, stretched out his arm, shook his hand a few times, and threw the webbing into the wind. As soon as it left his hand, it burst into fine dust and settled on the ground. There an image formed. An image of pure light replaying Oganna's recent duel. It showed her struggle, then destabilized, and disappeared.

The old man looked at Oganna. His eyes looked playful. "That is how you came here," he said.

"Here?" She grunted with frustrating. "I do not know where here is. Where am I?"

Once more he touched her forehead. "Does that feel better?"

She reached up to feel for the welt that the man's sword had given her, but it was gone. "Thank you," she said.

"It is not worth mentioning, my dear. Now, tell me, this man you were fighting, do you know him?" the old man asked.

She shook her head, trying to suppress her anger and frustration. "Not in the slightest! He has been deceiving the poor megatraths, leading them to believe that he is some kind of a spirit or a sorcerer, or something like that. Let's put it simply. He relies on their fear of him."

"Sounds like a clever fellow," the old man laughed. "Albeit, there is no honor in deceit. You have taken up the cause of creatures needing justice. Good, then I will send you back so that you can finish your fight." He walked off at a brisk pace and called for her to follow.

Within half an hour they topped a rise and stared down a hill at a great lake that was rimmed by a vast city. "My home," said the man, "and also your pathway back to Osira."

"Osira? What is Osira?" Oganna asked.

The old man swallowed hard. "My mistake! I meant to say it is your pathway back to Subterran."

She furrowed her brow. "I am not on Subterran? Are you trying to say . . . What? That I am on another world?"

He pointed at the ground behind her. "You didn't notice that you have two shadows?" When she looked behind, she saw that he was right. He told her to look at the sky again. "Does your world have two suns?"

She looked up and couldn't help gaping in astonishment. "I am on another world. How is this possible?"

"Yes, you are on mine." He waved a hand toward the city and beamed with pride. "We have perfected our society. Unlike your world, we do not need instruments of war. We rest in the Creator's peace. But come! I mustn't reveal all mysteries to you, for then I would be at fault for interfering in your future."

"But how do you know of my world?" she asked.

"We are familiar with it, but little more than that." He halted and faced her. "Let me give you a word of advice."

"Certainly." She shook her head. Her sudden transference to this place felt like a dream. A dizzying dream.

"When you get back to your fight, don't rely as much on your physical strength." His eyes roved from the sword to her silver garb. "There is a lot of strength in you. Yes, much potential! I see that you can use the power of dragon blood, and you are not an amateur at it." Leaning closer, he winked. "I would say you must be part dragon."

She started in surprise, and he laughed. "When you return to your fight, use your dragon side. That is your powerful side. The side that grants you the use of potent energies unique to your species' blood."

They had not reached his city before he stopped, stooped, and pressed his hand on something in the ground. Then he stood up and waited as an exquisitely carved gazebo rose out of the ground before them. "I regret not having the time to show you more," he said. "I have thoroughly enjoyed meeting you."

He led her onto the gazebo platform and ordered her to stand on a pad at its center. Then he bowed low, kissed her hand, pulled a lever, and she found herself lying at her opponent's feet in the subterranean antechamber.

The old man's words flashed through her mind. "Use your dragon side," she repeated.

The 'spirit' looked down in shock and his sword shook in his hand as he pointed it in her face. "How did you do that? You were out cold." As she rose, he struck at her.

This time she closed her eyes and felt the substance of everything in the surrounding area. She could feel the walls, the floor, and the electrical energy running through the ancient platform. She drew power from her sword and reached out with her mind. She raised her hand and clenched her fist, pulling the stones from the ceiling and from the walls so that they broke up.

Her opponent screamed and dropped one of his swords as the stones pinned him to the floor. "Please. Don't kill me! I beg of you, please let me live. I meant no harm to the megatraths."

She scowled. She wouldn't leave him to die. Besides, Vectra had to be shown the truth. She reached out with her mind, throwing the stones off of his body with a mere thought, and then dragged him toward the door she'd entered previously. The anteroom collapsed. Stones fell on the wall panels and sparks sailed in all directions. A string of energy lashed at the man, drawing blood from his chest. As he grabbed at his wound, a stone slammed into his shoulder, cracking bone. A panel loosened from the wall and flipped end-over-end onto the lighted floor panels. Electrical current raced along the panels, snapping at the soles of her feet. Bolts zigzagged along the walls, and an explosion rocked the chamber floor.

After pulling the pretender through the door, she closed it behind her. Letting out a long breath she leaned against the wall, and slumped to the floor. Her shoulder hit an ancient lever that flipped and turned the lights on, illuminating the main chamber. Stones grated again and two more doorways slid open along the opposite wall.

The mighty Vectra raised her head slowly and stepped forward. The chamber was large and the ceiling high. She glanced at the tiled walls and squinted at the bulbous orb glaring from far above. Then she looked at Oganna and bewilderment reigned in her eyes. She lumbered forward, towering over the wounded man.

Oganna kicked rubble to the side and shook her head at Vectra. "There is no spirit in these walls. There never was. He is only a man utilizing the strange mechanisms of this buried civilization to further his own esteem in your eyes." She looked at the humbled pretender. "I wonder how long he has lived down here. Apparently alone. Vectra, you said that you came to this place as a megling. Did you see the spirit then, too?"

"Yes, I have seen him my whole life," she said, staring wide-eyed at the imposter. "And I have lived a long time. Longer than any human would."

"Well," Oganna said as she laid her hands on the man's wounds, "then he must be very old. For a human that is." Ignoring her exhaustion, she poured healing energy from her blood into the man. His bruises and wounds slowly healed before her very eyes.

She patted his cheeks. "I think he's fainted. He has lost a lot of blood." The wrinkled man stirred, his eyelids fluttered open, and he looked in defeat up at her and the megatrath. "Well, sir," Oganna began, "you had better explain yourself."

"Please, wizard," he said. "I meant no harm." He swallowed hard. "Six hundred years ago I was a guest of the megatraths, and while I was exploring these ancient passageways I happened upon this chamber. Please do not take me away. Let me die in the home I have found within these ruins."

"You have deceived me ever since I was young?" Vectra exhaled a noxious fume. "You do not deserve an honorable death. I should kill you here and now."

The gray-haired man grasped his sword and held it between him and the creature. His voice trembled as she said, "This weapon allows me to command these ancient workings to do whatsoever I will, and if I wish it, I can destroy you."

Smoke roiled between Vectra's teeth. She pointed at Oganna, and her retracted claws slid out of her fingers. "This coming from you who failed to defeat a young woman? You should be in dread of me, deceiver. I can almost taste your blood in my mouth and feel your arms crushed between my jaws as I suspend you above the depths of my underground realm. I would drop you into the abandoned cities and, before your demise, you would curse the moment you challenged me."

Oganna stood between them and shook her head. She glanced at the megatrath and then at the man. "It was a cruel thing you did to Vectra when she was young. Was that your reward for her kind's hospitality?"

"But I did not do that on purpose. I swear!" He cupped his hands and looked at Vectra's toothy face. "There was a mechanism. I did not know what it would do, so I did not plan to touch it. But my elbow brushed against it and—"

"And my body burned with inner fire," Vectra spat. "Something I have not forgotten, deceiver." She exhaled another yellow vapor.

"But I found a way to shut if off. The pain stopped. Didn't it?" His face brightened, and he brushed dust from his beard.

Vectra stared at him for a moment, then her jaws parted and a quick stream of fire shot out. It burned his beard and hand.

At first the man cried out, then he shook his singed hair out of his eyes and gritted his teeth. "I will accept that as your forgiveness, megatrath. My debt to you is paid."

"I concur," Vectra said with a growl, and she scraped the floor with her claws. She glanced down at Oganna. "You have exposed him, and I am grateful. Name a request so that I may grant you a reward." The creature's offer hung in the air for a few moments. Oganna circled the man and then faced the megatrath. "His debt to me has not yet been paid."

The man's mouth opened wide, and his eyes reflected fear.

Oganna held her head high and gazed down at him. "Vectra and I have come here to make a pact of alliance, but I see now that her plan for binding it for eternity will not work. However, you can still serve as witness to this event. If you will serve as witness to our oaths, then I will forgive and forget your misconduct, and we will leave you to your solitude." She looked into Vectra's dark eyes. "He is harmless. I do not sense wickedness in his heart. What he has done is wrong, but I will forgive if he does this for us."

Gruffly, the megatrath agreed.

Oganna glanced down at the man. He smiled his gratitude and mouthed a "Thank you."

"One thing I will correct you on, sir. I am not a wizard." She held her hand to her chest. "I am the human offspring of a dragon. Please do not make me cringe by associating me with demonic forces."

The man smacked his knee. "No. You are an angel." Thereupon, he stood as witness while Vectra and Oganna declared an alliance between their nations and pledged to hold to their vow no matter what the future might bring.

The man raised his sword with both hands. "This vow must be maintained," he said with a snorted laugh. "Or I will come back to haunt you." His whole personage phased, the sword disappeared, and so did he.

The megatrath stepped back when he disappeared. As did Oganna. Vectra dropped her deep voice to a whisper. "Maybe he is a spirit."

Oganna rolled her eyes. "If he is a spirit, then maybe I am too." She straddled Vectra's neck and the megatrath shook its hide, then turned in the direction they'd come. With powerful strides the megatrath carried her up and out of the chambers. Behind them the lights flickered and extinguished, leaving the chamber once more in darkness. It took a while, but gradually Vectra climbed out of the subterranean world's depths. On the way Oganna occasionally peered into the deep crevices bordering the trail and wondered what mysteries remained to be solved in the still-deeper regions of this place. A shiver ran down her spine as an image of abandoned cities haunted by a creature dwarfing the megatraths painted itself in her mind. Deep, deep underground. She shuddered and forced her thoughts elsewhere.

This alliance that she had formed with the megatrath could greatly benefit her father's people. But what would he think of her committing herself to this pact without his prior consent? And what would Caritha and the other Warrioresses say? She ignored the doubts and determined that, whatever might happen, she would remain a faithful friend to the megatrath. She would keep her oath.

The future belonged to her and she had vowed to be prepared for it.

They reached a higher elevation where the firelights lit the way. She glanced back one time, wondering what had become of the man who lived down below. His wounds had been severe and even though she had tried to heal him, he was old and would likely die. But then again maybe she was wrong. After all, he had an extraordinary knowledge of the Ancient Ones' technology. Perhaps someday it would be possible for her to return. Perhaps one day the secrets buried here would be revealed to her. Perhaps.

ALLIES

In the morning Oganna followed an underground stream out of the chamber in which she's slept. She was holding her glowing sword in one hand, lighting the path ahead of her. The narrow stream bent around a corner and angled down, leading her into a tunnel that she had not yet explored.

Before she saw the waterfall, she heard it thundering from high in its cavern. Soon it came into view, plummeting to a circular pool carved in the stone floor by centuries of erosion. A hole in the roof of the cavern far overhead was letting in a beam of sunlight from the desert above. The beam illuminated the pool, reflecting off of the water, and danced in white and silver patterns along the walls.

She sheathed her sword, knelt, and drank deeply, savoring the cool, refreshing liquid. Submerging her hands, she cupped them. Next she splashed water on her face and wiped it with a handkerchief.

Someone walked from the other side of the pool. She could hear the gentle slapping of their feet on the stone, and she discerned the naked figure of another woman in the reflected light.

"Good morning, Oganna." It was Caritha's voice. "You were up late last night?"

"Vectra was showing me around," Oganna said.

"Um, hum. I see," Caritha said as she washed her face in the pool, then she stood and walked to Oganna. The reflected light created wild patterns on her dark hair and highlighted its reddish tinge. "Well, as soon as Laura, Rozel, Levena, and Evela wake up, we can say our farewells to the megatraths and be on our way."

Oganna bit her lip. "No. No, I am afraid it will not be that simple." She folded her hands behind her back. "Last night I took an oath of alliance with these creatures, namely with Vectra." She told Caritha of the old man dwelling deep in the caverns, whom she'd fought. But she left out the part where she had ended up on another world. She told her how the man had borne witness to the pledge of alliance between the megatraths and the Hemmed Land. "So," she said, "today we will leave, but we are not going to travel alone. Vectra is coming with us."

Caritha took a stunned step back. "What?"

"She wants to meet Father and, if she is able, to help him with his troubles in the north. The megatraths are desert creatures after all," Oganna said.

"Oganna, I know that you did this with the best of intentions. But I do not believe you considered all of the facts before you made this commitment. These creatures are a race bent on conflict, and they revel in testing one another's physical strength. You may respect Vectra, yet I see no reason to believe we can trust her followers." She put a hand on Oganna's shoulder. "I have serious reservations about this. However, you are the princess and thus the future queen of your father's people. The decision is not mine to make, it is yours. I may not fully agree with it, but I will support it unless your father sees fit to rule differently on this matter."

Oganna smiled and stood. "Will you tell the others for me? They will not object if they know that you stand behind my decision."

"Of course, although I doubt that will stop them from objecting. Rozel, in particular, is not going to like this," Caritha said. Her hand slid off Oganna's shoulder and she started to walk away.

Oganna held up her hand. "Oh yes, there is one more thing."

Caritha turned back to her curiously. "And what would that be?"

"We leave within the hour," Oganna said. "Tell them that you are all to meet me at the ledge where we first came into this place. And everyone should make sure to grab breakfast first. Bring your packs with you to the ledge."

Caritha nodded with a smile, then walked to the opposite side of the pool and stooped to pick up her clothes. She slipped them on but as she did so something shiny fell out of her dress pocket. As it clattered to the stone floor Caritha gasped, immediately dropping to her knees. Frantically she searched the floor with her fingers.

"Aunt Caritha, did you drop something?" Oganna stepped toward her but the woman held up a hand.

"Yes I did. Please do not come any closer." Caritha laughed with relief and picked something off the stone surface. She stood and clutched it to her breast, then raced out of the cavern.

Oganna stripped off her own clothes and stepped into the cavern pool. The water felt warm and she thought it likely that its source was heated by the desert far above. She stepped deeper into the water, soaking her skin and marveling that so much water was available beneath the desert's surface. The diversity of the world's geography fascinated her. Someday, she hoped, she would lead her people to meet new civilizations, other creatures, and to explore more strange lands.

When she had finished bathing she walked out of the pool. The beam of sunlight from above cast itself on a large rock a few paces from the water. She sat on the rock and let Yimshi heat and dry her body before she returned for her clothes. Today was going to be a monumental one in the history of her people, as well as for the megatraths.

She left the cave, belting her sword to her side, and made her way through the megatrath tunnels. At last she stood in the cavern she sought.

Sparks flew from the stones above Oganna's head as Vectra dug in with her claws, swung her body out of her cave, and slid down the cavern wall. "A good morning to you, Princess. Did you sleep well?"

Oganna bowed as the creature thudded to the

ground. As Vectra loomed before her, Oganna said, "Very well, thank you, and I found the pool to wash in. It is a lovely place to bathe!" Then she hesitated, glancing around the cavern as a few other megatraths lumbered out of their caves. "Is everything ready for the march?"

"Yes." The creature stretched and yawned. "My horde has finished preparations, and I must say that many of them seem as eager as I am to meet your people. There is much work to do before our alliance can stand the test of time, but I do believe we will succeed. And I look forward to proving the might of my horde to help your father find his enemies."

"It is a moment that we can be proud of," Oganna agreed. "The Warrioresses will meet us at the rendezvous point within the hour."

Vectra hunkered on the stone floor and rumbled an invitation. "Care to ride my neck from here to the ledge?"

Oganna laughed lightly. "No, but thank you for that. I think I'll stretch my legs before the trek across the desert. To ride on your back at that time will be a vast improvement over walking."

Vectra lumbered into the tunnel that led up and out of her subterranean home. Oganna followed close on her heels. The megatrath dug her claws into the stone walls, and her powerful legs pulled her up the tunnel at an astonishing pace. When they reached the cave at the tunnel's end and stood on the ledge that overlooked the sunlit desert, Vectra angled her long head to look down at her. "What do your people call my desert, Oganna?"

It was a startling question from Oganna's perspective. She realized for the first time how limited was the view of her people. They had taken to naming their land and its towns, but other than the infamous Sea of Serpents they had not placed importance on understanding the lands around them. She let out a slow breath and said, "We do not have a name for this desert." Oganna walked toward the edge of the cave, feeling the mighty creature's gaze follow her. She looked out over the sands that stretched to the horizon. "It is known to my people as the southern desert, but it has no other designation." She glanced back at the creature. "Why? Do you have a name for it?"

Vectra chortled. "When all megatraths were united as one nation, we called it Resgeria."

"Then it will be called Resgeria by my people as well," Oganna said. She peered over the ledge. Several dozen megatraths lumbered down the cliff's face and onto the baking-hot sand, aiming their long bodies in the direction of the Hemmed Land. "How many of your kind are coming with us?"

Vectra threw the front half of her body over the ledge. Her rear legs dug into the cave floor, holding her in place. Then she turned to Oganna as she held up the front portion of her body. She counted off thoughtfully on her claws. "It is one hundred of my finest followers," she said.

The Warrioresses stepped up on either side of Oganna. Their mouths dropped open, and Rozel looked at Oganna and clacked her tongue. She edged closer and lowered her voice so that only Oganna could hear. "I hope you know what you are doing, young lady."

"Wait a minute, Oganna," Laura said as she glanced at the megatrath horde and swallowed hard. "You can't bring all of them with you. What would your father say? The people will be frightened beyond belief."

"This is a token of Vectra's commitment to our alliance, and of my trust in her," Oganna stated. She rested a hand on Vectra's side. "They will bring us to the Hemmed Land, and we will bring them to meet Father."

Vectra spun around, jumped backwards, and grasped the cliff's face with her great claws. "Coming?" she asked as she skidded down the cliff, leaving fresh gouges in her wake.

Oganna and the sisters followed her to the desert floor with all due speed, but compared to the megatrath their going was slow. Oganna gazed down the cliff at the remaining distance that she must descend to the desert floor. She shook her head and clambered back to the cave opening, ignoring the quizzical expressions on her aunts' faces. After pulling a thin rope from her pack, she tied it around a boulder in the cave, pulled it taut, walked backwards over the ledge, and rappelled down the rock's face. In this way she passed the sisters and reached the desert floor ahead of them.

The Warrioresses descended foot by foot and finally arrived on the desert floor. Rozel glanced at the rope and shook her head. "Humph! You could have saved that. It's stuck up there now."

"Maybe not," Oganna grinned. She held the rope out to Vectra. "Do you think you can snap it off for me?"

"With pleasure," Vectra said, and she jerked the rope so that it fell to the ground. Its end had frayed where it had broken off but the rest of it was still usable. Vectra bent low and addressed the Warrioresses while Oganna climbed to the nape of her neck. "You may ride on my back or on the necks of other megatraths if you so choose," she said. "You are light, so please do not consider it an inconvenience to us. It will ease your passage and hasten our journey to your homeland."

"Riding the neck is smoother," Oganna advised. She tucked her skirts under her bottom and bounced a little. "Believe me. I've tried both."

In a graceful move, Caritha sidled up to another of the megatraths and bowed to it. "May I?" she asked.

A pleased rumble came from the creature's long mouth, and it crouched to the sand. She clambered onto its neck, the creature stood, and she spoke to her sisters. "It really is quite comfortable up here."

Laura and Rozel murmured to each other, then led the others to Vectra. They sat on the hard scales of her back and held on to the short horns that protruded from her spine. Oganna shrugged. "All right, but I think you'll regret it!"

Having all of her passengers on board, Vectra dug in her heels and dashed northward. A strong wind bit the sand, spinning it in thick clouds. Visibility fell to zero but the megatraths charged through.

Oganna put her cheek against the creature's neck, reached to her back, and pulled a shawl from her pack to wrap around her head. The sand stung her skin without relenting. When at last the wind let up, Oganna unwound the shawl from her head. Hot, dry air had chapped her face.

One glance at the sisters riding behind her on Vectra's back, and she smirked. Sand had attached itself to their sweating faces. They bounced with each stride and clung tightly to the creature's body. They looked as if they would fall off at any moment, their faces grim. Caritha's mount ran fast on Vectra's heels.

Yelling over the din of six hundred pounding feet, Oganna twisted to look back. "Comfortable back there?"

"Very funny," Evela said, spitting sand from her mouth. "Just you wait. Once we get off, I'll teach you a lesson or two in manners, young lady."

The megatraths did not stop until midday, and then it was only to take a short rest. Several of them ripped up a portion of the desert floor with their claws until they reached clay soil about fifteen feet down. Digging a little farther they hit an underground spring. A pool of water formed, and everyone drank. Afterward the megatraths rolled in the mud.

Oganna watched with fascination, then looked up at Vectra. "Why are they doing that?"

Vectra rolled herself in the mud before replying. "Yimshi's rays will bake a crust of mud over our scales, allowing us to maintain a cooler body temperature for a longer period of time." She motioned over to one of her followers and ordered him to clean the mud off her neck and back. "Unless you prefer to sit in mud," she said to the women. They assured her that they were indeed more comfortable without the mud.

Oganna touched the abrasive scales on the side of her new friend. Her comfort against that of the Warrioresses was not a reasonable trade for Vectra to make. "Do not worry about us, Vectra. We can clean our clothes later," she said as she stared meaningfully at Laura, Rozel, Evela, and Levena. "Isn't that so?"

They nodded their heads vigorously, and she could see that they felt ashamed of their selfish behavior. Without further ado all of the sisters with the exception of Rozel humbly approached separate megatraths and requested rides on their necks. Each of the creatures hunkered on the sand so the sisters could climb on. Rozel held her head high and took a lonely spot on Vectra's back, grasping a horn.

Oganna swung her legs over Vectra's neck while the other creatures lined up behind her. She caught sight of Caritha conversing with her mount before getting on its neck. The creature looked very pleased with her passenger. In an instant the cavalcade took off. They raced on through the heat, never slowing, never stopping, until nightfall. Then at last, when darkness had fallen, the air cooled.

As the stars began to stud the sky, the megatraths lay down in a protective circle with Vectra, Oganna, and the Warrioresses at its center. The exertions of the day had exhausted them and before long everyone, with the exception of Oganna and Caritha, had fallen into a deep slumber.

Lying there under the stars awakened Oganna's imagination and brought to mind some questions she had been meaning to ask. She waited until Caritha had comfortably situated herself before initiating a conversation. They talked on several insignificant matters for long minutes until Caritha propped herself on one elbow and raised her eyebrows. "You are trying to lead the conversation around to something, aren't you? What did you really want to talk about?" she asked.

"Father once told me that the dragon who is called Albino made my mother and all of you," Oganna said. "Is that true?"

"Ah, I think I see where this is leading." Caritha adjusted the rolled blanket under her head. "You want to know where we came from, or more specifically where your mother came from. Very well, only bear in mind that there are some things I am not at liberty to tell you. I wish I could reveal everything to you, for your sake, but I am bound by the dragon's wishes." She ran her finger in the sand. "The Albino is our father, Oganna. He alone is responsible for our existence, in that we have no mother to speak of."

The cold desert wind breathed across the sand, sending shivers down Oganna's spine.

"You are probably wondering what land Albino comes from, and for that matter where your mother grew up." Caritha shook her head. "To that question I can only give a vague answer because neither I nor any of my sisters knows exactly where. He has his own domain. A wonderful land rich with resources and full of nature's marvels. So strong is he that his land has never been invaded and no one who opposes him survives. Only he and those closest to him know its location. I myself do not know how to reach it. Even if I wanted to."

Oganna pushed herself up on her elbows.

"What can you tell me about my mother?"

"She was the closest of us to the Albino, and she spent a great deal of time with him. I attribute her greater power to that fact above all, for if I and the others had also focused on spending time with him, no doubt we would have learned a greater mastery of our powers. But as it is, we did not, and I am ashamed to admit, his fondness for Dantress caused us to grow a little jealous. When we were young, the dragon gave us these rusted swords, and later when we were not much older than you, he set us in the forest where your father and mother later met. He intended for us to use our weapons and powers to defend the helpless and to destroy any wicked creatures we came across, and for a time we intended to. Then we grew lazy and stayed very near to our woodland cave. Your mother, though, continued to seek ways to fulfill our mission. She had a soft heart and would often go off alone to explore, to find creatures in need and aid them.

"We had an adversary in those days whom we had believed was dead. A witch. But she was hunting us and she nearly succeeded in killing your mother. If it were not for your father's intervention, she would have. Your mother fell so completely in love with him. She spent more and more of her time away from us, and we soon discovered it was to be with him. We knew that having a child would kill her, so we did everything we could to discourage her from making that choice." Caritha paused to stare at the sand. She sighed and covered her face with her hands. "This next part is very hard for me to admit, and even harder to tell you, but when your mother followed your father to his home, we followed her with the intention of ending her pregnancy. We hid ourselves in the forests of the Hemmed Land, biding our time to save her life and take her back. "We believed that your father had deceived Dantress, leading her to believe he loved her when he only planned to use her. Because our blood is that of our dragon father, none of us can give birth to a living child without giving up the life in our blood. We knew that giving birth would kill her. But when your mother died to bring you into the world and your father wept for her, I saw in his face a greater devastation than I have ever seen a person endure. Guilt finally caught up with us. Our presumptions had led us to false conclusions, and we'd nearly killed a good man. That day we revealed ourselves to him and followed him to bury your mother."

Tears welled in Caritha's eyes as she said, "Dantress defended you against us. She told us not to interfere with your birth, and when we did, she received a power to defend you that I still cannot explain. Perhaps it was our dragon father interceding for your life. Perhaps it was the intervention of the Divine himself." She folded her hands. "She had such conviction, such fury in her eyes, but at the time I could not see it. Now, so many years later, I understand what she meant. I look at you and know that her sacrifice was not in vain. That it was not a thing to be feared, but a joy. Her sacrifice was a joy to the Creator because she put another's life before her own." She sighed and reached out to pat Oganna's cheek. "I am tired and we have a good way longer to go tomorrow. Get some sleep."

As she lay back, Oganna listened to the heavy

breathing of the creatures around her. It sounded like a constant wind protectively encompassing her. She thought of her mother, wondered what it would have been like to know her, and promised herself that she would live worthy of that sacrifice.

* * *

The unmarked trail across the Resgerian desert to the Hemmed Land's southern border proved wearying for the megatraths. When they at last came in sight of a town, Oganna ordered a halt. "I think it would be wise if I went on ahead with the Warrioresses." She patted Vectra's side. "The people will probably be shivering in their shoes, wondering if you have come to destroy them as Loos did to the town of Bordelin."

Vectra dipped her head in agreement, then growled out, "Do what you think is best. My guards and I will wait here until you send for us."

As Oganna led the Warrioresses into town, Caritha kept pace beside her. "This is really embarrassing." She patted her dress and a cloud of dust arose. She coughed. "I am not at all presentable for a matter of state. We should take time to clean first, then approach this matter."

"What about me?" Rozel said as she brushed sand off her cheeks. "I've been bouncing on Vectra's back for an intolerable period of time, and I can't walk straight. And did I forget to mention that the seat of my dress is covered in mud?"

Oganna shook her head at Rozel. "That creature saved us a lot of walking through a harsh environment. Come, we must arrange accommodations for the megatraths and calm a throng of terrified people. Then we can worry about cleaning ourselves."

The town's main street was deserted, except for a couple of cats and a yellow dog. The dog loped up to them and lolled its tongue out while Oganna scratched its head. The air felt good, refreshingly moist and cool after the desert's dry heat. "We do look quite dirty," Oganna said as she dropped her hand from the dog's head. "I wonder where everyone is. Perhaps they don't recognize us?"

"Who are you talking about?" Rozel asked. "Do you see anyone around here? Because I surely don't!"

Out of the corner of her eye, Oganna caught movement in a second-story window. She drew her sword and raised it above her head, sending streams of energy throughout her body to transform her filthy attire into that of her silver-clad self. The dog stuck its tail between its legs and darted into an alley, but the townsfolk rushed from their dwellings and businesses.

"It is Princess Oganna and the Warrioresses!" They gathered around and knelt before her.

"We saw the creatures come from the desert, and we feared the worst," a short, thin woman said.

"Why have they come and why are you with them?" a husky fellow shouted. He was wearing a white apron and holding a pair of scissors in his hand. Oganna smiled inwardly at that. He was a barber and he had left off cutting hair when he had seen the megatraths' approaching.

The questions poured in like rain until she raised her hand for silence. "The creature that destroyed Bordelin has been slain. I killed him. I watched him die. His blood stained my sword," she declared. "No longer will that creature invade our land. No longer will you live in fear. And in appreciation to the murderer's species for their help in bringing justice upon him, I have extended a hand of friendship to the leader of the megatraths. These creatures are going to ally themselves with us. Her name is Vectra, and the desert she rules is called Resgeria. I proclaim a formal alliance now exists between Resgeria and the Hemmed Land. Treat these creatures as you would your closest friends. You will find that they are gentle giants and intelligent beings of remarkable potential." She scanned the crowd. "Who here speaks for this town?"

A short man clad in loose tan trousers and a white collared shirt stepped forward. "I do," he said as he bowed low. "I am Mayor Gregory Grenenwill, at your service, my lady."

Oganna acknowledged him, then continued. "Mayor Grenenwill, will you be so kind as to find accommodations for the megatraths? I know that this is a lot to ask of you, but they have had a long and exhausting trip, and I wish to start this alliance on the best relationship possible."

"Think nothing of the difficulty of your request. Of course, if it is your wish it will be done," Grenenwill said gently. He turned to some men standing nearby. "Let's organize everyone into large groups. One group can see that a tent is made to shelter our princess and the Warrioresses. The other group will prepare food for them and these creatures. Maybe a bunch of us can see about finding the best place to let the creatures sleep for tonight. They will need a large space. Maybe an open field."

Splitting up, the people went to their assigned tasks. The mayor came forward again. "If it would please my lady, may I offer lodging in my home to you and the Warrioresses?" He puffed out his chest. "My wife is a superb cook!"

She accepted and told the sisters that she would meet them at Grenenwill's home later. "Is there any news of my father?" she asked the mayor.

"Afraid there is, my lady," he said, lowering his voice. "But it doesn't sound encouraging. Seems that he hasn't been able to stop the vipers from killing people up north, even though his army is still patrolling the border. It's a mystery and many people are panicking. Some say only half of the original population remains up north, some having been slain by vipers and others moving out of the territory."

Thanking him for the information, she walked out of town. She waved to Caritha as she left. "I will be back soon, but I must see to it that Vectra knows what is going on."

She found Vectra in a large field by the town. Townsfolk ran hither and thither laying straw inside of large tents for the megatraths to sleep on. They glanced up at the enormous creatures, but for the most part ignored them. Vectra raised her long mouth out of a creek and let the water run down her neck. "Ah, my friend." Vectra's teeth chattered as she spoke. "Your people have been very kind and are taking good care of us."

Oganna chuckled as the creature shivered. "Are you cold?" she asked.

"Goodness, yes! How can you bear this temperature? It is as cold as nighttime in the desert, and yet the sun is still up," Vectra said. She grimaced as a strong gust of wind cooled her hide. "I'd heard that you humans like cooler climates, but until now I didn't know for certain that it was true."

Oganna looked out over the field and changed the subject. "Tomorrow, if you are still willing to help my people, we must proceed north. I've been told that my father is still engaged in some sort of trouble along our border with the northern desert."

Vectra licked her scaly lips. "Ah, a desert! That sounds much better. I will look forward to passing northward through your land tomorrow then."

That night the horde slept on the straw beneath the tents that Oganna's people had set up for them, and the next day the creatures followed Oganna and Vectra northward. At Caritha's suggestion, the Warrioresses went on ahead to tell people of the new alliance and to spread good will toward the creatures among the populace.

Vectra seemed fascinated by the Hemmed Land's culture, and she inquired into many things that she saw as they passed. "It is serene here, and beautiful," she remarked after passing several large fields of flowers. "My race has not strived to create beauty. Instead we have worked to harden ourselves and cast off fleshly frailties. Perhaps this is a weakness?"

"Perhaps it is merely a pursuit of serenity," Oganna mused as she plucked a flower and held it up for Vectra to sniff. "Your race has preserved a far longer history than mine has. In that area my people could learn from yours."

"We don't laugh very much." Vectra rumbled

in her throat. "Your people seem to laugh a great deal of the time. It would be good for my people to learn again to love life through things other than combat. We used to. At least, it is a conviction of mine that we megatraths used to be cultured, like you humans are. But we lost that over the ages. Perhaps when the Ancient Ones separated from us."

Two blond-haired women were standing behind a white picket fence, watching with three young children as the procession passed. Vectra grinned at them with her snoutful of teeth. The humans' faces paled, and they stepped back. The creature sighed heavily, her head drooped, and her gait lost its enthusiasm.

Seeing this, Oganna went to the fence and called to a young lad who stood nearby. He eagerly approached, blushing a bit and bowing awkwardly to her.

"Can you run fast?" she asked him.

His eyes shone, and he bowed again. "Yes. I am the quickest in the land!"

No doubt this was a mere boast, but she did not care. His enthusiasm would lend his legs speed. "Very well, then listen carefully to what I have to say. Go ahead of us along the roads for a few miles and spread the word that any megatrath that makes an attempt at a friendly smile or gesture should be regarded with the utmost courtesy. I want everyone to make them feel wanted. I want everyone to welcome these creatures!"

"Yes, my lady!" He vaulted a fence and raced like a deer across a field to the north. Oganna smiled. He might not be the fastest in the whole of the

Hemmed Land, but perhaps today he would prove that his boast had carried a grain of truth.

On the next day as they passed through a smaller town made of wood and stone houses, Vectra curled back her lips to reveal her teeth to an onlooker. The people waved, grinning up at her, and the megatrath's face lit up. She swung around, facing Oganna.

"Now that is what I call a good beginning to a long relationship," the megatrath exclaimed.

Oganna, riding on Vectra's neck, waved back to the townsmen. But she hardly noticed their faces. The closer they came to Fort North, the more she wondered why her father had not yet been able to stop the vipers from attacking human settlements. Had he run into a deeper problem than he'd anticipated, or were there simply more of the creatures than he'd assumed?

Surely with the sword that had been given to him by the dragon, mere desert vipers did not present a continuing threat. If, however, the Art'en had returned . . . She set her face north, determined to root out whatever evil lay there.

LOVE'S WATCHFUL HALO

Darkness shrouded the forest as Ilfedo watched the desert. He stayed silent and still beside a large oak tree. Beyond the trees, the late evening mist curled its blue fingers over the desert sand. The viper snakes were not known to leave the safety of the desert climate, but for some time now they had been seen within the Hemmed Land's borders. The reports had come in sporadically at first, then deaths were reported and people were found poisoned in their beds with viper's fang marks on their skin.

Something strange was happening in the unexplored north. Ilfedo could feel it. The viper attacks indicated a level of coordination. Ever since he had first organized an ambush for the vipers, he had felt moody. The slightest remark from a close friend sometimes made him angry. His shortness of temper had started after his first night, when he was standing guard, just as he was now. A feeling of evil had loomed over him, only for a moment, but it had been long enough to make the hair on his head prickle.

A splash of cold wind blew across his face and he blinked his eyes. His ears listened for a sound and with his eyes he searched the forest floor. The leaves by his feet rustled, and he discerned a reptilian head tasting his boot with its tongue. He slid his hand deftly over the pommel of his sword and wrapped his fingers around the handle. The sound of the viper's soft, dreadful hissing caused him to tense. The creature reared back its head and moved to strike.

In a flash he slid the sword of the dragon from its sheath. The living fire leaped forth, and he severed the snake's head in a precise stroke. The armor of living fire covered his body and he scanned the ground. It was as he'd suspected. The forest floor's leafy carpet teemed with desert vipers. Their hissing grew in volume as they all turned at the sight of him burning like a candle in the dark. He dove to the side as several flung themselves out of the trees. Their fanged jaws snapped as they struck where his head had been.

He held his sword at arm's length, pointed its blazing tip at the invaders, and spun. The fire of his sword spewed forth, set the ground ablaze, and drove the serpents back. Hundreds of smoking snake corpses twisted on the ground. He walked forward, sidestepped a burning log, and continued to burn out the vipers.

Once the vipers had begun to retreat, he raised his other arm, motioning for his hidden warriors to join him. He had two hundred men with him that had been trained by the Warrioresses. Each of them drew a sword made by the master swordsmith Linsair, and armor of light covered their bodies. The light from their swords combined with his own and blazed beneath the trees as if a couple hundred lanterns hung from the branches.

Ilfedo wrinkled his nose at the smell of burnt flesh mixed with the freshly spilled blood of those serpents chopped up by his men. An oppressive darkness began to cloud his mind. It bore into him as if stifling his ability to think for himself. He felt enraged, furious . . . yet he could not explain why. The men had moved a little distance off. He could see them combing the forest and slaying vipers as they went.

The feeling of darkness maddened him, and he found himself gritting his teeth. "Get out of my head!" he screamed. For a moment he felt relief, but the oppression returned, and he spotted a serpent slithering up a nearby tree. He gripped the sword of the dragon in both hands and swung it with all of his strength. The blade glowed white as it divided the serpent and then buried itself deep in the tree's trunk. He stepped back and breathed deeply as the tree toppled and crashed to the ground.

Enraged that the darkness still stuck in his mind, he rushed into the forest, joined the fray, and slew every serpent he came upon. The remaining vipers rushed toward the desert, and he scorched them with his weapon.

Ombre ran up to him at that time, and pulled him aside.

The fog in Ilfedo's mind lifted and he calmed

himself enough to talk. "What is it, Ombre? I am a little preoccupied right now."

Ombre slid his drawn sword into his sheath and nodded. "These vipers are acting possessed. What do you know about them?"

"Know about them? What do you mean know? They are poisonous serpents. Reptiles, if you like—," Ilfedo began to say.

"And they are intelligent," Ombre interjected as he jabbed his thumb over his shoulder. "One of our men claims that one of these serpents just begged for its life."

"Impossible!" Ilfedo felt a growing frustration. He fought it back in order to retain control over his actions.

Ombre beckoned to a stocky man standing a short distance from them. His head hung as if in shame, his glowing sword lowered so that its point rested on the ground, and the light of his armor dimmed. As he stepped forward, he gave Ilfedo a quick bow.

"Dispense with the pleasantries, warrior." Ilfedo thwacked a tree root with his sword. "Tell me what happened."

"Well, my lord, I found a viper in a tree as it attempted to evade our attack. I swung my sword to cut off its head, but before I killed it the serpent gave me a piteous look and cried out, 'Mercy! Oh, please have mercy!' It was too late to withhold my blade, and I ended up killing it. I once vowed, as did all warriors trained by the Warrioresses, that *I will bear the sword of light with wisdom, so that I will live to serve justice. I will die to protect the innocent. I will die to protect my brethren. I live to serve justice, and I am committed to showing mercy rather than vengeance. This say we all!* It is our code of honor, and I do not want to bring shame to it."

Ombre patted the younger man's shoulder. "You have not shamed it," he said. "The remorse you have shown proves to me that your heart is right. These things have invaded our land, killed our friends, and they are reaping the death they sowed. Now, I want you to go back to the fort. We are about finished here."

"Yes, my lord." Sheathing his weapon, the young man ran into the forest and was lost to sight.

"Well, what do you think of that?" Ombre asked. He shook his head.

Ilfedo grunted back, "Of what?"

Ombre laughed nervously. "You are kidding me, right? Brother, this alters our perception of these creatures. If they are intelligent, then we could consider negotiating with them and finding out what has driven them here. If nothing else the fact that they are intelligent means we should consider alternatives to exterminating them."

"It changes nothing, Ombre!" Ilfedo recognized how wrong his words were as soon as he said them. Yet, somehow, he could not change his attitude. He jumped up a nearby tree and snagged a four-foot-long viper that was hiding in the crook of a branch. "Well now, if these creatures are intelligent, and they can talk, then I think it's about time we took a prisoner." He ignored his friend's frown and squeezed the viper so that it could not move.

"Ilfedo, what's wrong with you? I am going to dare and say it! You are not acting like yourself,"

Ombre said. "Sure, I can agree that we should take a prisoner. After all, if they are intelligent then we will need to conduct some sort of interrogation. But you seem so angry, and it came over you quite suddenly."

"I am rather angry," Ilfedo said with an uncomfortable laugh. Even as he spoke he felt the oppression filling his mind again. It weighed like a burden on his shoulders. He shook it off and faced his friend. "War is war, Ombre. If these creatures are intelligent, then they also have a choice. They have made theirs, and I have made mine."

The viper in his hands opened its fanged jaws. Its round eyes looked desperate, and its plea sounded almost like a whimper. "Mercy?"

Ilfedo shook his head at Ombre. "See what I mean? Even a hint at going soft on our enemies, and they take advantage of us."

Ombre glared at him. "You are in command, Ilfedo, so what are your orders?"

Glancing back toward the desert, Ilfedo laughed. "Eradicate them." He handed the viper to his friend and ordered him to bring it to Fort North. His friend growled at him through gritted teeth. Ilfedo couldn't blame him. Why was he acting this way? What was this dark oppression that wouldn't release him? He knelt with his sword and held it as if begging for it to drive away the darkness that was trying to imprint itself on his spirit.

A halo of white light surrounded him and peace filled him. He felt a woman's hands caress his neck, he heard the sound of her breathing in his ear, and he recognized the voice of his wife. "Take care, my love, for the wicked are seeking your destruction," she said.

Daylight replaced the night, and a lush field stretched as far as his eye could see. Dantress stood before him, just as lovely as the day he'd met her. Her smooth, olive skin felt warm to his touch, and her lips dripped with sweetness. She smelled like spring flowers and a fresh breeze. He wrapped her in his arms, wishing with all his heart that this was not a dream.

She laughed and a smile spread over her face as she tickled him until he laughed too. He knew that he should not get carried away with this dream, but he couldn't help it. He did not care. The world meant nothing to him when she had been in his life and now . . . now that she was dead, he cared even less. Often he'd hoped and prayed for death because it alone could reunite him with her.

Dantress embraced him and looked up into his eyes. "This moment cannot last much longer, my love. I am here now, not because I wished it, but because it was allowed. You are in grave danger and so is our child. You must not let anything happen to her."

"Danger." He looked around. "Danger from what?"

She leaned against his chest, and her eyes burned with flames. "Beware of them, Ilfedo. They are an ancient race, full of evil." She directed his attention to the darkening sky.

Creatures having the bodies of men and the wings of eagles dove toward him. He felt their evil pressing upon him, yet he could also feel her body against his. He clutched her close, shut his eyes, and kissed her.

"The Art'en will not harm you as long as I am with you," he said as he stroked her long, dark hair.

She laughed a quiet laugh, then turned to him with sober eyes. "No, my love, they will not harm you, so long as I am at your side. And I will be with you whenever you need me, even when you don't believe that it is possible."

The creatures and the daylight dissolved around him, replaced by the forest where he knelt. He rose, sheathed his sword, and then fixed his eyes on the desert. Something moved from behind a tree, then hid behind another. A dark-featured man sprinted out of the forest and raced across the desert sand. The fellow glanced behind him and leaned on a tall staff with an orb at its head. Ilfedo knit his brow. The figure stopped for only a moment, then ran on. But Ilfedo knew that it wasn't one of his own men. He puzzled over it for a few moments as the man disappeared across the distant sands. He shrugged, and walked away.

There would be another day to find out who or what that had been.

WHEN A GOOD MAN FALLS

Ilfedo strode down the main hallway on his way through Fort North's primary structure, his boots clapping the rough-hewn wood floors. The smell of fresh pine boards lay heavy in the air. He waited for the guards to open the door to his right, then entered and shut the door behind him.

"Well, my little prisoner, are you enjoying your stay with us at Fort North." He took a seat opposite a metal cage and stared at the four-foot viper that had curled into a corner of the small prison. The metal bars were spaced close together in order to keep it from escaping. It stared back at him with wide, black eyes.

"Do you have a name?" he said.

The creature remained silent.

Ilfedo crossed his arms and shook his head. "You've already been in that cage for several days. Do you want to remain there without food?" He paused before continuing. "I can get you out. Back to your little home in the sand. But first you have to answer my questions."

It cocked its head and opened its mouth. "Mercy?"

"No. No mercy today, my little enemy. At least, not until you help me learn what I want to know. You and your friends have been thorns in my side, viper, and I want to know why."

The viper lunged against the bars, showed its fangs, and snapped its jaws.

Ilfedo stood and kicked the cage to vent his frustration. "Have it your way, viper. But you may regret it." He left the room and out in the hallway, paused. He turned on the guards and shoved them against the wall. "Make sure that thing stays locked up!"

"Of . . . of course, my lord. That is why we are here," the shortest man said, his eyes wide.

Ilfedo returned to his quarters. The room also served as his office. Animal pelts draped the large chair behind his desk, and an embroidered rug covered the floor. Furs overlaid the sofa against the back wall just under the window. Two chairs for guests sat across from his desk. He'd had the walls built with oak boards, and painted a cheerful white. Then he had hung the heads of some of his kills on pegs. Behind his chair he had tacked a map of the Hemmed Land.

His finger traced the northern boundary until it rested on their current location, and he sighed. "Cursed creatures. What could they possibly want here? They belong—" He jabbed his index finger into the map. "They belong in the desert."

He sat down and looked out the window. Thunderhead clouds rolled from the eastern sky, and a stiff wind bent the treetops. Rain was sure to follow. He watched Yimshi's yellow disc fight with the clouds until it gave up and cast brilliant rays between the billowing clouds hiding it. He remembered how the white dragon had shot away into the sky.

His hand touched the pommel of his sword. He ran his fingers over it, feeling the superior craftsmanship. He thought back to the day that Albino had given him the sword. What a dark day that had been for him.

Why, of all people, had the dragon given the weapon to him? Of course, he knew the answer. Because of Oganna. The Warrioresses had told him that the dragon created Dantress. If that was true, then that would make his daughter the dragon's granddaughter. *My daughter, the descendant of a dragon.* Sometimes he worried about that. If she was not fully human, then there was an element to her being that surpassed his comprehension. She possessed abilities that could not be explained, such as the time that she had shot an arrow without a bow, and when she had eased his sorrow almost at the expense of her life.

"Deep in thought?" asked Ombre as he stepped through the door. He sat in one of the guest chairs across from him and stretched his arms behind his head as he leaned back.

Ilfedo nodded thoughtfully. "You might say

that."

"When in doubt ask a friend," Ombre said with a nod to the map on the wall. "It's been almost a week since we took that viper as prisoner, and I still don't see what good it did."

Ilfedo gave him a wry look. "I already apologized for my behavior. Can you please let the issue go?"

"Well, seeing as I am a soft-hearted individual." Ombre chuckled. "All right, I forgive you."

Ilfedo glanced out of the window. In the distance a bolt of lightning zipped to the ground, and shortly afterward a clap of thunder followed. He turned from the window and leaned against his desk. "Ombre, that night when we captured the viper did you see anything odd?"

His friend leaned forward. "Other than a swarm of disgusting snakes all over the ground and the trees? No. Why? Did you?"

At that moment, Honer came in, and Ganning limped in after him.

"The wind is kicking hard out there," Ganning said as he crossed the room. He dropped his sheathed sword onto the couch, and sat down. "Do you think we should call off our night patrol? The vipers have not been seen since you scorched them that last time, and it doesn't seem likely they will come in this weather."

Ilfedo drew his sword and let it clothe him in the armor of living fire. "If you were the enemy, Ombre, when would you make your next attack?"

"On a stormy night," Ombre admitted.

"Exactly." Ilfedo sheathed his sword, and

his attire returned to normal. Then he directed his friends' attention to the map. "On the same night when we took a viper prisoner, I saw a man retreat from the forest and escape into the desert. I did not get a very good look at him, but he carried a staff with a sort of ball on top. I suspect he is somehow connected with the vipers." He paced back and forth across the floor as he spoke, his sheath clinking against his leg.

Ombre stood and scratched his chin. "Hold on there," he said. "You didn't mention this before! You saw a stranger out there that night? With a staff? And he headed into the desert after the attack. Why didn't you say something?"

"I am sure I mentioned it," Ilfedo mused. But in truth he could not think why. His mind was confused in that regard.

"And you think this man may return tonight?" Ombre said.

"It seems to be a fair assumption because he was hiding, and what better time for him to return than in the midst of a lightning storm?" Ilfedo said, pausing for effect. "Tonight, I suspect, the vipers will attack again, and I am hoping the mystery man will be there as well. You, my friends, are my best chance of catching him. I do not care if he is dead or alive, though it would be useful to take him prisoner."

Honer looked confused. "Why do you need us? You have a good many of the Elite Thousand available to comb those woods."

Ilfedo nodded, then he said, "Yes, their service will be invaluable. But I will need men who are able to hunt as well as I can, and men that I can trust to work rogue. If you all help me, I am sure we can bag our prey."

* * *

The final flash of lightning vanished with a distant rumble. Ilfedo, Ombre, Honer, and Ganning stood in the shelter of darkness, awaiting the vipers' attack. It came soon enough. Wave after wave of the slithering vermin slithered through the trees. The glowing swordsmen attacked with a vehemence. Warriors with the swords of light swarmed through the trees. Keeping the serpents in front of them, they formed an impenetrable line and marched forward, driving them into the desert where the squirming assassins skittered away.

Sheathing his sword, Ilfedo sneaked toward the forest's boundary in search of the strange dark-featured man that he felt certain was waiting for the vipers somewhere nearby. He kept as quiet as possible and left his sword sheathed so that the living fire would not betray his presence.

At last, having explored the ground, he peered into the trees. To his horror he recognized an Art'en perched high in the branches. Ilfedo approached through the darkness until he stood by the base of the tree. "Ho, there!" He drew his sword. "Come down peacefully, and I will let you live."

The wild-haired man lighted down gracefully. Too gracefully, even for an Art'en. He had a grayish face chiseled as if from stone. Ilfedo tensed as the figure crept toward him. The wildhaired man bowed and a feeling of utter darkness bore down on Ilfedo. He dropped his sword, then picked it up again. He had to rid himself of the evil oppression. His head felt like it would collapse under the pressure, and he felt his mind leaving this world and sailing to the next, as if he was dying.

Through delirium he saw dark, feathered wings spread from his opponent's back. Just as he'd seen in the vision. Dantress had tried to warn him of this. The wings snapped against his face, and he fell to the ground. Nausea overcame him as the winged creature stood over him. "The vipers will soon return," it hissed. "Maybe I should let them finish you. Ah, but no. This will be very pleasurable to do myself, and Razes will be most pleased."

"You will not slay him," another said from the trees. A dark-featured man stepped up next to the Art'en, and the creature bowed away, spitting on the ground. The man stepped closer to Ilfedo and lowered the glowing black head of his staff. "I will finish the spell and all will be well with you. Do not fight this. Hear the spirits that you have denied. They are calling to you."

Whispers filled the air, and a plume of smoke fell through the trees. The Grim Reaper rose from the smoke and pulled back its serrated scythe, though it had only one arm with which to wield the weapon.

"No!" The dark-haired man with the staff jabbed his finger at the Reaper, though his finger trembled. "He must live in order for the full plan to succeed."

The Reaper's hood turned into smoke, and it flew around Ilfedo and the man. Its skull emerged from the smoke, and its empty eye sockets stared at the man.

"Oh, you know I fear you," the man said as

his body quivered. "But there is one I fear more, and because of that there is nothing you can do."

Spinning in a tornado of smoke Death vanished. But the voices ceaselessly, though unintelligibly, hissed and whispered in Ilfedo's ears. The oppression filled his being, latched onto his heart, and ripped it apart. His mind flashed back to the day his wife died, and the bitterness of defeat clung to him. He felt separated from himself and unable to connect to his actions. The darkness of this creature's soul spread over him and he felt powerless to stop it.

In another moment he lost all sense of where, or when, he was, and he found himself in the same field that he had seen in his vision. Once again, Dantress reached out, this time to comfort him. "Stay with me, my love," she said as he knelt and wept against her breasts. "Do not let the evil control you. Fight it, stay with me. Do not let him control you!"

He heeded her words though anxiety clouded his mind. Looking into her face gave him the strength he needed to hold on to his sanity, to hold on to life. In her eyes he saw peace, in her eyes he saw hope. And that hope cradled him as his mind screamed that he had stepped into a nightmare.

* * *

Ombre stood back-to-back with Honer as a dozen bold vipers attacked them from the ground and the trees. His skill with a sword had developed over the last years. He moved his blade with speed and precision, cutting the creatures to shreds in moments, and then looked around. "Honer, have you seen Ilfedo?"

Lopping off another viper's head, Honer

turned to him with a look of consternation on his face. "He's gone off alone?" he asked.

They called Ganning over, and he pointed to the desert. "I think he went that way."

Ombre wiped the blood stains off his blade and beckoned for them to follow as he set off in pursuit of his missing comrade. He looked through the trees ahead, stopped dead in his tracks, and shushed his companions.

Ilfedo stood next to a large tree at the forest's perimeter and his sword was not drawn. Suddenly a man dropped from one of the trees, approached Ilfedo, and spread dark, feathered wings from his back. The wings snapped forward, throwing Ilfedo to the ground. The man folded his wings back and stood over the Lord Warrior. His hands were moving in circular patterns, and he muttered something unintelligible.

"Now!" Ombre cried out as he rushed toward the creature with sword raised. But his head slammed into an invisible barrier, and he fell back. Honer and Ganning fell beside him. Shaking his head, he rose but could no longer see his fallen friend. Smoke filled the space between them.

"Something very strange is going on," Ombre shouted. "Honer, Ganning! Come on and get up. Ilfedo is in serious trouble this time." He pulled both men to their feet and stabbed his sword forward, it hesitated at the barrier then pierced it. He grunted and slashed at it. Feeling for an opening, he slipped through and ran toward the smoke.

When he reached the spot, the smoke vanished. The Art'en spun on him, but he twisted around as the winged man moved and he slashed his blade along its back. Deep red blood drained from the wound. With a screech that sounded more like a bird than an injured human, the creature dashed into the desert and flapped its wings until it achieved a low altitude. Gaining speed it receded from view.

Honer and Ganning grasped Ilfedo's shoulders and helped him to his feet. "Whoa, there. Take it easy," Ombre told him.

Ilfedo shook himself. "You see," he said. "The Art'en have returned."

"Yes, but only one of them. Thank the Creator for that," Ombre replied. Against the backdrop of stars over the sand Ombre's eyes detected the dark marauder's winged form. "I hope it doesn't bring back its relatives."

"It is only a single creature," Ilfedo said. "Surely nothing we need to burden our minds with at this time."

Ombre turned and looked into Ilfedo's eyes. They did not return his gaze. "Are you all right, Ilfedo? Your eyes look glassy."

"Yeah, Ombre's right. Your eyes are kind of glassy," Ganning said as he leaned closer. Both he and Honer held on to their friend's shoulders and steadied him as he teetered.

Ilfedo hung his head and shoved them aside. He walked off without another word.

Matching his friend's pace, Ombre followed. "Ilfedo, where are you going?"

"Since when do I have to answer to you, warrior?" Ilfedo demanded.

Ombre shook his head and uttered a curse.

"Answer to me? What are you talking about?"

Ilfedo waved him off and said, "Never mind, warrior. Goodnight."

Speechless, Ombre shrugged at Honer and Ganning. They seemed not to notice. They stared wide-mouthed into the distance. He followed their gazes to the forest's edge.

The warriors that bore swords of light chased the remaining vipers back to the desert. Their glowing ranks formed a line of light that was a perfect backdrop against which he discerned another Art'en flexing its wings. He blinked his eyes and watched the creature follow its accomplice into the desert. More than one Art'en had come back to the Hemmed Land, and where two survived there could be many more.

Other warriors of the Hemmed Land pushed through the forest and, when he glanced that way, he saw yet another winged human take to the skies. "Three?" Ombre was incredulous. "What is going on here?"

Unable to answer his own question, Ombre left the area, gathered the warriors of light, and marched them back to Fort North. Along the way he kept an eye out for Ilfedo. Something sinister had clapped its hand on this place. He could feel it. Ilfedo had been acting strange of late, very strange. And now he'd encountered an Art'en alone. Ombre remembered the glassy appearance of the Lord Warrior's eyes, and he shuddered.

Ombre breathed in the crisp night air. The dew had wet his clothing, and he was looking forward to changing into some dry clothes. He said goodnight to Honer and Ganning as he entered the fort, went to the main building, and entered his quarters. He lay in bed and tried to sleep. Troubling questions ravaged his mind and his dreams were filled with screaming Art'en. At last, in the midst of his troubled imaginings, he turned his thoughts to Caritha, and with her lovely face in his mind he was at last able to rest.

* * *

The dinner bell rang through the compound, and Ombre rose from his bed. He donned a black shirt and trousers, threw a white sash over his shoulder, and tied it to his belt. The leather strap for his sword's sheath lay nearby. He put it on his other shoulder and dropped the sheath to his hip so that he could easily reach for his sword with his right hand.

He paused at the door to fix his eyes on the gray wolf's head that he had hung on the wall. The days of hunting with Ilfedo had long ago passed, and he missed them. He'd kept the trophy as a proud reminder of how he'd saved his best friend's life. Best friend. Lord. Brother. Ilfedo was all of those things to him. With a frustrated growl he left the room, slamming the door behind him. He made his way to the parade grounds where most of the warriors had gathered to eat at long wood tables.

"Ombre!" Ganning beckoned with a grin. "Hurry along we've saved a seat for you."

Ombre walked to the barrack's far end. A tall middle-aged man with curly dark hair was flipping eggs on an outdoor grill and stacking them on a nearby table. His other arm skillfully stirred sliced potatoes and blueberries in a pan. Thick slices of bread soaked in a bowl of milk. The man flopped the slices onto the stove and chuckled to several warriors near-by who had their plates in hand, as if sharing in a joke that Ombre had been too late to hear.

"There's plenty, plenty, plenty for everyone. Take your fill and take your pick!" The man sounded like an auctioneer, only he wasn't getting paid for this.

"James McCormick," Ombre interrupted him, pushing his plate forward. He grinned. "It took me a few moments to place your name with your face, but I remember you. How are you getting along here at the fort?"

"Pretty good. I can't complain." James wiped his goatee with a sleeve and picked up the plate. "You want something fresh?"

"Watching you, I just know that you do love to cook," Ombre said.

"Yes. I don't do it too often, but I have to admit, I do enjoy it." James said. He flipped eggs and toast onto Ombre's plate and sprinkled cinnamon on top. "Are you feeling all right, Commander?"

"To be honest . . ." Ombre shook his head and sighed.

James set the plate down and glanced at the line of men waiting behind Ombre for their turn at the food. He reached for a selection of spices and held a straight face. "I could spice up your toast with a little jalapeño pepper."

Ombre picked up the plate and chuckled. "I'll be fine without that. But thanks for trying to boost my spirits." He started walking away, but the cook held up a hand.

"Here," James said. He stabbed a fork into a thick steak at the rear of the stove and set it on Ombre's plate, holding up his forefinger. "You've gotta have steak."

"Thank you, James." Ombre left the line and walked to the table, sitting next to Ganning. The morning chill refreshed him, though the heat of the rising sun soon warmed his back. Honer and Ganning, between mouthfuls, talked about the Hemmed Land and reminisced about their hunting days.

"Seems like it was only yesterday that we could travel for hours through the forest and never run into anyone," Ganning commented. He let the steak juices drip between his lips and he closed his eyes with a grin. "Oh, James knows how to make these."

Ombre played his fork in his eggs. "Nowadays . . . now there are people every few miles."

Honer dug his fork into a stack of pancakes. Butter oozed between them. "I miss those days. Back then we hunted to our heart's content and roamed freely. Sometimes I worry about our children."

Ganning paused midway through his steak. "How do you mean?" he asked.

"They are growing up in a changing culture, a society that is gradually rejecting its heritage in favor of a more comfortable life. People are chopping down the trees and trampling the wild animals' habitats without a second thought. They build new homes, new towns, and new roads. They are making for themselves an easier life. Yet they are forgetting that nature is not their slave to be used and abused. It should be cared for and respected."

"In all fairness," Ganning noted. "I must point out that nature is our slave and without its resources we would be unable to live. We kill the creatures and eat them. We take timber from the forests and build homes."

"But, Ganning, how long do you think this prosperity will last? The trees we take down are not being replaced quickly enough. It will take decades to grow large oaks to replace those that we have lost. Then there are the wild animals that are being driven farther from us. Unless we conserve the Hemmed Land's resources, we will end up exhausting them. There will be nothing left for our children. Do you see what I mean?"

Ombre felt compelled by Honer's postulations to break into the conversation. He put his half-emptied plate to the side. "There will be new challenges and different lessons for the next generation. They will face new frontiers and build on what we have started."

"Ah!" Honer raised his finger to emphasize his point. "But the question is, are we laying a proper foundation?"

"How do you mean?" Ombre said.

"If we continue to destroy the forests and kill off the animals, there will be nothing left for the next generation," Honer told him. "Will the Hemmed Land be able to sustain our growing population, or will subsequent generations drain its resources further? In fact, at the current rate, I foresee that our country's natural resources will reach a critical low even before I'm an old man. To our north is desert, to the south is desert, and the Sea of Serpents guards our eastern border. The western forests may permit a little expansion, but that is a small territory. We are cut off from the rest of the world, and we know little to nothing about it. We really are hemmed in, just as the name of our land suggests." He bit into his last pancake and swallowed. "I mean, if we ever need to expand, I suppose we could explore beyond our borders and scope out the territory. But if hearsay is true, the western forest is cut off by a vast swamp, in the midst of which is an active volcano."

"I never knew you had such an interest in geography," Ombre said. "Since when have you become an expert on these matters?"

"Since I finished the National Archive building. There are all sorts of little-known facts in our ancient scrolls, and I've been reading through them." Honer shoved his plate to the side and wiped his mouth. Crumbs fell from his pants as he got out of his seat. "We'd better get going, Ganning."

"Get going?" Ombre stood up and started toward the kitchen. "Why the rush?"

"Haven't you heard?" Ganning grabbed his plate, took Honer's, and waved him away.

After putting away his dishes, Ombre turned to his friend. "All right, Ganning, what was Honer referring to?"

"Ilfedo called for a special meeting this morning with all of his counselors. You weren't informed?" Ganning asked.

Ombre frowned and stomped toward the main building. Ganning limped after him and whispered into his ear as they walked into headquarters. "Take it from me, Ombre, Ilfedo is acting strangely."

"Yeah, I'm beginning to notice," Ombre replied sourly.

"Do you think it has anything to do with that

Art'en creature we saw last night?" Ganning whispered.

Ombre shook his head. "I wish I knew." He stepped into the council chamber. He wished the Warrioresses would make a surprise visit. They would know what to do. Women sometimes had better insight into men's souls.

The room wherein he now stood contained a circle of highbacked, wooden chairs, one for each of Ilfedo's military commanders and a few extras for invited guests. Ombre sat with Honer and Ganning, fairly close to the seat Ilfedo occupied.

"My subjects, my lords," Ilfedo said as he rose from his chair. He spread his hands and leaned on the table. "We are at war with an unknown enemy that comes at us in the dark of night. It surprised me more than anyone else when that viper that I captured turned out to be intelligent, rather than another dumb brute. How intelligent? We don't know. But smart enough to know when it is being asked a question and cunning enough that it plays on our perceived weaknesses. That explains its continual request for mercy." He gazed around at his counselors with a hard expression. "But this is war and I judge it in our best interest that, if the creature doesn't want to talk, then it shall be forced to. Therefore I have called this meeting to give my permission to torture the viper."

The members of the council looked horrified and each and every one, much to Ombre's relief, rose and offered objection.

"This goes against our moral standards," one of the captains said.

"Not to mention a few of your stated policies," said another. "Why do you even suggest such a thing? It's a damn viper. Just kill it, if it is not providing anything of use. But there's no need to enact torture."

"Silence!" Ilfedo roared. "Sit down, all of you. Who is in charge of this council?" Then he answered his own question. "I am in charge here."

Ombre gazed at the enraged Lord Warrior's eyes. They reflected the light as if they had been made of glass. It was even more apparent now than it had been the previous day. Ombre stood and addressed Ilfedo. "My lord, as commander of your army and as your friend I formally add my objection to your proposal. If it were a matter of extracting information from an intractable criminal, then I might agree with reservations. But with this there is nothing to gain. Nothing to justify it."

"Sit down!" Ilfedo's face reddened, and he breathed in rapid, short breaths. "Your objection is noted, but my plan goes forward. Order the guards to do as they please with the creature. Whatever it takes to get information out of it."

Ganning rose and put up his hand, opening his mouth as if to speak. But Ilfedo turned and punched the wall. "Any more objections, and I will consider it an act of betrayal to me and the country. I did not call you all in here to voice your opinions, but to back my policies! Now, go. All of you."

Heaving a sigh, Ombre left the room. Outside the door to the viper's prison he spoke to the guards. "Lord Ilfedo wants you to torture the prisoner, then to report any and all information that you glean directly to him." He started to walk away, then thought better of it and added a final word of advice. "For your own good I recommend that you disregard this order. The Warrioresses will not be silent on this matter when they return."

The men nodded their heads, but their mischievous eyes told him that they lacked sincerity. He shook his head and left the fort. He strode through the south gate and walked into the fields. A lot of the forest in this part of the country had been cleared long ago to construct the fort. He was alone at last, and he breathed deeply of the air to let it clear his troubled mind.

In the distance a flock of black birds rose from the trees with loud cries. He strained his eyes. What was that coming over the rise? He could just pick out several massive forms lumbering into view. Was this a new enemy? At a time like this? Heaven help them, please let it not be so! He turned to the fort and called to the watchmen. "Summon the Lord Warrior! Summon Honer, and Ganning as well . . . and hurry!"

A PRESENCE OF EVIL

"Fight, my love! Fight! Don't let him win," Dantress said. Her tears splattered on his neck as he knelt at her feet and clutched her to him.

Ilfedo felt the warmth of her body against his. He could feel a cold darkness surrounding and choking his willpower, but with her staying this close to him he fought on, determined to win the battle. "What is happening to me? Why am I here?" He looked into her eyes for an answer. "Am I dead?"

Dantress pulled him roughly to his feet, wrapped her arms around him and laced her fingers behind his neck. She held his gaze. "You are not dead. Not yet," she said with a sniffle. "Fight it, Ilfedo, don't stop resisting, or you will die."

He put his fingers in her hair and ran them through the soft, silken strands. It smelled like freshly cut roses in spring. His resolve faltered. In his being he longed to let the darkness win. Then he would die and enter the afterlife to be with her again. "I am tired of fighting, my love," he said. "I want to be with you. Don't you see that I am wearied and sick of this world? It is filled with violence. The Hemmed Land is a mere speck in the vast stretches of existence, a glass that may easily be broken. I want to get away from it all, to leave and be rid of the physical elements. You are all that matters to me, and all that has ever mattered since I met you."

Waving her hand in a semicircle, Dantress brought forth an image of their daughter. Her gaze searched his face as she said, "There is nothing there for you? What of Oganna? Are you ready to leave her alone?"

He pressed her closer to his body. "She has your sisters and Ombre to guide her. What can I give her that they cannot?"

"Hope," Dantress whispered.

"You mean that I am a beacon while I wield the sword of the dragon," he said. And he sighed as he acknowledged to himself that it was true.

"The future is dark, Ilfedo, and without you this world will fall without hope of redemption." Her eyes pleaded with him. "Do this for me. Do this for our child. Fight this evil, and vow to do so until the day your purpose is fulfilled."

"What do you say, Ilfedo?" another voice said. In a flash, the albino dragon loomed beside them. A gentle smile showed on his boney face. "Are you up to the challenge?"

Ilfedo's jaw dropped open in astonishment.

"How are you also here?"

"Never mind the details when death is on the line, my friend." The magnificent creature dipped his head, and smoke curled from its nostrils. "Just answer the question that my daughter has asked you."

Ilfedo solemnly nodded, then he said, "First, we need a moment more of privacy."

Albino turned his pink eyes to look away. He did not even smile, and Ilfedo was grateful for that.

Bending over Dantress's tear-streaked face, Ilfedo kissed her with all the pent up passion in his heart. "We will be together again, someday," he whispered in her ear. "A love like ours will never end."

The dragon grabbed him from behind. "Brace yourself, Ilfedo. The battle for your soul has only begun." Albino's claws clasped Ilfedo's body, and lit up with fire. Searing heat shot through him. The pain was immense and then it grew unbearable. Tears sprang from his eyes, and he dug his fingernails into his palms until he drew blood. The darkness within now became more apparent. It was a presence, an evil, trying to drag him into despair. A name appeared in his mind. The name of his oppressor.

"You don't want to live," his unseen adversary told him. "Stay here, die here, live here, and be with the woman you love."

A growl from Albino shook the ground. The dragon roared, "Show thyself to me, sorcerer! Show yourself to me and release this man."

Mist rose from the ground. It twisted into the form of a man that cried in tortuous pain. "Oh I will not reveal that," the mist cried. It bowed to the dragon. Albino's scales radiated light, and he roared again at the mist. "Revealed you will be, for you have a twisted soul and have rejected the mercy of God."

The misty form screamed again, and this time it solidified into the form of a dark-featured man. The dragon roared again and the claws of his other hand split the ground, causing the mist to fall therein. "Auron, I see you. You have fallen too far this time and retribution is upon thee."

Ilfedo cursed himself. This being, whatever it was, had tried to get him out of its way. It had wanted to dispose of him, to rid itself of the threat he posed, and it was assaulting his soul to attain victory. How selfish he'd been to entertain such a thought! "You cannot win," Ilfedo told the figure. "I'm coming back, and I will stop you." He struggled against the presence, wishing it would give up the fight. But it only grew stronger, and he grew weaker.

* * *

Oganna alighted from Vectra's back and ran ahead of the megatrath horde to the gates of Fort North. "Father!" She wrapped her arms around him, and he stiffened. She backed away, hurt by his apparent rebuff of her affection.

Ombre strode over and clutched her in a bear hug. "What are you doing here?" he asked, but his eyes looked past her. An expression of relief passed momentarily over his face. "Ah, you came with your aunts."

The five sisters lined up beside her and greeted the men. But Ilfedo did not respond to them either, and Oganna frowned. His eyes did not meet hers when she glanced at him, and there was something strange about the way he studied the approaching megatraths. "Father, what is wrong?" she asked.

He glared at Vectra as she came to stand behind Oganna. His voice dripped venomously. "Aren't these the creatures that I wanted you to slay?"

"Slay?" Caritha asked as she turned a withering gaze upon him. "You sent us to deal with the creature that murdered the people of Bordelin, not to wipe out its species. This is Vectra, leader of the megatraths and ruler of Resgeria, the land we know as the southern desert. She has come in peace as your ally."

Ilfedo kicked his boot into the dirt. "Oganna, why are you here? I sent the sisters, not you, in pursuit of the creature. Yet here you are as if you took part in their mission."

The sisters spoke up. Taking turns in their eagerness to show how well their pupil had performed. They told him, from start to finish, how Oganna had followed them, and later rescued them from death in the arena. "If she had not engaged Loos and his cohorts in combat, we would not have been able to recover from the first attack," Evela said.

After the sisters had finished their story, they stood silently, waiting for him to reply.

When Ilfedo did not speak up, Vectra did. She rested her hand on Oganna's shoulders and spoke to him. "It is as the Warrioresses have told you. Your daughter achieved a great victory against discouraging odds. She has earned a place of legend among my people, and I am honored to join with your great nation as allies."

"And you think that I will go along with this alliance?" Ilfedo said. He tilted his head back and laughed harshly. "I would die before joining forces with a low, dirty race of desert dwellers!" In the stunned silence that followed, Ilfedo spun around and re-entered the fort. He shot out a final insult as he departed. "The sooner you all leave us to our own troubles, the better it will be for you, megatrath."

Oganna turned to the megatrath and tried not to cry. "I'm so sorry. I don't know what has happened to him. Believe me, please believe me. That is not like him at all." She gritted her teeth and glared at the fort. "Do not worry, Vectra. The Warrioresses will find out what is bothering Father. He always listens to them."

"Humph! It did not seem to me that he was in the mood to listen to anyone," Vectra said in a growl. Having spoken her mind, the megatrath made a stiff bow and thundered away, muttering something under her breath about how dumb Ilfedo was compared to his daughter. "A fighter without honor," she called back to Oganna.

With a sigh, Oganna shrugged and shook her head at Caritha. "What did I do? I truly did not think he would respond like that."

"Leave him to me and my sisters," Caritha said. She grasped Oganna's shoulder and whispered in her ear. "Just wander around the fort and find out if anything else seems amiss. I feel that something strange is going on here, almost evil, and it may have something to do with your father. We will speak to him, and if Ombre is willing, he will go with us."

"There is something strange about Ilfedo, and I am more than willing to discuss it," Ombre grunted as he joined the conversation with a furious eye. He fingered his sword's pommel. "He hasn't been right ever since we started making nightly ambushes on the desert vipers. On the last attack he encountered an Art'en." Oganna's jaw dropped. He nodded his head and raised an eyebrow. "This one targeted your father on our last raid. I'm not sure why, but he has been exceedingly moody and indifferent ever since."

Ombre crooked his arm, and Caritha took it, letting him lead her into the fort. Laura and Eve-la chattered back and forth as they followed. Rozel went too, her arms crossed again. Levena paid them no heed, though she trailed along. She had her sword unsheathed and was picking at the rust with a cloth. Oganna watched them enter the main building, then she started to wander the fort. She was going to leave nothing to chance. Even if her aunts found out nothing, she would.

* * *

There was no answer to Caritha's knock as she stood in front of Ilfedo's office door. She could feel the tension hanging in the air as Ombre and her sisters hovered behind her. They all felt as she did. Uneasy, confused, and concerned. Ombre's recounting of Ilfedo's behavior in front of the council earlier that day greatly troubled her.

She shoved aside the questions that were pummeling her mind and braced herself as she opened the door. Ilfedo was sitting at his desk, his head buried in his hands. He was digging his knuckles into his skull. If she hadn't known better, Caritha might have attributed this to a severe headache. However, when he looked up, she put her hand over her mouth and gasped, for Ilfedo's face twisted in a sneer and his

478

eyes gazed without seeing.

"My brother, what has happened to you?" she cried as she skirted his desk. She bent over him, and grasped his arm. Laura, Evela, Rozel, and Levena filed into the room and stood in a line facing him. Ombre stepped past them and leaned his shoulder against the wall, looking out the window.

Rozel leaned over the desk and stared into Ilfedo's eyes. After a few moments she frowned at him and raised a fist in front of his face. "Just give the word, Caritha, and I'll gladly slap him back to his senses."

Caritha rested her hands on the desk. "That won't be necessary. Stand back. Let's talk civilly about this."

"You mean that you will try," Laura said. The words seemed to twist her mouth uncomfortably.

Caritha ignored her. "Ilfedo, what is wrong? Let us help you through whatever this is. You know we can."

For an instant his face softened and his gaze relaxed. "Help," he said. "I need you to help. Pull me from this. Get me out of here." His eyes hardened again, and he stood up. "Get out! Leave me be."

"Ilfedo," she said, "you can't mean it."

"Oh yes, I do. Leave now, or I will call for the guards." He glowered at Ombre. "You too, get out of my sight before I thrust you through."

Caritha frowned deeply. "What's wrong with you?"

Ilfedo's body twitched, and his eyes looked normal again, but then they reverted to their former condition and he clenched his fists as he spoke. "Do not make me hurt you."

She rose to go, but he grabbed her and slapped her across the face. As the tears spilled from Caritha's eyes, Ombre rushed over. His fist smashed with brutal strength into Ilfedo's head, sprawling his friend over the desk. Caritha wept as she stared at her unconscious brother-in-law.

Ombre pulled out a handkerchief, wiping her cheeks. Then he kissed her stinging cheek, reached his arm around her waist, and guided her out of the room. All of her sisters except for Rozel followed them into the hallway. Rozel clutched the edge of Ilfedo's desk and said, "I'll teach him better than to hit one of us!"

"Come on, Rozel. Can you not see?" Evela said timidly. "Ilfedo is not himself."

The sisters pulled Rozel out of the room, closing the door after her. She cursed Ilfedo and growled. "Let me kick him. Just one kick between his legs, and I'll bring him back to his senses!"

"Enough, Rozel." Laura grabbed her arm. "Let it rest."

Ombre ran a hand over Caritha's cheek. "Are you all right?"

"Yes, but shaken." She hung her head. "What will we do now? He doesn't even want to speak to us and—"

"That is not the man I know," Evela gasped. All of the sisters grew silent as she covered her mouth with her hand, stifling a sob. "He has become . . . I do not understand how this is possible. He has become something evil."

"Well, does anyone have a suggestion how we

can help him?" Laura asked.

As they stood there mulling things over in their minds, a lad ran past them into Ilfedo's office and emerged a minute later. Ombre pulled him aside and inquired what he'd been doing.

"The Lord Warrior is furious about something." The lad's voice trembled. "He is demanding to meet with his counselors right away. I'd better go now and do as he told me. He started to run down the corridor.

But Ombre held the lad's shoulder and turned him about. Ombre dropped onto his knees and held the boy's hands, looking him squarely in the eyes. "Thank you, my boy. You know who I am?" When the lad nodded, Ombre said, "I need you tell me if Lord Ilfedo said anything else."

In a whisper the messenger told him more. As the lad left, Ombre folded his hands behind his back and stood again. "Well, ladies, it seems that our friend has stipulated that we are not invited to attend this forthcoming meeting."

"Of all the nerve!" Rozel started marching down the hall.

"Where are you going?" Caritha asked.

"To the council chamber. Where else?" Rozel said.

* * *

To Caritha it felt as though she was waiting for a storm to strike, and in reality she knew that she was. The council chamber had been constructed on the fort's ground level. It was rectangular, and a circle of wooden chairs occupied its far end. Animal skins draped the chairs, and a handsome array of swords hung on the walls. When Ilfedo came in he would find that she and Ombre had disregarded his directive to attend this meeting.

The double doors swung open, and Ilfedo's commanders trooped in. Each of their eyes popped open upon seeing Caritha with her sisters and Ombre. But the commanders also nodded at them and several of them smiled with relief. Laura sat next to Caritha, but Ombre switched with her and gave Caritha's hand a comforting squeeze. "Don't worry," he said. "Every man here will stand with us. They are men of conscience, not blind obedience. Just do what you feel is necessary. Honer and Ganning will back me all the way."

Honer and Ganning sat down across from Caritha. She acknowledged them with a nod, hoping to lighten the tense atmosphere. Both of the men smiled back.

Ganning cleared his throat. "It's good to have you with us again."

"Yes." Honer heaved a breath, then exhaled slowly. "We've missed you all. You provide a much needed emphasis on grace and mercy."

Ilfedo slammed the chamber doors open. He glowered in Ombre and Caritha's direction, then strode to his seat. The sword of the dragon was still girt at his side. His eyes were darker now, yet still hazed as if he did not really see with them. After sitting down he gestured to two men by the door. "Guards, bring in the prisoner."

All heads turned to the open doors as a cage was borne into the room. Caritha could hear the caged viper hissing and snapping its jaws before she could see it.

"Behold our enemy," Ilfedo said. "This creature is a low desert dweller, and it is capable of talking with us. So far, it has refused to tell us what I want to know. Instead it repeatedly asks for mercy." He let out a sardonic laugh before continuing. "Lord Ombre and other members of this council have opposed the use of torture to get the information that we need from this creature, and so I have personally accepted responsibility for the task. He strode to the center of the ring of chairs and waved a hand in the direction of the guards. "These two men have performed the task for me . . . and, so far, I am very pleased with their work."

He pointed a finger at Ombre. "You, my commander, should have obeyed me. For the time being your command will be handed over to another man." He looked around the room. "Are any of you—" his body twitched and his face contorted in pain before he could go on. "Are any of you ready to obey me without question? If you are, then I will give to you the rank that Ombre now holds."

Ilfedo's counselors gasped in horror at his words. They talked amongst themselves, seeming to debate the truth of Ilfedo's words and looking at him as if he were a ghost. Ilfedo rushed forward, smote one of his counselors on the face, drew the sword of the dragon, and poised it against the man's throat. Caritha felt faint as Ombre stood to his feet with his hand on his sword's pommel. The sword of the dragon, given to Ilfedo by the dragon, did not blaze, the living fire did not come forth, and the light did not shine. Caritha remembered Albino's promise concerning the sword. If Ilfedo killed that man, the sword would, of its own accord, come around and slay him in turn.

* * *

Oganna steeled herself against what she was about to face. She stood outside of the council chamber, trying to calm herself. Even though the council doors were closed she had been able to hear much of her father's rant, and her heart had fallen. Something had happened along the border. She knew it in her spirit. Her father had found something or been found by something that was truly evil.

Two large men stood guard at the doors. They were trying their best not to stare at her, but they were having difficulty doing so. At last, one of them said, "Shall we open the doors for you now, your highness?"

Oganna stood straight, stood proud, and commanded them to be opened. She stepped through the doorway and dropped her hand to Avenger's hilt. "Have I missed something?" she declared to those seated around the room. She took a step toward her father and slapped him across the face.

His eyes and mouth widened and, again, the assembly gasped. "This is none of your concern, young one," Ilfedo yelled as he leaned over her. "Now, leave this room and do not dare enter again unless I give you permission."

Every muscle in Oganna's body screamed for her to get out. To obey her father, just as she had done when she was a little girl. But she fought the instinct. She was not a child anymore. "Oh, I think it is my concern," she declared. "After all, the leadership

484

of the Hemmed Land will one day fall into my lap."

"Hah!" Ilfedo spat on the floor. "Then I do, here and now, take away your right of succession."

Suddenly she noticed the cage and the viper. Blood had caked the creature's head, and its lower jaw hung loose. A fire burned in her soul, and she turned to the guards. Her hand tightened around her sword as she spoke. "Who has done this?"

"It refused to talk, and Lord Ilfedo gave us permission to torture it," they answered.

It would have been better for them if they had remained silent. Oganna drew out her sword and transformed herself into a goddess in silver, wielding a blade that glowed red. She thrust the nearest guard straight through his shoulder, pulled out her blood-stained blade as he fell to the floor, and struck the floor with her blade's tip. "Behold, the Avenger!" She burned her gaze into the faces of those around her. "With it I have and I will execute justice upon all. Honored members of this council, are you so blinded by the chain of command that you have lost all sense of moral responsibility? Why did you wait for me to come before putting a stop to this wickedness?"

Out of the corner of her eye she caught sight of the remaining guard jabbing the viper with his sword. She slid her blade around and struck at him, but her father drew his sword and parried the blow. "Do not make me hurt you, little child."

As soon as his blade touched hers it melded to it and, together, the sword of the dragon and the Avenger slew the guard. The people around them cried out in horror as the guard dropped to the floor, but Oganna reached out with both hands and took back the swords. As she grasped the sword of the dragon, it blazed with brilliant light, and a jab of current touched her mind.

"Oganna, my daughter, can you hear me? I am here." It was Ilfedo's voice inside her mind. She felt the presence of another with him, between him and her, blocking her path to bring him back. "Father," she said, stepping closer to him, "I can feel the darkness waging war inside of you. I can see something wicked controlling you. Let me help."

Before he could react, she dropped the swords, reached up, and pressed her hands on either side of his head. Her hands glowed, and she felt the powers of her mother surge against the tide of darkness and attack the evil that had rooted itself in Ilfedo's being. The resistance was strong. Too strong. She closed her eyes against despair, and the pain that suddenly assailed her mind. She held her ground. Yet the darkness, though not overcoming her, refused to be overcome in turn. She opened her eyes and strained to cry out. "I—can't do this alone."

The Warrioresses dashed to her side. Caritha spoke to the members of the council, though Oganna could not hear what she said. Ilfedo's counselors rose from their seats, bowed their heads, and knelt on the floor with hands folded in prayer. The sight of it renewed Oganna's hope.

The Warrioresses laid their hands on Ilfedo and on her, reinforcing her powers with their own. Dragon blood melded with dragon blood, allowing them to focus on the foreign presence in Ilfedo's subconscious. They surrounded it and pressed in. The presence was strong, like a black knife that had been buried deep in Ilfedo's soul. A knife that was held by an invisible hand from far away. But their unified minds suffocated it, separating the wound from the attacker until the demonic presence released its hold with a terrifying scream.

Oganna's exhausted arms fell to her sides, and her legs gave out under her. Beside her, Caritha, Laura, Evela, Levena, and Rozel followed suit. The last thing she remembered seeing was Ombre as he and other members of the council stumbled to catch them before they hit the floor.

RENEWED MAN

Ilfedo was still struggling against the evil that was trying to overcome him. The dragon remained beside him, as did his deceased wife, encouraging him in this dream-like state. But he felt an infusion of selfless love beat back the evil one. His chest heaved in rhythm with his labored breathing. He felt disoriented, yet energetic. He flexed his arms and shouted in triumph to the sky. Though he could not see them in his vision, he knew that, somewhere in the world of the living where he'd left his body, his wife's sisters and his own beloved daughter were fighting to bring him back.

The dragon rested a hand around his shoulders and spoke in rumbling tones. "You have seen through your own eyes the harm that your possessed body has done to your alliance with the megatraths. Vectra is a proud creature and a powerful one. Make it your priority to mend your relationship and treat her with respect."

"I will," Ilfedo vowed.

"One more thing, Ilfedo. Don't ever again be caught in battle without your sword, for it alone can prevent this incident from reoccurring." The dragon stepped back and moved his hand in a circle over Ilfedo's head. Blue-white light streamed from its claws and fell in waves to the ground until a bubble of swirling light surrounded Ilfedo, separating him from Dantress and the dragon.

He blew a kiss to his wife and mouthed, "I will be with you again. I promise." She and the dragon dissipated, and he found himself standing in the council chamber at Fort North. He stumbled and fell to his hands and knees. To his side lay his sword on the wood floor. He reached out and grasped it, then raised himself to his feet. The living fire sprouted from his weapon and decked him in the magnificent armor of light.

His counselors stepped back and then knelt before him, but this time their faces were full of joy. Ombre came forward, grinning from ear to ear. "It's good to have you back, my friend."

"It's good to be back," Ilfedo said as he embraced the man. Then he nodded at his unconscious daughter and the sisters. "They need rest. See to it that they are cared for." He turned to leave.

Ombre was aghast. "Ilfedo, where are you going?"

"Do not worry about me any longer," Ilfedo assured him. "I will be back in due time. First I have to mend the wrong that I did to the megatraths, and

I suspect such a thing will be far more difficult to achieve than I care to admit."

He sheathed his sword, left the fort, and found the megatraths camped to the south around a stand of widely spaced trees. The creatures stirred and raised their heads as he passed between them. Evening was falling, and the cool air felt moist.

"Explain your errand, sir." One of the creatures rose to its full height and peered down its snout at him.

"I have come to speak to your leader, Vectra," Ilfedo said.

The creature snarled. "She is busy right now, lord of the Hemmed Land. I suggest that you leave before I remember your insult to our noble leader."

Right then and there, Ilfedo almost apologized to the creature. But he thought to himself of how that would appear at this moment. "You are bold to address me so freely," he told the megatrath. "I could cut you down right here and leave you to die in the grass far from your home, and there would be little consequence to me." He held his ground as the megatrath evaluated him, drool dripping from its long jaws. He had to show strength with these creatures if the alliance was going to be salvaged. Had not Oganna won their respect through combat? He growled up at the megatrath and stared boldly into its dark eyes. "Do you think that I fear you?" he asked.

"Yes," the megatrath growled back.

Ilfedo laughed and drew his sword. The flames sprang forth and covered his body, causing the megatrath to stumble backward. "This weapon contains great power, megatrath. It is an extension of my will, and I am not one you should trifle with. I suggest that you permit me to pass before I force you aside."

"Enough!" Vectra roared as she lumbered into view. She circled her loyal bodyguard and gazed upon Ilfedo. "You are not a friend of ours, Ilfedo of the Hemmed Land. The child you had may be pure, but I have seen that you are not."

"I was not myself." Ilfedo bowed. "A dark spell had been cast over me, and I could no longer control what my body did. In fact, my mind has only just been freed from the sorcery and my freedom is in large part due to Oganna's intercession." He took a step forward and raised his sword in both hands. "This weapon is an instrument of the pure and will only respond to those that are worthy. Surely if I were deceiving you this weapon would not now clothe me in light."

"Humph, for all I know you could be a sorcerer. This sword proves nothing," Vectra said.

"If you do not believe me." He extended the sword's handle to her. "Take it and see if it will discern your heart."

"What? Is this a trick?" She rumbled deep in her throat and yellow vapors drifted into the air while flames burst from her mouth. "Father of Oganna or not, you will die!" She charged at him, spun around, and hit him broadside with her tail.

The impact threw him into the air, and his back hit the trunk of a large tree. All wind left his lungs as he fell to the ground, gasping for air. His fingers drew energy from the sword and sent it into his chest, allowing him to stand quickly. The megatrath wanted a fight, so he would have to test himself against her. Very well, he would give her a duel that she would not be able to forget. He waved the sword over his head, blasting the surrounding trees with fire until the other megatraths backed a safe distance away from him.

Vectra charged in spite of the fire and spun around. This time, instead of hitting him with her tail, she crushed him with her side. She stood, grabbed one of his legs in her gnarly hand, and flung him through the trees. As the branches scraped along his armor, he clung to his sword and sent a torrent of flames ahead of him. The fire slowed his plunge and he landed softly on the ground.

He raced back to the burning ring of trees, faced the megatrath, and poised his sword into the flood of fire that she now flung at him. He felt himself at one with the sword. He could feel the heat of Vectra's flames touch the sword's point, and he heard the fire crackle as the sword redirected it and threw it into the creature's face.

Vectra shook her head and roared. "Is that all you can do, Lord of the Hemmed Land?" She advanced, pouring vapors over him.

Coughing, Ilfedo slipped around her flank and stabbed his blade into the scales on her tail. Vectra screamed in pain, and the sword's power siphoned the energy from her body until she lay on the ground, helpless and weary. He withdrew the sword from her body and circled to her head. "I will not slay you, Vectra, I have need of your friendship and of your respect."

The other megatraths surrounded them. He

looked into their eyes, trying to read their expressions. "Do not worry, my friend." Vectra parted her lips to reveal rows of deadly teeth. "You have earned our respect this day and reclaimed your honor in my eyes."

He nodded and passed his sword over her body. "Then rise, my ally. We have work to do."

The megatrath stood and shook her tail and then her whole body. "How did you do that? I feel strong again," she said.

He glanced over the weapon in his hand, confused. "I don't know. It just came to me."

* * *

That same night, beneath the trees, Ilfedo stood at the ready. He did not bother to look at the ground. Instead he searched the trees' branches. At last he spotted his quarry. A winged man was perched, as one had been before, on the branch of a tree on the edge of the desert. Ilfedo called out, "Ho, up there. Do you dare try me again, but this time without your companions? Where is that human master of yours? Auron I believe his name was."

The creature dropped on top of him, knocking him to the ground. "The spell was not strong enough last time," it hissed. "This time I will try it myself."

"That was," rumbled a voice from the shadows, "if you got to him before I got to you." The alligator-like head of a megatrath came into view and snapped its jaws over the Art'en's head. The megatrath picked it up, and growled deep in its throat. Ilfedo cringed as he watched yellow vapors drift from Vectra's mouth around her struggling victim. Vectra shook her head vigorously and dropped the limp body.

"Well done," Ilfedo murmured. He perked his ears and glanced to the east and west where the sand ended and the forest began. Yellow clouds of the megatraths' poisonous vapors wafted through the tree line.

Vectra picked up her victim with one hand as if he were a doll and stepped out of the forest where all could see her. Several other Art'en flitted out of the trees and flew in vain toward the desert, but the vapors had robbed them of oxygen. The megatraths plunged into the desert, caught them, and slew them. The ground shook as the creatures roared their victory and beat the sand. A few others chased the surviving vipers into the desert.

"My horde will follow the vipers for a couple miles," Vectra said. "That should give us a good idea as to which direction we should search for the perpetrator behind these attacks. However, I doubt the vipers will ever return after tonight." She nudged the dead creature she had dropped. "And it looks like we killed the last of these."

Together they examined the creature. His clothes were black, and a rope had been tied around his waist. His face was boney and dark, and his nails were as long as a bird's claws. Flipping him over, they noted that his feathered wings were dark brown.

Ilfedo scratched his chin thoughtfully. "Before they appeared in these forests several years ago, I had never heard of creatures such as these. Not even in my ancestors' legends. Have you?"

"No." Vectra lumbered farther on, and they

looked at the next body. "This one's face is different, and he looks shorter. Other than that, he is almost identical to the first one." She turned to Ilfedo. "What should we do with the bodies?"

He considered for a moment before pointing to the desert. "Pile them over there and burn them."

Lines of men emerged from the forest. They carried seven Art'en into the desert, and the megatraths picked up another five. The creatures tossed the bodies into a heap, then formed a ring around it and poured flames from their mouths. The bodies smoked, and the burning clothes turned them into a sickening bonfire.

Ilfedo disintegrated the heap with a focused flame that he shot from the sword of the dragon. As he finished, the remaining megatraths returned from chasing the vipers and reported to Vectra. She in turn lumbered over to Ilfedo and growled. "The vipers are fleeing to the north. Their lair must lie somewhere in that direction."

"Then we will need to plan a campaign to hunt them down and discover if there is anything beyond this desert that provokes these attacks," Ilfedo said.

Vectra stomped her foot in the sand. "The vipers will perish for what they have done to your people."

Ilfedo sheathed his sword and gazed back into her dark eyes. "My primary concern is to find the man behind the vipers and the Art'en. Who is creating this conflict and why? Someone is masterminding all of this, and I don't think it was the sorcerer Auron. But I do not know how to find that individual."

Vectra roared into the night, and the megatraths pivoted to face her. "We are finished here. Return to the place of our lodging," she told them.

The creatures lumbered together, formed a group, and thundered into the forest. The stars shone brilliantly that night as Ilfedo and Vectra returned to Fort North. Every now and again a shooting star burst in the heavens, and they stopped to watch. Once, as they passed through a meadow, a fireball blasted from the west and blazed a bold trail in the velvety sky. It exploded moments later without a sound.

"Looks like a good night for stargazing," Ilfedo said as they passed into the trees on the other side of the meadow.

The megatrath bent a tree to the side so that she could pass without breaking it. "Indeed, it does," she said.

Ilfedo frowned, thinking of the campaign he would need to organize into the north desert. "Vectra, it will take a few days for me to assemble my army and prepare it for a campaign through the desert. I don't want to pack light for this trip. Whatever lies out there, we must be ready to deal with it at our first encounter. Supplies must be packed, organized, and distributed. Equipment has to be readied, and I must arrange for matters to be tended to in my absence. By the time I set out to find my enemy, they will be ready and waiting for me. I would prefer to take the offensive and strike before they have time to prepare."

With a nod of her heavy head, Vectra agreed. "Then I and my guards will move out tomorrow morning in advance of your army. I have a hundred of the most loyal in my horde, a significant enough force to follow the vipers and scout out potential hostiles. Besides, desert travel is what we are made for. It will not take us long to track down the serpents, and it will be easier for you to follow our tracks than the viper trails. If we wait even one day, the wind may erase the trail, and we would have difficulty finding it again."

Ilfedo thought for a moment. If he refused her offer, she would likely take offense. If he sent her ahead of his army, it would give him the time he needed to prepare a substantial force, but it might also place his new-found ally in great jeopardy. He took one look at her thick, scaled hide and laughed inwardly. What was he thinking? A force of one hundred megatraths could easily deal with a small army and stand a fair chance of victory.

He bowed to her. "Very well, we will do as you suggest."

* * *

Oganna's eyelids felt heavy. She yawned as someone stroked her brow and she grinned when her father's frowning face came into focus. "Father, you are better?"

"Yes, Oganna. Thanks to your efforts the spell was broken, and I am myself again." He took her hand and held it with both of his larger ones. "I've patched up things with Vectra, too. She and the other megatraths have helped us drive the vipers back into the desert."

She sat up slowly and put a hand on her head to soothe its ache. "I discovered a presence in your mind," she said. "It was so vile. It fought me hard when I started to break its control over you. It was a man. He must be very strong with magic if he was able to control you from afar."

"Well, you don't have to worry about him anymore," Ilfedo said. "Vectra killed him, and her companions took care of his partners."

Oganna smiled at first. She wanted to believe that it would end so easily. But, then, she knew better than that. "No." She withdrew her hand from his and held it palm up toward the ceiling. "I can sense his presence still. It is no longer in you, and it is far weaker, but whoever our enemy is, he is still a very great threat. I can sense it. He is lying in wait for whoever first searches for him. I am certain of it."

He shifted in the chair by her bedside. "The megatraths are leaving in the morning to track the vipers. I need a couple of days to ready the army for the march, so it will be a little while before I catch up with them."

"Then I will go with the megatraths," Oganna said.

Ilfedo touched her forehead as if checking for a fever. "I don't know if that is wise. You look weak after that battle for my mind."

She squeezed his hand and looked into his eyes. "Father, please do not try to stop me. Vectra will need me on this quest. Did Caritha tell you how I slew Loos, the megatrath that attacked Bordelin?"

He nodded. "Caritha informed me short while ago."

"Then you know that I can do this," she said.

He rose from the chair, kissed her forehead, and smoothed back her hair. "Your mother would be so proud of you." He walked to the door, and she saw his shoulders droop before he answered her. "All right, my daughter. I will not stop you, but you must be careful on this quest. We still do not know who is attacking us, and we don't know why. I will follow with my army as soon as possible."

Oganna relaxed and his newfound confidence in her bolstered her weak body. "Thank you, Father," she said as he left the room.

Instead of going back to sleep, she threw on a robe and strode to the council chamber where the prisoner lay in its cage. She lifted the viper out. The creature offered no resistance. She brought it to her room, closed the door, and laid it on the bed. Gently she placed her hands on its skin. "Do not be afraid," she said in hushed tones. "I am not going to hurt you."

As she began to heal its wounds, she felt resistance. At first she didn't know what it was, then she recognized an oppressive darkness. Some kind of spell was eating at the creature's free will, in the same way that Ilfedo's will had been ruined. "Oh no you don't!" she cried as the presence attacked her.

Forcing her will to concentrate, she sought to cast out the presence. But, though it could not overcome her, she could not overcome it. She brought the Avenger, laid it against the viper's skin and, adding its power to her own, surrounded the seed of evil in its mind. She choked out the demonic influence and killed it. Then, weakened by the effort she slumped over in a faint.

She did not know how long she lay there, but when she awoke it was to a strange voice hissing in her ear.

"Psst! Mistress?" the voice said.

Oganna rubbed her eyes. Who had called her?

The viper slithered to her arm and raised its venomous head. At first she cringed, believing that it would strike her, but she saw that its mouth framed a rather cute grin. "Mistress?" it asked again.

She pointed at her chest. "Me? You are talking to me."

"Psst! Who else?" The snake coiled its tail gently around her arm.

Oganna stood and smiled back at it. "You have changed for the better," she commented.

The viper rubbed its head against her skin. "Psst! Mistress, you saved my life. That makes me your lifetime friend. Do you know what that means?"

Oganna laughed inwardly. She felt funny talking to a serpent. "No, what does it mean?" she asked.

"That I will be with you until the day I die," the viper said. "I am called Neneila, and I will protect you with my life and offer advice if you want it." The creature curled the remainder of its tail around her arm and tasted her sleeve with its forked tongue. "Mistresssss you are very pretty."

Suppressing a giggle, Oganna left her room with the viper wrapped around her arm. This arrangement suited her. She could imagine it would be nice to have a constant companion to share her thoughts with. Much as her father had the nuvitors. She left the fort and found her father, the Warrioresses, Ombre, and Vectra conferring by a stand of trees. The members of Ilfedo's council stood nearby and the megatraths lumbered into a line behind Vectra.

A murmur passed through the air as Oganna approached. The men pointed to the viper on her arm and whispered to one another. Ilfedo glanced at her arm. "Well, my dear. You have worked another miracle overnight." He smiled and patted her shoulder. "If your little friend is comfortable, let's get down to business."

"Psst! Mistress, I don't like being called 'little.'" The viper raised its head in disdain and eyed Ilfedo. "Psst! Psst! Psst!"

But Ilfedo did not seem to hear the creature. He addressed those assembled and introduced Vectra. "My lords and counselors, please join me in welcoming our ally, Vectra, the ruler of Resgeria."

"Men of the Hemmed Land," Vectra growled. "Let your enemies be mine, and mine yours. I have brought a force strong enough to search out and discover your enemy. We will repay them for all the harm they have done to you." She held up her hand, and claws emerged from her fingers.

The counselors raised their hands and cheered.

Vectra gazed upon Oganna. "Your father informed me of your decision to accompany us. All I can say to that, is that I will be honored to have you by my side."

"Psst! What's this?" the viper hissed. It twisted its head around in order to see the megatrath from head to tail. "Big, bad, ugly, scaled—"

"Shush, Neneila," Oganna said. She tapped the little creature's head with her fist and glanced at Vectra, hoping no insult had been perceived.

"Look who's talking," the megatrath grunted. "A tiny, insignificant, beady-eyed—"

The viper slipped its tongue in and out of its mouth and showed its fangs. "Psst!" Venom glittered on its fangs. "I am also poisonous. Sssince I will be traveling with you . . . treat me with respect."

"Please stop, both of you," Oganna interjected. She shrugged her shoulders, and gazed up into Vectra's face. "Can't we all get along?"

The megatrath drew back her head and crouched to the earth. "You are right, princess. I shouldn't let such a small creature bother me."

"Small! Psst, you rude, fat," the viper started to say.

But Oganna clamped her fingers over the viper's mouth. "No more insults. Okay?" She swung her leg over Vectra's neck and held on as the creature stood to her full height. She spotted her father. His brow furrowed as if questioning the wisdom of her decision to go with the megatrath horde. "Don't worry, Father. I will be careful," she called to him.

Vectra lumbered up to her fellow megatraths and opened her jaws wide, emitting a series of high-pitched shrieks that rolled across the fields until answering calls from the other megatraths filled the morning air and sent shivers up Oganna's spine. She imagined that the forests and hills of the Hemmed Land continued to ring with the megatraths' cries, and at the sound of them the inhabitants would flee in fear of their lives. The great creatures formed a line with Vectra at its head.

"Hang on tight," Vectra advised her. "We will be moving fast, so this is going to be a rough ride."

Oganna could feel the megatrath's body tensing, its mighty muscles rippling. Like a flood, the horde raced over the fields and crashed through the forests until they passed out of the Hemmed Land and into the northern desert. They kept up a fierce pace for a long while, then slowed their pace and maintained steady progress across the sand. Oganna felt as if she was roasting under Yimshi's rays.

"Ah, this heat feels wonderful." Vectra's words stretched and rumbled in her throat, and she lengthened her gait. "This is more like my land. Except there are far fewer boulders in Resgeria."

Oganna sneezed as Vectra stirred the sand. "This climate may be all right for you. But to me it is stifling hot," Oganna managed to say. The viper slithered up her arm and settled around her neck. The collar of her garment provided some shade for its body.

Vectra snorted and picked up her pace again. "For your sake I will cross this area as quickly as possible. Deserts do not continue forever and I doubt not that your enemy is coming from somewhere beyond this place. Likely it is a land not unlike your own with cooler air and lots of trees," she said. "Hang on! This is going to be a long run.

NETROTH, THE CITY OF THE GIANTS

After enduring three days of travel through the boulder-strewn wastes of the northern desert, Oganna felt relieved to see green hills rise on the distant horizon. She dismounted and ran until her feet touched grass, and she found a tree to shade her. The cooler air kissed her sun-burned skin. A few trees stood out on the grassy rises. She climbed to the crest of the first hill and gazed down the opposite side. A deep blue stream gurgled out of the hill's base and ribboned across the flat landscape that stretched out behind the hills.

She left her shoes and socks on the stream's bank, then waded into the gentle current. She splashed the water on her face, and washed the dust from her hair. The cool water felt good on her skin. The first relief that she'd had in days.

The megatraths lumbered over the hill behind her and drank of the fresh water. Several of them rolled in the grass, growling with delight. Oganna wrung the water from her hair and washed her legs off while the viper dropped to the ground and curled up on the stream's bank. "Psst, Mistress what's all the fuss?" it asked.

Oganna did not answer, instead she laughed as she lay back on the grass. The green blades tickled her bare feet and the ground received her with its soft soil. The sun was setting and the sky in that direction turned orange and purple. Wispy clouds dotted the sky, each one a unique and evolving shape.

Vectra sloshed into the stream. "We'll rest here for now. Before we explore this strange land I want my horde rested. Tomorrow we continue north."

One by one the megatraths curled beside the stream, and soon their labored breathing filled Oganna's ears. Vectra brought over a supply pack that had been tied to another megatrath's back during the trek, and she set it at Oganna's feet. "Goodnight, Princess."

"Goodnight," Oganna said, and she watched the creature curl up nearby. Soon Vectra lay asleep and her snoring reached Oganna's ears. The viper slithered under her legs and came up by her side. "Are you ready for sleep too, Neneila?" Oganna asked.

The viper stretched its jaws until the fangs were fully exposed, then it yawned.

Oganna pulled her bedroll out of the pack,

rolled it out, and snuggled into it while the viper curled beside her head and dozed off. Soon she too would fall asleep with the sounds of crickets singing in the night. To her their songs were not mere vibrations wrought on the delicate tapestry of their wings, for she could hear the words. Now, as the crickets sang, she hummed along and repeated their words in her mind. Strange that listening to crickets sing came so naturally to her.

"In the darkness Netroth's bell tolls for the dead:
The unavenged slain that once roamed her streets.
They toll for the mighty king that into doom was led,
And the citadel that stands in the wake of his defeats.

Hearken to the pleas of the cities' murdered inhabitants.
Cry now for children torn from play,
For mothers slain by the corrupted giants,
Weep for the king that should not have lived to see this day.

Will not a champion rise to stay the wizard's hand?
When will justice be dealt to end his dread?
Who will save this burning land?
Who will rise to deal justice upon the wizard's head?"

It seemed a strange thing for crickets to sing. She whispered their phrases into the night, then closed her eyes and fell asleep.

The next morning Oganna rose with the dawn. The air felt strangely warm for so early an hour. Putting away her bedding she roused the viper. "I'm going to explore this place. Do you want to come along?" she asked.

"Certainly, Mistress. Psst! I wouldn't miss this," hissed the viper. It wrapped itself around her outstretched arm and settled its head over her shoulder.

Oganna walked beyond the hills and across the fields. Then the land rose again and she ascended a few more grassy hills. The last stood higher than all the land ahead of her. To her astonishment she saw a vast stretch of rolling hills that extended from the base of the hills on which she stood to a trio of mountains in the distance. It was a stunning scene, such a wide open territory. It made the Hemmed Land seem small. Smoke rose from the smoldering ruins of innumerable buildings throughout the region and geometrically laid out roads converged from the horizon, allowing access to the buildings and a main highway that drew a straight line to the mountains.

A multitude of dead domesticated animals dotted the landscape in dried pools of their own blood. Arrows lay strewn on the ground with broken spears and an occasional sword. She descended the hill and tried to pick up one of the swords by its handle. But it was twice the size of Avenger and at least three times as heavy. She released her hold.

Kneeling next to an arrow, she ran her finger along its shaft. It was as long as a man, and its head dwarfed any she'd ever seen. Not far off lay a spear with a shaft at least sixteen feet long. She stood and walked to the nearest structure, a four-walled home with its roof caved in. The doorway was nearly twice her height, as if fashioned for a giant to use.

From behind her Vectra's voice called out, "Oganna, what have you found?"

Oganna turned as Vectra's massive foot splintered the spear. Behind her the other megatraths lumbered over the hills, and suddenly the objects scattered about seemed smaller.

Vectra picked up the sword and stabbed its blade into the ground. Then she raised the front third of her body and picked up a couple of arrows in each hand. The megatrath cracked them in her teeth. "I was worried about you, princess. You should not wander off alone. This land is foreign. We do not know what creatures inhabit it."

"I had no idea that there were people living this far north," Oganna admitted. She shook her head and gaped at the structure. "Look at this place. It's as if giants built it."

"And fought a war here," Vectra said as she lumbered through the field, picking up various weapons. She lifted a shield and smashed her fist into it. But the shield held, and she pulled back her hand, shaking it and growling. Vectra strode back to Oganna, hunkering down beside Oganna and eying her quizzically. "Did you imagine that this part of the world would be any less interesting than ours? Take my word for this." She wiggled her claws at the territory ahead of them. "Subterran is full of other civilizations, some old, some young, some wicked and some good."

Oganna nodded thoughtfully. "It looks as if someone burned this place out and it wasn't with the consent of the inhabitants. Look at the weapons and livestock. You are right! Someone made war on these people. Recently, too, I should add."

"It does look that way," Vectra said as she

kicked another shield aside. "And I have little doubt that this devastation is somehow linked to the viper raids on the Hemmed Land."

"No doubt," Oganna mused. She walked to the main highway and followed it toward a large hill. Vectra lumbered beside her, a comforting reminder that Oganna was not alone. Smoke rose from behind the hill, and the point of a spire stabbed at the sky. The highway disappeared over the hilltop. Without warning her companions, Oganna ran to the crest and peered beyond.

In a very deep and wide valley rested the ruins of a mighty city constructed of stone. A wall rose over forty feet high around its perimeter. Streets had been laid through the city in the shape of a sailing ship's wheel, with four highways that formed the spokes that ran from the center to the four gates below the valley's rim. A wooden archway, inscribed with letters from the ancient alphabet, crowned the nearest gate.

"Netroth," Oganna read aloud.

Vectra, coming up from behind, caught her breath and laid a restraining hand on Oganna's shoulders. "Take care, Princess. I have heard tales of this place. It is a city of the giants. Little bodes well with those creatures, for they are warlike and powerful."

Oganna couldn't help smiling at that. "That sounds like another race I know," she said pointedly. Vectra ignored her comment.

Instead they descended into the valley and passed under the arch into the city. The one hundred megatraths pounded after them. Every footstep resounded through the empty streets, and the air smelled mildly of rotting eggs. Dead animals lay everywhere and most of the buildings had been burned.

The spire that Oganna had seen belonged to a citadel at the city's heart. It spiked above the four highways that led to the gates and intersected beneath it. A gargantuan stone ramp appeared to be the only way to enter the structure. The ramp dropped at least a hundred feet from the citadel entrance to the highway ahead of her. At its end, not thirty paces from the ground, it split to form an arch. This unique design would allow for visitors to ascend the ramp to the citadel from either side of the highway, or they could choose to continue straight and the highway would lead them under the ramp. Deep chips had been cut into the citadel walls and chunks of broken stones lay around it, apparently evidence of a recent bombardment.

Nevertheless, the city itself had fared far worse. Whether that was due to the weaker construction of its buildings, or to a greater focus of the enemy's wrath she could not determine. Oganna felt as if she was walking through a land of ghosts.

She climbed a thick stone step into one of the houses and gazed at the ceiling rafters above her head. It was tall. Again seemingly suited to a giant rather than an average human. Several spiders were crawling over thinly spread webs between the rafters and two beams that crossed beneath them for structural support. It didn't smell musty, but something putrid made her pinch her nose. She wandered past the kitchen table where two oversized chairs stood on either end. A third lay on the floor with a broken leg. A pair of cockroaches skittered out of sight into a cabinet. An iron stove sat against one wall. She stood on tip toe to see the stovetop. Burned eggs and several strips of bacon filled a pan that had been left there, and to the side a raw egg had broken on the cooling shelf.

She stepped away from the kitchen, spotted an open door in the far wall, and peered into the next room. It was large, as she'd expected. There was a bunk bed against one side with its dusty sheets neatly tucked under the mattress and the fluffed pillows. Someone had called this home. Someone had been happy here. Oganna could almost hear the laughter of children playing about in that room. But she tore herself away from the ghostly sight and left the building. Morbid curiosity compelled her to check the next building as well, hoping against reason that she would find signs of life. A broken table and chairs littered the wood floor, and to her horror, when she knelt to inspect the floor planks they were speckled with red. Someone had been hurt here. Perhaps they had even died. The plaster wall a few paces ahead of her had cracked where something had struck it, and a telltale red stain streaked from her eye level all the way to the floorboards. Almost worse was the torn shirt that lay on the floor farther into the room. It was large enough for three men to fit inside of.

In each home that she searched she found not a soul. She found meals left uncooked on the stoves, and in others the tables had been set and the dinner unfinished. Either the giants had fled the bombardment, or they had chosen to leave before their enemy arrived. Judging by the blood she had found, the giants had remained for too long.

She stood on the steps of one huge mansion, feeling like a midget, and watched the daylight fade. "It appears as though the citadel is the sturdiest structure remaining in this city," she commented. She glanced back at Vectra. The megatrath was sticking its head into another doorway. She waited until the megatrath pulled its head out and returned her gaze. "We should take residence inside of it for tonight," Oganna said. "Just in case whoever did this comes back."

Vectra nodded and roared down the city streets. The other megatraths emerged from various buildings, and walls collapsed in their wake. They came at her summons and stood attentively while she pointed out the citadel. "We will take refuge in there for the night. Tomorrow we will do a more thorough search of these buildings."

One megatrath lumbered out of line. "Vectra, I don't think that would be the wisest course of action," he said.

Vectra wheeled on the creature, grabbing its neck in her claws and driving its head into the stone pavement. "Dare to question my word again, and I will personally crush you into this rubble."

"But Vectra, I only wanted—" he began.

But she spun in a tight circle, crashed her bulk into his and sent him flying into a pile of loose stones. He shook himself as he rose from the rubble. She roared in his face, spewed fire until he cried for mercy, and thwacked him with her boney tail before eyeing the others. "Any more objections?"

Oganna shook her head and set off after Vectra in the direction of the great ramp. The megatrath's way seemed strange. Effective, to be sure, and yet strange. It would encourage obedience, but a blind obedience at that. She observed the creatures' expressions. In spite of their leader's apparent lack of sensitivity or perhaps because of it, they were grinning.

The viper's tongue tickled her ear. "Psst, Mistress! Your companions are very strange."

"Shush, now," Oganna said as she stroked Neneila's head. "You are also a strange companion."

The viper pulled its head away from her hand when she said that, and its strange face stared up at her. "Psst, no I am not."

Oganna could not help chuckling at the offended creature. "Oh? So you think that you are superior to a megatrath?"

"You will see, Mistress. I am not the first viper that has bound myself to a human, and you will find it to be very advantageous. Psst! Wait, and you will see what I mean," Neneila said.

The citadel ramp lay before her. Vectra and two other megatraths led the way as Oganna followed in their wake. The stone construction fascinated her. Stone tiles had been cut in the shape of diamonds to cover the walkway. She peeked over the edge. There were no railings along the sides, in spite of the fact that anyone who stumbled was in danger of plunging over the edge to their likely death. A sudden blast of cold air threatened to throw her off, and she shuddered, imagining herself slipping and then falling over fifty feet into the streets below.

At last Vectra reached the Citadel's entrance and Oganna admired the hefty iron doors that had been built into it. "Goodness!" Vectra exclaimed as she threw her weight against the doors. "How did the giants manage to open these? Even for us megatraths this will be difficult." The other megatraths lent their weight alongside of Vectra, struggling against the doors until they finally opened inward.

Oganna expected a loud squeal of protest from the iron doors, or lots of squeaking at the least. Instead they swung open noiselessly on their hinges, but a clatter of falling objects behind the doors did arise.

The megatraths pushed inside and unpiled an assortment of heavy objects that had been blocking the entrance. Oganna pointed to a heavy, square stone that had been set against the inside of the doors. "There's your answer, Vectra. I don't think the giants intended for these to be opened."

The citadel was incredible. It could have defined the word incredible. A pillar rose from the center of the floor to a junction where eight arches met high in the structure. Several stairways were recessed into the walls, and each of them spiraled upward. Doorways had been opened in the walls along the stairs. All around her, she saw furniture strewn on the cold floor.

"Oganna, this is something you will want to see," Vectra rumbled as she stood in the doorway to an adjoining chamber.

Peering around the megatrath, Oganna let out a long breath. "Wow," she exclaimed. Ornately carved wood covered the room's high walls. Flowers, swords, spears, scrolls, and people that had all been carved from wood adorned the upper half, as well as the ceiling. Chest-high wood rails ran the room's perimeter until they were hidden at the far side of the room behind an empty stone throne. Chiseled into the wall above was a sentence written in the ancient alphabet. "Vectra, what does it say?"

"'The voice of the One speaks for all,'" Vectra read off.

Oganna stepped into the room. "One thing is now certain. This place was built by a race of giants. I don't know if we should be thankful that they aren't here, or if we should pity their apparent demise." Almost as soon as she spoke the words she regretted them. She hung her head in shame. "How could I be thankful that they are not here? No, I do pity them and I wish that we had come here in time to help them. If I find the enemies who killed the women at their stoves and dragged the children from their beds, then for them I will seek vengeance."

She ran her fingers down the wood panels that formed the walls. Each one was covered with a uniquely carved image. Some depicted battles, others showed ceremonies, and others displayed families fitted in fancy clothing. "So many souls," she said in a hushed voice. "So many nameless faces." She gazed upon the image of a father holding his infant child in his arms and she glanced at her feet. How many innocent lives had been ruined in this place?

The viper reached out with the tip of its tail and caught her tear. "Psst! Mistress, you should get some rest."

"For once I agree with the serpent." Vectra growled and beckoned with a massive hand. "Come. We'll need your help to set up the tent your father's men packed for you."

An enormous fireplace had been built into a wall in the main chamber. Several megatraths left the citadel via the ramp and reappeared minutes later with armloads of timber. They stacked some of it in the fireplace and breathed gentle flames on the wood. The fire flickered and burned hot, warding off the night chill.

Oganna pulled out her bedroll and placed it near the fire. Vectra started to take out the tent from one of the packs they'd trundled along, but Oganna raised her hand to stop her. "This will do fine," she said, and the viper slipped under the bedding. Oganna lay down as well and the heat from the fire filled her with toasty warmth.

All of the megatraths were inside of the citadel with her now. She would sleep soundly tonight with the knowledge that she was safe in their mighty company. Yet every time that she heard a stone shift in the darkness it startled her wide-awake, and every howl of the wind outside of the citadel sent shivers down her spine. The place seemed to invite her worst nightmares to come true.

She thought of the empty city. What had happened to the people? Even if most of them had been killed in a war, shouldn't there be some survivors from such a vast populace? And why weren't there any human bodies? She had seen the bodies of animals, but the human corpses could not simply vanish. Especially not those of giants. She pulled the blanket closer to her chin and steeled herself against morbid thoughts.

Tomorrow she would get a fresh start and find

out what happened here. Maybe if she discovered what became of the giants' civilization she would find out who had sent the vipers and the Art'en to attack the Hemmed Land. Her father had called the wizard responsible for placing him under a spell by a certain name, but for the moment it escaped her. Feeling tired from her long day, she rested her mind.

* * *

The next day a cold drizzle of rain fell on the city. Vectra roused several of her fellow megatraths by punching them in their sides. They growled as they rose to their feet, and lumbered to the enormous doors of the citadel. Other megatraths pulled the doors open, and the horde plodded down the ramp.

Oganna stepped onto the walkway. Neneila the viper draped over her shoulders and lashed a forked tongue into the air. The megatraths thudded into the city and spread through the streets, poking in and out of buildings. Another line of them passed her and followed the first group into the streets. Oganna craned her neck to see the entirety of the citadel.

The stone structure rose majestically, almost touching a dark cloud. She returned inside of it and gazed around the interior. At the stairs she lifted her foot to the first step. It was twice as large as the ones back at her father's house.

"I see what you are thinking, but be careful," Vectra said as she loomed next to her, her dark eyes probing the stairwell. "If there are any survivors they may be up there."

"Do not worry, I'll be fine. I have my weapons

with me and you know that I can handle myself in a fight." Oganna climbed each of the stone steps to the second level, a wide-open room with a floor of stone blocks. No wonder the reinforced arches in the main chamber were necessary. Anything less and the ceiling below could not support the weight of this floor.

Continuing to the third level, she entered a broad hallway. To one side a wooden door with a heavy iron latch blocked her way. The latch was at eye level and quite thick. Perhaps for a giant it would have been doable to lift that latch, but it was beyond her strength.

Drawing Avenger from its sheath, she waited for it to turn crimson before thrusting it through the wood and cutting out a hole that was large enough for her to pass through. The room into which she now stepped turned out to be the giants' armory, and what an armory it was. Swords, ranging in size from six to nine feet long rested in velvet-lined, wooden cases along the walls. Each of the weapons shone like polished silver. The room smelled stale, as if it had not been opened for some time, and a layer of dust hung in the corners.

An assortment of spears and halberds hung at the far end, their shafts decorated with dyed bird feathers and silken streamers. Wooden shields covered in thick leather lined the left and right-hand walls, and a few maces lay on a table in the center. She imagined what it must have been like to see an army of giants wielding these weapons in battle. What a magnificent and terrible sight they must have made!

She left the armory and found more stairs

leading upwards. The steps brought her above the armory to the interior of the citadel's spire. It was breathtaking. Steel beams rose on all sides, crisscrossing one another to a great height before joining at the roof's peak, which stood at least a couple hundred feet. Along the interior of this structure another staircase snaked upward, its steps clinging to the inside walls as they circled the spherical interior. "Here we go," she said as the viper gaped at the ascent.

"Psst! Mistress, are you sure this is a good idea?" the creature ventured.

Oganna started to climb the stairs, grunting against the aches in her leg muscles. "Of course it's a good idea. Where else can I get a full view of the city?"

The viper tightened its grip around her arm and gulped. "If we fall. Psst, we go splat!"

Oganna laughed and continued the climb. There was a railing, but it rested just above her head, so she kept as close as possible to the wall in order to avoid the steps' edges.

As she climbed the stairs she gained a more intimate view of the awesome structure. The roof had been covered in some kind of metal plates. Steel reinforcements held it together. It took her a while to reach the top. Standing on that final step, she faced a metal door set up against the inside of the roof. Pushing the iron latch upward to open the door proved impossible, for it was exceedingly heavy. Instead she wedged her sword under it and broke the latch. She waited for the severed metal to fall away, then she opened the door with relative ease and stepped through onto an observation platform on the roof.

From this vantage point the city buildings looked like miniatures. The rising smoke from some of the buildings mixed with a steady rain to form a haze. The highway by which she had come to Netroth shot out of the valley to the hilly region beyond, where smoke still rose from some of the burned dwellings in that direction.

Bringing her attention back to the citadel, she examined the platform on which she stood. It circled the steeply inclined roof near the top of the spire. She walked to the opposite side of the observation platform and looked to the north. Things appeared to be much the same, except for the mountains that loomed in the distance. Smoldering, ruined buildings and slaughtered livestock dotted the landscape.

Just beyond the grass-covered terrain, a dark hill stabbed skyward. Try as she might she could not see it clearly, partly because it was so far away and partly because smoke rose from it at several points.

"Neneila, do you see that?" She pointed as best she could toward the distant dark hill. "Can you make out what that is?"

The creature squinted and stretched out its neck, then wrapped itself over her shoulders. "Psst! If only I could remember what happened to me after the spell took hold. Then I might know. After all, if it is your enemy that did this, then I was likely involved."

"Perhaps," Oganna said, and she left the platform, returning into the citadel. "Perhaps Vectra can help us find out what that is."

She descended into the citadel's main chamber and spoke to Vectra, describing as best she could what she'd seen from the platform. Vectra scratched her head. "Hmm, you say this hill that you saw was burning?"

"It appeared to be," Oganna said.

"It would take us too long to go there if you walk. I will carry you." Vectra hunkered to the floor and waited for Oganna to get on her neck.

After Oganna had climbed on, Vectra gathered her guards on the ramp. Then she raced north along the highway until she passed out of the city. The megatrath shook the rain out of its face as it ran. Oganna shielded her own face with her arm and her now-soaked clothes clung to her body.

They ignored the buildings that smoked around them and came within sight of the smoking, black hill. Broken pieces from machines of war littered the hills for as far as Oganna could see. A catapult and a giant crossbow, along with a few broken battering rams. Along with hand weapons and shields stood several trebuchets of extraordinary size, standing like sentinels in the wake of a battle.

The rain slackened, and the smoke rose thicker from the heap. Oganna turned up her nose as they approached. The stench of burning flesh overpowered her senses. Her horror intensified when Vectra began to tremble and growled a stream of curses. "Oganna, look. It is the giants. We have found them." The dark heap of tangled bodies of the giants stretched for a long distance. Their arms and legs stuck out from the pile, and a few scarce flames licked at their corpses. Women and children, warriors young and old. All of them lay together in death, their faces frozen in wild fear.

Oganna gritted her teeth, dismounted, and picked a child's doll out of the mud. Here lay the inhabitants of Netroth, slain without consideration of age, gender, or social standing. This was a massacre. She looked at the ground around the heap. Rage boiled in her heart, and she clenched her fists, drew out Avenger, and sent a wave of energy from her hand to the sky. "Before I leave this land, I swear that justice will be carried out upon whoever did this," she cried out. She turned to the milling megatraths. "The rain has all but quenched the flames. Burn this heap before the rotting flesh finishes poisoning the ground."

The creatures hesitated as they waited for Vectra to confirm the order.

But Vectra spun upon them and drove them toward the heap. "You heard her. Burn it!"

The megatraths drew in deep breaths and poured steady streams of fire on the bodies. The smoldering wood ignited, the flames wrapped around the heap, and before long the bloated funeral pyre roared heavenward.

THE TOLLING BELL

Upon returning to the citadel in Netroth, Oganna saw uncertainty in the megatraths' eyes. Their gazes were shifting back and forth between one another and the imposing structure that surrounded them. She understood how they felt, for she felt it too. They were camped inside of the great citadel, surrounded by thick walls of stone, and yet they were haunted by an unsettling fear of an unknown enemy that had brutally wiped out an entire city. What kind of an enemy was her father going to have to deal with here? They must have been strong in order to besiege and take a city as great as this one.

Vectra shivered in her hide and forced a smile at her companions. "Don't look so depressed, my brothers and sisters. We are safe. We have food to last several more days." She threw wood into the fireplace and shot a lazy flame into the midst of it. "And we have heat." The others gathered around, and soon the warmth from so many bodies filled the massive room, driving away the dampness.

First one megatrath and then another brought more wood to the fire until it roared. They heaped the excess wood to the side of the fireplace and settled down for a nap while Oganna and Vectra stayed alert. They did not want to be caught unprepared if the enemy showed himself.

Suddenly the citadel doors burst open, and a blast of wet air surged into the citadel. Oganna and the megatraths shot to their feet. She half-expected to face an army of foes. Instead a lone giant stumbled inside. He was dressed in ornate armor, and a tattered yellow cape hung from his broad shoulders. He leaned on a longsword that he held in his right hand. His eyes blazed with hatred and blood ran from his many wounds. On his head rested a silver crown with a large diamond set in its face.

His eyes darted about. Pain twisted his expression. He staggered toward them and lowered his head, spreading his legs wide and holding his sword with both hands. "Wh-what? How did you come to be here? I know none of your faces, nor am I familiar with your race. If you follow the wizard, then stand ready because you will fall by my sword!"

Vectra growled and the other megatraths pressed closer to the giant.

"I have given all of you fair warning. Now speak!" His eyes rolled back into his head, and he took a ragged breath before shaking his head and refocusing his eyes.

Gazing up at the imposing figure, Oganna stepped forward and laid her sword on the floor. "If you are not here to harm us, then let there be peace between us." As she spoke she edged closer to him.

In a deft motion he grasped her by the throat. Vectra rushed forward, clamped her claws on the man's arm, and forced him to release his hold. His head drooped, his eyes rolled back in their sockets, and he collapsed.

Oganna bent over, grabbed her throat, and gagged. "Whew! Thanks, Vectra, he has a fist of iron."

They laid the giant on the floor by the fire, and Oganna unbundled the tent that she had brought along. She glanced at the citadel doors. They remained open after the giant's unexpected arrival. "I would close those doors if I were you," she said to a nearby megatrath.

The creature lumbered to the entrance, closed them, and leaned its bulk against them.

As Oganna looked at the giant, she gasped. "What in Subterran happened to this man? It looks as though someone sliced him all over with razor blades!" Dried blood caked the man's body, and fresh blood ran from numerous deep gashes in his skin. In several places his bones lay exposed.

"This man must be someone of great importance," Vectra said as she helped Oganna set up the tent and slide the giant inside. Oganna had intended to set up the tent for her own privacy, but giving it to him . . . it felt right. "Look at his crown. That is no mere decoration. It is possible that the throne we found is his," Vectra whispered.

Oganna slipped the weighty ornament off his head and set it aside. "I must tend to his wounds. Otherwise, he will soon die."

Vectra held up a hand of caution and said, "Take care, Princess. This giant could be the very villain that we have come to find."

"No. I don't think so. Our enemy would not have come alone to this place if he had won the battle. However, if I can heal this man, then he should be able to tell us what is going on around here," Oganna said.

The megatrath chortled. "And what if he doesn't know? What if we are chasing a ghost that has long since departed to a different land, and there is no villain to be found?"

"Then we have come here for nothing, and the answer to the mystery of the winged men and viper attacks lies elsewhere. But I do not believe this devastation is coincidence," Oganna mused. "Rather I think that we have stumbled upon the place my father is seeking. All that remains is to find and deal with the sorcerer."

"An admirable analogy, Oganna, and I hope you are right. I too would like to deal with the perpetrator. I'd like to give him a piece of my mind, a sniff of my vapor, a scalding by fire, and I'd like to tear him limb from limb with my claws." Vectra gave one of her horrible grins as she finished speaking.

As the megatrath spoke, Oganna set to work carefully cleaning and sewing the unconscious giant's wounds. "Vectra, would you send out some of your guards in search of drinking water? There must be wells in this city and barrels that they can use to bring the water back here. I will need lots of it." As her friend moved away, Oganna said, "And tell them that any clean cloths they can find will be greatly appreciated."

"Hmm, will there be anything else?" Vectra raised her eyes in mock sarcasm. "Perhaps you want them to find a certain type of food as well?"

"That would be nice, thank you." Oganna laughed and drew the needle through the giant's skin, pulling together the sliced sections of his flesh.

Over the next couple of hours Vectra sent search parties into Netroth, and they brought back all that Oganna had required and more. They gathered more wood for the fireplace, too. Soon the citadel felt nice and toasty. It had been a long day for the mega-traths. As the room heated, the flames glistened off their hides and they fell contentedly asleep.

Oganna stayed awake, tending to the giant's wounds. Several cuts proved too deep and ragged for her to sew together. These she laid her hands on and probed with her mind to find that source of extraordinary strength and power within her blood. There! She pulled with her mind, feeding off the strength and healing with the powers therein. Energy surged through her and blossomed, its aura enveloped her, and the giant's deep wounds healed. The exposed flesh turned pink, and the skin closed over it.

Exhausted by her labors, she sat back. "Now, Mr. Giant, your body must heal the remainder on its own." She rose and left the tent. Within the shadow of Vectra's bulk she unrolled her bedding. The firelight flickered cheerily as she lay down.

The megatrath stuck her snout in Oganna's face. "You don't trust him, do you?"

The viper slid from around Oganna's neck and onto the blanket. "Psst! What do you take my mistress for? A fool? She won't trust unless she knows she can." The creature slipped out its tongue in a derogatory gesture. "Psst! You may have a large brain, megatrath, but sometimes I wonder if you know how to use it properly."

"True, I do not trust easily," Oganna said. She folded her hands behind her head. "I don't trust the giant because I do not know him." She chuckled as she continued. "Would you trust him if you were my size?"

The megatrath grunted, settled her head to the floor, and fell asleep, breathing rhythmically. Oganna lay down as well while the serpent remained on top of her blanket. She stared up at the citadel's stone walls. The flames in the fireplace threw a flickering light over the interior. These sturdy walls were a comfort to her, standing watch as a guardian, never resting. Needing none.

In her mind's eye she saw night falling over the city of Netroth. It was full of haunting sounds that echoed down the abandoned streets and traversed the empty buildings. She saw a knife that had never finished cutting a loaf of bread, and a child's doll neglected and alone. The entire city dressed in black, mourning its children, mothers, and fathers. In its sorrow a city bell tolled eerily in the darkness.

She opened her eyes, stunned. The bell was tolling! On its own? She doubted it. She glanced at the doors to the ramp. Two megatraths, sleeping soundly, were resting against them. If someone tried to sneak in they would be unable to. Vectra jerked up her head, then curled tighter around Oganna. "Don't worry, princess. Nothing will happen to you on my watch," the megatrath promised.

The bell ceased tolling. A restless megatrath stirred, rose, and stoked the fire before curling up again. Oganna glanced up at Vectra. The bell tolled again. Had the conquerers of the city returned? She looked again at the citadel above her. They were safe within these walls . . . she hoped.

In the middle of the night she still could not calm herself. She felt as if a pair of eyes was spying on her and her alone. She glanced at the citadel doors and the door to the giant's throne. No one was in sight, and she breathed a sigh of relief. She turned toward the fireplace, and a man's hand clamped over her mouth.

"Shhh, dragon child. It is only I." Specter released his hold on her mouth and stood before her, shimmering in and out of sight. "It took me a long while to find you. You are becoming quite skilled at protecting yourself," he said with a smile.

"What are you doing here?" she whispered.

"I am looking out for you, little one. And a quest of my own has intertwined with my duty to the dragon and you." He stepped close to the fire and stretched his hands toward the blaze.

Oganna gazed upon the warrior. How in Subterran he had managed to slip in unnoticed was beyond her. But he was here now, and her heart had slowed its wild pounding. Somehow, even though she was surrounded by creatures as large as dragons, this invisible guardian allayed her fears more than they. "What do you mean by a quest of your own?" she asked.

He stared into the flames and for a time said nothing. Then he closed his eyes. "The wizard who placed your father under a spell is familiar to me. I have waited for so long to meet him again, and now your path and his have crossed. If they cross again, I will be ready."

Turning to her, Specter looked at her with bright eyes and a grim expression. "I need to ask that, if you come across him, you leave him to me. Nothing would please me more than to end his evil."

"But," she said with a frown, "you don't have any powers. Do you? If he serves the powers of evil then I should face him, not you."

"Please," he whispered, "I will ask nothing else of you. Only this one thing do I require. Leave the wizard Auron to me."

Something about his manner made her cringe. "You mean to kill him, don't you?"

Specter turned back to the fire.

"If you do face a wizard then you will die," Oganna said. She shook her head. "No, I'm sorry, but I cannot let you do that."

"What makes you so sure that I would die in combat with him? Did I not protect your mother and your aunts all the days of their youth? I stood with them when they faced a witch and a wizard." He gazed over his shoulder, meeting her eyes. "You are young, Oganna. Trust that I know what is best. For I would do nothing to harm you and everything to protect you. I always have."

"But you wouldn't care if you are harmed in the process," she pointed out. Then she frowned as the viper blinked its eyes. The viper glanced at Specter and popped its eyes wide open. Its mouth opened in a little scream, but Oganna clamped her fingers over its mouth and put a finger to her lips. "Silence, Neneila! He is with us. Now go back to sleep."

The viper took another look at the cloaked warrior with the scythe blade in his hand. Then it slithered out of sight under the blanket.

Oganna burned her gaze into the eyes of her silent guardian. ""You don't care if you live or die. Do you?" she asked. "But know this! I do."

At last he dropped to one knee and looked at her with a smile. "I have lived two lifetimes, child. I have seen the ancient fall and this generation rise. Long ago a great sin was committed against a pupil of mine, and today you live in a darkening world that is a direct result of that event." He waved his hand at the sleeping megatraths, the citadel, and the doors. "These creatures would not be here, and this land would not have fallen if I had long ago seen the coming evil. Everything is a direct result of what this wizard did a day that was long, long before you, your father, or even his father were born. Auron knows this, and I must bring him to justice!" He clenched his fist and vanished.

"Specter?" She called his name softly over and over again. But he did not respond, and when she spread her other senses into the surrounding room she found nothing except for the megatraths and Neneila. With a resigned sigh she laid down to sleep.

WRATH OF THE MEGATRATH

The heat from the fireplace felt good on Ogan-na's back as she opened the tent flap and peered inside. The giant was lying in there, wrapped in cloth bandages from head to toe. He stirred from his sleep and groaned. His eyes blinked open, and he raised himself on his elbows before calling out in a weak voice, "Hello? Is anyone here?"

She stepped into the tent, gave him a warm smile, and rested a hand on his shoulder. "Easy there, you are still very weak," she said. "You've been out for two days, and your wounds are still healing."

He gazed around the tent, observing that she had neatly stacked his crown, cape, and boots in one corner. His sword lay next to him. "Where am I?" he asked.

"You are in my tent." She knelt beside him and dipped a cloth into a nearby bucket of water.

"Lean forward please."

The giant glanced at her face. Then he bent forward. She wiped the cold cloth over his forehead and felt his temperature with the back of her hand. "Your wounds are healing better than I had expected them to."

The giant relaxed his tense arms. He stretched his shoulders and looked at her with eyes as soft as a bed of Night Grass on a cool evening. Even though he was only sitting up, he was a little taller than Oganna was when she was standing. He had shoulder-length brown hair, a handsome face, and muscles like wrought iron. "Well, young lady, it appears to me that you have saved my life, and I don't even know your name."

She felt her cheeks flush and she smiled. "I am Oganna, princess of the Hemmed Land."

"Strange," he murmured. "I have never heard of a land by that name, and I thought that I knew of all within reach of my kingdom. But it is my pleasure to meet you, Princess. Now would you mind telling me where I am?"

Wondering if his injuries had affected his memory, Oganna returned his gaze. "You are in Netroth. Don't you remember?"

"But I was entering—" He closed his eyes and bit his lip, holding his head in his hands. "The day before last I came into the city. I was entering the doors to Ar'lenon when—"

"Ar'lenon?" She hesitated. What was Ar'lenon? But of course he must have meant the fortress. "Is that what you call this citadel? Ar'lenon?"

"We are in the citadel?" he asked.

She solemnly nodded and waited to see his reaction.

A relieved smile curled his lips, and he clenched his fist. "Then Ar'lenon does still stand. Despite everything, it still stands." He sighed. "Forgive me, I have not answered your question. And yes, this mighty citadel is called Ar'lenon."

Oganna smiled back. "It is a remarkable structure. Did your people build it?"

He skirted her question. "What does it matter now? They are . . . gone."

She wrung the cloth, returned it to the bucket, then stood. "I have told you my name, Sir. Will you tell me yours?"

"You may call me Gabel," he said simply.

"It is a pleasure to meet you, Gabel." She curtsied. "I couldn't help noticing that you wore a crown, and your cape is sewn from a rather rich material. Are you the lord of this land?"

"Yes, I am. I was. But now I am nothing. The land has been destroyed, and no one remains alive. I—" His lips quivered. "I am all that is left among the living in Netroth."

She could tell that he was struggling with memories that she could not share. He wanted to appear strong, but the man inside lost the battle, and he wept. She reached out and embraced his neck. "It's all right," she whispered. "You are among friends now and thus you are safe. Do not be ashamed to cry."

Gabel sobbed, then choked and cleared his throat, shaking his head. He lay back, growling. "Oh, Razes! I will make you pay for the evil you have done to our people. You will beg for mercy at the end and regret the day that you slaughtered the innocent and brought ruin to my land. I will make you pay with your life for this evil." He looked at her, speaking again with strength. "This war turned into a slaughter because we were betrayed by one of my own people. His name is Razes and he sought out evil counsel in the distant east. He returned with winged men to fight for him." Gabel blinked his eyes against his pain. Weakened, he lay back and fell into a fitful sleep.

Oganna left the tent, tiptoeing so as not to disturb him. "He is asleep," she said before Vectra could ask.

"That I guessed," the megatrath grunted, and she carved a circle in the stone floor with her claw.

Oganna reached down, and Neneila slithered around her arm. She held the viper in front of her face and lightly stroked its head. The viper closed its eyes. She looked past the viper into Vectra's enormous face. "Did you hear him ranting about the massacre?"

"Yes. Whomever this Razes character is, he must be bad news to incur such bitterness," Vectra said.

Oganna began to pace the floor. "On Gabel's word, Razes is responsible for butchering the inhabitants of this region. I suspect he is also the villain behind the attacks on the Hemmed Land. Gabel mentioned winged men fighting for Razes." She stood still and nodded in the tent's direction. "At least Gabel bears no hostility toward us. In fact he seems to feel indebted because we are caring for him. If Razes is enemy to us both, then we share a mutual problem. Perhaps when he is feeling stronger, Gabel will be able to tell us more."

Vectra cocked her head and listened to the monotonous sound of rain pummeling Ar'lenon's outer walls. Oganna kicked at a loose pebble on the floor and watched it roll over the stones. "The rain is not letting up, is it?" she commented.

The megatrath sighed. "Two days of constant downpour. I'm beginning to wonder if Yimshi will ever come out again. Surely this will delay your father as well." Twisting her head around, Vectra barked an order to one of her guards and gazed up one of the stairways that led into the spire of Ar'lenon. "If I was certain that those steps could hold my weight, I would go to that observation platform you told me about and stand watch. If Razes pummeled this city before, he might come back to search for survivors . . . and he might bring friends."

"Setting a watch up there wouldn't do much good," Oganna said. She set Neneila around her shoulders. "The climb is too high, and it would take a long time for you to come back down and warn us if you spotted trouble. Besides, if Razes came here he would have to come by way of the ramp and knock on the doors to find us."

"Then I will post guards on the ramp outside of the citadel doors," Vectra said. "At least then we will have warning if trouble comes."

Oganna thought for a moment. "That would be a risk. Anyone standing out there will present an inviting target."

"Nevertheless I am willing to take the risk. Besides, if anyone did attack, they would have to do so first from a distance, and our scaled hides are too thick for a mere arrow to pierce." Having thus decided, Vectra posted two megatraths on the ramp and set up a rotating schedule to change the guards frequently. "Do not worry, Princess." She curled up on the floor. "My bodyguards are more than capable of this task. They will not be caught by surprise.

Deep down Oganna hoped the megatrath was right. It would be a shame to lose two megatraths before a fight even began. Then again, maybe Razes would not return to Netroth. Even if he did, one hundred megatraths garrisoned within Ar'lenon posed a formidable force. She should stop worrying and just pray that her father arrived before Razes.

The next morning Gabel's face displayed more color. Oganna brought him oatmeal for breakfast, and he dug into the bowl with a vengeance. "Thank you so much for everything you have done for me." He grinned at her, and she laughed.

"It feels good to see you doing so well," Oganna said.

Vectra's enormous head poked through the tent flap. "How is he this morning?" Her question had been directed to Oganna, but then her dark eyes focused on the giant. "Oh, I see you are awake and feeling better now. Good!" She backed out of sight, and the flap fell back in place.

Gabel's eyes almost popped out of their sockets. "What was that?"

Oganna could not help it, she laughed aloud at his reaction. "That was a megatrath. Her name is Vectra, and she came with me to find out what is causing the viper and Art'en raids along my land's northern border."

He chuckled. "You keep interesting company, Princess."

"I prefer to think of it as making interesting friends. My father and I are very grateful to have the megatraths as allies," she replied. "They are fierce fighters. I fought them once, and I hope I will never have to do so again."

The man looked thoughtful as he stared at the tent flap. "How many of those creatures have you brought with you?"

She eyed him quizzically. "It would be more accurate to say that they brought me. But why do you ask?"

"Because if my enemy returns, he will try to kill you, too," Gabel said. "Razes is not a selective killer. He does it because he finds pleasure in making others suffer."

Oganna debated in her mind whether or not to press him further. Gabel had sustained significant injuries, yet he had been healing well and it was apparent that his great strength was returning. "Gabel, who is this enemy of yours?" she asked finally. "Tell me all you know so that I can make a fair judgment on what happened here."

"There is a lot to tell," he began wearily. He clenched his fist and looked into her eyes. "Where is my sword?"

In answer, she pointed to where it lay behind him. The weapon was longer than she was tall. "It is a wonderful piece," she said.

He clutched it to his chest, then relaxed his grip and lay it across his knees. "This sword has belonged to every king of Burloi since my distantly great-grandfather built this city and established the monarchy. From generation to generation it has passed from father to son as a symbol of our strength to deter those who would destroy us." He paused and lovingly eyed the blood-stained blade "But that was before Razes's rebellion."

"You mentioned him the other day, though only in passing. Who is this Razes?" She pulled away one of his bandages, saw that the wound was healing well, and smothered it with fresh salve.

Gabel eyed his injury as well. "You have the hands of a healer, little lady. I wish there was some way I could reward you."

"You can." She sat back. "You can tell me what happened here."

"Oganna. That is your name?" After she nodded he continued. "Razes is another giant, though younger than myself. When he was a youth I incorporated him into the Ar'lenon guard. But he was very ambitious and, desiring power, he led an uprising to dethrone me. It failed and I, in an attempt to show mercy, sent him into exile instead of to the guillotine as he deserved."

He gritted his teeth, then spat on the stones. "He and his followers fled Burloi and disappeared into the east. We thought they were gone for good. That was years ago. Then, a short while ago, Razes returned from the east. He was not the same youth that had left us. He had acquired a terrible weapon that gave him seemingly unlimited power. With a word he was able to demolish a building and with another he could manipulate the weather. My people have long known that there are evil beings that practice magic, but we had never been face to face with such blatant proof of their abilities. Razes declared that he had become an agent of wizardry in our land and that this entitled him to whatever he desired. 'Those who resist will die,' he declared.

"The population split over loyalty to me and fear of the sorcery. Almost half of them sided with Razes because they believed that it would be useless to resist him. Burloi erupted in civil war. I fought hard for every part of my land, but he repeatedly defeated me." Gabel spread his arms and gazed up as if seeing through the tent fabric to the stone ceiling. "Here in Ar'lenon, I and my counselors made our last stand.

"In his wrath, Razes destroyed Netroth. Then he and his wizard apprentice, a human, ascended the great ramp. I fought them. However, Razes's companion also wielded magic. I was outmatched and defeated. They threw me off the ramp and the last thing I remember is seeing my remaining counselors struggling against them. If they had survived, I would know it, for they would never have abandoned me even if they had thought that I was a lifeless corpse." Striking the floor with his fist, he said, "Those who practice sorcery should be cast into fire!"

Oganna folded her hands in her lap. "There are powers for good and powers for evil. For example, some would call the things I can do magic." She held up her hand, and it pulsated white and blue light. "But all good things come from the Creator. I truly believe that, and that is what my father taught me."

"You . . . you are a sorceress," he gasped.

"I am not," she was quick to say. "I am the blood descendant of a dragon, and as such I have their seemingly magical abilities. It is my inheritance, and it is a blessing."

"Inheritance?" he asked.

"Yes, a parting gift from my mother. She died shortly after giving birth to me. In order for me to live she had to give up the life energy in her blood. But she paid that ultimate price to follow the Creator's will." She stood to her feet and parted a fold of her garment to reveal the crystalline blade of Avenger. "I made this weapon, using the power in my blood." Gabel looked skeptical, so she proceeded to draw the weapon and array herself in silver.

He drew in his breath. "Whew! What I wouldn't give to have a weapon that could do that." Chuckling, he glanced down at his sword. "Actually, there is a legend among my people that our northern brethren once had swords that could render them invisible and that there was no sorcery involved. So, I suppose, it is possible that, as you say, God can give his creatures special abilities."

Oganna nodded thoughtfully. "Sorcery draws on some kind of connection that is corrupted. Like the spirits of the cursed, or the energy of a demon. My teachers have told me some of how to discern the one from the other, and it is honestly terrifying. I think the difference with my power is that the Creator could take it away from me, because it is a gift." Oganna slid the Avenger back into its sheath and returned to her normal state. "We will talk more later, Gabel. Your wounds have not finished healing, so for now I want you to rest."

He leaned forward and lightly kissed her forehead. "For a normal-sized human you are quite interesting. I have enjoyed our discussion."

As she left the tent, Oganna glanced over her shoulder and shook her head with a sudden amused thought. "I can't help but wonder. How tall are you?"

"Last I measured?" He laid his head back and scratched his chin. "Ten feet plus two inches. Scurry along now, little lady. As you said, I should rest."

Oganna went to the fireplace. The viper untangled itself from a broken chair, slithered up her outstretched arm, and rested about her neck. "Psst! Mistress, when can we leave this place? In case you haven't noticed the megatraths' body odors are increasingly stronger."

Vectra lumbered over and nodded at the tent. "How is King Gabel doing?"

"He is doing a lot better. His wounds are healing well. He shouldn't need bed rest for much longer," Oganna said.

"Good, he seems like a nice man, and I would like to get to know him better." Vectra jerked up her head, and she stretched her neck toward the ceiling. "Did you hear that?"

"Hear what?" Oganna asked.

Vectra lumbered to the citadel doors, threw them open, and walked out on the ramp. The rain had stopped. "Do you hear it now, Oganna?"

"Hear what?" But the viper spoke into her ear, and she bit her lip. "The vipers are coming."

Vectra shook her head and stamped her feet in impatience. "No, no! Quit listening to that little creature for a moment, and you will hear something else." She swiveled her head toward the north, and Oganna gasped.

Over the valley's rim poured a dark flood of giant men. Their tramping resounded through Netroth's vacated streets, a terrifying unison of clanging armor, rattling shields, and stamping feet.

"I don't think—." Oganna was about to say that the enemy had not spotted them when a screech from behind made her duck just as an arrow shot over her head. She spun to find a winged man swooping through the moist air. "Never mind what I was about to say. They've found us. Come on, Vectra! You must go and warn the others."

Oganna slid the blade boomerang from under her belt and into her hand. A dozen Art'en dove from the dark clouds, joining the first. She threw the boomerang into their midst, watching its trajectory as it severed four of their heads before returning to her palm.

In the distance line upon line of armed giants descended into Netroth from the north. Like a wave they rolled into the city and onto its streets. Another winged man with a shield and a sword in his hands, swooped around Ar'lenon Citadel, his brown wings fanned out. He landed on the ramp and sprang at her.

"The Art'en will reign again," it hissed. "Die, human!" But it had landed between her and Vectra. The megatrath's clawed foot crushed the man's wings to his sides and raised him off the stone ramp. The Art'en struggled in the mighty grip of the megatrath.

"She will not die on my watch!" Vectra hissed back. Her mouth opened and clamped down on his midsection. Then she cast the Art'en off the ramp so that he fell into the city.

Oganna turned toward the sky and raised her

sword as two others spiraled to the ramp and rained blows upon her. They each bore a shield and a sword. She parried their blows and struck back in rapid succession until one of them slipped around behind her. She raised her boomerang to block his attack, but Vectra rolled into him. The megatrath's six legs worked methodically, tearing the Art'en into bloody pieces before she scorched with fire that which remained.

The other creature proved agile and a capable fighter. He dropped his weapons and avoided every thrust Oganna attempted. Then he kicked her jaw with his bare foot and smote her face with his wings so that she fell. "At last I have you," it cried as it grabbed for her neck.

In an instant, Vectra stood over her and smashed her fist into the creature's chest. "I don't think so," the megatrath growled. She skidded around and pulled him back by the wings, then held him suspended in the air.

Oganna ran back to the citadel doors and shouted to the two megatraths standing guard. "Hurry, that army is getting nearer, and they far outnumber us. We must get these doors closed." She turned and looked for Vectra.

The megatrath leader gave the Art'en a rigorous shake. "So you like heights?" she screamed into his face, and the Art'en cringed. "I'll give you a height to remember me by," Vectra said. Before Oganna could say anything to stop her, Vectra barreled into the citadel with her captive in hand. Without thought to the damage she was causing, she punched through the stairway entrance and the stones crumbled away, leaving a space large enough for her to pass through. There was just enough time for Oganna to grab onto Vectra's tail and vault onto her neck.

Vectra rushed up the stairs as if her life depended upon it. In her fury she did not heed Oganna's protests. The ascent, which had taken Oganna a long time, lasted for what seemed like only moments. Vectra burst onto the observation platform and screamed her victory to the encroaching enemies before breaking her captive's wings and tossing him to his death. His body crashed onto a roof far, far below and rolled onto the street.

Art'en swarmed through the air toward the platform, screeching and clawing at the wind. They ascended and circled Oganna and the megatrath before drawing bows and arrows. A hail of arrows sped through the air. Oganna dismounted. Vectra stood in between the arrows and her, and the projectiles bounced off Vectra's scales.

The Art'en flipped through the air. Several landed on the platform and a couple on Vectra's back. They drew swords, stabbing at the megatrath. Vectra bellowed the louder and caught a couple of them with her forearms. A tornado of flames issued from her mouth, turning the others into living torches. After breaking those in her arms, she threw them over the platform. Their screams echoed into the city and faded.

"Vectra!" Oganna beat her fist into the creature's neck to get her attention. "Enough of this. We have to get back to the others." The creature hunkered down, and she remounted.

Another Art'en swooped over Vectra's head,

and she swiped her claws at it, but missed. The creature hovered just out of her reach.

"Oganna, now! Decimate them," Vectra demanded.

More Art'en dove from above. Oganna gritted her teeth. Vectra was right. It was time to show the enemy what they were capable of. She raised Avenger and fed it her power and rage. Electrical current enveloped its blade, knifed into the air, and struck the Art'en. They froze in the air, their feathers starting to smoke, and their hair stood on end before they crashed into the roof. They grabbed at the roof tiles but rolled off and fell into the city.

BATTLE FOR AR'LENON

Far below on the ramp to Ar'lenon the stones appeared to be changing color, starting with the end touching the city streets and progressing upward toward the citadel doors. Grays and browns shifted into hues of blue, black, and rusty red. Vectra and Oganna both looked down from their lofty citadel view. "Oganna, what is that?"

"Psst!" Neneila's forked tongue tickled Oganna's ear. "I was right. My fellow vipers that are still under the wizard's influence are coming."

After one more glance, Oganna clung tighter to the megatrath's neck and leaned forward. "Come on, Vectra. We have to get down there, now!"

Vectra lowered her head and smashed through the stone walls of the citadel. Oganna cringed as shattered stones sprayed over her face and body. The megatrath thrust the front of its body through the hole. Its rear feet held to the platform while its head and forearms angled dangerously into the gaping heart of Ar'lenon. The stairs curved some twenty feet beneath them.

"No, Vectra, don't," Oganna said.

But the megatrath leaped, dropping them through the massive structure. As the walls streamed by, Oganna gritted her teeth and stiffened her body around the creature's neck. Landing with a thud that shook but did not break the massive stone steps, Vectra raced down the remaining stairs. As they careened around the structure's interior, Oganna prayed that she would not fall off as she held on for her life. Every jolt of Vectra's body threatened to throw them into the heart of Ar'lenon and to certain death. They dropped beneath the spire and descended the next stairs, passed the armory, and jumped into the main chamber wherein they'd encamped.

The megatraths rose on their thick legs and shook their hides. Vectra rumbled in her throat and flashed her bloodied claws in their faces. "Today let this city be shaken with the cries of our victory. Let this citadel ring with the battle we bring to the treasonous giants, the Art'en, and the vipers. Teach them to never again oppose a megatrath in battle!"

Roars of approval deafened Oganna, forcing her to cover her ears with her hands until the megatraths quieted. Hisses filled room, and she turned as vipers slipped through the arrow slits along the citadel walls nearest the ramp and swarmed inside.

"Burn them out!" Vectra screamed as she rose on her rear legs to an imposing height. Flames sprang from her tooth-ridden mouth and splashed against the arrow slits, turning squirming vipers into blackened, smoking skeletons. From either side of her the megatraths lumbered forward, opened their jaws, and took turns burning the vipers until they had blackened the ancient walls.

Oganna sprang to the floor, her sword swiveling in her hand. Its blade turned crimson, and her glowing silver dress replaced her former garment. The megatraths growled, rumbled in their throats, and threw open the heavy doors. She stepped into the doorway, drew on her powers, and blasted the ramp before her.

A mass of desert vipers slithered around and over one another to reach the citadel. They covered the ramp knee-deep in a grotesque writhing mass.

"Wipe them out before they get inside," Oganna called. She advanced with the megatraths lined up behind her. Everywhere she aimed, her sword sprayed fire upon the vipers. Megatraths flanked her, Vectra to her right, and another to her left. They added their flames to hers until half the length of the ramp had been charred black and the air smelled like steam and wet, burned wood. Before long many of the vipers had receded from before her, disappearing into the maze of ruined buildings in the city.

But in the streets of Netroth the wizard's army was taking up positions to assault the citadel. With the vipers out of the way, the giants now plowed into the streets, a thick mass of humanity that seemed to increase in number with every moment. They raised their shields and advanced toward the ramp.

Oganna took her boomerang in hand again. She drew back her arm and threw the crystalline weapon with all her might. It shot in a long arc, descended through the giants' ranks, and lopped off several heads before it returned to her hand. Oganna resisted the urge to vomit when she felt and smelled the slick of thick red blood that now covered the crystalline boomerang. It had done its work well, but bloody work it truly was.

Next to Oganna, Vectra shook her head as if she was struggling to stay awake. Then she stumbled, shaking her head again. The creature collapsed beside her and six other megatraths fell behind her. Vipers emerged again from their hiding places beneath the ramp, swarming over the megatrath's bodies.

"No!" With a single thought Oganna reached out her hand and willed destruction on the vipers. Balls of energy gathered on her palm and she shot them against the ramp, blasting it with such force that the enormous stones trembled.

Fearless and angry, she raised Avenger and charged down the ramp. The standing megatraths roared and raced passed her. They lowered their heads and spun into the first rows of giants, sending the large men flying over their companions' heads. Oganna blasted the ramp with balls of energy. The glow in her hands spread up her arms, and most of the vipers perished by her hand.

Vectra's side heaved, her nostrils quivered. Oganna knelt at her side and laid a hand on the creature's cooling body. She had to do something, but what? The poison had rooted itself in the creature's blood. She could sense it and the weight of death that it was inviting.

The giants lowered spears and pressed upon

the megatraths, forcing them back to the ramp. Time was running out. Oganna raced to the ramp's base and pulled aside a couple of the megatraths, then she pointed up the ramp. "Bring those wounded into a circle around me," she commanded them. The megatraths bowed to her and barreled up the ramp. They dragged each of their sickened companions into a circle, and Oganna stepped inside and raised the Avenger.

As she held the sword in her hands, a pillar of smoke fell into the circle, and the specter of Death congealed before her. His bashed skull peered at her from beneath his cavernous hood. He raised his scythe with his only arm. She froze. Terror seized her like the morbid cold of a plague.

The Reaper stabbed his blade into a fallen megatrath, and his black robe swung around his skeleton legs. The megatrath's body convulsed, and its eyes glazed.

"You vile creature!" Oganna screamed, and she ran forward and swept Avenger's blade from the Reaper's head to his foot.

The Reaper stood his ground, his jaws open in a soundless laugh as her blade cut through him without so much as touching him.

"No, no, no," Oganna whispered, and she drew back, stunned.

The giants grappled with the megatraths at the ramp's base. They sank their huge blades into the creatures' bodies and speared their sides. Two megatraths roared and threw themselves into the giants' midst. The giants speared them also and marched over their corpses with a shout that rang in her ears.

The remaining megatraths, except for the two with her on the ramp, tried to stem the giants' advance. But one by one the giants cut them down.

Deep down Oganna realized that the battle could not be won. As she turned to face Death, she was powerless to stop him. His bashed in skull, a gift from her father, grew back as his blade sucked the dying breaths from the megatrath. He was using the dead to restore his grisly strength.

As she stared helplessly, a figure coalesced between her and the Reaper, a figure that held another scythe in its hand. Specter's gray cloak shimmered as he faced Death. "At last we meet again," Specter said as he swung his blade toward the Reaper's whole arm.

With a quick twist, Death pulled its scythe out of the megatrath, and floated to the side. The two scythe blades clashed together. Specter dropped to the ground, spun, and kicked the Reaper's feet from under it. The specter of death fell, and Specter crushed his boot into its ribs.

"Dragon child, tend to the megatraths," Specter ordered. He fell to the stones as the Reaper pulled his legs from under him, but Oganna knew that he had spoken to her. Her eyes followed him as he rolled across the stone ramp, grappling with the dark being. He tumbled over the ramp's side, pulling Death with him.

Oganna focused on the megatraths. Back in the desert arena Starfire had drawn the poison from her body and saved her life, but how had she done it? Oganna held out her hand, palm up, just as she'd seen Starfire do. She closed her eyes for an instant to strengthen her focus. When she opened them, she knew what she must do.

She pointed her sword at the sky and reached out with all her strength to the heavens. Thunder rumbled, and then lightning crackled before it split the air. Another bolt of lighting followed, spiked toward her, and fastened itself to Avenger's blade as if the sword was a lightning rod. The portion of clouds directly overhead parted, and Yimshi's warm rays poured through onto Oganna and the wounded. Avenger's blade glistened in the sunlight, and absorbed the tremendous energy the storm unleashed.

Oganna trembled under the force of it. The energy coursed through her body, igniting her blood like fire. It caused an intense pain like she had never experienced before, where the pain started beneath her breasts and spread through her skin. But the blood of dragons was strong enough and she held her place.

Tendrils of electricity spiked from her crimson blade and latched onto the prone megatraths. The poison drained from their bodies, forming a sphere of venom above her hand. Their life forces were restored. Against all visible odds, the megatraths rose to their feet and shook themselves awake.

She felt a thrill pass down her spine as the clouds continued to clear in the wake of her miracle. "Rise, my friends," she told the megatraths. "Let us send retribution upon these vermin." Thereupon she spun around, the sphere of venom hovering above her hands. Of its own accord, Avenger slid into its sheath. She lifted the sphere and flung it into the oncoming giants, and it burst like an egg on a giant's helmet, splattering its poisonous contents over the enemy lines.

Vectra and the other megatraths rose on their rear four legs and clawed the air with their other two, roaring at the enemy. But Oganna focused cold eyes on the assembling giants. They had halted as if waiting for someone. She only hoped they weren't waiting for Gabel's enemy, Razes.

Their ranks parted, and a human strode through the gap to the ramp's base. Compared to the giants he at first seemed small, but as he approached Oganna saw that he was not. He was clean-shaven and dark-featured. Scars spider-webbed over his face. Unlike the giants, who were decked out in heavy plated armor, he wore only chain mail to protect his head, neck, and shoulders. His pants were pitch-black leather, and an equally black plate covered his chest. He was carrying a curious weapon. It had a handle the length of a crowbar with dual serrated blades that speared out from either end. He walked over the dead megatraths and stepped onto the ramp, gripping the leather-handled weapon with both hands. A staff with a dark orb at its head was strapped to his back.

Oganna held her breath. The effort it had taken for her to draw raw energy from the sky had taxed her strength. She needed rest. But she rebuked herself. Rest would not come any time soon. She might as well settle in and pray that she and the surviving megatraths could withstand this onslaught. She glanced again at the man's weapon and hoped he couldn't handle it as proficiently as her father handled the sword of the dragon.

A sneer curled the dark-haired man's lips. "A

girl? Ha! Battles have no places for women."

The viper reared its head and slicked its tongue at him. "Psst! Get closer leather-brain, and I'll stick my fangs into you."

"So, I see that you are in the habit of keeping snakes," he scoffed. "My master also enjoys their company. They can be . . . useful . . . for the dirty work. Maybe after I show you a trick or two in combat techniques my master will see fit to give you some lessons of his own."

She searched the crowding giants' faces. "Your master. Ah, you must mean Razes. I know of one particular individual that is not too happy with him."

For a moment the man faltered, then he narrowed his eyes at her. "I don't know how you know my master's name, little waif. But I'll soon show you that making light of him is not a wise course of action."

The giants charged up the ramp and around her. They collided with the megatraths while the man sprinted toward her. Vectra would have to fight the giants alone this time.

The man swung his double-sword. Oganna parried and followed through with a thrust at his abdomen. He also parried, but she swung around, drawing her boomerang, and sliced it along his arm.

As the man's blood oozed from the cut, the viper sprang from Oganna's neck and inflicted its deadly bite on his neck. "Ssssweet revenge," the viper slurred in his ear. "Now you taste death from the bite of one of your master's victims." It swung around his neck and sprang back to Oganna.

The wizard stabbed at Oganna but she sidestepped his blade. His blades whirled expertly in his hands, and he was adept at keeping her off balance. Nimbly she avoided him, letting him wear himself out and allowing the poison to do its work. He cursed profusely and stumbled back. "You are insignificant beside my master. He will have vengeance, and beneath his fury you will fall," he promised.

Not bothering to answer, she drew back her arm and thrust Avenger's blade through his leg. "Mark what I say," the villain spat. His eyes grew bloodshot, and he dropped to his knees. "You think you're strong. You think you can win? The battle has not even begun." Drawing the staff from his back, the man held the sphere against his body, and his flesh closed around his wounds.

But Oganna kicked his head, and as he reeled from the blow she held Avenger's point to his throat. "I could kill you, Auron. I recognize you now. You were responsible for my father's insanity. I recognize your presence in my mind."

He cackled. "Truly the powers of darkness are harnessing Subterran for me and those like me." He raised himself enough to spit on her blade.

Oganna had to fight the urge to drive the blade through his foul neck. She wanted to. Oh, she wanted to end the misery he had caused and that he might cause again if given the opportunity! But she had made Specter a promise. A promise she would not break. "With God as my witness, I must save this duel for someone else," she said as she twisted the blade in his skin, drawing blood. "Specter will deal with you. Your fate is in his hands." Then she kicked the side of his head as hard as possible. His body went limp, and his eyes closed.

She glanced at his scarred face as she held her blade inches from him. What a waste! A surge of hate for the enemy poured into her heart, but she suppressed the feeling before it took root in her soul. Hate, it was the mother of great wickedness and she would not give in to it.

All around her the battle for Ar'lenon raged. The megatraths rolled into the midst of the giants' forces, struck with their tails and claws, threw vapors and fire, yet they were heavily outnumbered and began to lose ground. Oganna retreated up the ramp with them.

"We cannot continue like this," Vectra growled above the battle's fray. She blew a weak flame and coughed. "We must slow their advance."

Oganna raised Avenger and sprinted into the advancing giants. She slashed two giants' legs and, as they fell, pierced her blade through another's breastplate into his heart.

Vectra swung her tail into the giants, killing two more. She whipped it back, stabbing its boney point into a giant's abdomen. Another megatrath rose to a great height on its hind legs and fell upon the giants, raking them with its claws. The remaining megatraths poured a mixture of flames and vapor, funneling it down the ramp to incinerate more of the giants. Then they charged down the ramp.

Oganna stood alongside of her monstrous allies, and she struck down giants on every hand. But even though dozens fell, there were always more to take their place. Thousands of them had filled the city. They were yelling at one another and pushing past each other for a part in the fight. They poured through Netroth's northern gates and flooded through the streets. Oganna slashed a giant's arm, then ducked as another jabbed his spear at her. He missed and the spear's head stuck into the street. Its shaft, as large as a sapling tree, quivered from the force of the blow.

As Oganna struggled to maintain her ground, the giants pulled down several megatraths. One giant rose above his fellows and swung a war hammer of tremendous size, bashing in several megatraths' skulls.

"Vectra, we cannot win this battle," Oganna cried out. She blasted energy from her hand, killing another giant. "Help me onto your neck."

The creature knocked down several giants that stormed between them. She lowered her head and sent fire issuing from her mouth into the enemy ranks. "Climb on now. Quickly!" Vectra roared as she slashed at their nearest enemies.

As Oganna straddled the megatrath's neck, Vectra stood again to her full height. Oganna could now see over the milling heads of the giants in the streets. She pulled out her boomerang. With all her strength she flung it at the level of their necks. It spun through the masses and decapitated a dozen or more giants. It arced through the air and returned to her hand light as a feather, though soaked afresh in blood. She secured it under her belt. Other giants were getting too close to Vectra and, in such tight quarters, the boomerang was less than effective.

She held Avenger with both hands and dug her knees into Vectra's scales to maintain balance.

Yelling for all they were worth, they charged toward the giants, Vectra blowing fire and Oganna striking with her sword. They left a mass of wounded and dying giants in their wake and finally a number of them turned to flee from the attack.

One braver giant swung a sword at Vectra's side, and as Oganna blocked him with Avenger, she braced for the impact. The sword he was using had to be at least eight feet long. He pulled back and attacked again. This time she fed her power into her sword. Avenger's blade became almost invisible, and when it met the enemy's blade, it cut it in half. Her weapon flamed, and the attacker retreated into the sea of other giants.

Several giants managed to separate another megatrath from its fellows. With halberds, swords, and battle hammers they pummeled it. Oganna directed Avenger's blade in their direction and sent out a devastating fire that washed over their backs and left them screaming and burning alive. Still, she had been too late to save the megatrath and it fell.

Vectra rumbled deep in her chest and snapped her jaws at her fellows. "Everyone get into the citadel. Now!" She stood alone with Oganna on her neck. Her claws opened giants' arms, and she ripped their bodies apart as her faithful guards raced up the ramp into Ar'lenon. Oganna counted the survivors. There were only fifty of them left.

Vectra drove the giants back from the entrance to the ramp with a cloud of vapors, then spun on her rear four legs, and dashed up to the citadel. The megatraths met them at the doors. Once they were inside, they closed them and barricaded the entrance. Oganna wiped her brow and dismounted. "This battle is lost unless we get reinforcements," she gasped.

Vectra heaved a sigh. "Even if they did come, I doubt they could break through those lines to rescue us. No, I think we are on our own."

Oganna did not want to admit that, but it seemed to be the truth. But she said to herself, "Father, if you are coming, please hurry! We need you. We are dying here."

* * *

Ilfedo patted his Evenshadow's neck. "Whoa, boy." He sat up in the saddle and wiped his sweaty palm on his trouser leg. He would be glad to get out of the desert heat. Ahead of him lay a line of green hills, a welcome sight after the rocky wastes behind him. He held his saddle horn with one hand and looked in the opposite direction. "What do you think, Ombre? Journey's end?"

Ombre smiled, but as he did, thunder clapped in the distance. His jaw dropped, and he pointed toward the sky. "Look!"

In the distance, over the green land, heavy rain clouds stretched into the north. The clouds split open and a beam of sunlight followed a bolt of lightning toward the ground, only to be hidden behind the hills.

The Warrioresses walked up between the men and gazed at the sight. "That storm is not of natural causes," Caritha said, and she swallowed hard. "The power of the heavens has been drawn upon."

Ilfedo turned her way. "Do you think that is the direction in which we should head?"

She did not immediately answer. She gathered

her sisters in a circle. "If we unite our minds, then we may learn more." She drew her rusted sword, and the others followed her example. The five weapons touched at the tips, and static energy buzzed along their blades. After a few moments the sisters drew back their weapons.

"Ilfedo!" Caritha cried out. She grabbed his arm and pointed north. "We must go now! Oganna and the megatraths are in serious danger. I sense a great darkness closing around her. We must get to her before it is too late!"

He spun in his saddle, drew the sword of the dragon, and held it above his head. Flames licked from the blade and a torrent of fire spat into the air. Before him, stretching back into the desert as far as he could see, line upon line of sword-wielding men cheered. Seven thousand voices shook the earth, for he had brought the collective might of the Hemmed Land with him.

The divisions stepped aside, clearing a highway through their midst for the Elite who had marched in the rear. One thousand men separated from the main force. In a steady, practiced line they marched forward. He raced his stallion to their lead. "Draw your swords, warriors of light!" The sweet sound of one thousand metal blades slipping out of their sheaths answered him. The desert rang with the warriors' shouts, and Yimshi glinted on their blades. A flash of light followed, and Ilfedo's magnificent army was arrayed in white armor. Their blades glowed.

Division after division of men stretched into the distance as far as he could see. Eight thousand men ready to follow his bidding. A tremor of reality struck him but he wheeled his mount and urged it toward the green hills.

He waved his hand at Ombre. "Will you do the honors, Commander?"

"Gladly," replied Ombre.

Behind Ilfedo, Ombre called out to the main body of troops, and a man clad in green armor brought forward the lord's personal mount. Midnight whinnied as Ombre slid onto his back and shouted at the top of his lungs, "Forward!"

The order passed from mouth to mouth with growing enthusiasm, and the army followed Ilfedo toward the rising terrain. He rode into the hills, stopping only a moment to cool his face in a stream and let his horse drink. The sound of eight thousand men tramping into the foreign land filled his ears as he left the stream and walked off alone into the hills. His army would need to refresh themselves at this stream before going farther.

The clouds continued to dissipate. He thought he smelled a whiff of smoke. He came to a rise taller than those around it and climbed to the top. Smoldering ruins stretched across the rolling hills, and in the distance a dark mass moved over the land, coming from the north and descending into a valley.

"Like ants swarming to their prey," Caritha uttered as she stepped up beside him. She laid a hand on his shoulder. "Oganna is in that city. I'm certain of it."

Ilfedo turned to her and sudden fear birthed a rage in his bones. "What? In there!" He could have asked her for verification. He could have questioned how she knew, or even if her dragon senses were really that sensitive. But he could see the certain impending doom written all over her face.

He dashed back to his Evenshadow and drew the sword of the dragon. The living fire lit him up like a match and then the flames returned into the blade, leaving him decked in the armor that only he wore. The warriors of light raced with him toward the valley. A line of warriors that seemed to stretch endlessly in either direction. He raised his sword and wheeled his stallion before them.

"March, men! March!" shouted their captains. Their enthusiastic cheers deafened him, and the warrioresses stepped up beside him. They drew their swords and walked toward the main highway. In the distance the din of battle grew. Ilfedo dug his heels into the Evenshadow's flanks.

Patience was no longer a virtue.

THE ULTIMATE SACRIFICE

The heavy double doors trembled as the giants tried to break inside Ar'lenon. The surviving megatraths shook their bloodstained hides. Oganna massaged her sword arm. As sore as it was, how would she handle another assault if the giants broke down the doors? Could she and the megatraths hold them back?

Outside of the citadel the giants set up a cheer that filled Ar'lenon.

With Vectra's help Oganna climbed to one of the arrow slits that overlooked the ramp. Giants packed the ramp. Five of them relentlessly swung spiked battle hammers against the doors, and the doors were buckling.

She unfastened her boomerang, held it out the opening, and flicked it into the giants. Once again it brought down several of them before settling back in her palm. Hopefully that would make the others think again before attempting to bring down the doors. "All right, Vectra, you can let me down now. They have backed away."

Taking advantage of the giants' hesitation, the megatraths opened the doors and sent a tornado of fire and vapors onto the ramp. The enemy retreated, and the megatraths closed the doors and rebuilt the barricade.

"Oganna, you look exhausted," Vectra said. She rolled Oganna's bedding outside of the tent and next to the fireplace. "Catch some sleep. I'll keep watch."

Oganna peered into her tent for a moment. Gabel lay fast asleep. If the enemy broke into the citadel it would be his life under threat as well. She dropped the flap over the opening and went to the water barrels. She poured the cool liquid over her arm and cringed as she rolled up her sleeve. The dried blood came with it. It wasn't a terrible wound, but it was enough to weaken her even more. Exhausted, she bandaged her wound and fell asleep.

* * *

Ilfedo raised his hand, even as he reigned in his mount. He had thought of sending scouts ahead of the army to ascertain the position of the enemy. But that would be senseless now. The enemy lay ahead of him, coming out of the valley and from hills to the northwest, marching as an unbroken line of giant men clad for battle.

Ombre rode up beside him and shuddered at the sight of the giants. Truly they looked formidable.

"How many do you think there are?" Ilfedo

said.

"It's difficult to say," Ombre groaned. "A few thousand at least, and there could be more in the valley."

The Warrioresses lined up beside him.

"My sisters," Ilfedo said as he gazed upon them. He had to make certain they stayed safe. Caritha's eyes narrowed as she returned his gaze, and Rozel slapped the flat of her sword into her palm. They looked ready to do something rash. "I want you to stay by my side, Caritha. If we are going to find out what is happening in that valley, then we will first have to break through these giants."

Caritha nodded and scanned the advancing enemies. "Night is falling," she said.

He glanced at the reddening western horizon. "Good. That works to our advantage." He twisted in his saddle to face Ombre. "Send the Elite Thousand ahead of the regular troops. Their swords will give them an advantage in the dark, as will their superior training."

Drawing his sword, Ombre signaled to Honer and Ganning. They in turn signaled to the captains, who in turn led the warriors of light by two-hundred-dred man divisions. Two of these fanned out to the east, one forming an arrowhead to strike the enemy's opposite flank, and the remaining two divisions proceeding toward the valley.

Ilfedo kept his eye on the two divisions moving to attack in the east. Suddenly the giants cheered, and the hills trembled as more of them marched from the valley. Their ranks swelled to the east and directly ahead. "Well, Ombre, how many are there now?" he shouted.

His friend hesitated and started counting. At last he stopped. "Who cares?" He adjusted his breastplate. "Oganna and the megatraths are out there, so let's go get them!"

The Warrioresses stretched their arms and twirled their swords. "A wise swordmaster once taught me that in the heat of battle, victory favors the bold," Caritha said, and her rusty blade glowed in her hand. "I am with Ombre on this. If we do not bring the fight immediately to them, then they will bring the fight to us, and they probably know this land far better than we do."

"Yeah, and I'm hungry for a good fight with whoever has done anything to Oganna." Rozel grunted. "If we stay here we'll end up on the defensive. And I hate being on the defensive."

Ilfedo rode ahead, and the Warrioresses ran after him. Ombre, Honer, and Ganning led the Elite warriors in their wake directly toward the heart of the opposing force. Ilfedo reached the giants first and cut into their ranks but found that he had left everyone else behind. Alone he battled the enemy, and on every side the large men fell beneath his sword.

He turned his stallion, then hacked and burned his way back to his own force. His warriors were locked in battle, unable to get past the giants and into the city. "Fall back!" he commanded, and he led an orderly withdrawal from the giants. The giants must have been stunned by the ferocity of his attack, for they did not immediately follow but stayed where they were.

Ilfedo summoned messengers. "It is time to

bring all our forces to bear," he called out to them.

The messengers scattered from him, running to carry out his orders. The Elite Thousand regrouped, and the regular army stormed into position behind them. Their ranks covered the hills. He set his mouth in a firm line. The army of giants was formidable. He wanted every one of his warriors to go home to his wife and children. But to the army of giants he shook his head. A heavy price would be paid for the future queen today.

Dismounting, he sent his Evenshadow to the rear of the army and unsheathed his sword. With the living fire licking his armor he marched down the highway. Eight thousand men shouted behind him.

The giants marched toward him, then broke into a run. He let them eat up their energy. As they drew near, he sprang upon their front line. His sword cleaved the first giant's shield in half, and he stabbed him through the heart, then spun his blade behind him, impaling another.

Caritha sprang to his side, and Rozel followed. Laura, Evela, and Levena brought down three giants simultaneously. Six strong, they advanced at the front of the army, stabbing and slashing until the giants' hammering blows slowed the Warrioresses.

Ilfedo stabbed his sword into another giant and grabbed a fallen spear. The sapling-thick shaft made him stagger under its weight. But he felt the sword of the dragon infuse his muscles with energy, and he lifted the spear with a shout, throwing it into his foes. It pierced a giant's breastplate, passed through the man's body, and impaled another that stood behind him.

Several giants gathered around Ilfedo. They glared down at him and cracked their hammers and swords against his sword, driving him to the ground. The darkness of night settled around him. He could see the divisions of warriors with swords of light pressing upon the giants, but they were battling beyond his reach.

He drove his fiery blade into a giant's chest and severed the man's head before his body hit the ground. Another giant stepped up and stabbed at him with a sword. He brought his blade down and cut it in two. Fire shot from his sword's blade and set the giant's head ablaze. He ran the man through and turned to the next opponent.

A wave of winged men sprang from deep in the giant's ranks. They soared high, a hundred of them at least. Ilfedo grimly watched as another hundred Art'en sprang into the air, joining their fellows. Their screeches shot across the field of battle as they dove in one massive horde toward his army.

"Archers!" Ilfedo heard one of his captain scream. The call rang through his army. "Take aim! Fire!" A cloud of arrows rose from the army behind, like a protective cloud passing over the warriors of light. The Art'en flapped their wings as if trying to slow their descent. But the arrows found their marks, and the wave of flying creatures fell from the sky into the giants' ranks.

Blood ran down Ilfedo's blade and collected at its tip, dripping to the ground in a red stream. The light of his armor lit the area around him as brightly as day. One of the giants drove at him from behind and smashed its battleaxe into his helmet. He fell to the ground as his opponent pulled out a sword to run him through. Twisting away, Ilfedo jumped back up, grasped the giant's arm, and thrust him through his heart, dropping him like an oversized bear.

He felt his helmet with his fingers, running them along its unmarred surface. If he hadn't had the armor of living fire protecting him, that blow would have killed him. Three other giants raced upon him. He arced his sword behind his back, holding it with both hands, then brought it forward at their knees. They too fell, and Ilfedo drove deeper into the enemy lines with a surge of victorious adrenaline that would not be denied.

* * *

It seemed that mere moments had passed since Oganna had fallen asleep, when a dreadful cheer startled her awake. Neneila the viper slipped around her neck. She rose and made her way out of the tent. Morning light streamed through the windows and arrow slits along the citadel walls. "Vectra?" she called.

The megatraths stood facing the doors, their claws digging into the stone floor. Vectra ambled over to her side and spoke so low that only Oganna heard her. "I happened to look out the slit in that wall when the giants cheered. There is a new arrival in their ranks. I think this is the one Gabel called Razes."

"Razes?" Oganna rubbed the sleep from her eyes and drew the Avenger from its sheath.

The doors groaned and shook. Outside the cheer rose again, stronger, and then the wooden doors splintered into thousands of tiny chips. A cloud of dust hindered her view of the ramp for a moment. When it cleared, the figure of a giant stood there alone. He was at least ten feet tall, though he seemed taller because of a steel helmet on his head.

Razes cleared his throat and looked down on her. "There now, you must be the little dame about which I have heard so much." He curled his fingers tighter around the long metal staff in his hand.

Oganna advanced onto the ramp.

The wizard pointed his staff at her, its head twisted into blades around a small white globe. Too late, she realized his intent. A wave of energy rippled against her, throwing her down and throwing several megatraths to the floor behind her.

"He is mine!" Vectra spat as she and her companions charged onto the ramp.

Oganna struggled to rise but invisible bands forced her shoulders down. She could hear Razes cackling as he backed down the ramp, just out of Vectra's range. "You are such loathsome creatures," he said. He waved his hand, and the other giants collided with the megatraths and knocked them into the street. Now nothing stood between her and him.

The wizard sauntered up the ramp, stepping over bodies. "So this is the mighty and beautiful princess of the Hemmed Land. Too bad your father isn't around to save you from me," he laughed. "He's busy elsewhere."

In Yimshi's light his black armor shimmered. Oganna stared in horror. Every surface of his apparel had been outfitted with protruding blades. Even the backs of his leather gloves were barbed with razor-sharp metal. She struggled to rise and fought to lift her sword. The bands holding her broke, but she felt too weak to stand.

Razes twirled his staff in a circle, built speed, and brought it to bear against her head. The impact nearly knocked her out. Blood ran down her face. Pain knifed from her skull to her nose. The wizard swung again, and she cringed, unable to stop him.

This was the end. She knew it to be so, and all she could think of in that moment was how her death would destroy her father.

But an enormous sword slipped in front of her and parried the wizard's blow. Gabel stepped over her and snarled at his nemesis. "Seeking to add yet another crime to your sins, Razes? Does it please you to see the innocent suffer?" The former king of Burloi stood strong between Oganna and the wizard.

"Ah, your Majesty." The wizard mocked a bow. "So, you have survived the purging of Burloi. I should have guessed that you would come back." He spun his staff around his waist and declared, "The Valley of Death has made me strong. Very strong."

Gabel took a step toward him. "If you are referring to the dark magic you wield, then you are mistaken, for it has allowed you to do terrible things and taken from you that which is most important. Your soul. This power has consumed you and you are a slave to it, not the other way around."

Razes grinned. "You are the one that has nothing, Gabel," he said as he spread his arms. "Look around you, old king. I have everything."

"Everything? What you have is the support of a blind mob that destroys everything in its path," Gabel said.

"Ah, but even a mob can serve a purpose."

Razes thumped his staff against the stone floor. "Just to show you how good of a person I am, I will give you one last chance to join forces with me. If you refuse me, then I will cut you up before I set to work on your little lady friend. Now step aside and prove your new allegiance by watching her die."

Gabel's knuckles turned white as he held the sword more firmly. "You have killed all of the people that I loved, Razes. Except for this little angel. Your corruption ends here."

The wizard guffawed. "You could not end it before—"

"Don't act so confident, you slime pit! When you beat me, you had your apprentice with you. Now it is as it should have been. Just you and me." Gabel circled left. His eyes resembled cold steel, and every muscle in his body tensed. Oganna could only imagine the hate that swelled in his heart as he slashed viciously at his adversary. He stabbed his sword into stones, and they blew up in the wizard's face.

Oganna sat in shock. Gabel's sword had powers. Why had he not mentioned it to her?

Razes leapt out of the way, pointed his staff in the king's direction, and hit him with a blinding flash of light. He laughed as Gabel stumbled, and despair crept into Oganna's heart. The wizard spread his arms. "Are you having trouble with your eyes, old man?"

Gabel staggered closer to Razes and then sank his sword into the wizard's leg. His gaze shifted to the wizard's face. "Sorry, my mistake, I guess I wasn't stunned by your blast after all."

Screaming in pain and anger, the wizard

grasped Gabel's neck and raked his blades down the length of his chest. Blood pooled on the stones as Gabel dropped his sword. Razes brought his knee up, driving its blades into the king's abdomen. He let him drop to the floor. "Did you really think you stood a chance of defeating me, old king?"

Still weak and a little dizzy, Oganna struggled to her feet and held her sword. Avenger's blade turned crimson, and the silver garments covered her. She looked upon her fallen defender with all the love she could have given a second father, and tears flooded her eyes. Gabel's eyes looked back at her from his mutilated face. They were sad, yet fulfilled, then as they closed forever, he murmured, "There is great potential in you, Princess Oganna. Don't let anyone tell you differently, little lady."

Gathering her last strength, Oganna darted behind Razes and stabbed wherever his body presented a target.

"Is that all you can do?" Razes asked as he dodged her blows and thwacked her sides with his staff. She felt Neneila fall limp under her shirt. Razes growled at the sky and hit his wounded leg with the head of his staff. The wound cauterized, and he thrust his blade-ridden fist toward her.

She stumbled, and then stood still. Desperately she tried to understand why her senses seemed impaired. Why couldn't she attack him? An oppressive darkness crept over her. At last she recognized the spell he was using against her. Her mind was in a panic. His power bound her, reached inside of her, and stole her will. Then it struck something else, a residual strength innate and untamable. The blood of her dragon ancestors.

With all her will she pushed back and vented against the spell. "Depart!" she screamed.

The force of her refusal threw Razes backward, and he screamed in frustration. "You little imp! Do you really believe that you can last long enough to survive against this?"

Oganna cast fire from her blade, but his staff absorbed it. She struck with lightning, yet his staff resisted, and he remained unharmed. "Your powers cannot match mine. I have been trained by the greatest of wizards in all deadly arts. Now, witness my power." He stretched his hands to the sky. Far above them lightning flashed in the clouds. The wind whipped through the city and swirled the clouds until they tornadoed far above. Lightning flashed, zipped beneath and into the clouds, then spiked toward the earth. The bolts wove through one another, gathered speed, and headed toward the place where she stood.

The bolts blasted against her head and shoulders, but she pulled the first one down and wrapped it around her body as a shield so that the other bolts entwined themselves about her, then simply dissipated. "How little you know of the power of good," she said to the stunned wizard. She gazed up at Razes and frowned. "It will overcome you." Thereupon she pummeled him with blows from the Avenger. On every side she poured her fury like rain and sought to find a weakness.

Razes blocked her sword, and the head of his staff slipped past her defenses, landing blows on her thighs, shoulders, and then her chest. She gasped for air, drew back Avenger, and charged him with her blade aimed for his chest. But Avenger's point clinked against his armor and slid over it. She widened her stance, seeking to rebalance herself.

Raising his staff above his head in both hands and pointing it at her, Razes sneered. Black and red energy blasted from the staff's end, striking the ramp at her feet. The stones trembled and cracked. They crumbled into dust beneath her, and she fell. A moment of weightlessness and a glance downward as the ruins of stone buildings rose to meet her. Her spine impacted on a large stone block, snapping her head toward the ground. Every bone in her body burned as she tried to raise her head, and she screamed.

Razes leapt down after her, and his staff appeared to absorb the shock of his fall. "Poor, poor thing." He clacked his tongue and held the razors on the back of his hand against her face. "What a pity," he muttered.

Her vision blurred, and she breathed in rapid, short bursts that seemed devoid of air. She glimpsed his evil face as he sliced into her skin. The pain compared to nothing she had ever experienced. If she could have cried out she would have, but she had run out of tears. Before she lost consciousness, she felt his staff crush into her face and then chest. She could no longer feel any pain.

* * *

Specter had been grappling with his adversary through the night inside a ruined building. Now in the daylight he gritted his teeth and drove his blade into the Reaper's leg, pushed him against the stone walls. Death fell again, and this time Specter fell upon him and tore the scythe out of the Reaper's boney fingers.

He lifted his face toward the sky and laughed as the Reaper squirmed beneath him. Its feet and hand transformed into smoke. "Oh, you cannot run forever! I have seen the wickedness you and your kind would unleash on this world, and I loathe you. Now with the help of God I bring you to a just end," Specter said.

Holding the scythes tightly, he clubbed the Reaper's skull repeatedly until cracks spread through it. He hammered the scythes into the skull in quick succession. Fury filled his arms, and Death's skull broke into a thousand fragments.

Something exploded on the ramp above, and he stood to his feet, holding the Grim Reaper's headless body in his hand. Oganna fell off the ramp, and Avenger slipped from her hand. She crashed into a ruined building, stirring a cloud of dust.

A giant arrayed in armor unlike anything Specter had ever seen jumped down after her. The giant raised a wizard's staff in its hand and crouched over the dragon's offspring. He held his blade-ridden fist against the young woman's lovely face and viciously cut it open. Oganna's body collapsed and, in the stones beside her, Avenger's blade ceased to glow.

"Master," called another voice, and Specter recognized it. "Let me finish her," the voice begged. A dark-featured human stumbled up the heap of stones to the ruins, leaning on a dark staff.

Razes glanced down at the man and laughed. "You have a lot to learn, Auron. You fell at the hand of a girl? Wait until Letrias hears of this." He stood aside and pointed at Oganna. "She's all yours."

Specter roared with rage and dragged Death's carcass into the sunlight. He raised his scythe and faced the giant, rolling the Reaper's remains down the rubble. The carcass slid down the rubble to land at Razes's feet.

The giant picked up the carcass, and his eyes narrowed as he looked upon Specter.

Specter caused his cloak to render him partially visible and set his feet in the debris, frowning at Auron. "Rise, traitor!"

The man spun, glanced at Specter, and stumbled back. He pointed the staff at him. "W . . . what? Who are you? I do not know you."

"Think again, Auron. You know me better than your new master knows you." Specter slipped the hood off his head and smiled. "Brian's blood still stains your soul, and now I will exact retribution on you so that none will forget the cost of shedding innocent blood."

"No," Auron gasped and his lips trembled. Specter advanced as Auron shook his head vigorously, rattling his chain mail. "I saw you fall. I saw you die."

"Hmm," Razes said with a laugh, and he kicked his pupil toward Specter. "It looks like you have a fresh opportunity to prove yourself, Auron."

"This man. He died long ago. I saw him die," Auron said as he retreated a step. "Master, do not make me face him. You must slay him now before he brings death upon us both."

Razes shrugged his enormous shoulders. "Very well." He swung his staff but it passed through Specter as though he were a ghost.

Specter swung his scythe past Razes, cutting the traitor's arm. Auron screamed and then struck back with such speed that his staff cracked Specter on his cheek, and he fell into the rubble.

Auron sprinted after him, thrusting his staff into Specter's mid-section. But Specter kicked the man in the chest and, when he had fallen, laughed. "God has shown me favor today, Auron. Your master cannot touch me while your traitorous debt remains unpaid. Did you believe escape from the Creator's retribution would be possible? Were you fool enough to rank yourself above the will of Providence?"

The traitor stood and swung his staff at Specter's legs. Specter blocked it with his scythe's handle. "You can never beat me trading blow for blow, Auron. Or have you forgotten?" He spun, cutting the man's side with his scythe blade.

* * *

Ilfedo wiped his brow and paused a moment to allow the sword of the dragon to energize him again. All night he had been fighting. All night the sword had kept him from tiring, and now he stood far ahead of his army and his friends. He thrust through another giant, and another, and another. One more approached and he jumped into the air, holding the sword above his head, and cracked the giant's helm. After landing in a crouch, he spun. Fire spewed from the blade, and he straightened and stepped passed giant human torches of his own creation.

He crested the valley's rim and glimpsed the megatraths. They were desperately fighting around the ramp to the citadel. Dead and dying littered the city. The knowledge that Oganna was there too drove him mad, and he continued on without consideration to the danger. He was an island in a bloody wasteland with death threatening him on all sides. He descended into the city by way of the roads and fought within visual range of the ramp.

Then he saw her glowing silver figure, and the giant man opposing her. The giant blasted the ramp, and she fell a long, deadly distance into one of the demolished buildings. Her adversary leapt down after her.

His daughter, his most precious companion! He cried out, and his sword incinerated those closest to him, reducing the giants to piles of ash. He stabbed and hacked all in his path as if they were hay in a field until at last he stood at the base of the ruined structure. The giant had his back to Ilfedo and was laughing hysterically as he pounded Oganna into a mutilated pulp. The wizard spun his staff to strike again and spoke to the motionless body. "You have failed, young one! But at least you died at the hand of I, Razes."

Ilfedo smashed his fist into the giant's lower back and toppled him with a stiff kick to the back of his leg. Razes's head crashed into a large stone, and when he picked himself up he had to wipe blood from his mouth.

A JUST RECOMPENSE

In Ilfedo's hand the sword of the dragon blazed as never before, and the living fire upon his armor burned with unparalleled fervor. He felt the rage boiling inside of him, and when he looked again at his daughter, he was filled with a justified hate. He stepped over a foundation stone and held his sword with both hands before his face. Only one thing mattered to him now. Vengeance.

The giant looked down at Ilfedo and spat. The staff in his hand dripped with Oganna's blood.

Ilfedo stepped closer and menace filled his words. "Don't you dare touch my daughter again."

"And what if I do?" the wizard mocked. "Will you kill me?" He spun his staff and scoffed. "Do you think that I fear you? You are lower than the dust and worthy only to be ground into powder. Your body will hang in my hall alongside that of your daughter, and it will be a warning to all who oppose me in the future."

"You are mistaken, wizard, for it is you that will be an example to my enemies. By making an enemy of me, you have doomed yourself. And when this day is done and your soul has fallen into eternal darkness, then I will laugh at your corpse and feed you to the birds."

Razes stomped toward him and sneered. "Prepare to die!"

A series of cries and roars echoed around him. Caritha appeared from behind a pile of rubble. She pulled her rusted blade from a giant's breast and let him fall beside her. Another rushed her from behind, but his eyes opened wide, and he fell forward. Laura took her blade from his back and stood side-by-side with her sister. Beyond them, cutting a path through the enemy masses charged Levena, Evela, and Rozel. They reached Caritha and Laura, then formed a line.

Rozel eyed the wizard. "So, this is the big, bad enemy. I'd expected more than a coward that cripples young women!"

"Just say the word, Ilfedo, and we'll help you cut him into a thousand pieces," Caritha said. She stepped through the rubble, and her sisters formed a half-circle around the giant.

"Yeah." Rozel pointed her blade at the giant's head. "I'll take that part off!"

Razes advanced and spread his arms. "Is this supposed to make me afraid? You are like insects beside me." He beckoned to his forces, and a line of giants stamped toward the Warrioresses.

The sisters touched the tips of their blades

together and sent out wave after wave of energy into the giants' midst. The wizard's forces fell back, their hair smoking and their faces red.

Ilfedo let his sword shoot fire from its tip, drawing the wizard's attention again, and addressed him. "It looks to me like you are outnumbered," he said.

Cackling, the wizard raised his staff toward the sky, and lighting struck, opening a large hole in the ground. Razes sneered and looked into its depths. "Come, my children, you have work to do." Out of the hole slithered a multitude of vipers that swarmed around him in a protective circle.

Ilfedo dashed to Caritha's side and shook her shoulder. "I cannot fight as fiercely as I must with those I love standing near. Get Oganna out of here. Now! Leave the wizard to me."

* * *

The sisters climbed the rubble into the ruins and looked upon their young charge. "No, it cannot be," Levena exclaimed as she clamped her hand over her mouth.

Evela screamed and tears ran down her cheeks. Laura closed her eyes and knelt in front of Oganna.

Rozel swallowed hard. Her body trembled, her shoulders quaked, and her eyes moistened. "Is she already gone?" she asked.

"Hurry, she isn't breathing," Caritha said. She grabbed Oganna's blood-soaked legs, and Laura held the girl's arms. Both of them gasped and stared in horror at Oganna's mutilated face.

"Is she, is she, is she dead?" Laura choked back a sob.

"Not yet. Come on!" Caritha said.

Levena, Rozel, and Evela charged into another wave of giants, stabbing every which way. Caritha and Laura grunted under their burden as they followed the path that their sisters carved through the dead and the dying. They carried Oganna along the highway. As they approached the valley's rim, a shout caused them to look up.

Ombre and the Elite Thousand crested the hill. The warriors of light stretched in both directions for as far as Caritha could see. The giants were losing ground, and the swords of light could be seen everywhere, piercing hearts and severing limbs.

The regular army charged into the city, leaving heaps of dead giants in its wake. When they reached the citadel, they protectively surrounded the surviving megatraths. Hopefully Oganna's friend, Vectra, was among them.

Caritha helped Laura set Oganna down on soft grass. All five sisters knelt around her. "What can we do?" Evela cried. "She looks dead already."

"But she isn't. Not yet," Caritha said as she drew her sword and touched it to Oganna's chest. The others followed her lead. "Draw upon the strength that Father gave us. The powers within our blood. Use it up if necessary! Drain yourself completely of it if necessary. Feed it into her."

The viper's head peeked from under Oganna's collar. It rubbed its head gently on the young woman's neck.

Caritha sent the powers within her blood into her sword, and the weapon glowed. Tendrils of blue and red light latched on to Oganna's chest from all five swords. Caritha screamed in pain and her sisters soon followed. It felt as if the fabric of her existence was ripping out her heart. But she held on as the power left her blood.

A cocoon of light cascaded around the body, and through its veil she saw Oganna's wounds close and the blood dry. The energy receded and snapped back against the swords, throwing Caritha against the ground. When she sat back up Oganna's chest heaved steadily, and her eyelids fluttered open.

Caritha embraced her and cried on her shoulder. The others wept too, for Oganna's beauty was forever gone. Her face and arms bore the ugly scars inflicted on her by Razes.

* * *

"It's all right," Oganna said through her own tears. "I'm here. I'm alive." She gazed heavenward. "Thank God for that."

The sisters looked at each other, unable to reveal the horrible truth. Oganna's eyes froze as she glanced down at her arms. Her skin felt rough, rather than smooth. She felt her face and the realization hit her. "Oh my," she sobbed. She tried to hide her devastation, but it refused to be buried. "Oh my," she managed again. She buried her face in her hands and wept.

Caritha and her sisters tried to comfort Oganna, but they could offer no consolation. How could they? They hadn't lost their beauty. And so they cried with her until a tremendous explosion rocked the earth and they spun around.

Evela pointed to the base of Ar'lenon and gasped. "Was that Ilfedo? What does he think he's doing? He cannot face that monster on his own!"

"Be still, Evela," Caritha said, and she laid a restraining hand on her sister's arm. "I think that you underestimate the fury of a father who is avenging his child."

* * *

Ilfedo drove his flaming blade into the ground at Razes's feet and blasted the rocks out from under him. As the wizard's vipers sailed through the air, he directed the sword of the dragon at them and roasted them alive before they touched the ground. He slammed his shoulder into the wizard's abdomen and brought his blade around in a swift arc, slitting the giant's arm just above the elbow.

Ilfedo's army swarmed into the street, and the wave of giants fled before them. Razes screamed after them, "Back into the fight, you fools! Destroy them." He cocked his arm and thrust his blade-ridden fist into Ilfedo's chest.

Ilfedo stumbled. He glanced down at the deep wound. But how had the wizard penetrate the armor of living fire? Ilfedo felt faint. The world spun around him, and he fell. As the world darkened, Razes cackled.

But the sword burned Ilfedo's hand, forcing him to drop it. It hovered in the air above him and shot the living fire into his body. It felt as if he had gone from a frigid night's chill to the warmth of a sunny day. The blood stopped flowing out of his body, and his flesh healed without so much as a scar to show for the deadly wound.

Razes stepped back, and Ilfedo saw astonishment on the wizard's face.

Ilfedo grinned up at the giant. "Nice try," he said. He rose, took his sword in hand, and stabbed its blade into the ground. The stones and dirt blew up again in the wizard's face and threw him against a wall of stone. Before the giant could rise, Ilfedo shot fire from the sword of the dragon. The wizard held his staff in the flame's path, and it absorbed the living fire.

Ilfedo jumped forward, smote him on the chin, and cut the wizard's staff in two. He stepped back, hoping to receive the giant's surrender. Instead, small orbs of energy formed in the wizard's hands. "You think that you have defeated me?" The wizard eyed his orbs greedily and then chucked them in rapid succession in Ilfedo's direction.

As the orbs broke harmlessly on the sword of the dragon, the sword left Ilfedo's hands and hovered before him. He felt as though he had left his body and was instead hovering inside of the blade. He shot like an arrow straight into his opponent's heart. When it was over, he returned to his body and opened his eyes.

Razes slumped against the wall, and his remaining orbs fizzled out of existence in his hands. His eyes froze open and his breathing stopped.

Ilfedo grabbed hold of his sword, drew it from the corpse, and sheathed it at his side. The armor of living fire gave way to his everyday apparel, and he walked out into the city. He could see the last of the giants scrambling out of the valley, heading north, and he knew that they would not be coming back. Several Art'en flew above the giants, yet they too did not glance back. Heaving a sigh he walked down the highway, stepping over the bodies of the giants on his way.

Ombre rode toward him and wiped his dirty blade on his trouser leg. "It is done, Ilfedo. I don't think those giants will give us any more trouble. The Hemmed Land is safe."

"How did our troops fare?" Ilfedo asked.

"We conquered in this battle," Ombre replied.

"Casualties?" Ilfedo said.

Ombre shook his head and lowered his gaze. "Yes, there were some. But they will be remembered forever among our people. Ilfedo, we have proven that we are not a nation of random villages any longer. We are stronger than we knew."

Caritha tapped Ilfedo on the shoulder, and he realized that all five sisters and his daughter were standing by him. Oganna's scarred face startled him at first, but he caught himself, reached out, and clutched her to himself. "It's all right, my daughter. The wizard is dead."

"Father, I am . . . I am ugly!" she wept.

Tears poured from his eyes, for he knew that it was true. "The blame rests with me," he said, choking on his words. "I should not have allowed you to come here."

"No!" another voice rumbled from the streets. "I am to blame." Vectra stumbled toward him with her head lowered. Blood ran from the many wounds she'd received, and her eyes overflowed until she too wept.

Oganna broke free of her father and ran to the trembling creature. She reached out and laid her hand gently on Vectra's snout. "It is no one's fault,

Vectra. What is done is done." She wiped her cheeks and continued. "Though I am ashamed to show this face in public, I do not hold you or anyone else here responsible for it. Did you draw the blades across my face and mutilate me? No. You would never. Razes alone carries the blame."

Ilfedo counted the megatraths gathering behind Vectra. Twenty-four remained out of one hundred. He shook his head. Seventy-six of the magnificent beasts had died.

"Oganna, Vectra . . . let's gather the dead and head home. Tonight we will camp along the border with the northern desert. There is fresh water there and space for our numbers to spread out," he said.

Oganna shook her head and looked at him with her bluegold eyes. They were still as beautiful as the day she was born. "I want to stay here for a while. There is one giant in this city that deserves a proper burial, and I intend to give it to him."

Vectra sniffled. "Indeed he does."

Ilfedo started to beckon the Warrioresses over to stay as well, but Oganna stopped him. "Please, Father, I want to do this alone. Unless, of course, if Vectra is willing to stay with me."

The megatrath rested a hand around Oganna's shoulders and said, "I would have it no other way." She bent down, and Oganna straddled her neck. As the pair moved off, Ilfedo heard Vectra command the remaining megatraths to follow his orders and leave her behind.

He organized his troops, and the megatraths into bands to collect the dead. Using materials from the demolished buildings, they constructed large sleds, then they laid the dead on them and hauled them toward the desert. Ombre sent messengers ahead of them to the Hemmed Land and to Resgeria to both report the battle's outcome and to bring more manpower.

Within two days reinforcements came and the last of the dead were hauled out of Netroth. Ilfedo mounted his Evenshadow and rode out of the valley. Only once did he stop to look back. The mighty citadel, where he had last spotted his daughter and the megatrath, stood as a grim reminder to him that all great things that have a beginning also have an end.

He wheeled the Evenshadow stallion and rode after his army. Maybe during this time alone Oganna would find peace with her new condition and realize that the love of those around her did not depend on her physical appearance. He had survived, and so had she. What more could he ask for? Nevertheless he could not prevent a few tears from straying down his cheeks as he rode off.

* * *

"Die, Xavion! Why can't you just die?" Auron screamed.

The traitor and his captain battled in one of the city's larger remaining buildings. Twilight lengthened and deepened the shadows. A warm wind whistled through the rafters.

Specter smiled as Auron stabbed at him again with the wizard staff. "That staff can only rejuvenate you for so long," Specter said. He cut the ancient traitor's leg, and Auron fell back, touched his staff to the wound, and it healed . . . but much slower than it had a day ago. "You see? While your dark powers falter, I remain unchanged. While you grow desperate, I grow confident. You should have learned from me all those years ago instead of betraying me." Specter grabbed the chain mail headdress and yanked it off Auron's head, throwing it ten feet away.

Auron sneered and looked back up at him. "I didn't want to be someone's servant!"

"Ha! Everyone is a servant," Specter said. "We only choose what master to serve. And we know why we are both here, at this place, now." He spun, and the blade of his scythe slipped behind Auron's legs and cut them behind the knees. With a cry the traitor collapsed. Specter knelt beside him. "You chose your master, and I chose mine, and now we must each face the consequences."

"No. No, this cannot be. Letrias promised," Auron groaned.

Specter stood and pressed his scythe blade against the man's throat. Then he kicked the staff out of Auron's hand. "I am a more honorable man than you, my fallen apprentice. I remember that you used to care for righteousness. It was not all an act. And for that reason I am going to show you mercy today." He grabbed the man's neck and pulled him bodily off the floor, holding him there with his feet dangling in the air. "Consider whom you serve and choose wisely, for the next time we meet in this way, I will come as your judge and as the specter of death."

Specter dropped the man to the floor. He pulled the hood over his head and faded into invisibility. Auron wept and wiped at his bloody nose, then he whispered. "If only I knew that repentance could bring me forgiveness, then I would." He frowned, jumped for his staff and broke it across his knee.

A pulse of energy shot down the broken sorcerer's tool, exploding through Auron's leg. The traitor grabbed his leg and screamed and wept.

Specter grasped a fallen beam and hung his head. He let a tear slip down his face. For there, not twenty feet away, groaned a man he had once known and loved as a brother and treated as a son. But maybe this time mercy would pave the way to repentance. Maybe a traitor who betrayed his new master could resurrect to new life.

Turning, he stepped down onto the street and knelt with hands folded. "Send thy prophet, my Maker. I pray."

THE END OF SORROW

Vectra motioned for Oganna to come closer to the wall of stone as she threw her weight against it. The stones grated, and the hidden door opened inward to reveal a dark corridor beyond. Oganna stepped inside as Vectra closed the door behind them.

"Vectra, do you see any torches in here?" she asked.

The megatrath grunted. "It's pitch black. I can't see anything."

Oganna drew Avenger and let the silver robes adorn her sore, scarred body. The air smelled stale, and the light from her weapon showed thick cobwebs on the walls. It had taken two days of searching for them to find this place. It had been cleverly concealed by a false wall in one of the buildings around Ar'lenon, in what appeared to have been a distinguished home.

"This place looks as though it could use a good cleaning," Oganna said as she ran her finger along the grimy wall. "I wonder why the giants didn't maintain it."

Vectra grunted again as they entered a large square room decorated with runes and carvings. A long and flat stone table adorned the room's center. Gently she laid the linen-wrapped body of the brave giant king onto the tabletop. Next she heaved aside a blank square stone from the front of one of the tomb's many recessed chambers. Behind the stone lay a hole large and long enough for the body.

"Here, Princess, the epitaph has not been written," Vectra said. She leaned the stone against the table.

An oversized chisel and a hammer rested in a cubby on one of the walls. Oganna fetched them to the blank stone slab. It stood as high as her head. The giants' tools were almost too big for her to manipulate, but she chipped away at the stone for the next few hours until she had engraved the words she wanted:

Here lies Gabel, King of Burloi
In life he was magnificent
In death he was immortalized
In memory he will be loved.
Our friend, may you rest here in peace,
Undisturbed, until the eternal God claims this world.

"It is a fitting monument for a brave man," Vectra said as she scraped her claws on the floor.

"Now, let us put him to rest." She slid the wrapped body, feet first, into its chamber, and then reached to a pack tied on her back and set it on the floor.

Oganna opened it and pulled out a rich purple cloth. This she laid over Gabel's body, then drew out his cumbersome sword. She had spent the better part of three hours cleaning it the other day when she had found it, and now the blade and handle shone as if new.

Vectra accepted the weapon from Oganna. Balancing its blade in her claws, the megatrath rested it lengthwise on the purple cloth.

Oganna reached into the pack for one final item: the giant's silver crown. "He said he was king of Burloi," she whispered. "No king should be buried without his crown." As she lifted the crown onto the king's chest, the diamond augmented the light emanating from her sword.

Vectra heaved the heavy tombstone with Oganna's epitaph in front of the chamber, sealing it against prying eyes. Oganna melted the seams together with Avenger's fire.

She knelt on the floor, and Vectra followed her example. They remained like this for a long while, paid their respects to the dead, then rose to go. Oganna glanced around the tomb, noting the other stones along its walls. She pulled her cipher from her pocket and translated several of the ancient writings. "Vectra, am I getting this right? Most of it is gibberish to me."

"That's because most of the things written on these stones are names and titles," the megatrath said.

Oganna put away her cipher and walked out

with Vectra. The creature closed the hidden door behind them and together they built a false wall out of the rubble to conceal it from any future explorers. Oganna, now that she stood in the light of day again, veiled her face with a white cloth and walked in silence up the ramp to Ar'lenon. She paused for a moment to admire the colors of the sky as Yimshi set toward the west.

Tomorrow she and the megatrath would start the return journey to the Hemmed Land. Oh how she dreaded what people would think when they looked at her. Would they keep their distance and avert their eyes, or would they gape and stare until she was embarrassed to tears? The 'hideous freak of a princess.' That's what they might call her behind closed doors. A freak! She scolded herself for wallowing in self-pity and reminded herself that she still had much to be grateful for. But though she tried to convince herself otherwise, she knew that her scars would forever change her.

* * *

That night Oganna watched Vectra lie beside the enormous fireplace in the main chamber for the last time. Neneila coiled next to the creature. It seemed the two had bonded. The megatrath closed its eyes and breathed deep and slow.

Oganna rose from the fireplace and wandered one last time up the steps to the observation deck of Ar'lenon Citadel. There she screamed out her pain to the sky. There she cried anew for her brave martyr Gabel. He was but one of many that had died in her defense, but he had done so without a hint of regret, and he hadn't even known her. Evil had risen and claimed the life of a noble king.

"Why did this have to happen?" she cried out. She leaned back against the roof and covered her face with her hands, but as soon as she touched her scarred self, she ripped the veil from her face and threw it off the platform.

In that moment the clouds flashed with white light and, looking up, she saw dragon wings spread in the sky. Albino descended upon the citadel and settled on its pinnacle. His claws gripped the roof's steep surface and held him with seeming ease in spite of his great size. His pink eyes glinted as they gazed into hers, as if seeing through the flesh to search her soul.

She caught herself staring, and she marveled at how calm she suddenly felt with him nearby. Even before he said a word, she felt as if he had done a world of good. She basked in his presence.

The dragon wrapped his white tail around the roof, and his boney lips curled into a smile. "Do not grieve for Gabel, my daughter. For what he did, he was pleased to do for you. Seeing you brought him hope for the future, even though all of his people had been slaughtered, and your innocence reminded him of the worth of self-sacrifice." Albino reached out one clawed hand and lifted her chin. "Your mother would be proud of you."

She lowered her eyes, ashamed to let him see what she had become. "It . . . it was not only for him that I was crying," she admitted.

He slid down the roof. His claws cracked the tiles, and their pieces slid off the roof, rolling over the platform and falling into the city as he came to rest on the platform. She could sense his penetrating gaze still upon her as he rumbled in his chest. "Hold still, my dear, this may hurt."

He stared hard at her and Oganna felt as if her skin was starting to burn. She cried out as the pain increased and clutched her hands over her face. Between her fingers she lifted her gaze to the noble dragon's white face. The mighty creature returned her gaze, unwavering.

Cracks formed on the dragon's facial scales and glowing red blood oozed forth. The dragon growled and shook his head. He grasped the citadel's roof with one hand and bent the metal supports, still growling softly. Suddenly she knew what he had done, what he was still doing. And he was doing all of it for her.

The wounds Razes had inflicted, the horrendous disfigurement, spread across the dragon's face and raced down his neck, even to his chest. But not a single tear fell from the dragon's eyes, though every fiber of his body trembled.

She ran to him, ignoring his glowing blood flowing over her body. His arm clasped her against his chest, and she wept. His cool scales soothed her skin. The pain in her face melted into warmth.

"Now," he said as he held her at arm's length and ran his eyes from her feet to her head. "Now the wizard's small victory has been erased. Ah, yes! That is much better."

At first she reached to feel her face, then she hesitated and gazed up. But a brilliant glow radiated from his face, forcing her to avert her gaze. She knew that scars had marred his noble image, and she wanted to weep on.

The dragon, however, whipped his clawed fingers around and held out a silver mirror. "You are the offspring of a dragon, my child. We are a beautiful race. Scars do not become you."

She beheld her face in the mirror. It was restored, whole and beautiful. She jumped up and wrapped her arms around his neck. Deep in his chest Albino rumbled, and then he laughed. His mighty arms held her in a tight embrace. The gratitude she felt could not be expressed in words, so she didn't say it. Instead she let him feel it.

At last he set her feet on the platform. She gazed up at him with tears of joy in her eyes and made the request that now burned in her heart. "What of Gabel? Would it be possible . . . to restore his life?"

"Oganna, my child, your heart is good, and you have kept your mind pure. But though there is a possibility that I could do that, yet for your sake I will not. Perhaps if I gave my life blood to Gabel, then he might rise again, but at the cost of my own life. The Creator has a plan for everything, and even this sorry event had to come to pass. The loss of a friend is a hard thing to bear, but in dealing with it you will be strengthened, for you must learn now how to cope with the loss of those to whom you are the closest. Nevertheless do not fear. You will see Gabel again, if not in this life then in the next." He angled his magnificent face toward the sky and snorted a gentle flame. "Just look at how those stars are shining tonight."

A tear for Gabel slipped down her cheek, for she knew the truth. She would see Gabel when she saw her mother. They waited for her beyond death's door in the life eternal.

"There, there, enough weeping." Albino's glowing face smiled as he flexed his wings. "This is the end of sorrow in this place, Oganna. Yet, this is not the end of your journey. Hard times lie ahead. Remember always that you are mine, for I will be watching over you through it all." With a final smile he spread his magnificent white wings. They seemed to cover the entire sky, and she wished he would stay and wrap her in them. His leg muscles rippled, his wings beat downward, and he ascended into the night.

As she watched him go, she ran her hand over her smooth skin before calling after him, "Goodnight . . . Grandfather."

Somersaulting through the air, his whole body glowing, he glanced back. "Goodnight, my precious granddaughter. And know that I am always watching out for you, even when it seems I am not near." Then he shot into the night sky, streaming away like a blazing comet of white over the distant horizon.

The cool night wind howled through the city streets, bearing a sad note of finality. A formerly powerful nation had been overturned, its people slain, and its buildings burned. Only Ar'lenon and its damaged ramp stood whole. She looked around one last time and then entered the citadel to descend the stairs.

* * *

In the morning Oganna packed her tent and goods and put them on Vectra's back. The megatrath glowed with ecstasy. "My goodness, don't you look lovely today," Vectra said. She gave a toothy grin, and Oganna smiled back. She had revealed the truth of her heritage to the creature, and the megatrath treated her with all the more respect.

Whatever the dragon had done to her had not only healed her body but had revived her spirits as well. His blood stains covered her clothes, reminding her of the pain he had suffered on her behalf. She slapped the megatrath in a playful manner, then waited for her to lower her neck so she could climb aboard.

When Vectra swung open the citadel doors, fresh morning air filled Oganna's lungs. The megatrath bounced onto the dimly lit ramp and rumbled contentedly in her throat. "We are finished here," Oganna said, and down the ramp and onto the highway they raced. The eastern horizon brightened, blazing orange and yellow streaks across the sky. Not a single word more passed between them as they left the city. Oganna felt Yimshi's rays warm her blood, and her hand dropped to the Avenger's hilt. She fingered it for a moment and then, as Vectra crested the rise out of the valley, she turned for one last look.

The bodies of the giants lay in the streets, on the collapsed buildings, and on the ramp to Ar'lenon. A dark cloud rose from the north and grew in size as it approached the city. The sounds of scolding birds fighting with one another to reach the corpses soon filled the valley as flocks of vultures and ravens came to the feast.

"The wizard has fallen, and now the birds will pluck the flesh from his bones." Vectra stamped her feet with satisfaction, pivoted on her rear four feet, and galloped to the south. Her six legs beat against the ground, carrying Oganna quickly away.

Oganna drew her sword and held it aloft. The silver robes covered her again, and her blade turned crimson. Whatever the future held, she would face it with the knowledge that she was the grandchild of a dragon. Around her neck the viper slept. Oganna sheathed the sword and leaned forward so that Vectra could hear her. "Let's go home!"

Other books by Scott Appleton:

The Sword of the Dragon series
Swords of the Six
Dragon Offspring
Key of Living Fire
The Phantom's Blade

The Neverqueen Saga
Neverqueen
Neverqueen 2: The Suffering Chalice

Anthology
By Sword By Right

For more info visit: www.AuthorAppleton.com

About the Author

Scott Appleton is the author of the novels *The Sword of the Dragon series*, and *The Neverqueen Saga*, which are widely read by adults and younger readers.

Besides these, Scott has also published a collection of short speculative fiction (*By Sword By Right*) which runs the gamut of science-fiction, fantasy, allegory, romance, poetry, and biblical.

Driven by a love of storytelling and an appreciation for the craft, Scott has spoken extensively at events across the United States. His specialization in fiction editing and writing has garnered praise from some prominent writers.

Scott was born in Connecticut and grew up there. He actively pursued astronomy through his teen years, built ships-in-bottles and, throughout his life, read and wrote extensively. Besides his writing he works in sales.

Currently Scott lives in Greenville, South Carolina with his wife, Kelley, and their five children. His activities of choice are reading with his kids, watching fantasy and science-fiction movies, reading, and playing the occasional Star Wars video game. You can find him at **www.AuthorAppleton.com** and **facebook.com/scottappleton.fans**

ACKNOWLEDGEMENTS

Reworking this novel from its original form was such a pleasure. It was with special love that I read again the story, and enhanced it with extra insight into the characters and the plot. God has blessed me in allowing me to fulfill my writing dream, and nothing reminds me more of that than reading the characters' stories and feeling their hurt and joy as if they were my own emotions.

This particular work was in-progress for several years before it was first published by Living Ink Books. Originally it was going to be the first novel in The Sword of the Dragon series, but the enhanced backstory lended to a separate novel, Swords of the Six.

I want to thank my wife for her steady support of my writing projects. She has been my advocate to many new readers, encouraging others to introduce their readers to these novels. She works tirelessly as a wife and as a mother to our five children, which is no small task.

To my son, Andrew. Someday, when you're old enough, I hope that you will pick up these books and know how passionate your dad is about morally strong stories. They can educate and teach, just as Jesus taught us.

To the wonderful people at AMG (who first published this work) thank you for making my publishing dreams a reality. Many readers know of me because of your hard work.

A special thanks to my friend Robert Treskillard for accidentally suggesting the fantastic change to Albino's interaction with Oganna after the battle for Ar'lenon. That scene became one of my favorites in this novel, and I was reminded of that when I read through it for this final edit.

For this edition, thank you to my proofreaders, without whose help this would not have been as quick a process! Joseph Ely, Stephen Wright, Ashton Medford, and Esther Hollingsworth.

And lastly to all my wonderful fans! This journey would not be as much fun without you.